Bryony Rheam was born in Kadoma in 1974 and lived in Bulawayo from the age of eight until she left school. She studied for a BA and an MA in English Literature in the United Kingdom and then taught in Singapore for a year before returning to teach in Zimbabwe from 2001 to 2008. Still a teacher, she now lives in Ndola, Zambia, with her partner, John, and their two daughters, Sian and Ellie.

Parthian
The Old Surgery
Napier Street
Cardigan
SA43 1ED

www.parthianbooks.co.uk

First published in Zimbabwe by 'amaBooks, 2009
This edition published 2012
© Bryony Rheam
All Rights Reserved

ISBN 978-1-906998-53-0

Cover design by James Fleming
Typeset by books@lloydrobson.com
Printed and bound by Gwasg Gomer

Published with the financial support of the Welsh Books Council.

British Library Cataloguing in Publication Data

A cataloguing record for this book is available from the British
Library.

CONTENTS

In memory of my grandmother,
Beryl Beynon Gillen,
who enjoyed a good story
and a strong cup of tea.

And for John
with lots of love, always.

Part One

Chapter One

On the 18th of April 1980, my grandfather burnt the British flag. I remember because it was my sixth birthday and he ruined it. My mother had made me a cake: it was in the shape of a heart, a big brown chocolate heart with white pearls of icing strung along the edge and 'Happy Birthday' written unsteadily across the middle. Gran had iced it, but she was feeling the effects of trying to give up smoking and her hand had wavered over the 'a' of 'happy' so it looked like an 'i'. 'Hippy Birthday,' Dad joked as he lit the candles. 'Hip, hip hooray.' Then Mom noticed that Grandad wasn't there, so the candles were blown out and Gran went to look for him.

Inside the house, my grandmother's lunch lay in the dustbin. It was beef stew with green beans and mashed potato. We had eaten lunch in silence. Dad read the newspaper that lay on the table. Mom hated that. She said it was rude: it 'cut off communication' were the words she used. Today she just looked down and ate. Her knife and fork occasionally scraped the plate, the only noise at the table. If I did that, I was told to eat properly and quietly, but grown-ups are always allowed to break the rules. Gran sat and looked at her food, pushing it round and round her plate. Mom eventually got up and cleared the table. Without a word, she took Gran's plate to the kitchen and emptied it into the bin. Grandad wasn't there. He was 'at the club'. That meant he was drinking.

The day of my sixth birthday was the day Zimbabwe got its Independence from Britain. No one went to work. Prince Charles came all the way from England to shake Mr Mugabe's hand and give back the country to the black people. Many white people had already decided to leave by the time the Rhodesian flag was lowered and the new Zimbabwean one hoisted. Grandad said we were in for trouble; this was just the beginning. That morning he disappeared, but returned in the late afternoon as Gran was making tea and putting the cups and saucers on a tray. I was in the small room that adjoined the kitchen and acted as a pantry, looking for the candles to put on my cake. I heard them argue as Grandad had been drinking and was leaning against the wall for support. Then Gran called me and we went outside onto the verandah as we always did around about four o'clock. Afternoons tended to have a pattern back then.

By the time we noticed my grandfather was missing from the circle around my cake, he had lit the stolen Union Jack and came running out in front of us, spinning furiously round and round in circles with it. He was turning so fast that the flames looked like a giant Catherine wheel, a great golden loop of fire. Then he let out a long deep mournful cry of sorrow that sounded like the very call of death and sent a chill through us all. I can see us standing there around the table, frozen as if by a sudden icy wind, the late afternoon sun retreating like a war-weary warrior trudging homewards, defeated. I can see my mother turn and rush inside the house to get water, my father speechless and still; I can feel my nails as I dug them into my palms in fright and then I see my grandmother run out of the house and over to our macabre entertainer, screaming at him, her voice like hot oil, hissing and spitting and boiling, 'I hate you! I hate you!' As she reached him, he threw back the burning flag and it fell on to her, the flames reaching out like fingers to catch hold of her skin. She stumbled back onto the grass.

What happened next is a blur. I cannot remember who helped her and what was said, what my grandfather did or what was done to him. All I know is that was how she got the scar on the underside of her forearm. It was dark and ugly and, as she grew older and her skin sagged, it reminded me of old tea. Unusually enough, it was in the shape of a teapot. I said that it looked like the shape of Zimbabwe etched on her arm. I think Gran was always a little proud of the mark, a symbol of the price she paid for freedom. Many years later, the man who murdered my grandmother would remember that mark as the last thing he saw as she raised her arms against him before he brought the butt of his gun down on her head.

Chapter Two

Smile though your heart is breaking
Smile even though it's aching

Where do you start to put a life together? The pieces don't always fit. Many are missing, or borrowed. From other people's lives, other people's memories. Their own puzzles. Where is the beginning when you have only the end to start with? How many lies are told over the course of one lifetime? What of all that is not said, merely meant, hinted at, subsiding beneath the surface of action and words? All that is yearned for and never had?

*

My grandparents separated soon after my grandmother recovered, at least physically, from the flag burning incident. Gran moved out despite much pleading from my mother, tears from me, and my grandfather's sorry silence. She got a job in the accounts department of Haddon and Sly and rented a small flat on Wilson Street. I don't think any of us realised how difficult it was for her, leaving her old life behind, especially in the face of such adversity. There was no one she could talk to; Mom couldn't see her point of view, couldn't understand why her mother, at her age, had to stop living with us and start out on her own. That my grandparents hadn't got on for years was no secret in our family, but my mother had never let that leak to the outside world. It was a long time before she acknowledged Gran's departure, if she ever did. Everything Gran did was judged within the context of her leaving us and setting up her own home.

In the days before she moved out, when her things lay packed in two suitcases and a large cardboard box, I cried every night as I lay in bed and, when I woke, my eyes were swollen and sore to open. Alone in the afternoons, I peered round Gran's bedroom door and looked resentfully at her half-packed things. The space she left echoed noisily when she had gone and we all stumbled clumsily around the house, not knowing what to do and what to say and everything sounded false and far too bright and cheery. We were like the Colgate advert, where a gleam twinkles off the man's happy white smile. 'He must use bicarb on them,' said Mom, when she first saw it, because everyone knows that brilliant white teeth aren't natural.

The routine that I had known was rudely disrupted. When she lived with us, Gran would often walk me home from school. Grandad and Dad would come back from work at one o'clock and have lunch. Sometimes Grandad had a nap, but Dad never did. He read the paper and drank tea and talked to Mom. Then at a quarter to two he would get in the car and drive back to work, dropping Grandad off at Fox's on the way.

Grandad was a mechanic. He wore blue overalls to work that were always greasy and he always smelled of oil, even after he had washed. In fact, even after he retired and lost all interest in fixing broken carburettors and cracked radiators, a thick smell of oil seemed to emanate from him at times, as though all the years of working at Fox's garage had ingrained themselves under his skin.

After lunch, my Gran would go for a rest for an hour or so and Mom would be in the kitchen sorting out dinner or making a cake or scones. The house would be very quiet. At three o'clock Gran would emerge from her room, mumbling about the heat and how much there still was to be done in the house. If I were bored I would sit outside her room and listen for the creak of the bed, which meant she was getting up. Hours passed slowly and often it seemed as though the afternoon would stretch on forever before that one silent hour would be over.

The hour before Dad returned from work was spent with my grandmother. Sometimes we would walk to the library together, my books to return in a bag in one hand, the other holding Gran's. She also listened to me read and would sign my reading card afterwards so my teacher knew I had done my homework.

At night she would read to me from one of my library books, mainly Enid Blyton – *The Magic Faraway Tree* and *The Famous Five* – stories of children who ran about the English countryside, finding fairies and elves, or smugglers, joining the circus or exploring the caves of Devon: so different to me in a dusty old town in Africa with snakes and mosquitoes and endless hot days and nights.

Now she was gone and the afternoons stretched empty and dreary with a longing that could not be filled. To try and make me feel better, Gran let me help her unpack in her new flat and let me choose where to put her ornaments, even if some were in slightly strange places. I placed her two silver candlesticks on the floor, either side of the table on which her television rested, and a huge pot plant on a small side table that it completely dwarfed. It was so big you expected the table to collapse at any moment.

When my mother first saw it, she moved the plant without saying a word, she was so used to arranging other people's lives. Gran told her firmly to put it back as it was 'fine there', and winked at me conspiratorially. Gran didn't have much furniture of her own as Grandad made a huge fuss over every piece she wanted to take. My mother said she wasn't taking sides over the issue, although really she did by doing nothing. Gran had no bookcase for her collection of paper-backs and her hardback Reader's Digest anthologies, so we piled the latter into two pillars, placed a plank of wood across them and arranged the rest of the books in a row on top.

She never spoke to me about her decision to leave or the whys and wherefores of her relationship with Grandad. In fact, no one ever spoke to me about it. Somehow I was expected to just know. When I was a bit older and watched television more, I was always amazed at American family sitcoms, where parents had heart to heart conversations with their children, conversations that always ended with each party saying how much they loved the other. I cringed to see such open shows of emotion, especially if Grandad or my parents were in the room.

9

My mom had told me not to tell anyone about my grandparents; if they asked I was to say it was none of their business. She was still hoping Gran would come back and the whole affair would blow over, even though Gran now had a job and seemed so much happier than when she lived with us. Mom had initially come up with a great convoluted story, which Dad had laughed at, much to Mom's chagrin.

The story was that they were moving out into a flat. However, the flat still had to be decorated and so Gran was going to live there while she did that. She had to sleep in the lounge and there wasn't enough room for Grandad as well. The flat would take a while to be finished, especially because Gran was so fussy about paint colours and it was hard to find good upholstery in Zimbabwe these days. I was relieved when Dad reminded Mom that I was only six years old and unlikely to remember such a story, although I was frustrated, too, that I had let her down.

In the first couple of years after Independence, both for Zimbabwe and Gran, she and I spent a lot of time together. To compensate for her absence at home, I would often stay the weekend with her. Mom or Dad would drop me off on Saturday morning and pick me up on Sunday evening. Even if I did not stay the whole weekend, I would at least spend a morning or afternoon with her.

In many ways I was the strongest link between her old life with us and her new life on her own. I was also the go-between. Gran never came to our house and Mom entered Gran's flat uneasily. She never stayed long. Although they spoke often on the phone, there was always an extra message that I was asked to relay, either to Gran when I was dropped off, or to Mom when I was picked up. 'Please give Gran these

lemons and tell her I'll bring some more round on Tuesday.'
'Tell Mom I'll phone her on Wednesday.' And it wasn't just
messages that I conveyed, but snippets of information about
each other's lives: what Gran made for dinner, whether she
was lonely or not, how Mom got on with Grandad now that
he was on his own, all the questions they couldn't ask each
other. For the most part, I answered all their questions as
honestly as possible, although I was protective of both. I
shielded Mom from Gran's often acidic tongue, and Gran
from Mom's pessimism, her certain belief that Gran had
done the wrong thing.

My grandmother had learned to drive when she was forty-
five years old and continued for the next ten years to drive
illegally, until she finally got her licence. When she lived with
us there was always a fuss whenever she wanted to take
Grandad's car into town. He would shout about the
insurance and ask who would pay if she had an accident or
even just backed the car into a tree. Gran said that was
typical – men didn't even take women's accidents seriously.
The glory of great accidents was denied women who were
left to reverse into trees and walls or run over the dog – or
their husbands, she had once muttered mischievously – little
accidents of no consequence that illuminated the whole
character of woman: irrational, illogical, untrustworthy.

A few months after leaving us, Gran bought a car, a 1969
Toyota Crown sedan. It was blue. And big. She called it
Shirley, for some reason. I forget now. Everyone knew Gran's
car. I used to look out for it when we went into town. If it
was outside Downings, I knew she was buying bread: a
wholemeal loaf and a stick of French bread if it was Friday,
for the weekend. If it was outside the bank, I knew she was

actually in the fruit and vegetable shop opposite and would be there for a while as she and Mrs Patterson, the cashier, would chat for a long time after Gran had paid. Even if the shop were busy, Mrs Patterson would carry on talking while handing other customers their change or weighing apples and potatoes, tying a knot in the neck of the plastic bags she put them in and sticking the prices on the side.

Next door was the butcher with only one arm. It was sawn off above the elbow and I always imagined that he had got it caught in his mincing machine. At other times, I half expected to see it lying amongst the cuts of meat on display, perhaps decorated with a bit of lettuce and cucumber and adorned with an orange star which said 'Today's Special. Arm half price!' Gran pulled a face when I told her and said that he had lost it in some sort of accident or other years before, but it didn't stop me thinking of the mincing machine and the noise it would have made as it chewed through the bone and flesh.

If I saw the car outside Mr Patel's, I knew Gran was looking for material. She would choose a bolt of cloth and the assistant would carry it down for her, heave it onto the counter and measure out a metre or so. Mr Patel could tell exactly how much you needed for trousers or a skirt or dress. He would slice through the material with a big pair of black scissors and then fold it again and again into a small square. I loved the way he did it, the motion of the scissors, the way the material surrendered to the blade. I loved the sound and the speed, the way he folded the cloth and put it into a plastic bag, sealing it with a piece of Sellotape, in one smooth motion.

One day I told Gran that I wanted to work there when I

grew up. She laughed. The next time we went to Mr Patel's she told him and he grinned widely. I felt embarrassed and couldn't understand why they thought this so funny. I didn't like not understanding. It was at times like these that I felt an enormous gap between me and a world I didn't, and perhaps still don't, understand. The truth, it seems, often lies further than where you look.

I wasn't the only one who looked out for Gran's car. Grandad did too. Whenever he was in town, his eyes continually scanned the parking bays along the side of the road. If he did spot the great blue machine that always, due to its size, stuck out into the road, he never had a good thing to say about it. He saw dents and scratches that weren't there. If the wheels were anywhere near over the line, he spoke of women's inability to park, let alone drive; if Gran parked in the sun he ranted about the damage it would do to the upholstery. He checked to see if the car was clean inside and out, whether she left any rubbish in it.

Once she left a red lipstick on the front passenger seat without its top on and it melted in the sun. The liquid colour, as it became, got ingrained in the seat, which had a pattern of little grooves in the middle and down the sides. I don't think Gran ever tried to clean the seat, so the colour stayed, giving the strange impression of blood, as if someone had been murdered sitting there.

I knew that Grandad missed Gran. I got tired of his complaining but, at the same time, I felt a knot of pain twisting itself deeper and deeper within me. I knew their separation had somehow resulted from Gran being burned that day but I couldn't understand why she could not forgive him for that. Even before that incident though, I couldn't remember my grandparents ever being happy together. Alone, yes, they each could be funny and laugh, but not together. Together there was always a sense of sadness and bitterness about them, as if the very air between them was eaten away, and hung, full of holes, like an old flag beaten about by the wind.

Chapter Three

There were many things my grandmother enjoyed doing. She loved going for walks in the park, but she didn't like the bush and even somewhere like Hillside Dams was a bit too rural for her. I think she liked the order that she found in the park: the pots and the carefully trimmed flowerbeds. She liked the fact that you could sit on the lawn and that there was plenty of shade. She wasn't one for anthills and snakes and sitting on a rock under a thorn tree. That isn't to say that she didn't appreciate the beauty of the bush, for she did, as long as it was from the comfort of a lush green oasis.

She also enjoyed cooking and baking, especially rich chocolate cakes and feather-light melt-in-your-mouth Victoria sponges. She was a stickler for ceremony and even the most mundane visitor was offered cake with their tea. She also made sandwiches with grated cheese fillings and slices of cucumber. She'd cut the crusts off and decorate them with shredded lettuce. Somehow they always tasted better than any other sandwich and, for a long time, I thought it was because she sliced them diagonally, rather than straight down the middle, which seemed so ordinary and plain in comparison.

I loved to watch her bake, to watch the wave of thick creamy batter turn over in the bowl as her wooden spoon ploughed under it. I loved the way it slid smoothly into the waiting greased tins, the way it baked, turning darker and firmer in the oven.

'It's all in the eggs,' she would say to me, as she folded them into the flour. 'Never scrimp on the eggs and never bang the bowl or the baking tin, or you'll knock all the air out.'

She also told me to always use less sugar than the recipe asked for as most recipes were from South Africa or the UK and they were not as high above sea level as we were. Nobody else believed me when I told them that and my cookery teacher at high school laughed when I told her. What had sugar to do with sea level she asked? Who knows, but it worked.

Teatime, whether in the morning or afternoon, was always a sign of something, a signal. When Gran lived with us, I loved the latter teatime best as it signalled the end of the afternoon for me. The long wait of having nothing to do while she or Mom was asleep was over and Dad and Grandad would be home from work soon. Although we of course carried on drinking tea after Gran moved out, my mother didn't make it as well as she did, or give it that certain sense of ceremony, and I always looked forward to teatime at my grandmother's.

Later on, tea became one of the benchmarks by which I used to judge my life in England. There, such formalities have long disappeared from everyday life and a teabag in a mug takes its place, for no one has time for the leisure and appreciation of tea drinking. Sometimes I have noticed people having four to six mugs of tea a day but it isn't the same as that one cup in the late afternoon with Gran.

Tea, my grandmother always maintained, was one of the great benefits of colonialism. In fact, she said, it was the one thing in the world that kept everyone together, the one thing everyone shared. Tea was originally grown in China, its popularity spreading to India and other surrounding countries. It was discovered by the Europeans on their exploring and colonising expeditions, but it was the British who really recognised the great quality of tea. The best thing they ever did was to take it to all their colonies, to insist that it was grown wherever it could be. Think of the Africans, Gran would say, they love tea, they have their own way of making it, but it is tea nonetheless and who do they have to thank for that? The British, who in turn must thank the Chinese and the Indians. We are all indebted to one another. Africans and Indians boil the tea-leaves with the water, the Europeans like theirs black and the British like theirs with milk; the Chinese drink green tea and the Indians have masala tea. Then there is chamomile, honeybush, rooibos, lemon: the list is endless. Tea is the one thing that links us all together.

Gran was a prolific letter writer. She wrote to everyone: friends, people she had met, me when she went away on holiday. She had beautiful handwriting, soft and curving, the kind of writing that made you want to carry on reading, as though it were the keeper of mysteries and secrets, and you were always vaguely disappointed when you came to the end of her letters, for the mystery and the promise were still there, unsolved and unravelled. She wrote copious notes, too: a note for the butcher when she ordered meat, for the plumber or painter or odd jobs man when he came round while she was at work, and for her once a week cleaner when she wanted some ironing done. I always felt that her notes gained her a certain amount of respect, that each recipient looked forward with a strange longing to those beautifully scripted lists: the meat or milk order, her grocery requirements. Even the instructions concerning her blocked drain.

'Nobody writes any more,' she lamented in one of her last letters to me. And it was true. She was the only person that I wrote to rather than e-mailing and shopping lists are now a thing of the past, bound to send busy butchers, bakers and candlestick makers into fits of exasperation over the dated habits of old ladies.

Gran was an avid reader. She mainly read detective novels: Agatha Christie and Ngaio Marsh. And she read a lot. She could read four novels a week easily. Too much, my mother complained. My mother never read. She didn't have the time, she said.

'The thing is,' Gran would declare every once in a while, 'crime writers depend firstly on stereotypes and secondly on routine. They depend on a certain character looking and acting a certain way and not everyone is that predictable. Sometimes someone behaves in a way that is totally out of character. People do the strangest things.'

I would nod my head sagely and agree, but it wasn't until I was much older that I fully understood what she meant.

'Imagine if someone asked you what you were doing on Wednesday last week at three o'clock. Would you be able to tell them? Have you got an alibi, they might ask? No? Well, how many people do have alibis for half the things they do? Does this automatically make us guilty of murdering someone? Crime novels don't take the individual into account, that's the problem. We are all subject to changing our minds and just because you have a three o'clock appointment in your diary doesn't mean you have to keep to it. Do you see what I mean?'

'What drives one person to murder,' she said to me another time, 'might not bother someone else. Just because your husband is unfaithful doesn't mean you're going to kill him, yet someone else might have chopped him into small pieces. In fact, most crime novelists presume that chopping an unfaithful husband into small pieces is a fairly reasonable reaction to his betrayal. Murder is often more understand-able than forgiveness. Isn't that strange? And yet,' she paused and pulled her lips together, her forehead locking in a frown, 'there are many ways to kill someone, some just take a little longer than others.'

We went to the movies once to see *Evil Under the Sun* and, on another occasion, to see *Murder on the Orient Express*. We went to the 2.15 Saturday afternoon show at Kine 600 and that night (I was staying with her) I had a terrible nightmare about it and crept into bed with her.

'It's just a story, you know. They're all actors and actresses and nobody's really dead. At the end of the day, they take off their make-up and go home for supper.'

Put like that, the film didn't seem so scary, but, when I closed my eyes, all I could see was the man being stabbed over and over again.

'Gran,' I asked, 'would you kill someone if they killed me?'

I could see her silhouette on the pillow next to me. She was lying on her back and had the sheets and blanket pulled up under her arms. I never knew how she remained so straight as she slept. Sometimes it looked the next day as though no one had slept there at all. She thought for a bit and then said 'I could kill them a thousand times but it wouldn't bring you back.'

'Would you cry if I died?'

'Of course I would,' she said and, although I couldn't see her face, there was a sad smile in her voice. Her hand rested on my arm and now she gently smoothed it up and down. I could feel the hair on my arm rise and flatten with each movement.

'Do you think you'll die before me, Gran?'

'I hope so,' she said, and I couldn't hear the smile any longer. 'Children shouldn't die.'

You'll never know just how much I love you
You'll never know just how much I care

She sang quietly as I fell asleep, the words subsiding into a gentle hum. Gran had a song for every occasion.

After my grandmother's death, I was assigned the awful task of going through her things. In her latter years she had worn mainly trousers and shirts, but in her cupboards I found ballgowns and cocktail dresses, silk shirts and pure wool skirts: even a cashmere jersey that I never remember her wearing. In her drawers were soft cotton slips and silky camisoles. 'It's not every girl who can be a lady,' she once advised me. 'Don't get drunk, don't swear and never, ever, laugh at a dirty joke.'

20

I packed her things in boxes. Things to sell, things to give away, things to keep. But there were some things I had no idea what to do with: half-used lipsticks, nearly empty perfume bottles, her hairbrush.

I learnt a lot from my grandmother. I may not be a baker myself, but I can tell when a cake is short of an egg or two. She didn't like literature (too heavy, she said, preferring her crime novels), but she showed me how to read characters, doubt the narrator and not fall for red herrings. Never squeeze a teabag, never blow your nose in public and never ever trust the man without the scar on his left cheek, for he's the one that did it.

*

The phone rings a couple of times and I lean over and switch the answering machine on. I don't want the present, although it insists on intruding. I turn to my notebook, in which I have written a couple of sentences. If only I knew where the beginning was. If only I could remember everything.

That's why, dar-ling, it's in-cred-ible
That someone so un-forgettable
Thinks that I am
Unforgettable too.

Chapter Four

My grandmother never cries in front of me. At her flat there is only laughter and treats; chocolate biscuits with tea at ten o'clock; jelly and ice cream to eat in front of *The Muppet Show* on Saturday nights. She always sets a tray for tea and puts a flower in a vase. She lets me have a bubble bath and stay up late. Sometimes we go swimming at Borrow Street and buy lollies on the way home.

I never see her crying. Once, years later, before I move to England, she tells me that the day her son died was the last time she ever cried. Nothing could ever make her feel that pain again. But I know, I know she cries when she thinks I am not there.

*

Back then Gran and I had one secret, although the number was to increase significantly in the next few years. Every Sunday, Gran would go to morning service. It was not held in a conventional church with stained-glass windows and wooden pews. Instead, it was in an old hall, also used by the Girl Guides and the Women's Institute for their meetings. It was run-down and needed a coat of paint, but it was clean and thoroughly swept out every week. There was a long trestle table near the front of the hall covered with a white tablecloth. On top were placed two vases of roses and a Bible. It was no ordinary church service either and my mother, even though she was not religious in any sense, would not have approved. There was no piano or organ; we had to sing without music. Two people sat at the table, one who read the prayers and the lesson, the other the clairvoyant who received messages from 'the other side' and relayed them to the congregation. At first I did not understand what was happening and why the messages were generally very vague.

'Is there someone here whose name begins with 'P'?' the clairvoyant might ask, or 'I have a message from someone who's holding a wooden spoon in his hand. Does anyone know who I'm talking about?'

I thought the clairvoyant had been given a message to give to someone in the congregation by someone alive. When I found out that the messages came from dead people I was horrified. I feared death, and talk of ghosts and spirits scared me terribly. Gran explained to me that these weren't the ghosts of storybooks: headless horsemen and monsters dragging chains across castle floors, but spirit guides or guardian angels. Gran said that when you died your spirit stayed alive and you became a guardian of someone on earth whom you had loved dearly. The way that you communicated with them was through a clairvoyant: a person with the ability to see and talk to spirits. When we first went to the church, Gran didn't receive any messages at all. Some people's guardian angels, it seemed, were very active, while others seemed not to care about their human charges, for I noticed that it was often the same people every week who received messages.

One night I was staying with Gran and looking forward to a night in front of the television. I was allowed to stay up much later with her than at home, a privilege I did not let my mother know about. Before the late night film started, she made tea in her big orange teapot and took out two cups and saucers. Two toasted teacakes lay on a plate, oozing with butter.

'Go and get me a clean tray cloth, won't you, Ellie?' Gran asked me, and I went obediently and looked for one in the linen cupboard. I couldn't reach the shelves where the cloths were kept, so I went and fetched a chair to stand on. I saw the blue cloth that Gran normally used, but I wanted to find a different one in order to give the evening some sense of occasion. I was rummaging in the back of the cupboard when I found a green beret. It looked like something someone in the army would wear. I put it on, pushing it down on my head as it was so big, jumped off the chair and marched into the kitchen where Gran was just stirring the pot. I saluted, stamped my foot and said 'Yessir!' Gran looked up, the beginnings of a smile curving her lips slightly. But it died at the sight of me. Immediately I knew I had done something wrong.

'Oh, Ellie, take that off, please,' she said, in a deathly hushed voice that was worse to hear than if she had shouted at me. I reached up and took the cap off.

'What's wrong?' I asked, turning it over in my hands.

She swallowed hard and put the lid on the teapot. There was a pause and then, 'It was my son's'. There was another pause. 'He died.' I looked down at the cap and my stomach contracted. I had held something of his. I had touched it. Not only that, I had joked about it: joked about someone who was dead. 'He was killed during the war,' she continued. 'Please put it back, Ellie.' I turned and went back to the cupboard, put the cap back and picked up the blue cloth. All thoughts of finding a more rarely-used one were gone. I thought it best to stick to the tried and known in case I opened up another slow-healing wound.

The next day we went to church and got there slightly earlier than usual. Gran got talking to Mrs Coetzee who wanted her to help out with serving tea every week after the service. Gran was unsure: she didn't know if she was going to carry on attending church, or at least as often as she had been. I think she was disappointed she hadn't received any messages. Every Sunday as she drove home she was very quiet and when she smiled it was sadly, as though she were trying to accept some terrible truth about life.

Mrs Coetzee was one of those people who talked incredibly slowly and who took a long time to get to the point, implying that making tea was a lot more difficult than it appeared and the responsibility it entailed was something that could not be bestowed upon just anyone. I stood by Gran's side, patiently at first, but gradually more and more restlessly. I crossed my legs and tried to turn my head as far back as possible but lost my balance and stepped on Gran's foot.

'Ellie!' she exclaimed, turning sharply to me. 'Stand still!'

A large lady in a purple and blue kaftan was standing

25

close by and saw what happened. She came across.

'Have you seen the library?' she asked me in that bright patronizing way I associated with aging primary school teachers: women who think they possess some charm irresistible to small children but who, in reality, actually scare them. 'Come with me, dear,' she continued before I could answer. She took my hand in an attempt to lead me away. I stood my ground and looked appealingly up at Gran for help, but it was not to come.

'Go with the nice lady,' she said, giving me a gentle push. I felt my heart fall to the bottom of my stomach, and had the incident the night before not happened, I may have become sulky and openly despised the large lady and tried my best to make Gran feel guilty. As it was, I allowed myself to be led away.

The 'library' was a small room at the back of the hall with two kitchen chairs in it and a coffee table. There was also a small cabinet with a rounded glass front. Inside it were two rows of books. The lady busied herself looking through them and emerged with three rather worn items. None of them were suitable for children and I looked at them despondently. Two were hardcover books with faded gold writing on the spine. They looked depressing. The other was a thin paperback with a plastic cover. The title read *Mind Power* and on the right hand corner of the cover was a yellow star with the word 'NEW!' in red letters. Underneath it said: '1978's US bestselling title!' All of a sudden I felt an overwhelming urge to cry. Here I was, abandoned to the whims of a large overbearing woman whom I did not know, being offered books to read whose hard, faded covers threatened some sort of punishment, a berating for the previous night's discovery.

The large overbearing woman left me after being called by another member of the congregation to meet a visitor to the church. I was left alone in the room, perched forlornly upon one of the chairs. I sat with one of the books open and tears welling up in my eyes. Just as I could feel the first trickles down my cheeks, someone came into the room. It was someone I hadn't seen before: a tall, thin, slightly stooping man with grey hair and trim grey sideburns. He had on an old dark suit and I remember that one of the buttons on it was navy blue whilst the rest were black. He had a slightly bristly chin and his breath, when he came closer, smelt of coffee.

'Hello, my dear,' he said, smiling and looking rather quizzically at my reading matter. 'What are you reading there?'

I showed him the books and his eyes widened comically. 'My, you must be a clever girl if you're reading these!' There was a pause. 'Are you reading them?'

I shook my head sadly, trying very hard not to cry.

'Are you here on your own?'

I shook my head.

'Is your mother outside?' he probed.

'My gran,' I answered. My voice was just above a whisper as I struggled to hold my tears back.

'And who's your granny?'

'Her name is Mrs Rogers. But her friends call her Evelyn.'

The man smiled. 'Is she the lady talking to Mrs Coetzee?'

I nodded.

'Has she deserted you then? Or did you get tired of the ladies talking? Ladies can talk for a very long time!'

I tried to get some sort of answer out, but suddenly found myself crying. I hated crying in front of strangers.

The man looked concerned and was obviously troubled by my behaviour.

'Are you in the dog box?' he asked. 'Is Granny cross with you?'

I nodded through my tears.

'Do you want to tell me what's happened?' he asked and I nodded again.

Eventually my tears subsided into a sniff and he handed me a handkerchief. 'Keep it. My wife gives me them every Christmas. I try and get rid of them during the year so I have a use for the ones she gives me the next time.'

I smiled weakly and dried my eyes with the large brown check handkerchief. There was something comforting about the man. I felt he was genuinely concerned that I was upset, not dismissive or derisive as many adults can be.

I told him what had happened the previous evening and he nodded sympathetically every now and then, his arms crossed in front of him. He didn't interrupt me at all and, when I had finished, sat for a few seconds in thought. I felt relieved to tell someone about the episode. It wasn't something I normally did; most of the time I kept things to myself. Finally he said, 'Has your granny ever told you about her son before?' I shook my head. 'I see,' he nodded his head slowly. 'She doesn't want it discussed.' He seemed to say the last comment more to himself than to me. Just then there was a knock at the door and a head looked round.

'We're just starting, Mr Philips.'

'Oh, yes,' he said, rather startled. 'Just coming.' The head disappeared and the man turned to me, 'Your granny's not cross with you, you know.' He got up and went to the door, still rather distracted. 'I must go. The service is about to start. She will be looking for you.'

I slid off the chair and put the books back in the cabinet, then followed him out of the room.

The man was right. Gran was looking around for me. She smiled when she saw me and didn't seem to notice that I had been crying. I was relieved. We found a place to sit just as the rest of the congregation started singing 'Guide Me O Thou Great Jehovah'. I looked for the tall man, but couldn't see him anywhere. It was only when the service started that I realized he was sitting up at the table. Once the prayers and the reading were over, Mrs Johnstone, one of the church organizers, stood up and introduced a visiting clairvoyant from their branch in Kwekwe, a Mr Philips. Suddenly I was seized with panic. I felt like I had told a teacher some secret that they felt must be told to my parents. My palms began to sweat and I kept looking down at my feet to avoid catching his eye.

Mr Philips was not much different to the other clairvoyants who graced us with their presence every Sunday. He spoke in vague terms about someone with a red hat, someone who liked pickle sandwiches and a man called Fred who wanted to tell his wife not to worry as everything was going to be all right. Then he looked our way. He stared for about half a minute. My heart was beating fast. What would he say? Would he tell her? His body trembled suddenly and he closed his eyes.

'I have the name Evelyn,' he said. I felt Gran start beside me. She put up her hand and I could see she was shaking. He opened his eyes, but although he was looking at us, it was as if he didn't see us at all. Instinctively, I looked over my shoulder, but the only people there were Mr Hunter and his sister, Mrs Braxton, sitting in the row behind us.

'I have someone here,' he continued. 'I don't have a name, but it's a young man.' Gran sat stock still beside me. Mr Philips's forehead furrowed slightly as though he were confused about something. 'There's something about his clothes,' he said, shaking his head. 'He's wearing a uniform... some sort of uniform.' His voice trailed off a little and then he added, 'I think he was in the army'.

I turned to look at Gran. She had her hand over her mouth and her eyes held a startled look. 'It's Jeremy,' she whispered. 'It's Jeremy.'

Mr Philips nodded and half smiled. 'He says to tell you not to worry. He's OK. He says something... something about tea.' There was a murmur of laughter in the congregation. Gran's love of tea was well known. Mr Philips closed his eyes and I could see his lips moving slightly, as though he was talking to someone. 'Yes, tea,' he said aloud, 'something about doing something with tea.'

'And otherwise,' said Gran, 'otherwise, he's all right?'

'Yes,' smiled Mr Philips. 'He's fine.'

When Gran and I left the church that day, she was in a very good mood, smiling and laughing with something like the relief of someone who has been dreading something that has turned out all right. Before we drove away she had thanked Mr Philips for the message. He shrugged and said it wasn't up to him: it was up to the spirits who communicated with him. He was standing with a cup of tea in his hand and, as Gran left him, he raised it and said 'Remember.' He smiled at me and turned away to talk to someone else. Gran looked for Mrs Coetzee and told her that she would help out serving the teas after the service. She left feeling very satisfied with life that day.

*

Three months after her funeral, I am back in England. I can't sleep at night. I am haunted by the loss of her: the letters that don't arrive anymore, the phone calls I no longer make. There is a space, a hole. I feel like a trapeze artist waiting for her partner to swing across to her, arms outstretched, but there is no one there. Would it have been easier if we'd said goodbye? If I could just have held her hand?

I find myself looking in the phone book for the address of the nearest Spiritualist Church. I sit through the service; I wait for the messages. There are none for me. I go the following week, and the week after that. Still there is nothing. I walk home in the rain, my coat pulled close. Part of me wants to let it go, to let it fall open and have the wind and rain whistle into me, through me. I want it to wash away all that I feel, to numb the pain.

I think: she is with him and she is happy. But what about me? What about me? I want to scream. What do I do now?

Chapter Five

A letter drops through the door onto the carpet. It is in a blue envelope. I feel a sharp stab of pain, a longing, and then I realise it is from her, from Gran, but it can't be. She's been dead for nearly six months. 'Missent to Malaysia' is stamped on the front. Malaysia? It was posted in Bulawayo on the 16th of October, five days before Gran died. I am afraid to open it. It is from a dead person. She was the last person to touch the letter inside. I can stand a trip to the Spiritualist Church in the hope that some message will come through from her, but not this, not so literal a message as this.

But I succumb, of course. I open the envelope with a knife... I pull the letter out carefully, fold back the thick paper and read:

My Dearest Ellie,

You are so much in my thoughts recently that I feel I have to write to you and let you know what I am thinking. I feel you are desperately unhappy, so unhappy that you have forgotten what happiness is and you accept this state as 'normal'. I think you'd take yourself by surprise if you were to suddenly find something funny and laugh. I do not feel your smile any more in our conversations, what few of them we have, and even your letters lack their old *joie de vivre*. And then your dream. That's why I had to phone you last week. Something is wrong and somewhere, somewhere in your consciousness you acknowledge this, but the thinking, rationalising Ellie won't do this. The ring around the bath – it's a warning. Of what, Ellie? You must think.

As I draw near to the end of my life, I realise what's important. What to keep and what to give away – what to cut out. There are things, too, that I want to set straight, sort out, explain. Not all of this includes you: much appertains to your mother and grandfather, but I doubt if it will ever be quite resolved.

I want to face death prepared. I will come like a thief in the night, said Jesus. I need to be ready. I need to talk to you, Ellie, properly, face-to-face, and that is why I have decided to come and see you. I have not been to England for many years. I thought I'd never return, but I need to see you. Let me know when the best time for me to come would be. I know you don't have a big house and I wouldn't expect to stay for a long time. A couple of weeks at most. England was my first home and I would like to say goodbye to it as well. Nothing morbid, mind. Sometime in the spring or early summer is what I'm aiming at.

You'll write soon, Ellie, won't you? I do worry about you so much and only want to see you happy.

All my love,

Gran XX

*

I first went to the Bulawayo Naval Club in 1983. If I remember correctly, it was a Saturday afternoon and Gran and I had spent the morning in town shopping. It was an extremely hot day, probably sometime in November. The rains hadn't started and day after day the sky stretched pale blue from one end of the horizon to the other. Gran had looked up at the sky that morning and shaken her head. 'Not a cloud in sight. Should've started by this time of the year.'

That Saturday was the same as any other except that Gran had bought me a new pair of shoes. They were red sandals. I had tried on just about every pair in the shop before choosing those and, to be honest, I had only chosen them because Brenda Thomas at school had a pair. I am not sure whether I liked them myself, but I remember that the shop assistant looked up at the ceiling and mouthed the words 'thank you' to an omniscient god. Gran laughed and said she, too, had been about to call upon divine intervention if I hadn't finally made up my mind.

As I wanted to wear the new shoes, my old ones were packed up in the shoebox and I carried it under my arm to the car, constantly looking down at my new red sandals.

While Gran unlocked the car, I stood looking at those new shoes, my feet placed firmly together. When I looked up, Gran was holding the door open for me and smiling at my behaviour. I leapt from the pavement on to the road and then climbed on to the back seat of the car.

'Someone's a happy girl,' said Gran, laughing. She took out her lipstick and hand mirror and 'touched up' as she called it, squeezing her lips together and then pouting. She dabbed them with a piece of tissue paper, applied more lipstick and then ran her finger around the edge of them. '*There may be trouble ahead*,' she sang, '*but while there's moonlight and music and love and ro-mance, let's face the music and dance...*' Finally, she squirted perfume on her wrists and neck. She gave me a little squirt too. I wrinkled my nose and blinked my eyes at first, but after a while I could smell lavender. She always wore lavender perfume, so much so that it became 'her' smell. Because she was so used to it, she tended to put too much on, so it was possible to smell her still in rooms that she hadn't been in to for a while. I once joked that she could never be a burglar because the police would know who it was straight away. They'd call her 'The Lavender Looter' or 'The Perfumed Pilferer'. Now the smell of lavender has an odd effect on me: it is more than a perfume, it is a touch like that of a hand stretched out to lead a child across a busy street. The effect is momentary, leaving a terrible sense of loss; a lost child looking bewilderingly for a familiar face amongst all the others that loom across its way in the busy street.

I wondered why she was 'touching up' then, when we had finished all the shopping and it was time to drop me off at home. I couldn't wait to show Mom my new shoes. I had asked her for a new pair just that last week but she'd said I'd have to wait for Christmas as they were too expensive. That was the nice thing about Gran now that she lived on her own. She didn't seem to worry about money the way Mom and Dad did. 'We only live once,' she'd say, 'so let's give it hell while we're here'.

'I thought we'd go out for lunch today,' said Gran as she reversed the car.

'Where to?' I asked, knowing that Mom was making my favourite meal of spaghetti bolognese.

'The Naval Club,' she answered, in the same tone of voice that one might say State House or 10 Downing Street, as though we were special guests of the Prime Minister.

'The Naval Club?' I repeated. 'What's that?'

The Naval Club had been started after the Second World War by a Major MacDowell, mainly as a social club for ex-Navy men and their dependents. As with most clubs of its type in Zimbabwe, it was mainly a drinking establishment, frequented less by able seamen than by aging alcoholics. It was different to the sports clubs whose bar counters were weighed down with the beers of their die-hard Rhodesian clientele, those who could've won the war if only Smith had not given in to Nationalist aggression, those who had always been on the brink of victory when Smith had surrendered. They were the same people whose stomachs got in the way of them playing tennis and for whom a game of squash involved trying to get behind the steering wheels of their cars at night to drive home, drunk of course.

The Naval Club was different in that those who frequented it were mainly British and older than the sports club types. For some reason there were quite a few Scots, a

Welshman called Taffy (as all Welshmen seem to be called, except in Wales itself), an Irishman called Paddy (as all Irishmen seem to be called) and a number of Englishmen (all from the north of England, whose accents made them hard to understand, especially after six hours of drinking). Even the born and bred Zimbabwean members had some kind of British connection, like a Scots father or a Welsh grandfather. Everyone was white. There were no women.

When we walked into the club it was like playing musical statues, when the music is cut off mid-song and you have to stand as still as possible, whatever you are doing. Had we been playing this game, it would have been difficult to judge who was 'out' as everyone stood so still. For a second we just stood in the doorway to the bar area and didn't move either. Then a waiter approached us with a message. Mr Trevellyan, he said, was sitting at the end of the bar counter. He signalled to the left of the row of stools and dishes of peanuts. Gran clutched my hand and we walked across the silent room with what felt like a hundred pairs of eyes following us.

'This is Mr Trevellyan, Ellie,' said Gran. 'Say hello.'

Still holding Gran's hand, I edged closer to her and, biting the fingers of my other hand, said 'Hello.' I looked down at my feet immediately I had said it.

'She's shy,' said Gran, with a rather high-pitched laugh.

I could see that the last person Miles Trevellyan expected that afternoon was me. He looked slightly annoyed, acknowledged my greeting with a light tilt of his head and turned to offer Gran a drink. I noticed he was wearing white canvas shoes that looked oddly out of shape, as though they had been shrunk in the wash and then someone had tried to

37

stretch them back to their original size. He was also wearing light yellow cotton drawstring trousers and a white golf shirt that had a pocket on the left-hand side with the words 'Club Med' sewn on in light-blue cotton. Underneath the words were three wavy dark-blue lines that represented, I supposed, the sea.

I made up my mind then and there that I didn't like Miles Trevellyan. Whenever anybody asked me why I never liked him, I always thought of that first meeting, his look of disappointment, his way of dismissing me as a child, an encumbrance, something that stood between him and Gran. 'What would you like to drink?' he asked Gran. 'Gin and tonic? Vodka tonic? Beer shandy?'

'Gin and tonic,' said Gran. 'With ice.'

'And you?' he turned to me, his thin blond eyebrows slightly raised. 'Cola or lemonade?'

I didn't answer immediately, not really wanting to accept anything from him but secretly wanting a Cola. I was never allowed it at home because Mom said the sugar would rot my teeth and they'd all fall out. I didn't like lemonade.

'Come on,' said Miles, 'it's not that hard a question is it?' His irritated tone made me feel even more shy and I quickly said: 'Lemonade'.

'Lemonade?' said Gran, tilting her head a little in surprise. 'But you don't like it. Are you sure?'

'Yes,' I replied, looking down at my shoes again.

'Sure?' she asked again. 'Not Cola?'

'No,' I said, wishing she'd just let the matter go.

'Final answer?' asked Miles. I nodded. 'One G&T with ice,' he said to the barman, 'one Castle and one lemonade, shaken not stirred.' He laughed at what he thought his own witticism and pushed a few coins towards the barman from a pile that he kept near his elbow. 'Let's go and take a seat.' He motioned towards some armchairs in the corner of the room. They were covered in green velvety material, worn away in places from prolonged use. They smelt faintly of beer and something greasy. In the middle of the circle of chairs was a small vinyl topped table with a wooden ashtray in the middle. A waiter was just wiping it of ash and beer bottle rings when we sat down. Miles placed his cigarettes and a box of matches on the table, which was still damp, just as the waiter was walking away.

'Hey!' Miles called after him, a finger pointing in the air, both motioning the waiter and warning him. The waiter glanced back and Miles pointed to a bottle top in the ashtray. It was removed without a word.

'Standards,' said Miles, shaking his head and pulling his lips back grimly. He placed his beer on the table, rich and golden with a thin head of froth. Next to Gran's small fizzing glass, it looked manly and proprietorial, yet at the same time, cold and self-absorbed in comparison to her excited leaping bubbles that seemed to throw themselves at the side of the glass, saying 'Look at me, look at me!'

'So how's things?' he asked Gran.

'Fine, thank you.'

'Work?'

'Fine, fine, thank you.' There was a pause while she seemed to search for something to say. 'Been a little busy lately. End of month. That sort of thing.' She smiled her shy smile, the one where she looked down and blushed slightly.

'Luckily, I don't suffer from that,' he said, picking up his packet of cigarettes and knocking it on the table. 'Business at the workshop is generally always the same for me.' He shook out a cigarette.

There was another pause. Gran was sitting rather straight and held her hands on her lap in much the same way that she did at church.

'How's Ronnie?' Miles asked, leaning back in the chair and putting the cigarette in his mouth. I watched, quite fascinated at the way in which he balanced it in the corner of his mouth. He was able to talk while it flicked up and down and only seemed to find stability when he paused to light it. He closed his eyes and took a long drag.

'Ronnie's fine,' answered Gran, with a laugh. 'You must know what she's like. She said she's known you for a long time.'

'About thirty years.' The cigarette burned slowly in his right hand.

'She's quite a character, isn't she?'

Miles nodded.

'She really brightens up the office,' continued Gran. 'Always laughing and joking.'

'Yes,' said Miles. Much later on, I realised that he never commented on anyone's character, except to make fun of them. When I realised that Miles was becoming a semi-permanent feature of Gran's life, I began to follow their conversations closely. Hating Miles, I looked for a way to undermine him, find something about him that would reveal him for the fraud I believed he was.

Ronnie was someone Gran worked with, Ronel van Staden. I had heard Gran mention her to Mom; she had the desk next to Gran in the accounts department of Haddon and Sly.

There was another pause and then: 'What do you do at the weekends?'

Gran smiled again, almost embarrassed. 'Not a lot. Tidy up, I suppose. Do a bit of baking now and then.' She turned to me and put her hand on my head. 'Ellie comes to stay quite often, don't you, Ellie?' I nodded once and looked across to Miles. His eyes moved momentarily across to me and then back to Gran. He didn't comment.

At that point, someone came across to the table, an incredibly thin and tanned man of about fifty. He had on a very short pair of shorts and a short-sleeved shirt. His socks stretched up to his knees.

'Your turn for a game, Miles,' he said, offering him three darts. 'Best of three.'

Miles took the darts and stood up.

'Excuse me,' he said to us, putting out his cigarette and blowing a long stream of blue smoke out the corner of his mouth. 'I won't be too long. Come and watch if you like.'

It was a scene that was repeated many times in my childhood. Gran and Miles would sit and talk and I would sit at Gran's side, lost in a world of my own. Often Miles would play darts and we would watch, though I don't know if Gran did really as she would often ask him who won and if he mentioned something that had happened during the game, a comment made or a particularly good throw, she couldn't seem to recall it. I didn't know why we were there. I didn't know Gran to have many friends and I'd never known her to go out and meet them. The ones I did know were the likes of Mrs Benson, the retired music teacher who lived in the flat above Gran's.

That afternoon Gran seemed so happy; shy at first but

then she couldn't seem to stop smiling. She laughed, excessively I thought, for Miles did not seem to say anything very funny. He bought me a hamburger and chips for lunch; more forbidden food. Mom had a rule about junk food and I was surprised Gran did not remember it. I thought ruefully of the spaghetti bolognese they would be having at home and wondered if Mom would keep me any. I supposed not.

Eventually we left the Naval Club. Miles walked us to the car and held Gran's door open even after we were seated. They chatted for a bit longer and then he closed the door and peered in through Gran's window.

'I'll call you,' he said and then, looking over to me, added, 'Bye, Shelly.'

'Ellie!' giggled Gran, but he didn't seem to have heard her. He gave her a long look and then turned with a backward wave and went inside the club.

It was late when we left. The last lingering rays of the sun gave the darkening streets the look of an old sepia photograph. I sat in silence as we drove home. *'Let's face the music and dance,'* hummed Gran, drumming her fingers lightly on the steering wheel. A slight smile played on Gran's lips. She drew up in front of my house and kissed me goodbye. Gran hadn't come inside the house since she moved out.

'Thanks for the shoes, Gran,' I said, trying to open the car door and pick up the shoebox at the same time. At that point all hell broke loose. My mother came running out of the house shouting, 'Ellie, Ma, you're OK!' She threw her arms around me and then turned to Gran who sat still at the wheel. 'Ma, where on earth have you been? We've been so worried. Andrew's been round to your flat twice and we phoned all the hospitals! Ellie should've been back at lunchtime. Where've you been?'

'Ma, Ma! It's OK,' I said, pulling her arm. 'Gran and I went out for lunch...' I was about to continue and explain the whole afternoon at the Naval Club, meeting Miles Trevellyan, having a hamburger and chips for lunch and two lemonades, when Gran suddenly said, 'I'm sorry, Frances, we went to the park and then Ellie wanted to go to the museum to see the natural history bit, you know – the stuffed animals. Then we had an ice cream. I don't know what happened to the time. It just flew by.'

Mom turned to me. 'Ellie!' she cried. 'We only went to the museum last weekend. Why did you drag your grandmother there again? Honestly! You and those bloody animals!' I stood dumbstruck. Gran had lied. For a few seconds the world spun and I couldn't seem to make sense of the voices or the words that crowded in. The growing darkness obscured Gran's face from me. I wasn't even sure if she was looking my way.

'But–' I began, but I stopped. Somewhere in my consciousness the knowledge that this was our secret, Gran's and mine, was dawning. Somehow, and for some reason, Miles Trevellyan must be kept from everyone else. The afternoon at the Naval Club sitting on the old green chairs suddenly seemed to take on some secret air; it was a place that could not be mentioned. Tears pricking my eyelids and feeling the back of my throat taut and dry, I turned to go inside the house. At the door I met the outline of my father.

'Don't worry, Ellie,' he said, stretching out a hand to me as I approached. 'She's overreacting again. '

As I entered the house, I heard Mom ask, 'How much do I owe you for the shoes?'

'That's all right,' said Gran. 'Early Christmas present.'

Chapter Six

She's still like that today, my mother, though perhaps not quite so overprotective and neurotic about my every move. I suppose it's hard for her to be. I am miles away in England and she is in Bulawayo. When I first left, she used to ring quite diligently every Sunday lunchtime. She'd ask about the weather and what food I was eating and warn me against walking home through parks at night.

Gradually, the calls became less frequent and not quite as intense as they had been, although she did ring me once to make sure I wasn't killed in a train accident she had seen on the news.

When my grandmother spoke of her, it was often with a sigh and a wish that she would let go and enjoy herself a little. Gran was right in many ways, but in others she was completely wrong. Supper was always on the table at the same time, and I was never allowed to eat it in front of the television, or leave my vegetables or go to bed later than nine, but Gran misread the tight control as strictness, not love. She failed to see how she had made my mother the woman she was, how she had made her afraid of her feelings and, most importantly, of an unknown future.

On my departure from my last visit, just before I left for the airport, my mother stood in the kitchen and wished me a safe journey. She was tired, incredibly drawn and haggard looking, but she had managed to get out of bed and dress so that she could see me off. Her beautiful rich chestnut brown hair showed signs here and there of age and the lines under her eyes cut smooth dark half-circles on her face. I could see she wanted to cry, and I did too.

'Give us a ring when you get back. Just a short one. Let us know you've arrived safely.'

I nodded. 'Of course,' I said, trying to hold back the tears.

'Ellie,' she started. The word came out in a dry rasp. 'Ellie, I didn't want you to know because I loved you, not because I wanted to keep something from you.'

I nodded again. There was so much to say. So much I knew that she didn't know, so much that I would have to keep from her.

'I made you some sandwiches,' she said in a forced bright voice and pushed a small packet of food towards me. 'There's some biscuits, too, and an apple.'

I took it and managed a half smile.

'I know what airline food is like,' she said, leaning against the kitchen counter. A remnant of her former matter-of-fact tone crept into her words and momentarily lifted my spirits. There was a time when I would have protested and tried to laugh her off, but I took the food meekly and put it in my bag. I wanted to remind her that I was still her child.

46

The phone rings and I let it go onto answering machine. It is Mandy.

'Ellie, where are you? Nobody's heard from you for days. I hope it's because you're having such a wonderful time that you've completely forgotten all your friends. Call me if you need to chat. I have plenty of peanut butter. OK?'

*

When I look back on my life, the thing I notice most, and now miss in my present life, is the pattern: the way one year rolled smoothly into the next. The way we didn't think of the future or question it, or feel separated from the time that had passed. Did I know that once I left I would never go back? Did I know that once I left, I broke the pattern and could only return as an outsider?

Mandy was part of that pattern of my old life. So were peanut butter sandwiches. She was one of my few, but strong, links, not only with a country, but with a time. I had known her since the age of eight when I was sent to Collingswood, a private primary school in Bulawayo. Some weekends we would stay the night with each other, normally just on a Friday because I went to Gran's most Saturdays. On the Fridays she stayed with me, Mom would pick us both up from school and take us to Haddon and Sly for lunch. Haddon and Sly was a large departmental store with a restaurant on the second floor. I always had a ham sandwich and a strawberry milkshake and Mandy always had a toasted cheese sandwich and a 'brown cow'. Afterwards, we would go down to the supermarket on the ground floor and, while Mom did the shopping, we'd push each other around in the trolley.

When it was my turn to go to Mandy's house for the night, her Mom would pick us up in her lunch hour in her yellow and white VW Golf. It had a sticker on the back that said 'Praise the Lord!' She always smelled nice and her nails were painted red. She would drop us off at home, arrange for the maid to make us something to eat and then she would go back to work and we'd be left to our own devices. For lunch we always had peanut butter sandwiches and raspberry cool drink.

Mandy's parents were staunch churchgoers who let no opportunity to inform you of their devout belief go by. Everywhere about the house were verses and quotes from the *Bible*. Even the toilet was not free of inspiration. '*The Lord is my Shepherd, I shall not want*' a picture read, and a man with a beard and a lamb in his arms stared down from above the cistern. Opposite it, on the door, was another plaque with the words: '*If you sprinkle, while you tinkle, be so sweet to wipe the seat*'. Next to the toilet, instead of the usual stack of *Fair Lady* and *Home and Garden* magazines to keep one occupied, were American magazines from a place in Wisconsin, dated 1972, full of men who looked exactly like the man above the cistern with the lamb in his arms, and a book of inspirational poetry by a man called Walter Johnson. It used to amuse me that the magazines were older than I was.

Mandy had a swimming pool and we'd sometimes spend hours in it, playing games like Marco Polo and throwing stones in that we'd then retrieve from the bottom. On Friday nights we'd watch TV programmes like *The 'A' Team* and *Knight Rider*. Monday always seemed a long way off then.

It was all part of the pattern of my childhood. What I expected, what I knew would happen. Although Mandy was my best friend throughout school, the strange thing was that I never told her about Miles until much later on and, even then, not in great detail; she remained as much in the dark about him as my family did. Nor did I ever mention my Saturday afternoons with him and Gran at the Naval Club. In fact, Saturday itself was a strange day for me, almost a time apart from time, a suspension of life and reality.

Chapter Seven

I have a dream. In it I have two jobs and am trying to do both at the same time. I am wandering about at night, going up flights and flights of escalators in a deserted shopping mall. It is late and I am exhausted. I am wearing my black coat, the one I bought in a charity shop. I am asking someone something, I'm not quite sure what. The person I speak to is one of those kind people who secretly think you're odd, or mad, and smile sympathetically. Coming down on the escalator opposite me is Janice English. She is smiling and radiantly beautiful. On the step behind her is a man. I know they are together. My coat is short, hers is long. She has make-up on, a deep plum lipstick. As we pass, she smiles absently. She does not know who I am.

Another night I wake up twice laughing, but can't remember why. Someone was telling me a joke, perhaps.

*

'Ellie? Ellie, if you're there, please pick up the phone... You can't go on like this for much longer... Please Ellie... Ellie? Give me a ring anytime. You know I'm here.'

A click and a beep and the answering machine switches off. I lie in bed a while longer, glad that Mandy has rung and yet angry at the same time. Do I just get over it? Is that what they want? A smiling face at the door, chatter on the end of the phone line. Everything forgotten.

But I'm glad she rang. I manage to open the curtain slightly without moving much from my position in bed. All I can see is the sky; a grey roof. I let the curtain fall back and think. Once again I am trying to find a beginning.

Later, I get up and sit in my dressing gown in front of the computer. I sit for a while, gazing at the wall and then I type:

The Matabeleland of the early 1980s was a place of fear. Dissident attacks on farms were common. The only way to make world news in Africa is to kill a white person. If you die in Africa and you're black, you fade into the statistics of civil war, famine and drought; proof that black people really can't look after themselves. In response to the murders, the government unleashed terror in the form of the Fifth Brigade, ostensibly to silence the dissidents but in reality to wipe out thousands of people, most unconnected with any form of dissident activity.

In 1980, many people left Zimbabwe for places such as South Africa, Australia and England, and, in the absence of skilled labour, many of those white people left made their way swiftly up the ladder of success. They bought property in Bulawayo's sprawling eastern suburbs with swimming pools and tennis courts; they went on overseas holidays every year and drove the latest Mercedes Benz; they sent their children to private schools. They were the new white elite and their children were my classmates.

I delete the last line. It's too personal and I don't want to be included in this history. I can't write anymore. I make myself some tea and move to the settee near the window. Will I ever finish this piece? I can't seem to finish anything. I look out of the window again.

Competition, I think, that was the whole problem: I could never compete with some of the children in my class to be popular. I didn't have nice enough crayons and coloured pens, or the confidence that having such things to flaunt brings. I feared becoming another Janine Summers, another butt of all the jokes. Janine Summers whose dad came every day to pick her up in an old brown pick-up that clattered and jolted down the road at a snail's pace. Janine Summers who wore her older sisters' cast-offs from the seventies: flares and wide collars with big, garish designs in bright colours. Janine Summers who sat by herself at break and read a book.

I move back to the computer and write:

They weren't the only children who went to private schools, however. There were children there who were paid for by the companies their parents worked for, and other children whose parents struggled financially to keep them there, having to pay the school fees on their own. It was an odd mix; some children had been to London and Disneyland on holiday, whereas others had not even been to Victoria Falls. Some pupils were dropped off in shiny BMWs and others in cars as old as Gran's.

I stop again and nearly delete the whole thing. Why have I mentioned her? I look to the left at a photo of Gran and me taken years ago with Shirley, her great blue bomber. I'm standing holding the passenger door open and she's standing to the right, smiling down at me.

'Come on, you funny girl,' I can imagine her saying. 'Let's get this thing on the road.'

I feel the tears again and look away.

The phone rings and I let the answering machine switch on again. It's Mandy, trying to be cheerful, but there is an edge to her voice:

'Ellie, we're going to Fat Sam's for drinks tonight. I know you don't really like the place, but the change will do you good. We're meeting at seven. Please, Ellie, come.'

There is a sigh and she hangs up. I'm pushing it, I know. She won't always be this patient.

A lonely child. That's how my grandmother described me. Too old for my age. Too serious. Mandy was my first friend at Collingswood, the private school I moved to after Attlee Primary. I joined late in the year and was too afraid to make friends. At break I tended to sit alone or go to the library to disguise the fact that I was on my own. That was until I met Mandy. I left my pencil case at home one day and had to

53

borrow a pencil from the boy sitting next to me. This in itself was not a catastrophe except that Miss Lowe had a strict policy about forgetting things. If anyone forgot anything they had to write 'I will not forget again' five hundred times. I borrowed Timothy's pencil and was managing to get through the day unnoticed when Miss Lowe announced that we had to draw pictures to decorate our history class work. Timothy didn't have any coloured pencils and I wanted to make my work look impressive so I decided to go and ask someone else if I could borrow theirs.

I waited until Miss Lowe was out of the classroom before I went up to Janice English and asked if I could borrow some of her crayons. She had a lovely set of twenty-five with three shades to each colour. Janice said no, I couldn't borrow them. I was shocked. At Attlee everyone had shared their things; no one ever said no. When I asked why not, Janice said her mother said she mustn't lend them out to anyone. I begged and begged but she was firm. No. A couple of other girls joined in and supported Janice. Where were my crayons they asked? Why did I want to borrow Janice's?

Unfortunately, at that point Miss Lowe returned to the classroom and wanted to know what all the noise was about. Everyone went quiet. I was the only pupil standing up so it was to me that Miss Lowe's eyes turned.

'Ellie?' she asked, folding her arms.

My heart started to beat faster and I looked down at the floor.

'Why are you standing up, Ellie?'

'I was asking Janice if I could borrow her crayons.'

'And where are yours?' A gasp of fright went around the class just then, as everyone knew what was coming next.

'I left them at home,' I said.

'You what?'

'I mean, I left them at home, Miss Lowe.'

'And what happens when we leave things at home?'

'I have to write lines.' The muffled gasp rose again.

'What's that?'

'I have to write lines, Miss Lowe,' I said again.

'Five hundred by tomorrow,' she said sharply and turned to write something on the board.

My face was burning with embarrassment as I went back to my seat. I heard someone snigger as I sat down, but I kept my eyes on my work to avoid meeting anyone else's. The lesson continued and I illustrated my work with the borrowed lead pencil, knowing that I would be punished again for poor work. I had just finished drawing when I felt a nudge at my elbow and I turned around, half expecting the mocking eyes of one of my classmates, but it was a packet of coloured pencils. I looked up at who was offering them. It was Mandy Whittaker, the girl who sat behind me. She didn't say anything and I took the packet, almost afraid to smile in case it was a joke. Mandy was my first friend at Collingswood.

More than anything, I hated swimming at school. At Mandy's house there was no competition, no need to swim lengths or divide into relay teams; I couldn't let anyone down. We lined up after break on Thursday and then all trouped down to the pool in single file. I didn't eat on Thursdays. My packed lunch lay neatly wrapped in greaseproof paper, the sharp corners neatly folded over my ham sandwich, a banana lying placidly beside it.

I clutched my towel, with my swimming costume rolled

up inside it, to my chest, a sharp contrast to those who slung their towels jauntily round their necks or spun their swimming costumes round their fingers. A swim was fun; it meant no work, no tests, but I would rather have had both. I couldn't dive, you see, I couldn't get my body to make that sleek curve into the water, parting it with my hands and then slicing through it with the rest of me. Miss Lowe sometimes held me by the ankles and dropped me in head first, but all this achieved was water up my nose and a coughing fit.

I came to fear the water, too, as it rushed up to my face and hit me spitefully. If I tried backstroke, as Miss Lowe suggested, I couldn't swim in a straight line and nearly always endured the wrath of someone in the next lane into whom I bumped.

So I was left to pretend I could dive and make the best of it: the cold splash, the scrambling, the frenzied attempt to get to the other side. The laughter at my belly-flop, the cynical despair of whoever I was partnering in a relay, the disappointment. Sometimes I wanted to hide away or I wished I was genuinely ill. Sometimes I wished I would drown, just to serve them all right. I imagined them all at my funeral: lines of sombre children, wishing they had never laughed or jeered or groaned as I had gaspingly made my way across the pool. All eyes would be on Miss Lowe, who would sit, eyes downcast, ashamed and ostracised on a back pew of the church.

All through my childhood, I had a recurring dream. In it, I was sailing down the Zambezi in a canoe. I was on my own and the canoe kept going faster and faster. Suddenly, I realised that I was nearing the edge of Victoria Falls and began to panic. Every time, I got close enough to look over into the boiling pot beneath, and just as I was beginning to feel the drag of the boat downwards, I would wake up. I'm not sure why I had this dream. I had never been to the Victoria Falls, but on the way up to the library at school hung a set of framed prints of pictures of the Falls by a man called Thomas Baines. There are two that I remember particularly well. In one, he sits in a canoe going down the Zambezi with a black man steering him. He looks uncomfortable in his safari suit and anxious for the safety of his belongings. He looks as if, should they flip, he would sink, his clothes heavy with the dark, muddy water. But the other man, the man who wears a loin cloth and necklace, he will float, no, he will swim. His powerful arms will take him to the shore.

In the other picture, a herd of buffalo is being driven to the edge of one of the cataracts by a herdsman. The terror in their eyes is what I can't forget. There is no way for them to turn around; no way to fight their destiny.

Chapter Eight

I used to think that if I died they would bury me beneath the earth. There would be worms. The worms could crawl out into the sunshine, but what about me? What if I wasn't really dead? I would lie in the bath and cry. My shoulders heaved and heaved in terrible aching movements. God, let me live forever and ever. Let my parents never die. Or at least let us live for a thousand years.

Deep from the blackness that swarmed in about me and hung like a heavy fog, menacing, knowing something that I did not, a voice spoke. It was low and serious, full of knowledge, and yet sad and hopeless. It was a tired soul that spoke and reminded me of my grandfather's resigned movements as he heaved himself from his chair on the verandah and shuffled drunkenly off to bed at night. It was a defeated song that it sang, rueful of decayed hope, of past optimism. But it stretched across the room towards me and placed warm, but old and gnarled hands on my shoulders and whispered close to me, 'You will live for a thousand years.' Then it retreated into the back of my mind and disappeared into nothing.

*

I did go to Janine's house once. We had mince on toast for lunch, and when I told Gran, she pulled a face and said, 'Shame, they're Afrikaans, you see,' and I nodded my head and felt sorry for them, as though they had a terrible incurable disease.

They had two sitting rooms; one for everyday use in which they kept the TV, and one into which we weren't allowed, although Janine opened the door slightly for me so I could peer in. There was a red velvet lounge suite with white crocheted head and arm rests and a shiny brown coffee table, in the middle of which was a bowl of red and white plastic flowers. On a small sideboard was a plaster head of Jesus with long brown hair and blue eyes. He seemed to be staring at me, reproaching me for having peeked into the room. I shut the door with a start. It reminded me of John the Baptist's head on the platter taken to Herod. I was glad we never had one at home.

The only other time I ever went to Janine's house was for her grandmother's funeral when I was about thirteen. Mandy and I both went. My mother took us and she wore black: a black dress and a black jacket and shiny black shoes. We hadn't any black clothes so we wore our school uniforms, even though it was a Saturday and everyone kept asking us if we were boarders out for the day. My mother was the only person in black and looked the most mournful of everyone there, even though she had only met Janine's grandmother once for about five minutes when we bumped into her shopping in Haddon and Sly. No one had known what to say besides 'Hello' and 'This is my grandmother' and

'Hasn't the price of meat gone up?' And then we had all smiled at each other and said goodbye.

The funeral was the only time I did go inside the second lounge. They had cleared the sideboard and laid the open coffin on top. Janine's grandmother lay there, still and peaceful, with her eyes closed and her arms crossed on her chest. Jesus had been put to one side, but his eyes continued to watch me as I filed past the coffin. 'Dear Lord,' I thought, feeling a prayer was appropriate. 'Please look after Mrs Bester and keep her safe.' Afterwards I thought the last bit was a bit ridiculous as she couldn't be safer than being dead. Hers was the only funeral I had ever been to. It wasn't eventful, besides an older cousin of Janine's throwing himself at the coffin and shouting, 'Ouma, Ouma, take me with you!' and having to be heaved away by Janine's dad before he got a clip round the ear from his mother, who set herself on him like a bulldog.

Afterwards, I told Gran about it and her only comment was 'I don't go to funerals,' and that ended the conversation. Perhaps she was afraid of death, like I was. I wanted to tell her that I had dreaded going to the funeral, dreaded seeing the body laid out and everyone crying. Yet when it came to it, it wasn't all that terrifying. I didn't tell her though. The subject, I knew, was closed.

I wonder sometimes if, when you die, you suddenly know everything. Like who built the pyramids and who shot JFK. Whether there are Martians or not and when the world will end. Does it all become clear, all your mistakes, all the things you should've done? Do you watch a movie of your life and say, 'Oh, so that's what really happened...' and, 'I always wondered where that went to.' Or is there just nothing? An everlasting nothing, a blank screen that declares with a high-pitched buzz: 'end of transmission'.

Chapter Nine

The last time I ever saw Miles Trevellyan was at Harare Airport after my Gran's death. He was a broken man, off to live in an England in which he had never set foot, to hide his broken heart. I would say he was off to start a new life, except that really he was going to die. Nothing stills a broken heart, I know that myself, not even the cold vacuum of England. He took my hand in his and said, 'We've seen the best of times, Ellie, the best of times.' I thought then that perhaps we had. But I know now that Miles was wrong.

Looking back on my life, there is only a small part of it that I associate with 'good times'. In Zimbabwe, we have known very little peace and security; we have never known stability. We've always lived in the shadow of the past; we've always lived with fear, and fear is a strange thing: it stays with you a long time, lying dormant at times but always alive, waiting to possess you again.

Miles owned a farm about twenty-five kilometres out of Bulawayo. Well, it wasn't really a farm as such, more like a smallholding. He didn't grow anything on it besides a few rows of tomatoes and mealies. Most of the land was dry, hard and infertile. His domestic worker kept a couple of cows on it, but they were thin, skeletal animals that wandered aimlessly about. Really there was no point in calling it a farm at all.

When Gran and Miles had been seeing each other for about a month, he suggested she come out to the farm with him for a visit. They could leave on Saturday afternoon, spend the night out there and come back early the next morning. Gran was excited; not, I suppose, about going to the farm, but because his suggestion pointed to some progression in their relationship. Up until now they had only met at the Naval Club for drinks and they were not always on their own. People would come up and chat, not so much to Gran, because she was still new to the Club, but to Miles. Miles played darts and many a time Gran just sat and watched him, smiling at me occasionally and sipping her G&T. This was an opportunity for them to be alone.

However, it came as no surprise when Gran asked Miles if I could come along as well. In fact, she didn't so much ask as tell him that I would be joining them on their trip. He was obviously irritated and I can't say I was much happier about the situation. It was bad enough having to spend an afternoon with Miles Trevellyan at the Naval Club, where at least we weren't alone, never mind a whole day at his farm, territory that was wholly his. Still, I felt protective towards Gran and had an idea that he might murder her and leave her body in the bush somewhere to rot. I suppose I was curious, too, and some spiteful part of me wanted to see this so-called farm so that I could deride it. I needed all the ammunition I could find.

Arranging the trip was the biggest problem. After the disastrous end to my first trip to the Naval Club, Gran was very careful not to upset Mom again, always making sure I was home on time. There was no way my mother would have let me go out to Miles's farm for the night at that time because of the fear of dissident activity. Luckily for Gran, my parents and grandfather had to go to a wedding in Harare that weekend and I was left with her. My mother would most certainly have taken me with her had she known of the plan to go to the farm.

I remember it being very hot, so hot in fact that my back stuck to the seat of the car with sweat on the way out to the farm. We were in Gran's car, as Miles didn't like taking his on long journeys. It overheated, he said, although I was sure he just didn't want to pay for the petrol. Gran's car had one long seat in the front that three people could sit on without feeling squashed. When Mom, Gran and I were together we all sat in the front. It was fun then, but when Gran suggested we do the same now, I inwardly grimaced. So too, I think, did Miles. I said I didn't think it was safe. Dad said so. He said that's why all the modern cars had two separate seats in the front. Gran said I shouldn't be worried; we always did it, she, Mom and I. But I said no and stood my ground.

'All right then,' said Gran resignedly, and opened the door with a roll of her eyes. 'Such a strange child,' she continued to Miles, as though I suddenly couldn't hear anything now that I was sitting in the back. 'One minute it's one thing, the next it's another. She doesn't want me to break the rules now.'

Miles half turned his head back towards me with a smirk. 'Well, we have to listen to the rules now, Ellie, don't we?'

I didn't reply. I felt a sudden surge of anger towards Gran then. Why did she want me to go with her to this stupid farm anyway? Why had I to go everywhere that she went with Miles? Couldn't she do anything on her own? Tears pricked at my eyes and I crossed my arms defiantly and looked out of the window.

When we finally reached the farm and got out of the car, I looked at the outlying buildings and land in dismay, not because I expected anything better, but because this was where I had to spend a whole day. The rains still hadn't started so the land lay bare and brown and dusty. The heat rose in waves from the ground and the sky was like the bottom of a flame, hot and white; all the blue had been burnt out of it. We went into the farmhouse first and Miles fetched us both some water that came out of the tap with a great burst, speckled with dirt. It was warm, too. The rooms were very barely furnished and had an odd unlived in smell to them. The lounge had a few old brown chairs in it and a couple of wooden tables. Nothing matched and the curtains were too short for the windows. On a shelf was a row of books and a telephone directory that was three years out of date. The cover was decorated with coffee stains from cups and stuck to one of the rings was a flying ant's wing. It must have got stuck there when the coffee was still sticky and not yet dried. I imagined the ant being caught and trying so desperately to fly away, that it left one of its wings behind. It couldn't have gotten very far, I thought. There seemed no worse a fate than dying here.

There was no phone. Miles said there was a radio somewhere, but he wasn't sure whether it worked or not. We went outside into the sun and Miles took us around the

65

various buildings, which were as equally run down as the main house. At some point, someone had kept cattle and pigs, but the pens lay unused and falling into disrepair. Miles told Gran that he had been left the farm by an aunt of his. She had been a pioneer and had come to Zimbabwe in an ox-wagon. He had little idea what to do with the place and not enough money to make it a viable business.

Miles wanted to take us down to the fields, or what remained of them, parched and empty as they were, but I was hot and a dull ache had started to thump on one side of my head. He and Gran walked off on their own, she squinting and shielding her eyes from the sun with her hand, and he pushing his hat further down on his head. I looked around for something to do.

To the right of the farmhouse were the servants' quarters, a rather tumbledown collection of once-white rooms at whose windows hung ill-fitting and dirty curtains, and around whose doors pecked a handful of chickens. A mangy dog lay in the thin shade of a pawpaw tree and a couple of children played in the swept area between the rooms and a small vegetable garden. As I walked over, I could smell *sadza* cooking and hear the sound of chopping from inside the first door.

The children, a boy and a girl, looked up as I approached and stared at me with the odd mixture of interest and fear that children often view new people with, especially those of a different race.

'Hello,' I greeted them, but they turned shyly away and smiled at each other. A head poked round from inside the room and regarded me suspiciously.

'Hello,' I said again, this time addressing what looked like the children's mother. She didn't say anything either and, after staring at me for a few more seconds, disappeared again into the room. I looked inside. On the floor was a pot of *sadza*, just cooked and, next to it, was a pile of white cabbage, cut into small pieces. The eyes of the woman were fixed defensively on me. I looked away and back at the children who laughed to themselves again and whispered something to each other. Their clothes hung in tatters and their brown skin was grey with dirt.

One of them then picked up a stone and drew seven squares in the dust with it, two next to each other, one on top of them, two on top of it, next to each other and two single squares on top of them: hopscotch. She kept looking up at me as she drew them and finally turned to me and handed me the stone. I threw it in the last square and jumped, on one leg and then on two, to get it. The children laughed out loud and seemed to find the whole thing hilarious. I thought I might be playing the game wrong so I handed the stone over to the girl, but she laughed and said something to her brother, who laughed too. She threw the stone in the first square and then jumped. Her brother played next and then they handed me the stone again. This time I played correctly.

The afternoon passed surprisingly quickly, as it always seemed to drag when I was somewhere I didn't want to be. I was surprised when I saw Gran and Miles walking up from the fields. They were holding hands, Miles helping Gran along as she seemed a little breathless. I felt embarrassed at this open display of affection and turned away.

Gran was carrying what at first looked like a flower in her left hand, but when she came closer I saw that it was a small bunch of leaves.

'What are those, Gran?' I asked, trying to avoid Miles's eyes and ignore the fact of him holding Gran's other hand.

'Well, that's what I want to find out,' said Gran, opening her hand and looking down at the small, dark green leaves. 'Miles says they are used by the Africans to make a type of tea. I'd be interested to know how.'

Just then Miles whistled over to the *kaya* and called, 'Raymond! *Buya lapha!*' Nothing happened and no one appeared. The children ran behind the *kaya* and took turns to creep round the side and stare at us. Miles called again, 'Raymond! Hey, Raymond, come here, man!'

A door opened and a man appeared, trying to put his overalls on at the same time. He looked as though he had been asleep.

'Yes, Baas, very sorry,' he said, coming up to us, grinning sheepishly and cupping his hands together.

'What you sleeping for now, hey, Raymond?' asked Miles.

Raymond just laughed, 'Ah, it's too hot, Baas.'

'Too much *Chibuku*, you mean.'

'Ah no, Baas,' said Raymond, now laughing even harder. Miles gave him a knowing look and rolled his eyes.

'Raymond, what are these leaves?' asked Gran, showing them to him.

Raymond looked at them and then called over to his wife who appeared once more at the door of the first room. She shouted something back and Raymond nodded.

'You must boil the leaves and then you drink.' He raised a cupped hand to his mouth as he spoke, an imaginary mug of tea.

'Is it like tea?' asked Gran.

'Yes, it is like tea,' answered Raymond.

'Is it good for you?'

Raymond looked a little confused and so Gran asked again: 'It's not a poisonous one, is it, Raymond?'

Raymond laughed. 'Ah no, Madam, it's not a poisonous one.' He called something over to his wife again and she came closer and said a few things in Ndebele. She rubbed her stomach as she spoke.

'My wife says it is very good for painful stomachs.' His wife rubbed her head as well. 'And she says it is very good for headaches.'

Gran nodded thoughtfully. 'That's very interesting. I must try some. I've got a bit of a headache at the moment,' she smiled. 'Too much sun,' she said to Raymond, patting her head.

In the late afternoon we sat in the shade of the old verandah and drank tea, which tasted funny due to the water and the fact that it was made with skimmed milk. Gran played patience and I sat and watched, and pointed out any cards she overlooked. Miles read a book with a half-naked woman on the front, with a gun in the garter round her thigh. Dad said any books that had half-naked women on them were trashy. That kind of woman was called a bimbo.

In the early evening, Miles brought out two beers for him and Gran and some lemonade to mix with hers. Gran said that when you mixed beer and lemonade, you called it a shandy. Mandy had a dog called Shandy because he was a mongrel, a mixed breed. It was a huge dog and fairly intimidating if it met you at the gate. Whenever Dad came to collect me from Mandy's when I had been playing there, he would chat to Mr Whittaker for a while and the dog would continually leap up at the gate and try and catch hold of

Dad's hand. 'Down, mutt!' Mr Whittaker would order. He often called it 'Mutt' rather than Shandy, but Dad said mongrels were the best: they hardly ever got sick and they were good guard dogs.

Miles handed me a lemonade. He never bothered to ask what I wanted anymore. The sky that evening was a tranquil blue and a few early stars were out, as though they couldn't wait for the others. If I had been with my Grandad, he would have told me where to find the Southern Cross and all the other constellations; I doubted if Miles even looked up at the sky. The moon rose swollen and golden. It was so warm still that it seemed like a second sun. Gran made a simple supper of sandwiches on French bread followed by fruit, which we ate outside as well, despite the mosquitoes that hummed menacingly around us.

A wind started to get up just before I went to bed and the sky clouded over a little, hiding the stars. Gran and I were to sleep in the same room, but I went to bed first. The bed was hard and smelled stale and old. I was afraid to push my feet down under the sheet and so lay curled up in a little ball. The wind blew against the window, making the mosquito net creak and clatter and the curtains lifted every so often and then drew back against the glass.

I started to feel afraid and all the stories that I had heard about the dissidents came to mind. What if they came here, I thought? What if they murdered me and Gran and Miles? Who would know? Who would find our bodies? I started to think of an escape plan. I would hide under the bed, I thought, and imagined myself lying there and hearing footsteps in the hall. In my mind's eye, I saw the bedroom door open and the light stream in. I saw the dissidents' boots as they walked in and heard them talk in muffled whispers as they looked for me. But the bed was too obvious. That was the first place Mandy said she looked for her baby brother when he hid from her. There were built-in cupboards in the room. I would hide right at the top and cover myself with a blanket. Would they look there? Would they pull everything out and find me? My heart raced and I pulled the sheet right over my head. It was hot though and I could feel sweat damp on the back of my neck.

I must have fallen asleep, because when I next opened my eyes, I saw Gran creeping softly into the room. She changed into her nightdress and lay on top of the covers. The wind was blowing more forcefully and she got up to close one of the windows. The air was full of the smell of rain and dust. Feeling comforted, I fell asleep again.

I awoke with a start to hear rain beating down on the tin roof. The other window was still open and it blew back with a crash. The curtains were whipped up in a frenzy, blowing into the room like a ship's sail. I got up to close the window and turned back to look at Gran's bed. It was empty. My heart skipped a beat and I crept closer to the bed and felt around. She definitely wasn't there. Thoughts of the dissidents came back to me and I was gripped with terror once again. I tiptoed down the corridor, all the time the storm blowing and banging outside and light dancing along the wall. I was too afraid to see if the electricity was still working in case, by turning a light on, I attracted any unwanted attention. I turned into the lounge, half expecting to see Gran's and Miles's bodies lying on the floor, pumped full of bullets, but there was no one there. No one was in the kitchen either but, as I passed the verandah, I noticed

71

that the door was slightly ajar. As I put my hand up to close it, lightning flashed momentarily and I saw a figure outside. My chest contracted in fear and I looked again. It was Gran.

She was in her nightdress, leaning against one of the wooden pillars on the verandah. She looked deep in thought, but quite at ease, her head on one side. She was not afraid of the storm at all and didn't seem to flinch at the noise or the sudden blades of lightning that sliced across the sky every few seconds. She jumped when I reached for her arm though and touched her chest with her hand.

'Ellie! God, you gave me a fright! What are you doing up?'

'The storm woke me. Why are you out here, Gran?'

'I couldn't sleep, I felt restless.'

'Aren't you afraid of the storm?'

'The storm?' she replied, as though she had just noticed it. 'Oh no. I love storms. They make me feel so... so alive!' She looked down at me for a second and then suddenly grabbed both hands in mine and started to do a little dance, turning me around. I started laughing.

'What Gran? What are you doing?' I asked through my giggles, but all she did was turn me faster. She was laughing loudly now as well and singing.

'When I give my heart, it will be com-plete-ly, or I'll ne-ver give my heart.' The rain was pounding down on the roof and I could feel the floor cool and wet under my bare feet. Then Gran ran out into the rain, pulling me by the hand as she did so.

'When I fall in love, it will be FOR-EVER,' we shouted. I wasn't frightened, not of the thunder, or of the lightning, or the rain, or any dissidents. I was happy, she was happy. We kept dancing, she and I. We were both drenched and my legs

were covered in mud, but I felt that night like a bird set free to soar above the storm and the rain, above the farmhouse and the land, above the whole aching, broken world. My spirit was set free.

When we eventually stopped dancing and the world stopped spinning, we turned to go inside. In the darkness of the verandah, the red glow of a cigarette caught my eye and a figure moved. It was Miles. He didn't say anything, but my eyes met his in triumph.

When the storm moved off, Gran ran a bath for me. The water was brown, but hot and, when I stepped out of the large old white tub, Gran wrapped me in a towel and rubbed my hair dry. As the electricity was off, she made tea on a small gas stove and I fell asleep soon after drinking it. This time, nothing kept me awake, least of all fear.

Chapter Ten

If the storm had cleared the sky and provided a brief respite from the intense dry heat, it hadn't dispelled any clouds in our own lives. In the morning, Gran was quiet and withdrawn. Her face was as grey as the exhausted sky. I spent the morning sitting on the verandah steps. I had played hopscotch by myself for about ten minutes, until I heard the shouting. I stood still. It was coming from inside, from Miles's room. I crept under the window to listen. I half-listened for the thud of a stick or a gunshot. I was ready to rush in and save Gran from Miles. I would just wait for a hint in his words that might suggest physical danger, and then I'd storm in and attack him.

But Gran wasn't crying out for help; not mine anyway. Her voice was full of sorrow and she was crying, crying in the same way I did when the puppy got run over, knowing that something could not come back to life and yet it lay there plump and soft and still warm. That's how Gran cried.

'Oh, no, no, it won't, it won't!' Her words fell like the tears that heaved out of her, swollen and heavy with pain. I could hear Miles's voice, but could not make out the words. He spoke gently and slowly, and every minute I hated him more. Sometimes the crying abated a little and I couldn't hear what Gran was saying. I stood, fidgeting with the stone with which I was going to play hopscotch, not knowing what to do, or how I would comfort her. Eventually, I couldn't hear any voices anymore, and I thought they may be coming out and didn't want to be caught standing under the window. I knelt by the remains of a flowerbed and pretended to have a great interest in the dead bush that protruded from it. Time passed and still no one came out. I decided then to go inside and investigate. Miles was in the kitchen, filling a glass with water from the tap. He took no notice of me. I went into his room. Gran was sitting on a chair, dabbing her eyes with a tissue. There was something girlish about her posture; there seemed to be little difference between her and I. She looked up as I walked in and quickly smiled and pulled herself straight.

'Ellie! What have you been doing? Not misbehaving, I hope.'

'No,' I half-smiled. There was a pause in which she continued to give me that bright, artificial smile.

'Gran, are you OK?'

'Fine, fine. Just got something in my eye, that's all. A bit of mascara. Silly thing, really. Why we girls use half this stuff, I'll never know.'

She and Mom were the same like that, always covering up their tears. It made me more embarrassed when I cried. I felt I lacked the strength to hold them back. Mandy was the only person I didn't mind crying in front of, and yet I'd never seen her anywhere near tears. Maybe everyone has someone they fall apart in front of; but did Gran have to choose Miles?

I wanted to reach out and hold her hand, or put my arm around her like people do in films, but she got up and put her tissue in her pocket and picked up her bag that hung loosely on the back of the chair.

'Come on. We're going to be late,' she said with sudden gusto. 'Last one to the car's a...'

'Fat pig!' I said, completing her sentence with equally forced enthusiasm. It was pointless playing that game with adults, anyway, because they never even tried to race you to the car, and, if they came last, as they invariably did, they never minded being a fat pig or a squashed banana or a whatever it was you had decided the last person was going to be.

We put what luggage we had in the car and sat waiting whilst Gran thanked Raymond for his help and tipped him a dollar or two. Miles rolled his eyes and muttered something about Raymond being the laziest bastard he knew. He took a drag of his cigarette and blew the smoke out of the side of his mouth. He hung his left hand outside the window of the car, keeping the cigarette away from Gran. With the flat of his hand, he banged on the door. 'Come on, let's go.'

Five minutes later we had left the farm and were on the road travelling back to Bulawayo. The rain, which had lain like a silver veil over the world, had begun to dry in the gathering heat. I sat in the back of the car and looked out of the window, breathing deeply the smell of rain and dust. Gran was silent for most of the way, and when she did talk, it was in that bright 'isn't-that-lovely' voice she used when she was trying to cheer me up. Except this time I wasn't upset; she was. I should have been comforting her. I retreated into silence the rest of the way home.

After lunch, Miles left. Gran was tired and went to lie down. She told me to do the same, but I was restless. I could never sleep in the afternoon. Gran's flat was very small and there wasn't a lot in it. It didn't provide much of a place to play in. Through a door in the lounge was a tiny verandah, which was full of pot plants and two hanging baskets, but there was no room to move. Outside the back door were the fire escape steps, which led upstairs; Gran lived on the bottom floor. I sat on the first landing and looked down. It hadn't rained as hard here as it had out at the farm, and what puddles had formed were now almost gone. I started playing a game where I had to flick stones off one step and see if they could land on the next. Sometimes I flicked them too hard and they landed two steps down, sometimes they fell off the back of the step and I'd have to run down and pick them up off the ground. It was just beginning to prove amusing, as I had two teams of stones who were competing in the world championship stone-jumping contest, when the first door along on the landing opened and Mrs Benson came out.

'Who is that making that noise?' she barked from her doorway.

'It's me, Mrs Benson, Ellie,' I said, blushing and turning round with a start. I hadn't been aware that I was making a noise.

'Ellie?' she said, not registering the name until she came closer. 'Oh, Ellie.' She squinted. 'Sorry, I forgot I knew an Ellie.'

I got up and moved a step down, as though I were going back to Gran's.

'Oh, don't go. You carry on with your game. I didn't know it was you, otherwise I wouldn't have said anything.'

'It's OK, I was just about to go anyway.' I took another step down.

'Is your granny sleeping?' she asked, holding the stair rail.

'Yes,' I replied. 'But she might be awake now.'

Mrs Benson turned her wrist to look at her watch. 'I doubt it. It's only half past two. Evelyn likes a full hour's rest. I presume she's been lying down since two.'

I nodded.

'I've known your granny a long time, and I know what she likes and doesn't like.'

I must have looked surprised because she said as a means of explanation: 'We're all creatures of habit, Ellie. It doesn't take long to work out someone's movements.' She smiled suddenly. 'Come in and have some tea.'

'Oh, no thank you,' I said, with an awkward stumble down the first step. 'I must go back. Gran might be up.'

'I doubt it,' she smiled again. 'Come, come and have some tea. I think I've got some biscuits somewhere as well.'

I followed her into her flat.

Going into Mrs Benson's flat was like walking into a spider's web. It was clean, spotlessly clean, but everything inside it was old. Age seemed to seep out of everything, as though it couldn't contain itself anymore. It saturated the air and clung to your clothes. There didn't seem to be any way out. A baby grand piano stood covered with a dust cloth in the corner of the sitting room, untouched for years, Gran had told me, because of its owner's arthritis. A faded rose carpet lay on the floor and heavy sage-green velvet curtains hung at the windows. Lace curtains were drawn across, darkening the room, which didn't get much light anyway. The main light was on, despite the time of day.

'Do me a favour, Ellie,' Mrs Benson said, as she precariously arranged cups and saucers on the tray with her gnarled fingers. I nodded. 'In the cupboard over there, at the top, is a blue box. Please could you get it down for me.' I went over to where she instructed and opened the cupboard. 'You'll have to stand on the chair.' I saw the box she was referring to. It was an old shoebox with *Bata* barely discernible on the side. I reached up and took it down and handed it to her. In it were old photographs, used stamps still stuck to the corners of envelopes, letters and three small books with hard covers. She sat down and opened the largest of the books and I moved close to her side so that I could look at it, too. On the first page was a photo of an old car with a white man in the driver's seat looking very sorrowful and dignified. Next to the car was a black man dressed in a very smart suit, holding a book.

'That's my father,' said Mrs Benson with a smile. 'He was a missionary out at Hope Fountain.' She tried fumblingly to turn the page of the book. 'You do it,' she said, trying to cover up her embarrassment. 'Or we'll be here all night.'

On the next page was an orangey-brown newspaper clipping and opposite that were more photos. I turned the pages for her, not knowing what we were looking for. I could hear her clock ticking methodically on the mantelpiece. There were more pictures; quite a few of a dog she told me was called Lucky, on account of his being found alive down a mine shaft as a puppy; some were of a young woman who mostly appeared with a tennis racquet and occasionally with two children. That was Mrs Benson's mother. Then there were some photos of scenes in which the sky and the horizon were barely discernible from each other and which Mrs Benson thought was great photography of the Nyanga downs – I just nodded – and lastly some group photographs. Here Mrs Benson bent lower and carefully scanned each one.

'Is that her...? No, no... maybe... no.' She looked up at me and pulled a face. 'I really thought I had one of her. Maybe it's in the other book.' We went through the next book and the next before she saw what she was looking for. It wasn't stuck in any of the books at all. It was loose, lying with the letters and stamps. She moved closer to me and I could smell her old, soft, powdery skin and a faint trace of perfume.

'There she is, Ellie,' she said, pointing to a young woman standing with another woman and two men on the steps of a house. 'That's your grandmother.'

I looked closely, but the picture was very slightly blurred. The woman had shoulder-length dark hair and the front piece looked as though it had been rolled back. She wore a dress and had a handbag on her arm. I couldn't tell if she were smiling or not. The man next to her was wearing a suit. He had a bald head and a big smile. The other man also wore a suit, but he was shorter and thinner and had dark hair. The lady next to him had blonde hair and was slightly plump.

'That's me,' said Mrs Benson, pointing at her. 'Your gran was the pretty one though. All the boys loved her.'

'Who's that with her?'

'Winston... No, something like that. It was short for something else. He was a funny man! Could make you laugh and laugh and laugh. That's my Bill,' she said, pointing to the dark haired man. 'That was the night we got engaged.'

I looked at her and she smiled the way people smile when they remember something they don't have any more. Gran had told me that Mr Benson had died a long time ago. Way before I was born.

She put everything back in the box and put it on the table. 'Now. Who's for some tea?'

I was still interested in the photo though. 'Was that Gran's boyfriend?' I asked.

'No, no, nothing like that,' she laughed, but the corners of her eyes narrowed as though she was annoyed. She put a cup and saucer in front of me with rather more gusto than the action demanded and the cup slid sharply into the saucer. 'Your grandad was the only boyfriend she ever had.'

My eyes widened in surprise and she softened. 'Nowadays girls change their beaux every two minutes, but back then we had more stamina, more staying power. We didn't just give up on something – or someone – we really made a go of things. Love lasted.' She stopped at some expression on my face and must've realised what she'd said for she carried on: 'Of course, some things don't last. Perhaps they're not meant to. Right, help yourself to sugar.'

'Who are the natives?' I asked Mrs Benson.

'What are you looking at there?'

I held up one of the old clippings and read: 'Two Natives Killed in Failed Robbery'.

'It's a rather old-fashioned word for the Africans. People don't say it anymore. It means the people who live in Africa.'

'Oh,' I said, looking back at the article. It was a funny word. It reminded me of the word 'knives'. I imagined the natives carrying knives. 'Am I a native then?' I asked Mrs Benson.

She laughed. 'Oh, no, my dear, you're a European. Natives are black people.'

'Are Europeans also from Africa?'

'No, we're from Europe,' said Mrs Benson, 'originally.'

'Oh,' I said and thought for a minute, 'I've never been there.'

'Never mind,' said Mrs Benson, mistaking the confused note in my voice for disappointment, 'I'm sure you'll go one day.'

When I went back downstairs, Gran was awake and speaking on the phone to Mom in Harare. In those days Dallas was on television on Sunday evenings. I was never allowed to watch it as it was on too late; anything after the news at a quarter to eight was too late for me.

Viewers in Harare watched Dallas one episode ahead of those in Bulawayo. Everyone said that was one of the many unfair advantages that Harare had over Bulawayo. Harare had everything. All we had in Matabeleland were dissidents, drought and delayed episodes of Dallas. Those determined not to be completely left out used to phone friends and colleagues in Harare on Monday morning to find out what would happen the following week.

Gran was asking Mom to watch Dallas that night so she could let her know what happened. Mom had obviously said something derisive and Gran said, 'Frances, you might enjoy life more if you weren't so critical.' There was a pause and I could hear Mom's voice rattle back like machine gun fire. Gran rolled her eyes and smiled at me.

'Where've you been?' asked Gran, when she put the phone down. She ruffled my hair. 'I thought I told you to lie down. You've got school tomorrow and we had rather a late night last night.'

I told Gran where I'd been and about the photo I had seen of her.

'Photo?' she said, wrinkling her brow. 'I didn't know Audrey had any photos of me.'

'It didn't look like you.'

Gran laughed and ruefully nodded her head. 'Thirty years does a lot to change one's looks.'

'What was Mrs Benson like when she was young?'

'Audrey? Much the same as she is now. I don't mean that in a nasty way. She's just always been old. Goes to bed at nine every night, has done for the last fifty years. That sort of thing. A bit set in her ways.'

'She says you always have a nap at two for exactly an hour.'

Gran let out a screech of laughter. 'Did she really? Well, perhaps we're just as predictable as each other.'

'There were two men in the photo as well. Mrs Benson said one was her husband and the other was a friend of yours.'

'Really?' replied Gran, frowning. 'Who was that, I wonder?'

'Someone called Winston or something like it.'

Gran rolled her eyes. 'Winston! Heaven forbid I ever had a boyfriend called Winston!'

I laughed. 'She said you didn't have any boyfriends besides Grandad.'

Gran shot me a look. 'Me? I had loads of them. I had to fend them off in the end.'

I giggled. 'Gran,' I warned, 'your nose is growing big!'

That night, Gran let me stay up to watch Dallas. She seemed her old self again: laughing, joking, making tea when the adverts came on. I felt a return of the comfort I usually felt with her and snuggled up close to her on the couch. (Just the nearness of *you*.) On the TV, J.R. Ewing had just completed some shady deal. He rocked back in his chair and smoked a fat cigar before laughing, self-satisfied, to himself. He looked how I felt. But things never stay the same way forever.

*

Another message on the answering machine. It's Mark. I leave it run.

'Ellie, it's me, Mark... Just talk to me, won't you? You can't cut me out of your life forever.' There was a pause and his tone changed. 'You give up on everything, do you know that? You're so high-handed about morals that we all have to be perfect around you. Well, I can't be. I'm sorry.' He puts the phone down.

Chapter Eleven

One night I dreamt of Jesus.

'What would you like?' he asked.

'I want everyone to be happy,' I said, and then I woke up.

*

Gran asked me once why I never liked Miles. I didn't know what to say, so I lied and said I liked him.

'Don't fib. I know you don't.'

We were sitting in her car, waiting for Mom to come out of some shop or other. It was a Saturday morning and all three of us were in town shopping. Later, Mom would leave me with Gran and we would have a hurried lunch before starting out for the Naval Club. Gran kept looking at her watch. We were going to be late if Mom didn't hurry up, but she couldn't say anything without letting on about where we were going. She reached into her bag and pulled out a couple of mints.

'Want one?' she asked, passing it back to me. '*When there*

are clouds in the sky, you'll get by...' she hummed absently.

If Mom was gone a long time, Gran could ask me all sorts of questions and, knowing her, she probably would. Luckily, however, Mom reappeared soon after Gran's questioning began and she looked in the car window and said: 'Ellie, come and try on these school uniforms, please.'

'Come on,' she added when I pulled a face. 'Let's get this over and done with and then we don't have to come back.'

The problem with school uniforms was that I always had to go back, no matter how much my mother said 'these will fit you for a good while' and 'let's leave some length so they'll last a bit longer.' The intervals between trying on uniforms seemed to be more like weeks than months or years. I wasn't going to argue though as Mom was in a bad mood. She had been all day. We had driven to Gran's with the intention of picking her up, but she had wanted to go in her car. Mom couldn't understand why as our car was more comfortable than hers and there didn't seem to be much logic in us getting out when all she had to do was get in. She wouldn't have it though and eventually Mom gave in. After that, they argued about everything: where to buy the freshest bread, the choicest cut of meat, the most economical washing powder. Gran's driving drove Mom up the wall, for she didn't look in her rear-view mirror too often and more than once, someone hooted at us as she changed lanes and narrowly missed bumping into them.

The shop was dark and stuffy. It was an old building with shelves packed full right up to the small high windows with box upon box of clothes and shoes. It was run by an Indian family called Doolabh and had been for about the last hundred years. Old Mister Doolabh had just died and his picture was propped up on the counter, surrounded by a garland of flowers. 'Good riddance,' Grandad had said when he heard of Old Mister Doolabh's demise. 'They say only the good die young. That bloody coolie was a right bastard.'

'Dad,' Mom had said despairingly when she heard him. 'Don't talk like that. He's just died.'

'Moslems – they're all the same,' said Grandad, ignoring her.

'He wasn't a Muslim. He was a Hindu,' corrected Mom. My mother was ahead of her time in being the type of atheist commonly found in Britain today: the type who show reverence for every religion except Christianity. Had Mr Doolabh been Catholic and my grandfather said he was Anglican, the error may have passed uncorrected.

'Whatever – they're all the same.'

'How can they be?' asked Mom, rolling her eyes. 'Muslims believe in Mohammed and Hindus believe in... in all that reincarnation palaver.'

'Reincarnation!' spat Grandad. 'I hope the bastard comes back as the rat he was.'

Young Mister Doolabh had taken over the running of his father's shop, although he had always worked there anyway, so nobody really noticed any change. Although he was always referred to as Young Mister Doolabh, he was in fact in his early sixties and had grandchildren older than me. Fortunately, he had no sons, which saved us having to address a Young Young Mister Doolabh. He was assisted in the shop by his wife and two of his daughters who worked the till and greeted customers. There were also a number of black workers who were generally used to climb a ladder up to whichever box was requested from the great pile stacked against the walls.

The uniforms were waiting for me when I entered the shop and I looked with severe displeasure at the three different sizes that I had to try on. I picked up the first dress and looked around for the dressing room.

'Sorry, sorry,' said Mrs Doolabh from behind the counter. 'No dressing room, I am sorry.'

I glanced at the curtained cubicle that I could see at the far end of the shop and had turned to challenge her on that point when she, reading my mind, said: 'Sorry, used for keeping stock at the moment.' She beamed self-satisfyingly at my mother and added: 'We stock every uniform for every school in Matabeleland.' My mother raised her eyebrows in a weary attempt at showing interest. 'Boys and girls.'

'Just change here, Ellie,' said Mom. 'No one's going to look.'

'Mom,' I said, horrified at the prospect of changing, not only in front of Mrs Doolabh and her daughters, but also Young Mister Doolabh and all the assistants.

'There's nobody here,' encouraged my mother, meaning that there were no other customers.

'Everybody's here,' I protested. 'I can't.'

Mom blew through her nostrils angrily, but I wouldn't relent on this one.

'You're eight years old. There's nothing to see, for God's sake. Let's just get this over and done with.'

'No,' I said, squirming with humiliation. 'Can't we take them home? I can try them on there.'

Mrs Doolabh turned to her daughter and said something in a language I couldn't understand. Her daughter laughed and the great row of bangles on her arms jangled as her bosom rose up and down. I could feel the tears building up inside. Suddenly Mom turned on me and pulled the zip of my dress down.

'No!' I shouted as I felt the material fall loose. Even Mrs Doolabh's face changed to horrified surprise as Mom pulled the dress off me and I stood there in my pants, my arms crossed over my chest. She looked uncertainly at Mom and then swung her thick black oily plait over one shoulder and passed one of the uniforms to her. I knew everyone was watching me. I knew more customers had entered the shop and that there was a man half way up a ladder who was grinning down on me, but I just looked down and let the tears come and blur my vision.

'Ellie, what's wrong?' I heard another voice, Gran's voice. She had got bored sitting in the car and came to see what was taking us so long. I couldn't speak and I couldn't look at her. I stood and cried with embarrassment.

'Frances, what's wrong?' asked Gran with concern. 'What are you doing? Why is she changing in the middle of the shop?'

Mom's resolve had begun to waver somewhat at the onset of my tears, but she tried hard to maintain the hardness in her voice as she pulled the second uniform over my head and said: 'We're trying on uniforms, Mum. What does it look like?'

Gran didn't reply. Instead, she leaned over the counter and called over to where Mr Doolabh sat balancing the books at a small desk rather hidden in the darkness of the shop.

'Mr Doolabh, excuse me, but I think my granddaughter

needs a proper changing room in which to try on these uniforms.'

Mrs Doolabh made as though to approach and explain the situation, but Gran silenced her with her hand and said: 'It's a disgrace to run a shop like this. It would never have happened in the old days with Old Mister Doolabh.' She didn't raise her voice or pound her fists, but Young Mister Doolabh got up at once, his chair scraping along the cold tiled floor and hurried over.

'Of course, of course,' he muttered, obviously flustered. He shouted to his daughters in more of the language I couldn't understand and I was hurriedly ushered into a stock room at the back of the shop. There wasn't much space to turn about in as it, too, was piled high with the entire range of school uniforms for the province, but it was better than stripping down to my underwear in public. Gran held my hand as we walked in and Mom followed behind. She didn't say a word.

When we got back to Gran's flat, Mom kissed me goodbye and squeezed my hand. Her eyes were brimming with tears as she waved goodbye from the car. She never said she was sorry, but I knew she was. Gran never mentioned the incident to me and the following week we picked Gran up in our car and did the shopping together.

Chapter Twelve

Ever since I can remember, my grandfather sits out on the verandah at night. In summer, he wears shorts and no shirt. The glow of his cigarette momentarily picks up the sheen of sweat on his chest and arms. In winter, he wears a jersey, but he doesn't seem to feel the cold. He drinks beer slowly from the bottle and sits tapping cigarette ash onto the concrete floor, even though Mom has told him off about it and leaves an ashtray on the table for him to use. He stares into the flowerbed, the canna lilies, the clear and cold or warm and dry or wet, liquid night. One beer, sometimes two, and three, sometimes four, cigarettes. If I sit with him, he doesn't talk. I think he resents my presence if I go out to him. No one else tries. Everyone leaves him alone.

On Sunday afternoons, I sit and watch old films with my grandfather. Everyone else is lying down and the house is cool and calm with the silence that only Sunday afternoon can bring. We watch John Wayne, Humphrey Bogart, Stewart Granger. Gangsters, cowboys, soldiers. The Alamo, the South Pacific, Dunkirk, Normandy, North Africa. Always heroes.

Men who lead soldiers across the battlefield, who fight the last Apache single handed, or the Mafia, the Japanese, the Germans. Men who lead and do not follow. Heroes. My uncle was a hero. This is all I know. No one else talks about it. Everyone else sleeps through. The house is calm and silent.

*

Things at home carried on much the same as they had done when Gran had been there, except that my grandfather was even more bitter a person, inclined to spend his evenings on the verandah looking moodily out into the night, and his weekends slumped in front of the TV. My mother tried to pacify him, tell him that Gran would return any day now, that soon she would realise the error of her ways.

But it wasn't just Gran's absence that caused my grandfather's permanent bad mood; it was the state of the country, too. He would continually rant about black rule and the certain demise it would bring. Look at Zambia, look at Malawi, look at Mozambique, he would rage. The end was near. Soon we would all be sitting in huts, eating *sadza* and relish with our hands, smelling like a pig's backside. My mother would try and calm him down. She felt uncomfortable when he got in one of his moods, which was often, especially if the servants were around.

I got on well with Jameson, the houseboy. He taught me how to whistle, not the tuneful whistle of the happy worker, but the short, sharp 'Hey, you!' whistle used to attract the attention of friends, attractive women and anyone of interest passing up and down the road. Sometimes in the afternoons, when it was too hot to be right out in the sun and even the dogs flopped about in the shade, I would sit outside on the kitchen step with Jameson while he cleaned vegetables for the evening meal. If there were peas to be shelled then I would help him, eating many along the way, which made him angry and he would tap my hand whenever he saw it raised to my mouth.

He had a great fear of snakes, but it was also his favourite topic of conversation and he would tell me of various encounters he had had with cobras that were twice the size of men, pythons that could swallow a fully grown cow, and boomslangs that threw themselves onto you as you walked through the bush. He would twist and turn slowly as he told the story, his eyes narrowing to slits in his face. He wove his left hand backwards and forwards in an 's' shape in front of my eyes, his fingers close together, bent in an arch, like the hood of a cobra, and then suddenly he would dart towards me and clutch my throat. I would scream or giggle or do both.

At school, a number of my classmates had left and gone to live in South Africa. One had even gone to Australia. He sent the class a postcard from Sydney. I remember it was of the Opera House and that he had written on the back that Australia was nice and hot but that Australians talked funny. When I asked my mother why so many people were leaving, she said that it was because they were worried. It was because of the black government. Britain, who had once owned Zimbabwe (when it was called Rhodesia), had given it back to the black people and, although the black people owned the country really, it wasn't a good idea as they wouldn't know what to do with their power. She said it was like giving Jameson a car to drive: he would crash it. I asked whether, if Dad could teach Jameson to drive, it would be possible for him to learn. Mom said she thought so, but the problem was that there were so many people who needed to learn, and not enough people to show them how.

'There's no way I would let that silly bugger drive me an inch out of the garden,' said Grandad. 'He's just learnt to control the hosepipe, never mind drive a car.' Mom winced whenever Grandad said such things, but she never really challenged him, preferring to try and change the subject. And so it was that my grandfather felt betrayed by both his country and his wife, both of whom had left him for greater things.

My grandmother wasn't born in Zimbabwe. She was from a small seaside town on the Kent coast called Goresdon. She said that it was the most boring place on earth and that she had no desire at all to ever return there. She had had a brother, Gregory, who dropped dead one day, at the age of forty-five; it was a heart attack. He had a wife and a child, but Gran did not keep in touch with either of them. When I asked why she just shook her head and said that's what happens sometimes, especially when you have been away for a long time.

Before Gran married Grandad, she was married to someone else. His name was Timothy Broughton and he was killed in the Second World War, two months after Gran married him. He was a Rhodesian who was sent to England to train as an officer in the RAF. He was shot down in the Mediterranean somewhere. After the War, Gran's father told her that she should go and visit his family. England was a bleak and desolate country and he was afraid that Gran would never meet anyone ever again. Gran told me he was bitter, bitter about the War and what England had to offer. He, himself, had served in the First World War and had the limp and ruined lungs to prove it.

Her father, on account of his father remarrying a much younger woman after his first wife's death, had a half brother who was only ten years older than Gran. Cadwallader, or Wally, as he was more commonly called, had moved to Rhodesia in 1937. If Gran were to get into any trouble, Uncle Wally could help her out. As it happened, his assistance was called upon as the Broughton family turned out to be less than accommodating of dead Timothy's widow.

'That's how I moved to Bulawayo,' Gran used to tell me. 'I was in Harare, which was then called Salisbury, and I received a letter from Uncle Wally who was living here. He arranged a train ticket for me and a job and accommodation at the other end. The rest, as they say, is history.'

Uncle Wally was an architect with a firm called Stoughton and James, a thriving company back in the forties. He arranged for Gran to work in the reception of the main office and, although it wasn't a great job and didn't pay well, it was something and it also gave her the opportunity to meet lots of people.

Gran's father died soon after she arrived in Rhodesia; she didn't go back for the funeral. Her mother came out to see her once in 1953. I found a photo of them together at World's View in the Matopos. Next to Gran is a stout woman with a calf length skirt and a short jacket. Her handbag hangs from one hand and she isn't smiling.

Perhaps the sun is in her eyes, I used to think, or she is hot. Gran told me the suit was woolen and I exclaimed in surprise, 'Woolen! No wonder she doesn't look too happy!' I couldn't imagine climbing up to World's View in a woolen suit. On the back of the photo in blue ink was scrawled 'Me and Mum, 1952'. It is the only photo I have ever seen of my great-grandmother.

I asked Gran why she called her mother 'Mum' and she said that's what you call your mother in England, well, in certain parts and if you are of a certain class. She said upper-class people called their mothers 'Mummy', but she thought that was silly after a certain age. Other English people said 'Mam'. In Zimbabwe, we said 'Mom'; Gran said that was because we watched too much American TV.

Somewhere along the line, my grandparents met and got married. It was only when I was about fifteen that I asked my mother where they'd met. She said it was at Stoughton and James. My grandfather started working there a year or so after she did. He was a builder then, although not in the sense of laying mortar on brick himself; he oversaw operations at the sites. Two months later they were married. My uncle was born a further nine months down the line.

My grandfather was a born and bred 'Rhodesian', as he always referred to himself. Way back in the mists of time, his family had come from somewhere in Britain, but he himself had never even set foot there. The furthest he had ever gone was South Africa and once to Zambia, when it was called Northern Rhodesia. During the War, he had served in East Africa. He talked often of his time there, but I couldn't help getting the feeling that he felt he had missed out on the real action, as though he had taken part in a sideshow rather than the main attraction.

Wally moved to Wales in 1973. He'd left Rhodesia two

years before and moved to Durban, hoping to set up his own company there but his plans fell through. Mom said the threat of majority rule in Rhodesia prevented him from coming back to Bulawayo and he knew it wouldn't be long anyway before South Africa went the same way.

About two or three years ago, before I moved in with Mark, Gran confided in me for the first time about her long-dead first husband. As usual, I had written to her for advice. Should I or shouldn't I, that was the question. She wrote back almost immediately. There was a time when she could post a letter in Bulawayo on Thursday and it would land with a fat plop on my doormat in England on Saturday.

'Go for it,' she wrote. 'I know there are many of my generation who feel that living with someone is not only wrong or sinful, but lacks the commitment that my generation had. Audrey was just saying to me the other day that nothing lasts anymore. Even marriage is undertaken with the feeling that if it doesn't work out, one can get divorced and give someone else a go. But I'm not so sure, Ellie. I'm not so sure that anything lasted when we were young. We just stayed with it, because that's what one did. Is it worth the unhappiness?

'I knew my first husband, Timothy, for less than a month before we married. Less than a month! What was I thinking and yet look where it took me! I didn't know him. He didn't know me. I didn't love him, either. He knew that, but it didn't matter, because he had already lost his heart to someone else and because it was wartime and war does strange things to people, Ellie.

'We spent our first night at a pub near Tunbridge Wells. We had one night together before he had to return to his regiment. We had supper in the small dining room of the pub. It was dark – we weren't allowed lights. I didn't know what to do, you know, or what to say. I was so innocent, so naïve, only seventeen. He stayed downstairs and had a drink at the bar. I went up to our room and jumped into bed with my nightgown on and pulled the sheets right up to my ears. He didn't come for a long time. I nearly fell asleep. My head kept rolling over to one side and then I'd jerk upright and I'd look around for him. In the snatches of moonlight that made their way into the room, I tried to see my watch, but I couldn't make out the time.

'When he did eventually come in, he was drunk. He fumbled at the door and appeared to be looking for a key, although it wasn't locked. He kept his head down when he came inside. It was as though he didn't want to look at me, as though the door was more interesting. He leant his face against it, his arms outstretched, as though he were dancing with it, as though it could give him comfort, give him something that I couldn't.

'I called over to him but he didn't answer, so I got out of bed and tried to remove his uniform, but he wasn't helping; it was as though he was dead. I had to move his arms myself and he was heavy and I kept stumbling backwards.

'"What's wrong?" I kept saying. "What's wrong?" He fell on the floor and slumped against the door and suddenly I saw that he was crying. He held his head in his hands and rolled on to his side and just cried. He was like a baby, a little baby, crying for his mother.

'I don't know what was wrong. The War, I thought then, but now I think perhaps he was crying because he had married the wrong person. In another life, in your life, Ellie, we may have had a couple of nights in bed together. Perhaps we would have made it to living together, though I doubt it. We certainly wouldn't have married. How different my life would've been. And yours. You are only here because of him, which only shows that each path we take has its own rewards and failures.

'Our marriage was never consummated and he was killed two months later. I spent a long time pretending that I was sad he had died, but I couldn't help a certain feeling of relief. I was glad I never gave myself to him in that way, that I could hold him while he cried and put my arms around him while he slept, but that when he died, he never took that little piece of me with him. I was left whole and I don't mean physically, I mean spiritually, in thought. It was a long time before I really fell in love, but when I did, I had everything to give.

'Go for it, Ellie, be free. Love Mark with all your life, but always hold something back. Never give a man everything, Ellie, for when they have everything of yours, you will have nothing but the memory of it.'

Chapter Thirteen

One day I heard my Mom on the phone to Gran; it sounded as though someone was coming to stay.

'So when does he arrive, Ma?' I heard her ask. 'Oh, lovely. It will be great to see him again after all this time. I hope he's not too old to travel. Sixty-seven – is that all? I thought he was older than that. God, he'll find things changed, I'm sure.'

Impatient to find out who exactly was coming to stay, I pretended to find something near the phone amazingly interesting. Mom pulled a face at me and smiled whilst talking away to Gran. I continued to fidget. When she came off the phone, I hopped about her, dying to know who the imminent visitor was.

'You haven't met him, Ellie,' Mom said, going into the kitchen and tying an apron around her waist. 'It's Uncle Wally.'

'Wally!' I laughed. 'That's a funny name!'

'It's short for Cadwallader,' she explained, but that made me laugh more. 'Uncle Wally used to live in Zimbabwe, but he left a long time ago, before you were born.'

This was indeed a long time ago. I couldn't imagine a world without me in it, couldn't quite comprehend that the world had gone on long before I was born.

Later, I heard her telling Dad about Wally's impending visit. 'Seems she heard from him last week and he's going to give her a call soon to confirm the dates.'

'Last week?' said Dad. 'She's taken a while to break the news. The man will be here soon.'

'I don't think she wanted to tell us too quickly in case he changed his mind. Mum's superstitious like that.'

'Like how?' asked Dad, being awkward.

'Well, she doesn't like talking about things before they happen. You know how she was when I was pregnant with Ellie. She didn't want me telling anyone until she actually popped out. I think she only bought my baby clothes once I'd been born!'

Uncle Wally was going to stay with Gran, although there wasn't much room in her flat. Mom offered to have him stay with us, but Gran was adamant. I think it was something to do with Grandad. For some reason she did not want them to be together in the same house.

Wally was going to come a couple of weeks before Christmas and leave just before New Year. Gran wanted him to stay longer, a couple of months even. Now that he was retired there wasn't anything to rush back for, she complained. But Uncle Wally was also adamant. Two weeks was long enough and, besides, his ticket was already booked.

In the days before Wally's arrival Gran seemed strangely quiet and lost in her own thoughts. It was the school holidays so I was around at her flat quite often. She had taken two weeks off work and would have another week off between Christmas and early January as Haddon and Sly's accounts department would be closed for business then. In those days many businesses shut over the festive period. Some people went away, visiting friends and relatives in South Africa or on fishing trips to Kariba or Lake Kyle. We didn't have any friends or relatives in South Africa and Mom said fishing was no way to spend Christmas: only Rhodies did that. Come rain or thirty-five degree sunshine we had a big roast turkey, pudding and carols around the tree.

When Gran lived with us she was very house proud. She would spend hours washing, polishing and shining so that our house looked like a showroom. Even if someone were just coming round for a cup of tea, the furniture would be dusted, the rugs shaken out and all the pot plants' leaves shined. I often wondered whether the visitors found the overwhelming smell of lemon scented polish suffocating. Now that she lived on her own, and had to go to work every day, she was more relaxed about her cleaning routine. Although everything was still neat and tidy, it was not the fastidious neatness and cleanliness of the past. It was strange that, in the week before Wally's arrival, she did nothing. She sat, seemingly immobile, in her chair in the lounge and stared off into space. Nothing seemed to be able to make her move, let alone become excited. It is perhaps the only time I ever saw my grandmother really sad. Even when she lived with us and had a row with my grandfather about something or other, I had never seen her look so forlorn. Miles called about twice a day, inviting her out or inviting himself round, but she put him off.

The way she had been acting that whole week, you

wouldn't think she was looking forward to seeing Uncle Wally at all. Maybe she was afraid it wasn't going to go well. Mom said he would find everything changed and, when I asked her what she meant, she said the country had changed so much since Uncle Wally was here, he might not like it. Grandad, as usual, said things had gone downhill fast since Independence and Mom reminded him of how lucky we were; Mugabe could have had us all kicked out in 1980 and then where would we be now? However, in some ways she agreed with Grandad. Not only had standards dropped, people had changed; they were less friendly, more guarded and money conscious. Maybe, I thought, Gran was afraid that Uncle Wally would want her to move back to Wales with him, as he had once persuaded her to move to Bulawayo.

I went with Gran and Mom to the airport to meet Uncle Wally. We stood on the balcony and saw him walk down the steps from the plane. Gran was waving like mad and he stood for a while on the tarmac and just looked. Then he waved as well.

Uncle Wally is the only person in my life I can describe as having a beaming face. It was huge and round and pink and his head was nearly bald. He reminded me of the pictures of the sun I used to draw at school; a great big shiny sun with a smiling face. When Uncle Wally smiled, you could almost feel the heat from his face. He smiled often, too, and was always telling jokes and making us all laugh.

The day after Wally arrived, I was at Gran's flat and we made gingerbread men. He joined in and mixed up the ingredients, singing away as he did. 'You are my sunshine, my on-ly sun-shine. You make me ha-ppy when skies are grey.' At one time he caught Gran round the waist and twirled her around the kitchen. Do you smile to tempt a lover, Mona Lisa, or is this your way to hide a broken heart? He was fun and Gran was relaxed and quite different to how she'd been before Wally's arrival. She talked away about where she was going to take him while he was in Zimbabwe and which of his friends still remaining in the country he should want to go and see.

While the gingerbread baked, Gran made tea in a pot and put it on a tray with three teacups and saucers. I loved the formality of the procedure: heating the teapot first with a little water, waiting for the tea to brew before pouring it, the clink of the china teacups and the silvery tinkling sound the beaded cover for the milk jug made as it was placed on the tray.

Over tea, Gran and Wally discussed the past: working at Stoughton and James, life in post-war Rhodesia, people they had known, places they had gone. The more I looked at Uncle Wally, the more I thought there was something familiar about his face. It didn't feel like he had just arrived and that I had only known him a few days.

He had a large watch that he carried in his pocket as the leather strap was broken. He took it out every so often to check it and I could hear the tick-tick-tick of passing time. I wanted to look at it, but he wouldn't let me touch it, whisking it back in his pocket when I stretched out my hand.

'Do you have any photos of the old days?' asked Uncle Wally, leaning back in the sofa with his tea in one hand and remnants of a gingerbread man on his chin.

Gran looked slightly uncomfortable and shook her head, 'Only the one,' she said and got up and went into her room. I heard her rummaging through one of her drawers and then she came back into the lounge, picture in hand. It was an old black and white one, printed on a piece of card. On the back of the photo, across the top and in faded grey letters, were the words 'POST CARD'. In the left-hand bottom corner were the words: 'Harry Llewellyn and Sons, Cardiff'. It seemed strange to me that people actually used to send postcards of themselves to friends and relatives. The photo showed Wally as a large, fairly stout man with a big round head and receding hairline, although he said he wasn't more than twenty years old when it was taken. He was dressed in a smart suit and had his hands clasped behind his back.

'That's the only one I have,' she said, passing the photo to Wally. I had a feeling that any other photos might be at home with Mom and Dad and that Gran had left them there when she'd moved out. Wally took it and laughed.

'Pity, I should have brought mine. See this,' he said, leaning over to me and showing me the photo, 'this was me when I was young and handsome.'

'And now you're old and fat,' said Gran, laughing. I giggled and Uncle Wally opened his eyes wide.

'And what are you laughing at, little lady?' He reached over and started tickling me and I screamed and kicked in self-defence. Gran laughed as well. We had a lot of fun that day.

Uncle Wally came round to our house as well. My mother was very fond of him and they would talk for ages, sitting outside on the verandah or at the table after dinner. Mom made her famous lemon meringue pie, which she only ever made for special visitors and on Dad's birthday. He and Grandad got on quite well, strangely enough, for Grandad didn't get on with many people and Wally didn't seem to bear him a grudge at all. I was used to playground politics where if somebody wasn't your friend, you weren't allowed to be a friend of their friends either. I thought that Gran probably hadn't told Wally about her arm being burnt or he might have beaten Grandad up. At first I thought maybe he didn't know that Gran and Grandad were separated. Perhaps he, too, had been fed the story about the flat being decorated. However, it became clear that he knew very well what had happened but chose not to dwell on the subject.

Once or twice I got the feeling that I had met Uncle Wally before, or at least seen a photo of him, although I couldn't remember any being shown to me. I suppose I just felt so comfortable with him, as though I had known him for a very long time.

One afternoon, I heard my Mom telling him how upset she was about her parents' separation and he listened attentively throughout. He never commented on anything she said or interrupted her. He was a great listener was Uncle Wally, sitting patiently and holding her hand until she had finished talking. Afterwards they both sat in silence for a while, looking out on the rain drenched garden of mid-December, but I could see that he cared very much about his great-niece's state of mind. Everyone loved Wally, my parents, my grandfather, my gran and everyone else he met or was introduced to. You just couldn't help loving Uncle Wally.

Chapter Fourteen

The Saturday before Christmas of 1984 is one I shall never forget. It had been raining all through the night, which was unusual as it normally only rained in the afternoon. The combination of the approaching festivities and the fact that I had woken to the sound of thunder made me feel excited, as though something special was going to happen that day. In Africa, rain takes the place of snow in instilling a feeling of Christmas cosiness and seasonal cheer. I chattered my way through breakfast, prompting my dad to ask whether I had been injected with a gramophone needle, and regaled my family with stories about my teachers at school that were so outrageous that my mother ordered me to go and get ready to go to Gran's as she was laughing so much. I liked being the clown at times, and at least at home I could be assured of being treated like a child.

On the way to Gran's I sat and made a mental list of what I would buy everyone for Christmas, including the dogs and the cat. I knew why I wasn't being taken shopping; Mom and Dad were going to buy my Christmas present and didn't want me around. Gran had promised to help me make decorations for the tree by rolling kaylite balls in glue and glitter and then threading a piece of string through the top. We had made some at school, but I had visions of covering the whole tree with them and surprising everyone with how beautiful it was. Uncle Wally was such fun that I was sure he would help as well.

In front of the block of flats in which Gran lived were a few parking spaces for visitors; the residents' car park was at the back of the building. When we arrived, parked diagonally across three parking bays, was Miles Trevellyan's white Ford Cortina. It looked like a shark or a crocodile, lurking quietly in the water, waiting to snap up an unsuspecting swimmer. It had what looked like a pair of wings protruding from either side of the rear lights, as though it were not entirely a water-borne creature, but might also rise up and gobble the beasts of the air, too. It was the first time I had seen Miles since Uncle Wally had come to stay. I had been hoping he would stay away longer. Dad pointed with an open hand towards the car, exclaiming, 'Some people have no consideration for others! Who's this joker, I wonder?' I sat nervously on the back seat, fearing that at that moment Miles would come out to get in his car and Dad would ask him who the hell he thought he was, parking like that. Then Gran would appear and take Miles's side and the whole affair would be revealed. Mom and Dad would find out that I had known all along and they would be angry. Mom would be hurt and would shun me. I saw her in my mind's eye, crying quietly and pushing me away every time I tried to touch her.

I hastily got out of the car, a plastic bag with kaylite balls, glitter, glue and string in one hand, and had already started walking away before Mom had finished giving me instructions on how to behave and not to tire Gran out. At one point I thought she was going to get out of the car and come in with me, but luckily she didn't. I felt incredibly relieved when my parents eventually drove away. It was with great trepidation that I approached Gran's flat. I had an ominous feeling that we would not be making Christmas decorations that day. I was right.

When I entered Gran's flat, it was in a state of commotion. Gran was there, sitting on one of the sofas in the lounge. She was laughing hysterically and trying to say something that kept getting lost in floods of giggles. Miles was seated opposite her and was talking to a man who stood with his back to me, a tall balding character dressed in a pair of shorts and a T-shirt. He had on long socks that had fallen down and gathered around his ankles and a pair of old takkies. Miles saw me arrive but kept on talking; Gran was too busy laughing to see me at first. The tall man turned when he heard the door close behind me and said, 'Well, hello, sonny! Come to visit your grandma, have you?'

Gran looked up, rather surprised to see me, and tried to compose herself. She smoothed her hair back from her face, 'Ellie. Oh dear, I forgot you were coming today.' She turned her head to the window and asked, 'Have Mum and Dad gone already?' as though she wanted to call my parents back to collect me.

'Yes,' I answered in a small voice, feeling unwanted.

'Oh well, we'll just have to make do. Did they say when they would pick you up?'

'This afternoon,' I answered, adding, 'like they always do.'

'Ellie?' said the tall man with a grin. 'I thought you were a boy.'

Miles laughed and Gran giggled and said, 'Don't be stupid! It's just her haircut. It's a bit short.' I was a funny-looking child at that stage, with long skinny arms and legs and a fat stomach. My straight brown hair was cut into a pageboy style, not perhaps very short by today's standards but short for that time. The fringe was too long and I developed a habit of pushing the hair out of my eyes, a habit I continued for a long time after my hair was cut into a shorter style. I felt self-conscious and stood still, holding the bag of unmade Christmas decorations. I felt my face reddening.

'Well, who's for some tea?' said Gran, getting up from where she sat and walking over to the kitchen. 'Miles? Trevor? What about you, Ellie? Have you had some this morning? I've got some chocolate biscuits somewhere as well.'

Miles and Trevor declined Gran's offer and she continued to offer different drinks.

'Coffee? Milo? Milk?' she called and each offer received a 'no' in return. Finally, jokingly, she said, 'Beer? Vodka? G&T?'

'Beer,' said Miles.

'Make that two,' called Trevor.

'Oh, go on, you two,' shouted Gran in return, coming back into the room with a tray of tea and two cups for her and I.

'Hey! What kind of a service is this?' said Miles. 'You offered us beer so where is it?'

'It's ten o'clock in the morning,' Gran laughed, putting down the tray and pouring out the tea.

'So?' said Miles, an incredulous look on his face. 'Who says when we can drink and when we can't? It's not against the law, you know.'

Gran glanced quickly over at me, now perched precariously on the arm of the sofa, still clutching my bag. 'Well, help yourself,' she said, and sat down.

Miles shook his head, rolled his eyes and got up from the chair. He went into the kitchen and came back with two open bottles of beer.

'Glasses, please,' said Gran, but Miles had already sat down.

'What do you need glasses for?' he asked obtusely, taking a swig of the bottle. 'Cheers,' he said to Trevor.

Trevor, as I gathered from the ensuing conversation, worked with Miles as an electrician. He was in his early thirties, was already divorced and lived with a woman whom he mocked all the time he was there. She was overweight, neurotic, paranoid, and too dependent on him. She phoned him up at work to make sure that he was there, phoned the waiters at the bar at Queens to check who he was talking to, phoned him to ask him when he'd be home, when she'd see him again. They had rows where she threw him out of the flat, where she threw his things over the balcony into the road and where she turned up at the bar and tore him apart in front of all those who were there. I felt sorry for Trevor, even though he had mistaken me for a boy. At that age I had not learnt to mistrust the storyteller.

'I really need to go,' said Trevor, sitting down with the beer Miles passed him.

'Bullshit,' responded Miles. 'No one never has time for a beer.'

Gran passed me a cup of tea that I took a long time to drink as it gave me something to do while I watched and listened to the conversation. All the time I was wondering where Uncle Wally was. Trevor talked about his girlfriend and all three of them talked about people they knew. Then the conversation turned to the previous evening. It appeared they had gone to the Naval Club for a Christmas party. Gran seemed to have enjoyed herself and was laughing about Miles's dancing and something that Uncle Wally had said about it.

'You've got two left feet, you have,' she said. 'Even Wally can dance better than you can. He said you danced like a duck with gumboots on.'

I laughed into my tea and Gran turned and winked at me.

'Couldn't care less,' said Miles, raising the beer to his lips.

'Anyway, he's not exactly Fred Astaire himself.' sighed Gran.

'Exactly,' said Miles.

We carried on sitting there for the next two hours. Miles and Trevor had a couple more beers each. Trevor had a biscuit, but Miles didn't eat a thing. He hardly ever did, whatever Gran had made. Every time Miles handed him a beer, Trevor said he really should be leaving. Every time he said that Miles scoffed at him and told him to relax. I was getting bored. Even though the shops closed at midday on a Saturday, Mom and Dad weren't going to pick me up until the evening. I wondered if we were going to make decorations that evening. Almost as though he could read my thoughts, Miles asked, 'What are you holding that bag like that for? It's not going to run away from you, you know.'

I blushed. Gran said, 'Oh dear, we were supposed to make Christmas decorations.'

Miles looked uninterested. I don't think he even knew it was Christmas.

'Decorations!' exclaimed Trevor with a foolish look on his face. 'Ooh, that's nice.' I looked at him with scorn, resenting the patronizing tone in his voice.

'The thing is,' said Gran, 'that I was hoping Uncle Wally might help you so I could have some time to make some mince pies, but he's gone out now. He's gone to meet an old friend.'

'Well, you can't make them now, that's for sure,' said Miles. 'We're too busy drinking.'

'Ellie,' said Gran quickly, obviously feeling guilty for sidelining me, 'why don't you go up to the garage and buy yourself some chocolate and a drink? They sell packets of mints up there, too, now.'

I hesitated.

'Go on,' she urged, 'take my purse and buy whatever you want.' She smiled.

I sighed, got up and took Gran's purse from her outstretched hand. I could feel the two men watching me.

'Not too many sweets now,' said Miles, 'or that belly of yours will pop.' His words were like a bitter acid that ate through me. I could feel a lump in my throat.

'Miles!' admonished Gran, 'Leave the girl alone!' She was laughing though.

'God. You should see Val's stomach,' said Trevor, rolling his eyes. 'So fat it's a wonder she can see her toes over it.'

As I walked to the door, I could feel myself blushing. I would have asked Gran if she needed anything else from the garage, but instead I just walked out.

The garage was at the end of the road. It had a small kiosk where you could buy bottled cool drinks, sweets, chocolates and chips. The sweets were of the cheaper variety and were often sold singly. They were kept in large glass jars; some of them didn't have wrappers. My mother never let me buy those sweets as she said you didn't know where they had been. The man at the kiosk took the sweets out of the jar with his bare hands and you didn't know if they were clean or not. I bought a bar of milk chocolate and began eating it as soon as I had paid for it. I started walking back to Gran's flat when I stopped. I didn't want to go back; the thought of Miles and Trevor was not a welcoming one. I went back to the kiosk and bought a handful of mints. I ate one and carried the rest slowly back to the flat. Instead of going in, I sat outside for a few minutes. The rain had cleared during the morning and a bright hot sun was drying up the puddles and the wet grass. There was a small wall outside the flats where I sat and ate another mint. I tried to suck it rather than bite it so that it would take longer to finish. I told myself I would go inside when it had.

When I walked back into Gran's sitting room, things hadn't changed much. Trevor and Miles had had another beer; Trevor didn't look like he was going anywhere and had given up saying he was. Miles was telling a story about something funny that had happened at work concerning one of the black electricians who had short-circuited the lights and been chased out of the building by the boss, a Mr MacGregor. Trevor was almost choking with laughter and Gran kept repeating 'You two, you are cruel.'

Someone else was there. I recognized her as Mrs James

who lived directly above Gran. She was about forty years old, divorced and worked as a school secretary. Mrs James had a soft spot for me and would always spend a lot of time asking me questions about my friends and my school and what I wanted to be when I grew up. Gran told me it was because she had no children of her own and had always wanted them. I felt sorry for Mrs James and let her talk to me for as long as she wanted. I didn't mind her questions as she took a genuine interest in me and wasn't trying to entertain me like some adults thought they should. She had a habit of calling me Eleanor for she thought that my real name, although it wasn't; it was just Ellie. In anyone else, such an error would be unforgivable, but I forgave it in her.

She had actually come to meet Uncle Wally as Gran had told her he was coming to stay. Finding him absent, she looked slightly uncomfortable in the present company, and when she saw me her eyes brightened and she smiled.

'Eleanor!' she exclaimed, 'Just the girl I was looking for. I've just made some shortbread for my nieces and nephews – the family's coming up from Durban this Christmas – and I need someone to be my chief taster. I haven't made shortbread before and I'm a bit worried that they won't like it.'

'Oh,' I said, smiling and blushing at the same time. 'OK.'

'Great,' she said, standing up a little too quickly and betraying her haste to leave. 'Come upstairs with me and we'll have a cup of tea and try it out. You don't mind, Evelyn, do you?'

'No. Of course not,' said Gran, standing up to show Mrs James to the door, 'and I'm sure Ellie won't. I am sorry Wally isn't here to meet you, Sally.'

'Never mind, he can try my shortbread another time.'

Upstairs in Mrs James's flat, I sat and drank orange juice and ate shortbread. She did most of the talking, telling me about her family and what each niece and nephew was doing and how old they were. Lunchtime passed and still she talked. She also got out an album of photos and showed me pictures of her family. Some of the photos were very old and weren't taken in colour. There was one of Mrs James as a baby in her mother's arms. Her mother was standing in front of an old car and a toddler stood on one side of her, holding on to her dress. Mrs James said that was her sister who lived in South Africa. She used to live in Zimbabwe when it was still called Rhodesia. It was funny to think that Mrs James had once been a baby.

When I finally left to go back to Gran's flat, it was two o'clock in the afternoon. I was quite relieved that I had spent such a long time away from Miles. It was very quiet; the sun had reached its peak an hour or so before but it was still hot and the afternoon had a dozy feel about it. Everything and everyone was hiding from the heat. The sun was bright outside the flat and I could feel it on the back of my legs and neck as I walked down the stairs to Gran's. I opened the door and walked inside. It was quiet in there, too. I went into the lounge. There was no one there. On the table were empty beer bottles and a couple of empty glasses. There was also a bottle of gin and an empty tonic water bottle. A bowl of peanuts had spilled across the tabletop. One chocolate biscuit was still on the plate; another lay on the table. On the sofa, a magazine lay open at an advertisement for a car and the small carpet that lay on the floor in front of the sofa was ruffled and askew.

When she lived with us, Gran didn't drink. She had a glass of wine at Christmas and that was enough to make her afternoon rest last two hours instead of the customary one. Since moving out, I'd seen her drinking G&Ts at the Naval Club on Saturday afternoons; or rather I should say she sipped a G&T all afternoon. Miles often commented on her speed of consumption. Gran always said she had to drive home afterwards and there was me to look after. Miles's eyes would flicker over me and I could feel his resentment, his wish that one day I would just not be there; that it would only be him and her. Perhaps I was more than her darling granddaughter; perhaps I was her assurance that she would behave herself.

A slight feeling of panic rose somewhere inside of me and I turned towards Gran's bedroom. The door was closed. I slowly turned the handle and pushed it open slightly. Inside it was dark, for the curtains had been drawn. Gran lay on the bed, asleep. I pushed the door open further as my eyes adjusted to the half light. Suddenly I noticed a pair of eyes on me; it was Miles. He was lying next to Gran with his arm around her waist. He smiled slowly and held my eyes with his. It was only then that I realised Gran was naked.

In my shock I let go of the door and it closed with a small bang. I moved away from the bedroom and sat on the sofa hugging myself. I thought the noise of the door closing would have woken Gran but no one came out. I sat for what seemed a long time in that position. I wanted to go home, but didn't know how I could. My parents weren't to fetch me for another couple of hours. The phone was on a small table near me; it looked so inviting. I just had to pick it up and dial home. I edged towards it and lifted the receiver. The

117

sound of the numbers dialling seemed to make a very loud noise. Once, I put the phone down and rushed to sit at the other end of the sofa as I thought I heard the noise of someone stirring in the bedroom. Eventually I got through and waited for someone to pick up the phone at the other end. I had no idea what I would say. My grandfather answered the phone.

'Ellie!' he said in rather more jovial a fashion than he normally did. 'Where are you?'

'I'm at Gran's,' the words falling like stones in a pond as the connotations spread out between us, wave after wave after wave.

There was a slight pause and then, 'Mom and Dad aren't here. They're playing tennis.' I had forgotten. My heart sank. 'Ellie, are you still there?' he asked when I didn't say anything. I felt like crying but held my tears back. 'What's wrong? Where's your grandmother?'

'Nothing's wrong,' I gulped. 'I just want to go home.'

'Why? Where's your grandmother? Why are you whispering?'

'She's sleeping,' I said, wishing I hadn't phoned. 'Anyway, I'll see you at home. Bye Grandad.' I tried to hurriedly end the conversation.

'Ellie, is it your grandmother? Is everything all right?'

'Yes,' I managed to say.

There was a pause and I heard Grandad sigh. It was typical of him that he would immediately think that something was wrong. 'Bye.'

I put the phone down and decided to go and wait outside for my parents to pick me up, however long a time away that might be. I was afraid that Gran might wake up and I certainly didn't want to see Miles again. Time seemed to pass faster outside.

I sat outside the flats in the visitors' car park. Miles's Cortina was still parked across three parking bays. It still looked like a crocodile, but one that had just eaten and lay sleeping self-satisfied in the sun. I had my bag of unmade decorations with me and played with the kaylite balls, rolling them down the steps, all the time thinking of what I had just seen. I was glad Uncle Wally was out so that he did not have to witness what I just had.

Suddenly I heard a great commotion coming from Gran's flat. I could hear her and someone else shouting. I got up and walked around to the back of the flats. To my horror, I realised that my grandad was there. I hadn't seen him because he'd used the other entrance; he had gone to the residents' car park at the back of the flats. Gran stood at the door in rather dishevelled clothes. She was shouting that this was her life and she could do with it what she bloody well wanted. Grandad was telling her that she was going downhill and how he had foreseen such a thing happening. How could she have left me alone? Had she been drinking? He could see empty bottles all over the show. The next thing he expected was for her to become an alcoholic. Neither of them saw me and so I turned around and went back to where I had been sitting. I stood shaking on the front steps. I finally got the resolve to walk around the side of the building to the residents' car park. Grandad's pick-up was parked there. It wasn't locked, but I didn't think I should get in. If Grandad was looking for me, the last place he would think I'd be was his truck. I had to go back.

I crept around to the front of the flats and a feeling like a cold knife drove through my chest; my mother was there too. My parents had come to pick me up and had parked at the front entrance. My mother had arrived to find her parents fighting and her daughter nowhere to be seen. Her father was accusing her mother, who was angrily denying it, of being an alcoholic. She immediately took her father's side, almost hysterical as I was missing. My father was standing rather gingerly behind my mother, looking as uncomfortable as I felt. Our eyes met and he smiled a rather wan smile that slid off his face and lay with all the other pieces of emotions that scattered about our family that afternoon. My mother saw me and rushed over and grabbed my arm. She pulled me in front of Gran like exhibit 'A' in a court case. I was crying, big soft tears that made marks down my face. I felt guilty. I had done this.

'You see!' shouted Gran, pointing to me. 'She's perfectly OK!'

'OK? OK?' screamed my mother in return. 'Is this what you call OK? Why is she crying if she's OK?'

'I don't know, Frances,' said Gran, her lips drawn back in a snarl. 'Why don't you ask her?' I noticed that Gran's blouse was on inside out and I wondered if anyone else would too. 'Come on, we're leaving!' said Mom, dragging me by the hand. 'Dad, come on. We are leaving.' She shouted the last word and turned to go, but her eye caught some movement in the flat. She stopped. 'Who's here?' she asked. She would have hated anyone to have heard the argument. Gran hesitated and shook her head. 'There's someone here,' said Mom. 'Who is it, Ellie?' She turned to me. I stood still and shrugged my shoulders.

Just then we heard the toilet flush and my heart sank even

further. What a fool Miles was, flushing the toilet like that. He probably had no idea that this argument was going on or, if he did, he couldn't care. Mom pushed past Gran into the flat and met Uncle Wally just as he was coming out of the bathroom.

'Oh, Wally, I'm so sorry,' she rasped. Her breath was coming hard and forceful and her cheeks were red with embarrassment. 'I thought you were out this afternoon.' I could feel her hand trembling on my shoulder.

'The party's over, it's all over, my friend!' he joked and then stopped. 'No problem. I've been back about an hour. I fell asleep for a while.' He looked rather bewildered at everyone standing around the door, my grandfather's face still black with anger, Gran's face white and pinched, her lips set firmly together, as though she were holding back a flood of words; my father standing rather timidly at the back of everyone and me with my tear-stained face, clutching a bag of tinsel and glitter and kaylite balls to myself. His eyes passed over all of us and rested on me. I knew he knew about Miles. Had he seen what I had, or had he just put two and two together? Miles must still be there, hiding in the bedroom.

'Anything wrong?' asked Uncle Wally.

'Oh no, no,' said my mother. 'We just thought we had lost Ellie for a moment.' Her hand was clammy and soft.

'Aha! And now the vanquished has returned!' he grinned, trying to break the icy silence.

I forced a smile and turned my head away, embarrassed. I had no idea what 'vanquished' meant.

*

I sat most of that evening in my bedroom, not even leaving to watch *The Muppet Show*. My father came in at one point. He pretended that nothing had happened.

'How about some cheese on toast for supper? I suppose you had a big lunch with Gran today and you're not very hungry.'

I nodded weakly and followed him to the kitchen. Grandad was sitting out on the verandah in the dark. He had a bottle of beer in one hand and rested his head in the other. My mother was sitting next to him and speaking in a low voice, 'I know you thought she'd been drinking, but I don't think she had. When have you ever known Mum to drink? At least Ellie's OK. That's the main thing... she's OK. If anything had happened... well... I don't know what I would have done.'

Although my mother was trying to smooth things over between her parents, I knew that really she was seething inside. She hated her mother at that moment. I didn't approach them.

Later that night as I lay in bed, I went over the events of the day in my mind. I wished the day had never happened. If only I hadn't phoned home, then Grandad would never have turned up. Mom might never have known that something was wrong if Gran and Grandad had not been having an argument when she arrived. She wouldn't have thought I was missing; it was Grandad who put that idea into her mind.

I tried not to think of what had happened. I tried to think cheerier thoughts: the approaching festivities, Christmas presents and the tree. I even tried to believe in Father Christmas again. Then, feeling guilty, I thought of the

Christmas story; about Mary and Joseph and the Baby Jesus and how Mary had no choice but to do God's will when the Angel Gabriel told her what would come to pass. As I fell asleep, the words we had read at school flew slowly and rhythmically round and round in my mind: 'And Mary kept these things... Mary kept these things and pondered them in her heart.'

Chapter Fifteen

You got to know when to hold 'em, know when to fold 'em,
Know when to walk away and know when to run.
You never count your money when you're sittin' at the table.
There'll be time enough for countin' when the dealin's done.

We didn't spend a lot of time together, my grandfather and I. Occasionally, we watched the Sunday afternoon movie on television and sometimes he took me to town with him on Saturday mornings.

He taught me how to play cards. Real cards: rummy, patience and, later on, poker. He taught me how to bet and how to bluff, how to maintain a straight face when looking at my hand for the first time. It was confusing sometimes and often I would get mixed up and he would get irritated with me. Sometimes ace was high and sometimes it was low and I often got lost in an adult world of changing rules.

For the most part, I saw my grandfather as a man who was in a permanently bad mood, whose moroseness created a wall around him, a wall that smelt of engine oil, beer and cigarettes and bitterness. At other times, he displayed a type of gentleness and he would show me something of interest in a book or magazine he was reading or tell me a funny story in his inimitable way: straight faced and serious. He was the archetypal Rhodie man and he wasn't. He was tough with anyone who had a black skin and his racist comments would make my skin crawl with embarrassment, and yet he could also be generous and many a time lent Jameson money or gave him his old clothes. I'd often seen him swing Jameson's little girl in the air above his head and stare up at her, cigarette hanging from his lip while she giggled and her little brother stood with his arms outstretched and cried that he, too, wanted to be lifted up.

When I was angry with my grandfather, I was angry with him for everything: for the arguments he had had with Gran and for the separation, for the scar on her arm. Beneath his hard exterior, though, I felt his aching heart. At times, when we had spent a while together, my heart beat in time with his and I could feel it, dull and slow and sore, not in my chest, but in my throat where the pain of unwept tears lay throbbing.

After his confrontation with Gran at her flat, I felt determined to spend more time with him, to look after him. Perhaps I could fill that space that he carried around within himself. Every good thing that I could find about him and every good time we had together was counted as a mark against Miles.

Grandad took me to Luna Park every year when it came to Bulawayo to coincide with the International Trade Fair. We'd go for rides on the roundabouts and the Big Wheel and buy candyfloss or toffee apples. We had to drive past Gran's flat to get to the fairgrounds and Grandad would always stare at it, looking for something upon which to comment. One Saturday in late April following that fateful Christmas, Miles's car was parked outside and I felt a pain in my chest as we passed by. Grandad didn't recognise the car and only remarked on the terrible colour the outside wall was painted, beige and impractical.

Suddenly, I didn't want to be anywhere near Gran's flat. Even if I couldn't see it from the fairground, I could feel its presence, as though something or someone was watching me. Miles's eyes, with their self-satisfied gaze, magnified in my mind and became a force that could follow me through walls and closed doors.

'Grandad,' I said quietly, 'can we go to Centenary Park instead? I don't really feel like going to Luna Park.'

Grandad looked a little surprised. 'What's the problem?'

I shrugged. 'I just feel like going to the park.'

At some level, Grandad probably felt the same way I did. He didn't want to be near the flat either, but not because of Miles, of whom he knew nothing, but because of Gran herself.

'OK,' he said and turned down another road. 'No problem.'

We drew up alongside the park gardens and got out of the car. Opposite us, on the edge of the grounds, there was a monument to those who died in the First and Second World Wars.

'Bloody British,' said Grandad, looking up at it and I knew what he was thinking: sold us down the river. Fought for King and country. For what? Where's their Empire now? He didn't say anything though and we walked through the gates. We walked around the park first and went to see the birds that were kept in an aviary. There were parrots and lovebirds and cockatoos, green and yellow and red. They sat on their perches and called to each other or sat together, whispering sweet nothings as we looked on. On the ground next to one of the cages was a beautiful pink flower. It was as brightly coloured as the birds who hopped and flew around inside the cage. As I picked it up the smooth curves of its petals drew back to reveal its centre, soft, vulnerable and still beating with life.

'Hibiscus,' said Grandad, looking down at my hands. 'Nice colour.'

I decided to take it with me and put it in water when I got home.

We wandered through the rest of the park, down the tree-bordered paths and past the roller-skating rink and the miniature railway. We went down to the large pond and looked through the fence at the ducks and swans and Grandad showed me the difference between the male and female ducks; the females were always dull and the males were always beautiful and brightly coloured.

'The females don't have to rely on their looks like you lot do,' he said, nodding at me as symbolic of the female human form. He tapped his head. 'They're the clever ones you see. They don't have to prove anything.'

We started walking back towards the car. The path was laid in small concrete squares and I was trying to walk without touching any of the lines.

'What are you doing?' asked Grandad, slightly irritated.

'It's bad luck if you step on the lines, Grandad,' I said, ignoring the tone in his voice. I carried on walking with my head bent down when suddenly I realised that Grandad was no longer beside me, but had stopped a few paces behind. I looked up and saw in horror that there, a metre or so ahead of us and coming in our direction, were Miles and Gran. They had seen us, too, and approached rather like an advancing army on a besieged town.

'Afternoon,' said Gran to Grandad, but looking at me. She ran her hand through my hair. 'Hello, darling,' she said to me and smiled. 'I thought you'd be at Luna Park this afternoon. Mum said you were going there.'

There was a silence and then Gran and Miles started walking away. 'I'll see you next Saturday,' she called over her shoulder. 'Go and have an ice cream; the Mivvies are delicious!' She waved in the direction of the ice cream man.

Grandad didn't say a word and we moved off in the other direction. I walked properly now, aware that I was walking over all the lines and cracks. Bad luck, I kept thinking, I'm going to get bad luck. My hands were clenched into sweaty fists. I looked down and opened my hand. The flower was bruised and damp and the edges were a light brown colour.

All the way home in the car I tried to smooth out the petals but its heart, too, was damaged. By early evening the thin brown fingers of a stain stretched their way up to the centre and the edges curled up limply in death.

Chapter Sixteen

A wind blew in from somewhere. A thin, cool wind that no one noticed, but which eroded and moulded with its insidious fingers the very landscape we lived in. Zimbabwe changed. Slowly but surely, some things died, crumbled and fell away. In the early years of Independence, some things stayed the way they had always been, but later, not long afterwards, things changed. Gone were the days when you had to queue to see a movie or a play; the queues were longer outside the video rental shops, which got the latest releases well before the cinemas did, and whose very nature – that of renting films to be watched in the comfort of your own home – seemed to offer what many wanted: privacy. Yet it was more than privacy: seclusion. The choice to mix with whom you chose, another invisible division between people. The large cinemas struggled for many years to fill auditoriums built to seat a few hundred people, prostituting themselves on billboards offering sex and violence in B-rated movies with unknown actors. The Thursday midnight kung fu double session replaced the *Casablanca* of my gran's youth and the *Love Story* of my mother's. The chatter and excitement, the rustling of crisp packets and chocolate bar wrappers was replaced by a silence, a sense of being left behind after everyone else had left.

In the early years of my life, many people went to the park on Saturday and Sunday afternoons. They played miniature golf or went for a ride on the train that went around the park. They fed the birds, the ducks, the swans. They bought cool drinks and sat on the grass. But soon that, too, became unpopular. People stopped going to the park; it became less frequented and more dangerous to walk around. Someone was stabbed there one afternoon, the train broke down and there were no spare parts with which to repair it, the ducks and birds and swans were moved. One day a child drowned in the black stagnant pond. Her body wasn't discovered for hours. Now the grass grows unchecked around it and broken white pillars lie where once greater things stood straight and tall.

White Zimbabwean society became less cohesive, more fragmented and unsure of itself, more paranoid and watchful. It hid itself at the sports clubs and the Evangelical Church; it counted its pennies from the distance of its suburban homes and every so often looked out to shake its head and feel better for its reclusive choice. Gradually it settled down to an all too comfortable snooze as the world passed by.

The worst aspects of white society were also evident in the worst of black society, the new elite. They were often insensitive to the plight of others and never thought of helping anyone who was less fortunate than themselves. 'So much for the liberation struggle,' my grandfather would say when a street kid came begging at the car window. Yes, it was a cool wind that blew and made us huddle together.

I stop writing. Is it all too personal, too subjective, too me?

*

When I was fifteen, my mother decided to go back to school. It was a bit of a surprise, but Dad and I were happy for her. It wasn't a proper school, of course, like the one that I went to, but a college, where she was going to do her 'A' levels. She had dropped out of school before completing them and the decision to do so had hung round her neck like a dead weight ever since.

The day she told Gran about it, she had been shopping for my birthday present. It was a Saturday in early April. I had spent the morning with Gran and Mom came to pick me up at lunchtime. She didn't usually stay for long when she picked me up; sometimes she didn't even come inside. Time lessens some things, but habit often steps in and takes the place of pride and hurt. This time, however, when Gran asked if she would like to stay for a cup of tea, Mom didn't refuse. She came in and sat down and looked oddly at ease in the flat. She even commented on a picture Gran had up on the wall. It must have been there at least seven years, yet it was as though she had only just noticed it.

'Any news?' called Gran from the kitchen, where she was filling the kettle with water.

There was a pause and then: 'Well, yes, some good news actually.' I knew what she was going to say. I had been dying to tell Gran all day, but Mom had told me not to say anything to her.

'Win the lottery?' asked Gran with a dry laugh, coming in and sitting down.

Mom ignored the comment. 'I'm going to go back to college to study for my 'A' levels,' she said with a somewhat bashful smile.

Gran looked at her sharply. 'At your age?' were her first words. 'What are you going to do with them?'

'Do with them?' asked Mom, confused. 'I want to finish my education, that's what.'

Gran nodded once and didn't say anything.

'What?' asked Mom, irritated. 'I've always wanted to finish them. You know I have. I'm not too old. No one is ever too old for an education. I might even decide to do a degree. Who knows?'

She wasn't too old; that was the truth, for she had had me when she was twenty, two months away from her twenty-first birthday. Gran had had Mom when she was twenty-six, so she wasn't old either, not like some people's grandmothers.

Gran got up and went back into the kitchen. Mom fiddled with her wedding ring.

'I have something to tell you, too,' said Gran, coming back into the room carrying a tray of tea and cups and saucers. Mom looked up.

'I'm moving house,' said Gran. She sat down with a sense of occasion. She was sitting very straight, the way she sat when she wanted to prove a point, and didn't move nearer to the tray to pour out the tea, preferring to keep it at arm's length, thus adding a slight flamboyance to the way she turned the teacups over.

'Oh,' said Mom. There was a silence and then, 'You're

not getting married, are you?'

Gran breathed out sharply and rolled her eyes. Her legs were crossed and one foot flicked ominously up and down, like a cat's tail before it digs its claws into you. 'I am married, to your father.'

'I know,' said Mom, defensively. 'I just, well, wanted to know, that's all.'

'No, I'm not going to get married. Not ever again. This is my life now.'

'Where are you moving to?' asked Mom, after another short silence in which the only noise seemed to be me swallowing my tea. I could feel it, hot and sweet, sliding down my throat, like a butcher's knife through liver.

'Suburbs,' said Gran curtly, decisively cutting a small piece of Victoria sponge into three even smaller pieces. 'Lawson Road. Cake?'

'No thank you. Suburbs? How are you going to afford to live there? You're retiring at the end of this year, aren't you? Or has that plan also changed?'

'I am still retiring and, yes, thank you, I shall be able to afford to live quite comfortably in Suburbs. I have savings, I have a pension and,' here she paused, 'I've decided to get a lodger.'

Mom closed her eyes for a second before saying, 'So you can't afford it, can you, otherwise you wouldn't need a lodger.'

Gran's foot flicked upwards again. 'It's a three-bedroomed house. I need the company.'

'Three bedrooms! God, mother! What do you want a three-bedroomed house for at your age when you've been living perfectly fine in a two-bedroomed flat for the last umpteen years?'

'This is not a two bedroomed flat, Frances. It has one bedroom and a large cupboard. I need somewhere bigger so I can have a nice bedroom, have a lodger for company and security, and have a third room to use when visitors come to stay.' Here, she pointed at me.

Mom rolled her eyes. I wanted to say that it didn't matter, I didn't mind the small bedroom where I slept, she mustn't move on my account.

'Think what you like,' said Gran, replacing her cup on her saucer very deliberately. 'I have never had to justify what I do in my life to you.'

'That's for sure,' said Mom, her tongue thick with sarcasm, 'When have you ever cared what I thought?'

When we got into the car that day, Mom looked very sad. There was a plastic bag on the passenger seat. I moved it to sit down.

'What's this?' I asked, looking inside.

'Try it on and see if it fits you. I didn't know what to get you for your birthday this year. Kids grow up so fast these days.'

Inside the bag were a top and a pair of jeans. 'These are nice.'

'You don't sound too enthusiastic,' said Mom, reversing the car.

'No, they're nice, really,' I assured her, wanting to make her feel better.

'I'm sorry,' she said when we stopped at the traffic lights, 'It's not much of a surprise really, is it?' She sighed as she leaned her head against her hand, her right elbow resting on the window.

'It's OK. It's not like I'm a child anymore.'

Chapter Seventeen

My mother's return to college, and finally to work, signalled a new freedom. No longer was my mother's attention focused on me. I began to spend an increasing amount of time with Gran, who had now moved out of her flat into a small, turn-of-the-century house in Suburbs. She retired as she said she would and concentrated all her energy on her new home. She had a beautiful garden, full in the summer months of flowers and shrubs and birds; even in the dry winter, of a large selection of the same. The long green carpet of a lawn was bordered by beds overflowing with flowers: petunias, marigolds, hibiscus, roses, hydrangea, lavender, geranium, African violets, sweet peas and poppies. She grew vegetables in the back garden: butternut, gem squash, beans, carrots, spinach, tomatoes, onions, potatoes, lettuce and cucumber. And then there were strawberries and cape gooseberries, mulberries and lemons, oranges and *naartjies*, and a large herb garden with everything from rosemary to coriander. It was a paradise; a place where everything wanted to grow, even the sweet peas, which Mrs Benson said would never survive in the heat of Matabeleland. In the small shed in the corner of the garden, she had trays full of earth in which she kept very young seedlings before they could be planted properly in the ground. There, too, she grew bulbs, keeping them in the dark and warmth of the shed.

After school, I would cycle there on my way home. Often I would sit and do my homework with her as she worked away at something: filling a flowerpot with earth, sewing curtains for the guest bedroom. This was hers, this house.

If my mother had returned to college to complete her education, Gran had left work to return to an old love of hers, the garden. The most she had had in Wilson Street were the pot plants on her verandah. Here, she practically had a kingdom. She told me once that no matter how hard and how lonely life becomes, one should always have a friend and that friend could be anyone or anything, even an African violet. In fact, they made the best friends of all. She was at pains to teach me how to look after plants properly, shaking her head at those who felt there was no more to gardening than shoving a plant in the ground.

'You've got to get it right, because that plant is going nowhere once it's in. It's like choosing a house; everything's got to be right: the shade, the sun, the soil, even the bedrock. Anything can flourish in the right conditions. Don't you listen to Mrs Benson. In the right place, anything will grow and the plant doesn't have to be taken to the right place, the right place can be made.'

'You've no idea how much the garden means to me,' she said to me on another occasion, although I think if anyone did it was me. 'It's got me through so much,' she added and it was here that I was not so sure of what she meant.

'It's therapeutic,' I said. I had read that somewhere.

She looked at me sideways then and smiled. 'Therapeutic. Yes, that's what they call it these days.'

Much later on, when she had died and I was sorting through her things, I found a poetry book, *Collected Poems* or something of the sort, and in it she had pressed about thirty different types of flowers, from daisies to elderflower. At first I thought she had placed the flowers randomly in the book, but then I saw that certain verses or lines were underlined as though there were a link between each flower and the poem it rested on.

'For I have known them all already, known them all –
Have known the evenings, mornings, afternoons,
I have measured out my life with coffee spoons;'

A dusty pink bougainvillaea crumbled as I read the words. It was in Thomas Gray that I found the daffodil:

'Full many a gem of purest ray serene
The dark unfathomed caves of ocean bear:
Full many a flower is born to blush unseen,
And waste its sweetness on the desert air.'

At the time I presumed she had picked all the flowers from her garden, although she couldn't have because, as far as I know, she never grew daffodils in that garden.

She didn't choose the largest of the rooms to be her bedroom, but the one with the best view of the garden, with double doors that opened onto the verandah that ran around three sides of the house. I don't think it had ever been used as a bedroom before, for there were too many shelves along the walls and not a lot of space for a cupboard. 'Perhaps it was used as a study before,' said Gran. 'But I like it, I just like it. It feels like home, like I know it somehow.'

I was at high school now and growing steadily interested in clothes, music and boys. Sometimes Gran would take me shopping for material. Mr Patel was still running his shop and every time we went in, he would leave whatever he was doing to come over and serve us. He would smile foolishly, his grin revealing the gaps between his teeth, and always compliment Gran on how she was looking.

'When you grow up, you want to be like Granny, heh?' he would say to me and I would smile shyly while Gran laughed off his compliment with 'And how many metres would you like me to buy today?'

At Gran's house, we would pin a pattern to the material and cut it out. Gran showed me how to use her electric sewing machine and we would sit for hours, pinning, cutting, tacking, and finally sewing the whole thing together. I loved it: the way you could create something with sides and pockets and collars from a single flat piece of cloth. My fingers would tingle as the scissors slowly cut their way around the pattern, or as the sleeves were tacked on to the main part of a shirt. Something was coming together, taking shape, forming. It was up to you what you wanted from the cloth; it could be anything; you were the master, tucking, shortening, lengthening; you were the creator.

There weren't that many places to go to meet potential boyfriends. There was church, which I didn't go to, a sports club, none of which I belonged to, and nightclubs and bars, which I wasn't allowed into. I had a dream that one day I would meet a poet or artist and we would spend all our time together saying deep and meaningful things to each other. In the picture that I had of him in my mind, he always wore a beret and had long dark hair tied back in a ponytail. He definitely wasn't Zimbabwean and often had a French accent, although it sometimes varied and sounded Eastern European. At those times he was a refugee, on the run from a cruel regime. I daydreamed about me helping him escape from secret agents sent to track him, a dream that always ended with him fleeing in the dead of night in a small aircraft. He would kiss me passionately before leaving, his last words always a breathless, 'someday I will come for you. Be strong until that time.' One long meaningful look later, and he was on the plane and flying out of my life, *Casablanca*-style.

Unfortunately, there was not much scope for meeting poets or artists in Bulawayo, especially those on the run from communist dictatorships. Gran said I was too fussy, I judged people too hastily. All I knew was that I didn't want a boyfriend like Miles, but that was all there was.

Mandy was different. She could get on with everyone and could laugh and joke with any kind of boy and not take any of them seriously. I didn't know how to be chatty, to talk brightly about nothing. I was always accused of being too serious and most people shied away from that. It wasn't always that I didn't give anyone a chance, but that they weren't interested in me either. What I hated most was the attempt at being interested that I had to make. For this reason I hated parties and other expressly social occasions.

I was at a party with Mandy one evening and, feeling rather self-conscious and clumsy, after having contributed not one word to a conversation that I was, to all intents and purposes, included in, I went outside to sit on the verandah. This is not where I will meet my poet, I thought, I will bump into him in the art gallery or our eyes will meet across a crowded café. I imagined reading a book of verse on a bus and him sitting opposite me and leaning over and whispering, 'Shall I compare thee to a summer's day?' My fantasy was slightly flawed by the fact that there isn't much romantic about a smoke-belching, air-polluting Zimbabwean bus. The fantasy then changed so that I was in Eastern Europe and we were on a bus full of peasants, women with flowers in their hair and baskets of freshly made bread on their laps; men with braces and goatee beards, playing the banjo and the flute. I was just figuring out what I was doing on a bus full of friendly peasants in Eastern Europe when someone plonked himself next to me.

Vance Taylor; *veldskoen*-wearing, beer-swilling Vance Taylor.

'Hey, howzit going? What are you doing out here all on your ace?'

'Minding my own business,' I replied, the curtness of my words slicing through his enthusiasm, cutting it down before it could get carried away. 'You should try it.'

Vance pulled a face. 'Jeepers. OK.'

He didn't move away though and appeared to find my attitude quite funny.

'So, who died?' he asked.

I rolled my eyes. Couldn't he just leave me alone? I didn't say anything. There was a silence and then, 'So I was thinking that you and I might go out sometime.'

'Really?' I asked, sarcasm thick on my tongue.

'Ja,' he replied, peeling the label off his bottle of beer, 'to the movies or something.'

I didn't reply.

'You don't have to,' he laughed. 'What's your number?'

'I don't give out my number,' I retorted, flicking my hair back and looking away from him.

'Jeepers, someone's seriously pissed you off, hey!' He wrote something on the back of the beer label and passed it to me. 'My number, in case you want to go out sometime. When you've come out of mourning, of course.' With that he stood up and left. I looked down at the piece of paper in my hands. This is not it, I thought. This is not 'Shall I compare thee to a summer's day' on a peasant bus in Eastern Europe. However, I didn't throw the number away. I put it in my jeans' pocket and went back into the party.

The following week, when I went round to Gran's, she told me that she had a lodger moving in. She had been phoned by the Publicity Association that morning to ask if she could provide a room only to a Englishwoman who had just arrived in Zimbabwe and was going to work here for three years. Gran had said yes and she was going to move in that day. Gran made the bed in the spare room and put folded clean towels on the chair next to it. I picked some flowers and put them in a vase on a table. We also put a pile of *Fair Lady* and *Home and Garden* magazines in the room and Gran decided to make a special meal for supper. She wasn't obliged to make her lodger food, but she thought it would be a welcoming gesture. 'She'll probably be tired after a long flight,' said Gran thoughtfully, 'and we also want to give her a good impression of Zimbabwe.' She made butternut soup and Beef Wellington with roast potatoes, courgettes and carrots. For pudding, there was crème brulée. Gran got her second-best dinner service out as well, the cornflower blue one with yellow flowers. You had to be a visitor to eat off that.

The next day I arrived at Gran's to find she had someone there. It was a young man with brown curly hair that sat on his head in a somewhat mushroom shape. He wore a black T-shirt and a faded pair of knee length denim shorts. It was winter, but he didn't seem to notice the cold. He had the whitest pair of legs I had ever seen and a pair of sandals on his feet. At one glance I could tell he was English.

'Hello!' he said cheerily as I walked in.

'Hello,' I answered rather shyly. I immediately started speaking to Gran, as though he weren't there.

'You should see how much homework I've got, Gran, tons! English, maths, French! I don't know how I'm going to finish it all.' I was aware of my voice being slightly louder than usual.

Gran smiled. 'This is Jason,' she said, pointing at him with an open hand. 'Jason, this is my granddaughter, Ellie.'

'Ah, we've just been talking about you,' said Jason. I blushed.

'This is my new lodger,' said Gran with a laugh, 'and I don't think he's going to appreciate the magazines we've put in his room!'

'Bit of a mix-up, I'm afraid. There are four of us who came out and Rosie was supposed to come here but, as she's working at Mapilo, which I'm told is miles away from here, due west, I think they said, it seems more logical that I take this accommodation and she stays somewhere a lot closer to Mapilo.'

I was a little taken aback. He spoke without taking a breath and with the very British trait of being able to pinpoint places and directions within hours of arriving in a place. Gran smiled.

'Rosie will be working at Mapilo, whereas Jason here will be working at the council offices. It's too far for her to travel each day, if she were to stay here.'

I nodded.

'Rosie's not arrived from England yet,' said Jason and then, suddenly, in a jovial, very British manner, 'Your Gran says that you love reading.'

'Yes,' I said, feeling stupid. I couldn't think of anything else to say.

'So does Jason,' said Gran. Jason smiled and nodded. He was seated at Gran's kitchen table with his hands cupped round a mug of tea.

'Everything. Yes, I read anything and everything. Who's your favourite?'

My mind went blank. For some reason I couldn't think of one author.

'Enid Blyton,' I said, trying to be funny. The attempt fell flat. I said it so seriously and with such a straight face that Jason looked quite taken aback and his smile wavered on his lips.

'Shakespeare's your favourite, isn't he?' said Gran, stepping in to help, but she couldn't have suggested a writer more unlikely as a favourite for a teenager.

'Shakespeare!' said Jason, more enthusiastically, although obviously surprised. 'You like the old stuff then, do you?'

'Sometimes,' I said and then thought how foolish and indecisive that sounded. Gran handed me a glass of orange juice, but I couldn't drink it. My throat felt tight and my hands were sweaty. I looked down at the glass.

'Well, our tastes certainly differ. I'm more of a modern man myself. I'm reading a lot of sixties stuff at the moment. Kerouac, Heller, Burgess? Heard of them?' I shook my head.

'No? I'll lend you some. See if you like them.'

The next day when I went round to Gran's, she wasn't there. I was a bit surprised as she was always there at lunchtime. I didn't usually knock on the door, but this time I did. No one answered so I knocked again. The door opened suddenly and Jason stood there, looking rather dishevelled and disorientated. He didn't seem to recognise me at first and his eyes flicked from my face to my school uniform. It was this that seemed to trigger recognition.

'Ah, right. Evelyn's granddaughter, yes?'

'Yes,' I answered. I thought he was a little young to call Gran by her first name, but I expected that that was because he was English and Grandad said they had different standards to ours. He said some kids even called their parents by their first names in England. 'Is my grandmother here?'

'Ah, no. She's just gone into town to get some wood.'

'Wood?' I repeated.

'Yes, I'm... Sorry, do come in. How rude of me to keep you standing outside.' He stepped aside for me to enter. I hesitated.

'Don't worry. I haven't murdered your grandmother or anything like that,' he laughed.

I stepped inside and he turned to follow me. We went into the lounge.

'Excuse the mess. It's all mine.'

'Can I help you with anything?' I asked.

'Um, no... no,' he said, looking around at all his possessions and empty boxes strewn everywhere, 'I think I've got it all under control. That's actually where your grandmother's gone.'

I looked at him, not understanding.

'Sorry, I'm not actually making much sense, am I? I'm going to put up some shelves. I've got loads of books, you see, and your grandmother's going to buy some wood so that I can make some shelves to put all the books on.'

He spoke a lot with his hands and every second or third word was emphasised by a firm gesture.

'I found that book I was talking about,' he said, kneeling by a pile of novels on the carpet. 'It was you I was talking to about *The Clockwork Orange*, wasn't it, um, sorry, this is really bad of me, but I've forgotten your name.'

'Ellie.'

'Ellie. It was you I was talking to, wasn't it?'

'Yes,' I said, too dazed by his rapid way of talking and moving around to think whether it had been or not.

'Well, I found it today.' He picked up a book from a pile on the floor and handed it to me. 'You can borrow it. I think you'll like it.'

Jason was about eight years older than me. He was good-looking in an academic sort of way with his curly dark hair and glasses. The fact that he wore shorts and sandals in winter added a certain eccentricity to the attraction. He came from a different culture to that I had grown up in and he was different to all the sports-loving, beer-swilling macho men that Zimbabwe generally produced.

From those first awkward moments, I started spending more time with Jason, reading his books and discussing them over tea and coffee. I usually listened and he usually talked.

My own books took on an almost childish air and I felt slightly ashamed to look at my copies of *Mansfield Park* and *Great Expectations* that lined, together with others of their ilk, the shelves in my bedroom. I read copiously and speedily, not always liking the content of what I read, but reading it anyhow. This was new territory to me and I didn't want to be left behind. The literature answered something inside of me, for it seemed to explain something I couldn't quite define: a sense of separation from the world, a feeling, not only of not belonging, but of not knowing how.

Chapter Eighteen

Jason spent a lot of time with Gran. He was working with the council as an engineer on a British-based voluntary scheme that meant he worked in a Third World country for three years, in which time he was to impart his First World knowledge to the poor peasants who ran the council. In exchange, he received a lowly salary in terms of money, but the 'African experience' he received more than compensated for this fact. He could go back to Britain in three years' time, confident that he had played his part in the reconstruction of Zimbabwe and had taught the poor natives more in three years than the nasty colonials had managed to do in ninety. In reality, he received a lowly wage and not much else. His 'African experience' tended to be constricted due to the fact that most of the money he earned went on paying his rent and buying food.

Although she was not bound to, Gran often made him lunch or dinner and, in return, he talked to her. He was a gardener as well, and often when I arrived there on a Saturday, he would be wheeling a wheelbarrow around, or digging up a bed. Once, Jason joked that if Gran were only thirty years younger, he would snap her up and whisk her off and marry her. Gran laughed and told him he wasn't her type, and I think he was a little hurt for he pulled a face, 'Oh, all right then. What is your type?'

'I've never found out,' said Gran. 'A bit more rough and ready. A bad guy, as the Americans would say. You're too good.' She laughed again.

'Get out of here,' joked Jason, smiling again. 'I see you with some posh gentleman type. Top hat and all that. Dinner and the opera. That sort of thing.'

Gran turned up her nose. 'Heaven forbid, I don't think that sort of man exists anyway. It's all a show.'

I, however, was convinced he did. About a month after I met Jason, there was a dance advertised at school. It was the first year that Mandy and I were allowed to attend such a function, as we were now in form four. I was excited. Somehow, although the dance was a school function and would be held in a school hall in Bulawayo, Zimbabwe, I imagined it to be a sophisticated, grown-up affair with a string quartet and someone like Frank Sinatra singing in a tuxedo and occasionally breaking into a tap dance. I would be dressed in a long ballgown and have long blonde hair, although in reality it was short and mousy in colour. I would look mysterious and exciting, men would vie for my hand in a dance that sometimes was a waltz and in other, slightly more exotic daydreams, was a tango. At those times I wore high, pointed black stilettos and a red rose in my hair. My chosen partner, the only man I would deign to dance with was always, every time, Jason.

I became so enrapt in this particular daydream, so much

so that even the Eastern European poet on the run from a Communist dictatorship was momentarily shelved, that I almost forgot that in reality I had no one to go to the dance with. I could ask Jason but I was far too shy. The confidence of the sultry tango dancer was, in actual fact, the painful lack of confidence of the sixteen-year-old schoolgirl. Mandy was going with a boy called Martin Payne, who was captain of the Matabeleland under-eighteen rugby team. A lot of girls were envious of her. I imagined how envious they'd all be when they saw Jason and I. The only problem was how to ask Jason.

My first plan of action was to reveal my intention to Mandy. She didn't really like Jason, though, and screwed up her face when I mentioned it.

'I don't know what it is about him,' she said. 'He's just weird, that's all.'

Nonplussed, and secretly quite glad that if she didn't like him, there was unlikely to be any competition between us, I pursued the topic with her.

'What would your gran say?' she asked. 'Isn't he a bit old?'

'Twenty-four,' I answered, with a nervous laugh. Mandy's eyes widened, as though I'd said he was over a hundred.

'Well, if that's what you want, go for it.'

'I don't know how. That's the problem,' I said, putting my head on the table we were sitting at as though I was in pain.

Mandy thought for a while. 'Ask your gran,' was her advice. 'She knows him quite well.'

I decided to approach the subject with Gran over a cup of lunchtime tea. My trick was to try and make Gran suggest the idea.

'There's a school dance at the end of the month.'

'Oh, yes?' said Gran. 'And are you going to go?'

'I don't know yet,' I replied sorrowfully. 'Mandy's going with Martin, the rugby guy.'

'And what about you? Who are you going to go with?' asked Gran, blowing on her tea before sipping it.

'I don't know. There isn't anyone.'

'Does Mandy know anyone you could go with?'

I shook my head. 'No. I've asked.'

'I'm sure she could find someone. She knows a lot of people.'

'They're not my type. Besides, I don't want to go on a blind date. I want to go with someone I know.'

'Well, who do you know?'

'No one.' I was being difficult, I knew, but I wanted to eliminate all irrelevant possibilities as soon as possible.

'There must be someone.'

'No. There isn't!'

'What about that boy who gave you his phone number?'

'On the back of a Castle label?'

'Well, we don't all carry spare paper around with us. It's creative thinking.'

I pulled a face. 'No thanks. I'd rather not go than have beer breathed all over me all night long.'

'I'm sure he's all right, really. Give him a chance, Ellie, you never know.'

'No thanks.'

'Right, well that's eliminated all our possibilities, hasn't it? You better get out there and meet someone soon.'

I nodded dejectedly and picked up my things in order to go home.

'Cheer up!' said Gran. 'When you do, we can make you a beautiful dress and you'll be the belle of the ball.'

I cycled slowly home and stayed in my bedroom for the rest of the afternoon. I felt like Cinderella, left all alone with no one to love and no one to love her. I imagined girls asking me why I wasn't going to the dance. I pictured them sniggering and whispering to each other. 'Too boring,' they would say, or, 'a bit odd.' I tried to change the picture in my mind so that when they asked me why I wasn't going to the dance I looked away mysteriously and later someone told them that the love of my life had been killed in a tragic accident and that I'd vowed never to love anyone ever again. 'What a pity,' they whispered to each other. 'She is so beautiful. What a waste.'

The phone rang. It was Gran.

'I had a thought, and I hope you don't mind, but I acted on it. I asked Jason if he would go to the dance with you and he said yes. Now, tell me what you think. I know he's quite a few years older than you, but it's only for one night. If you're not happy, I'll tell him.'

Not happy? Not happy? I was spinning through the air, I was mentally cartwheeling across the room, I was ecstatic; but I couldn't let my feelings show.

'Jason?' I said in the most surprised voice I could muster. 'But he won't want to go with me.'

'Well, that's not what he said,' said Gran, reassuringly. 'I said you could even take my car as he doesn't have one, and I doubt you'll want to go to a dance on the back of his bike. What's important is if you are happy with the arrangement.'

'Yes, I suppose so,' I said, miserably, although I was actually so happy that I wouldn't have minded if we did have to go to the dance on Jason's bike. 'Thanks, Gran,' I added.

'Well, it's still up to you, Ellie, dear. I only want you to be happy.'

That Saturday Gran and I went to Mr Patel's to look for dress fabric. I knew the style of the dress I wanted. I had seen it in a *Fair Lady* magazine. It was of white satin with a heart-shaped bosom. It was sleeveless and there was a white organza shawl that went with it. In the magazine, it was worn by a beautiful model as she sat on the back of her boyfriend's motorbike, laughing provocatively at the camera. I was going to look like that, I thought. That was going to be me.

Gran and I found a pattern for a dress very similar to that of the motorbike-riding model and spent a Saturday afternoon cutting it out. Jason had gone to Harare with another of his volunteer friends, a Scot working at a government college. They were going to see what the Big City was like and also meet another of their group who was arriving from England. They were going to travel by local bus in order to get a 'genuine feel for the country'.

Mandy came round to help pin and tack and we had a lot of fun talking to Gran. We discussed the dance and who was going with whom. We talked about boys in general and who we liked and who we couldn't stand.

'What's this Vance like?' Gran asked Mandy.

Mandy laughed because she knew I didn't like him. 'Oh, he's sweet, Mrs Rogers.'

'Then why doesn't Ellie like him?' asked Gran with a sideways glance at me.

'I don't know,' laughed Mandy. 'I think he's cute.'

'Well, would you go out with him?' I asked her.

She smiled, knowing she had been cornered. 'Weeelll, no, no... but that doesn't mean he's not nice.'

'See! See!' I exclaimed, triumphantly. 'He can't be that nice if you wouldn't go out with him either!'

'What about Steven Albright?' asked Mandy, with a giggle.

'Perhaps if I was a boy,' I answered.

'Oh yes?' said Gran. 'What's all that about?'

'He's gay,' laughed Mandy. 'A real mommy's boy.'

'Being a mommy's boy doesn't mean he's gay,' said Gran, cutting carefully though the material.

'No, but he is,' insisted Mandy, a little unkindly.

'I once thought I knew someone who was gay,' continued Gran, unpinning the pattern from the cut out material. 'Now I think he was just lonely.'

Mandy pulled a face that said she didn't understand what Gran was talking about. 'Being lonely's no reason to be gay,' she stated.

'Oh no. I'm just saying that I don't think he was really gay after all. Circumstances, that's all.'

Mandy and I exchanged a frown and raised eyebrows.

'I do feel sorry for you girls,' said Gran a little later. 'There's nowhere nice for you to go to meet young boys.'

Mandy and I looked at each other and smiled at the mention of 'young boys'.

'What did you do, when you were our age?' said Mandy.

'Well, we used to go to the cinema sometimes or for a walk around the park or along the sea front.'

This time Mandy and I giggled.

'The park?' I laughed.

'Did you go for a ride on the train?' asked Mandy.

'Watch it,' said Gran, jokingly, the needles she held

between her lips moved warningly up and down. 'That was the park in England before I moved out here.'

'What did you do when you came here?' asked Mandy.

'Much the same,' laughed Gran. 'Minus the walks along the sea front, of course. Picnics, walks, films.'

'The thing is,' she said suddenly, as though she were continuing aloud a conversation she was having with herself, 'with a man you have to remain aloof, apart. Even when you're married, they must never think that they have you, they must still be left wondering.'

'Why's that?' I asked.

'Psychology. Men always want what they can't have and, if they can't have you, then they'll want you all their lives long.'

I thought of Grandad then, how he was waiting for her to return. The memory of Gran and Miles lying in bed together momentarily rose before me and I felt a stab of pain but didn't say anything. I didn't want to spoil the good mood.

All afternoon we cut and pinned and tacked and in a few hours the outfit was roughly joined together and I could try it on. I stood in my bare feet, my legs cold in the early winter evening while Gran pulled at the sides and asked me whether I had enough room to move and then asked me how long I wanted it and pinned up the hem. I felt then like the most beautiful person on earth. To me, the dress was the height of sophistication and glamour and I couldn't help smiling. Gran noticed and smiled too, raising her eyebrows as she did so.

'You're going to look beautiful, my girl. You are going to be cold, though. I have a shawl you could wear that would go nicely with this.'

154

Shawls were old-fashioned and I smiled at Gran's naïveté in these matters, but I loved her so much then that it didn't matter. I'd wear the shawl, I'd wear ten shawls, I was just so happy.

'Where did you learn to sew, Mrs Rogers?' asked Mandy as we cleared up that afternoon. Gran was picking up scraps of material from the floor.

'Don't throw those away,' she said to Mandy who was just about to put a handful of scrap material in the bin. 'I'll keep them for something.' Mandy looked with surprise at the tiny scraps but obediently placed them on the table along with any pieces of cotton that she felt could still be used.

'I don't need those!' laughed Gran. 'Just the material.'

Mandy blushed and took to winding up the reels of cotton.

'The War,' said Gran, a little while later, 'has a lot to answer for. I haven't been able to throw a thing away since. We were rationed, you see, and so we didn't have a lot. Even if you had the money, you couldn't always buy what you wanted.

'You ask how I learnt to sew. Well, it was after the War. Only after I moved here. I couldn't cook either, you know. My mother wouldn't let me in case I messed up the recipe and that was it, our rations gone on something totally inedible. When I moved here, I couldn't believe what was available. There were things for sale that we in Britain hadn't seen for years. Ice cream, for one. I once ate three in one sitting. When you've done without something, you can spend the rest of your life trying to make up for it, but you never do.

'When I came here, I found the women had such beautiful

dresses. Material I hadn't seen my whole life. But I didn't have any money. I didn't have my own income so I learnt how to sew.'

'But who taught you?' asked Mandy, arranging the reels of cotton in Gran's sewing case.

'A friend,' said Gran. 'Someone who came to be a friend.'

'Now you're being all mysterious, Gran,' I teased.

'No, really,' continued Gran, seriously. 'She was a friend and she taught me to sew and I have been indebted to her ever since.'

'What about cooking,' I asked. 'Who taught you to cook?'

'That was another friend,' said Gran, winding a piece of cotton back onto a reel. 'Also in this country. After the War. As I said, my mother wouldn't let me cook in case I did something terrible with all our rations.'

'What are you going to make out of these?' asked Mandy, fingering the scraps and turning up her nose simultaneously.

'I have no idea!' she laughed with good nature, quashing Mandy's snub. 'What about a pair of trousers for winter?'

The day of the dance dawned clear and blue and cold. Gran took me into town that morning and I bought stockings, two pairs; Gran said that a woman should always have two pairs. 'One must always be prepared,' she said, with a serious nod of her head.

I wore black patent leather court shoes that made me feel grown-up and feminine. It took a while to learn how to walk in them though and they pinched my toes. Gran lent me her shawl and a pressed powder in a round gold box with mother of pearl inlay.

'That's another thing a woman should always carry,' she said, 'and perfume.'

156

I was so excited, I tried on the dress and shoes and stockings that afternoon. I locked myself in my bedroom and tried putting make up on and pouting my lips provocatively. What would have happened by this time tomorrow, I thought? Would I have kissed Jason?

When I got to Gran's, I could see her sitting on the verandah with Jason. I suddenly felt very nervous and took a long time propping my bike up against the garage wall. I didn't know whether to try and look serious or happy. As I walked up the path, I noticed that there was someone else sitting on the verandah. She had her back to me, but I could see that she had long black hair twisted up into a knot on her head. She looked like a ballerina and there was something about the way she was sitting that reminded me of the way a cat's back moves when you stroke it, almost detesting your touch on its silky smooth fur.

'Ellie!' said Gran, looking up. Although she was smiling, I could tell there was something wrong.

'Ellie,' echoed Jason. Unease permeated his voice and he stood up too quickly, his actions tainted with guilt. 'This is Rosie.' He went to get a chair for me to sit on from a corner of the verandah. His movements were excessively polite and unnatural. The coolness of the cushion when I sat down reminded me of the feel of chairs in a doctor's waiting room. They had just finished lunch and the table was littered with plates and crumbs and used cutlery. There was something about the screwed up serviettes that suggested a good meal had been had and all were full. I had broken the conviviality of post-lunch conversation.

'Rosie's just arrived from England,' said Gran. 'She was

supposed to be my lodger, remember?'

Of course I remembered; it was only a few weeks ago. Why was Gran talking so unnaturally? Her words were hard and forced and hung on the air after she had spoken, not dissolving completely. Rosie looked at me unsmilingly. She held a cigarette in her hand and, when she took a drag of it, her eyes narrowed slightly and she blew out perfect lines of blue smoke that disappeared quickly, as though they had orders to follow and couldn't delay.

'Would you like a drink?' asked Gran. 'You must be thirsty after your bike ride over here?'

I hesitated and Gran said quickly, 'Come into the kitchen and let's see what we can find you.' She stood up and went inside the house. I resented the tone of her voice; she was talking to me as though I were a child who needed entertaining. I followed her anyway, as I wanted to know what was going on. I could feel Rosie watch me leave.

'Gran, is there something wrong?' I asked once we were in the security of the kitchen.

Gran poured orange juice into a glass and filled it up with water.

'Well, unfortunately Jason won't be able to go to the dance with you, Ellie. Not now that Rosie's here. She arrived this morning apparently and didn't tell anyone about it. Maybe it was supposed to be a surprise, I don't know. Anyway, he hasn't seen her for a while and they want to catch up with each other.'

I looked at her, not quite comprehending her words.

'Rosie's Jason's girlfriend,' said Gran. 'I didn't know either,' she added, as if that would make me feel better.

I stood still, dumbstruck at what I was hearing.

'Don't worry,' continued Gran, as though she had some sort of plan in action, 'we'll find someone else.'

'Find someone else? It's half past five in the afternoon. Who are we going to...'

My voice trailed off as Jason entered, looking very sheepish. He had his hands in the back pockets of his jeans and pulled a face of apology at me.

'So sorry, Ellie. I really, really am very truly sorry. I didn't know she was arriving. Is there anyone else you could go with?'

'No,' I said, in a small voice. 'No. I don't know anyone else.'

'Oops,' he said, equally as quietly. He didn't say anything and then, 'I'll make it up you know. I'll take you somewhere next weekend.' He turned to Gran. 'I could still borrow the car next weekend, couldn't I?'

'Yes, yes,' said Gran, still trying to be jovial.

'Borrow the car?' said a voice suddenly. 'To go where?'

We all turned round to see Rosie standing in the entrance way to the kitchen. She had taken off her shoes and looked oddly at home barefoot. She had a chain around one ankle and was wearing a long blue and grey sarong. Jason looked surprised and started to explain about the evening. I felt myself going red and wished he would shut up.

'Oh,' was all Rosie said when Jason finished speaking, 'a school dance.'

She turned and went back outside, smoothing her hair with her hand as she walked. Jason made a feeble attempt at a laugh and then stopped and followed Rosie outside too. I couldn't bear it any longer and said I was going to phone Mandy. Gran said I could use the phone in her room so I went in but I didn't pick up the receiver. Instead, I lay on the bedspread and cried into Gran's pillow. My world had ended.

After a little while, Gran came in and sat beside me. She patted my back with her hand.

'Oh, Ellie, dear, I'm so sorry.'

I didn't say anything and we sat in silence for a while.

'I could ask my friends,' she said, suddenly.

'Ask your friends?' I said, angrily. 'What do you mean ask your friends?'

'Well, someone might know someone. They might have a grandson or nephew who could take you.'

A shiver of irritation passed through me. 'What are you talking about Gran? Whose nephew or grandson? You can't just ask people. This is not 1914, you know.'

'Well, there might be someone,' said Gran, soothingly, ignoring my sarcasm.

'I don't want someone,' I cried. 'I want Jason. I only want to go with Jason.'

Gran winced. 'I know, Ellie. I know.'

About fifteen minutes later, Mandy arrived. Gran had called her when I hadn't.

'I can call some people,' she said, 'I've already asked Martin to ask around.'

'Great,' I snapped. 'Now the whole of Bulawayo knows that I don't have anyone to go to the dance with. Thanks very much!'

'I'm only trying to help,' said Mandy, hurt. 'I thought you'd still want to go. You've got the dress and everything. It would be a shame not to go.'

'What's the point? What's the point of a nice dress if I'm

going with someone I don't even know.'

'Come on,' said Gran with sudden gusto. 'Stop feeling sorry for yourself and get out there.'

'Get out where?' I snapped again. 'Who would you like me to call? I don't know anyone!'

'What about that young boy you were talking about once? The one who wanted to take you out.'

My mind searched blankly for a few moments and then I said, 'Vance? Vance Taylor? You must be joking. Nooo thanks. I'd rather go with an inmate from Ingutsheni. They would have more to say for themselves anyway!' I put the pillow over my head.

'Yes, what about Vance?' said Mandy, picking up on the note of enthusiasm in Gran's voice.

'Mandy,' I said, taking the pillow off my head, 'you even said you wouldn't go with him.'

'That's me. We're talking about you.'

'Thanks!' I retorted.

'No. No, I didn't mean it like that. What I meant was that you two, well, sort of go together better.'

I rolled my eyes. I couldn't believe that someone would ever look at Vance and me and think we went together.

'At least he likes you. Which is better than someone who has a girlfriend.' She nodded towards the verandah.

Gradually my crying ceased and I looked resignedly at the phone.

'Maybe you're right,' I said in a small sorrowful voice. 'Maybe I should just give it a try.'

Gran got the phone book and we looked up Vance's number. I looked at it for a long time before finally picking up the receiver and dialling.

He was in. He was delighted. He had been planning to watch a video – *Die Hard* – had I watched it? It was going to be a classic. But no, the dance sounded much better. He had been looking forward to an evening like this for a long time. He'd pick me up at seven.

Gran was pleased. 'Great. If he picks you up at seven, then I'll go to the Naval Club and meet Miles at about half past. It looks as though we'll both have a good evening.'

'Fantastic,' I said, my voice flat with defeat. 'What I've always wanted.'

'Oh, Ellie,' she said, hugging me. 'One day you'll look back on this and have a good laugh, you'll see.'

'Can't wait,' I said, with a sniff. My eyes were swollen from crying.

'Listen, why don't you two come to the Club afterwards and meet us there?'

I wanted to say that the plans were getting better and better. An evening with Vance Taylor followed by a nightcap at the Naval Club with Miles Trevellyan. What could be better? But there was something in Gran's voice, some note of sympathy that I could not ignore. She was doing her best, I knew, and she really did feel as though she was to blame. I took a deep breath and managed to say, 'OK, maybe we will. If we have time.'

When we drew up outside the Naval Club later on that evening, I was feeling much more relaxed than I had done earlier. The dance was not as disastrous as I was sure it would be, although it hadn't started very well. Vance had arrived in a small blue truck with yellow wheels and I had truly wanted the ground to swallow me up when I saw it. Luckily we were a little late arriving and had to park quite far from the school hall. He'd offered to drop me at the entrance and go and find somewhere to park, but I'd hastily told him not to worry and pointed to a parking place near the fence which was dark and where we'd be fairly inconspicuous. Vance was also wearing a pair of brilliant white shoes that quite literally shone in the dark as we walked over to the hall. I mentally cursed Gran and Mandy and half wished I'd decided to stay at home.

However, the evening improved. I soon brightened up in the company of friends and even enjoyed myself. Nobody asked me what happened to Jason, as no one besides Mandy knew that he was supposed to be there. I had kept it a secret, as I wanted the whole thing to be a surprise. I had had a picture in my mind of Jason and I arriving and everyone turning around to look. Even the music would stop. People would glance at each other and whisper what a wonderful couple we looked and how handsome Jason was. When Vance and I walked in, the music didn't stop and no one turned around to see us, that is no one except those of his friends who were also there and greeted him with, 'Hey, howzit going, China!' and 'Jusus, man! Who let you in?' But the evening itself was not a disaster and I felt that perhaps I had judged Vance too harshly.

At the end of the dance, I decided to go to the Naval Club and see Gran so that she would also feel better about the way things had turned out.

'The Naval Club?' said Vance, as we left the hall and walked towards his car. 'Sheez like! Where's that?'

'I'll show you,' I laughed. 'Once seen, never forgotten.'

We drew up outside the Naval Club, but Vance didn't move so I relaxed my hold on the door handle and waited for him to get out. He turned towards me. I thought for a moment he was going to kiss me and fleetingly wished he would. Surprised at myself, I turned and looked out of the window.

'I've had a great evening,' he said, smiling. I didn't say anything. 'Have you?'

I thought momentarily of him in his white shoes getting out of his little blue truck with yellow wheels and hesitated.

'Ja, well, it hasn't been too bad,' I managed to say, in rather a formal tone.

'You don't sound too happy,' he said, still smiling.

'No, no really, it's been great. Thanks for coming.'

He pulled the handle of the door and got out. Rather reluctantly, I followed him. When we got to the bottom of the flight of stairs that went up to the Naval Club's bar, I turned to him.

'Vance.'

'What?' he asked. I went up to him, rather like a child approaching Father Christmas, and kissed him on the cheek. He laughed, a little embarrassed. Neither of us spoke.

'Well, let's go see if my Gran's here,' I said moving away from him and making towards the stairs.

Gran was pleased to see us and waved us over to the table where she and Miles were sitting. Miles was smoking, but he got up to get another chair, his cigarette hanging out of his mouth.

'How did it go?' asked Gran with a naughty smile.

'Fine thanks, Gran,' and Vance nodded his head in agreement.

'Heard the cricket results?' Miles asked Vance.

Vance looked surprised and shook his head. 'I'm not much of a cricket fan myself.'

'Oh?' said Miles, surprised.

There was a pause and then Gran heckled me with questions. What were the other girls wearing? Had anyone commented on my dress? What time had it all ended? Eventually Vance stood up and said he was going.

'Thanks for a great evening, Ellie. We should do it again some time.' He shook Miles's hand and nodded a goodnight over to Gran.

'Going so soon?' asked Gran, disappointed. 'Why don't you stay and have another drink?'

'No thanks, Mrs Rogers. I have an early start tomorrow.'

'On Sunday?' asked Miles, in a voice like a teacher who doesn't believe your excuse for not doing your homework.

'I'm off to Harare. Motorcross,' he said, moving his hands as though he were steering a motorbike.

'Well, goodnight then,' said Gran and, turning to me, she widened her eyes and nodded in his direction.

'Good night, Vance,' I said and he disappeared out the door.

'Ellie!' said Gran once he'd gone. 'You should've, you know, gone and said goodnight.'

I laughed. 'No, Gran, I don't think so.'

'Ellie, you're useless!' she laughed. 'Anyway, how was it... really?'

'Fine really,' I said, opening my eyes wide and laughing. 'Besides the fact that he wears white shoes and drives a blue truck with yellow wheels, fine.'

We started laughing. 'Don't be cruel,' said Gran.

'I'm not,' I protested. 'How would you like to go to a dance with someone whose shoes look as though they are powered by ZESA?'

Gran shrieked with laughter and even Miles half smirked.

'So you won't see him again?' said Gran.

'No. I don't think so. It'll take a while to recover from seeing him tonight.'

I knew I was being unjustifiably cruel, but I was aware of a pain beginning to throb inside of me, and I felt that if I made light of the matter, it would go away. I kicked off my shoes, which were hurting my feet, and snuggled up to Gran.

'I'm glad it wasn't too bad,' she said, kissing the top of my head.

'No, it wasn't too bad.' I sighed.

I could feel the pain long after I had gone to bed that night. I lay on my back and drew the duvet up to my chin. I was cold but couldn't be bothered to fetch a blanket. My feet stuck out the duvet but all I could think was why didn't he kiss me? Why didn't he kiss me?

Chapter Nineteen

August blows bush fires across the *veldt*; the kind of fires that burn with anger and hunger as they eat their way through the long dry grass and fallen dead leaves of winter. I loved that time before the rains, those halcyon days that stretch on, seemingly forever. Before the rain, before the storms, when *jacaranda* trees burst into purple splendour, when the air smells like newly ironed cotton sheets, when it trembles with life, like an over-full jug of water carried carefully lest it spill its contents, shivering and wavering. October shall drink ravenously of its contents; October shall quench its thirst and spit out the excess on the dust beneath its feet. November shall bring restoration and rain, but storms too, blades of lightning and swollen black skies. But for now it is time for September, September that heals and soothes and comforts.

September sees the start of the last term of the school year. Exams, concerts, rain and Christmas. There is a poetry to September, a song, a promise. It speaks of a new beginning, yet it heralds in an end. We are all wrong in the

Southern Hemisphere. It should have been our January. Every day, I cycled to Gran's along the wide tree-lined streets to lazy Suburbs. The air of early afternoon was silent except for the birds twittering gently to each other and the occasional car that ambled along. Late afternoon, the air was filled with the smell of water on dust and the tic-tic-tic of garden sprays. The *jacarandas* spread themselves out along the road, their branches reaching over to their counterparts on the other side of the tar, as though they were making a way for me to pass through. I was in love then, not with someone, but with life. Once I tried to write a poem about it. 'This September sun...,' I started then stopped. I could go no further. Words seemed useless. Nothing could explain it; nothing can. September: words are meaningless.

Jason left. He went to share a flat with some other expats in Northend. Rosie lived there as well. I never saw him again after he left Gran's and he never kept in touch with her. I thought it bad of him not to and I think she missed his company, but she never got another lodger and said she preferred things the way they were. She liked being on her own.

During my 'A' level year, I applied to many universities to study English and Art. I knew I could probably never go as my parents couldn't afford to send me, but I wanted to know that I could have got in, had the opportunity been there. I started to think about what I would do the following year. I had great ideas of working for a while and saving enough money to go to England. I would work my way across Europe as well, picking grapes, waitressing, eventually learning four or five more languages and living on the Mediterranean somewhere. The greatest obstacle was having to work in Zimbabwe first. I hated the thought of being a secretary or a receptionist somewhere, but there were not many other options.

One night I was sitting with Gran on her verandah, talking about the future and feeling down about it. All I wanted to do was read books and study.

'Don't worry, it's only a year and then you can go overseas and travel for a bit.'

'A year! A whole year of my life,' I said, miserably, 'being some pathetic secretary. "Hi, my name's Ellie and I'm a secretary",' I mimicked in a high-pitched voice. '"I'm really stupid, but I love typing and playing patience on the computer. I'm not ambitious because one day I'm going to marry my boyfriend. Ja, he's really sweet. He plays rugby."'

Gran laughed and I rolled my eyes contemptuously.

'Why do you say that, Ellie?' she asked more seriously. 'Even if you were a secretary, you're not stupid and you can do more than type and you are ambitious. Being a secretary doesn't make you stupid.'

'But that's what people would think.'

'That's what you think. Have more confidence in yourself.'

'It's not me. It's other people. They just look at women and think one thing about them. There's no room to be different here. If you are a woman, you're one thing and one thing only.'

'Well, that's not quite true,' said Gran, sounding rather offended. 'Look at me. I'm not like that.'

It was true, Gran wasn't like that, yet anyone glancing at her life would think otherwise: going to the Naval Club every week, being involved with a man like Miles. I didn't say anything. I knew I would hurt her feelings.

'The problem with you, Ellie, is that you think there is only one way of living and if you don't fit in you're an outcast. Well, you're wrong. There are many ways of living your life.'

'Not in this country,' I retorted.

'Yes, in this country,' she said vehemently. 'You don't have to be a Rhodie to live here, Ellie. Find your own space, your own way of doing things. You like it here, don't you? I mean the country, do you like it?'

'The country, yes, not the people.'

Gran sighed. 'Then stay for the country. You can meet the people you want to know as you go along.'

'And how long is that going to take?' I asked, throwing up my hands. 'Gran, I want to live, not just exist. I want to go to theatres and concerts and meet people, people who have something to say for themselves, who can talk about something more than... than drinking and parties. I'll die, Gran, if I stay here. I'll shrivel up and die.'

There was a silence as we sat and looked ahead of us, past the pot plants and the verandah steps, out into the warm late September night. I could feel tears in the back of my throat, but I didn't cry.

'When I first came out here, I knew no one,' said Gran after a while.

'It was different then,' I said, a little irritated. Why was it, I thought, that when you had a problem, someone always had a story about their own life to compare to yours? I didn't want to know that everyone goes through similar things. I wanted my own story, a unique story that stood on its own.

'Why? Why was it different?' asked Gran, a note of annoyance entering her voice.

'Because years ago, things were different. Women were treated differently and men were more romantic. There were dances and balls and... and... romance!' I declared, snatching the word out of the air.

'You know, Ellie,' said Gran, sitting up, 'it wasn't all like that. Yes, men treated you differently. That doesn't stop your heart being broken. Yes, there were dances and balls. That doesn't stop you being lonely. It wasn't all romance. It was hard. When I came here, I didn't know a soul. Not one person. I had to go out and meet people and that was hard. You talk about it being better for a woman in those days. I couldn't go anywhere without a male escort. You didn't just go to the pictures or go out for a cup of coffee. You had to wait to be asked. And if you weren't asked, you didn't go anywhere.'

'But you got asked, didn't you? You're always telling me how you went here, there and everywhere.'

'After a while,' said Gran, leaning back in her chair. 'But it took some time.'

'Anyway, I thought you knew Uncle Wally. You knew one person at least.'

Gran hesitated. 'Yes, I knew Uncle Wally but...'

There was a long pause and we continued looking out into the night.

'He didn't always understand though,' said Gran a while later. 'Being a man, I mean. He didn't always understand.'

I sighed. 'Gran, when you knew you were moving to this country, weren't you happy?'

'Yes, of course I was. I was also afraid.'

'Did you think of it as a new life?' I persisted.

'Definitely. Especially since the War had just ended and

Britain was so gloomy. I was...'

'Well, that's how I feel now,' I interrupted. 'I want a new life. I want to travel and see the world. Do you know what I mean?'

'I know,' said Gran, looking down sadly. 'I was going to see the world as well.' She gave a brief humourless laugh. 'I just stopped off along the way.'

A few weeks later, I rode round to Gran's on the way home from school. It was 1992, the worst year of drought we had had. She was in the garden, walking along the thin ribbon of dust that was the path, carrying a bucket of dirty bath water and pouring it sparingly on the straggly daisy bushes that bordered the verandah and the lavender bushes near the back door. The majority of the water she reserved for her roses, which lay open to the sun's brutal reign all day and which stood like a row of defeated soldiers, waiting, heads bowed, in front of their captor.

Gran waved and smiled when she saw me. She looked tired and, for the first time in my life, I thought she looked old. I felt a sudden rush of affection for her and wanted to throw my arms around her neck. I didn't though; instead, I took the bucket she was carrying and continued to water the garden for her. She wiped her hands on her trousers and sighed.

'Thank you, Ellie, you are a good girl, aren't you.'

'I wonder how long this drought will go on for?'

The blue sky looked blankly down at us in answer; it didn't care, I thought.

After watering the garden, Gran went to the kitchen and poured out two long cool glasses of orange juice and we sat in the shade of the verandah.

'Where did you say you would most like to study?' asked Gran.

I didn't want to get onto the subject again. I felt a little ashamed, not about what I had said before, but about what I had thought during our talk, that Gran was in some way a failure, that she had conformed to a society from which I wanted to detach myself, that she was part of what I hated. I hesitated and then said, 'England. Bristol, if I had the chance.'

'And you've applied? Is that what you said?'

'Yes, I've applied to lots of places.'

There was a silence.

'I have a plan,' said Gran at last. 'I have some money in England.' She looked down and ran her hand along the arm of the cane chair she was sitting on. 'It was left to me by my father when he died. Not much, but I invested it a few years ago and it's been earning interest ever since.'

I stared at her. 'You have money in England? You've never mentioned it before.'

'To tell you the truth, I didn't really know how much it was. When my father died, the money was put in a bank account for me and basically forgotten about. I was here when he died and I just never investigated it.'

'But Gran, use it, use it for yourself. You always need money, why don't you use it?'

Gran's lips twisted into a question and then she said, 'I do use it, some of it.' She waved behind her at the house. 'That's how I afford to live here. I couldn't do it otherwise.'

'I thought your pension...' I started, but Gran gave a short laugh that stopped me.

'Pension! It goes nowhere. To tell you the truth, Ellie, I

wouldn't be able to survive on my own without the money overseas.'

'Well, I can't take it. How would you survive?' I exclaimed.

'It doesn't take much to live here when you convert the money. And I only use it for the rent.'

'Well, why don't you use it for other things? Why don't you go on holiday?'

Gran looked down at her hands and turned a ring on her index finger.

'You know, Ellie, when you've been dependent most of your life on other people, you want something of your own. You want to be able to say, "I've done this or that. On my own."'

She looked really sad as she spoke and, when she looked up, she held my eyes with hers for a few seconds. 'That's why I don't use it on going on holiday.'

'But it's your money, Gran.'

'No, it's not,' she answered and pursed her lips together ruefully. 'It's not.'

'Does Mom know? About the money?'

'Yes,' Gran nodded. 'I told her when I moved here. She went on and on about how I couldn't afford to live here. I didn't want to rely on the money at all. That's why I got a lodger. But I like being on my own, Ellie. This' – she threw her arms open to the house and the garden – 'is mine.'

I didn't know whether to be happy or sad, accept Gran's offer or turn it down. The whole thing seemed unlikely to come to anything.

'You'll have to work though,' said Gran suddenly, with a smile. 'If I pay the tuition fees, you're going to need to support yourself.'

'That's fine,' I almost whispered, I was so close to tears.

By November, it was decided. I was going to study in England. I was overjoyed; I was ecstatic. I was leaving Bulawayo. The day that I got a confirmation letter from the university, I rode to Gran's, threw my bike down on the lawn and went round the back where I knew she would be, tending to her seedlings. She gave me a big hug and kissed my hair. My lips trembled slightly. Through my happiness I could feel the beginnings of sadness. I wanted to leave and I didn't want to. I wanted to go to England and yet forever live in Zimbabwe. Would I ever come back? Would this be the last November in the place I had lived all my life? I could see Gran's blue eyes clouding over a little with tears and she turned to go inside.

'Let's have a cup of tea to celebrate,' she said. 'I think it's going to rain.'

Chapter Twenty

And so it was that I left Zimbabwe and went to live in England. It was here that I found a voice I had never had before. I felt as though I had spent my whole life on a stage and yet had never managed to stand in the spotlight. Somehow it had always swung over or past me. Although I had once or twice waved my hands and tried to attract its attention, I had always been left in the dark. Now it stopped and held me in its glow and I, in turn, basked in its warmth and grew in its gaze.

Here was everything I had ever dreamed of. England had an absorbing culture; it had art and, above all, it had books. There was no pressure to conform, no need to be anyone but myself. It is strange now to realise that freedom, or an idea of it, is something that exists in one's mind. The England of my arrival was the same England as fourteen years later, yet by then it had become a prison.

I left Zimbabwe in January of 1993 and worked in a bookshop in London, in Golders Green to be exact. I had great intentions of reading all the books there, working my way through the classics and then modern literature and into the history of art and music. I wanted to read my way through all the gaps in my knowledge so I could nod my head wisely when asked about the Beat Generation or the Harlem Renaissance or Graham Greene's novels, whatever it happened to be.

However, I was really a glorified shelf stacker and the job didn't lend itself to the leisure of reading. I couldn't afford to buy the books for I only earned enough to support myself and anything left over was saved for my future studies. I learnt how to be poor, how to live on very little, but in many ways I did not need money. There was so much to see that I absorbed it through my skin. I would sit and watch people getting on and off the tube and this alone was food for a mind starved of variety and colour. If I couldn't afford to go and see a play, I would compare reviews of it in different papers. I learnt to appreciate the joy of saving all week to sit in a coffee shop and spend it all on a cappuccino while watching the world go by, how to save all month for a half price ticket to a concert.

When I first arrived, I stayed with Michaelea Loft, the daughter of a friend of my mother. She had lived in London for two years and was going to give it another two so that she could apply for a British passport. Even if she then decided it wasn't the place for her, the passport was all-important, as it was for so many like her. I suppose I took mine for granted and yet always felt slightly guilty for having had it bestowed on me without doing anything except being someone of British descent. Not only did I feel guilty next to the likes of Michaelea, but I sometimes felt guilty in the company of real British people, those not born and bred in a far away country, and now making claim to a land to which they bore no loyalty.

Michaelea had a small flat about two blocks from the bookshop in which I worked. It wasn't big enough for two people really and the room in which I slept was really a large cupboard. There was a bed pushed up against one wall, which the door bumped against when you opened it. There was a small chest of drawers at the foot of the bed and the only hanging space was a hook at the back of the door. But anyone who's been in the same position will recognise the sense of freedom, even pride, that the room gave me. It was my first step away from home, my first step on a road I felt would take me towards success, romance and the kind of completeness only found in Jane Austen novels and romantic movies.

Michaelea herself had a large room with space for a dressing table, a desk and even a couch. This last item was generally covered with clothes and towels and it was where she threw her handbag when she came in from work. I didn't see much of her as she left before I did in the mornings. It took her over an hour to get to work in Fulham, where she worked as a secretary in a building firm. She returned home late at night, often going to meet friends for drinks after work and her boyfriend would appear from Liverpool at the weekends. I would hear them in her bedroom at night and try not to think what they were doing. I wasn't envious; I thought myself better than her as I was going to wait for The One, the one who was going to change my life.

I envisioned meeting Him at the bookshop. He'd be an academic type, a research student probably or a struggling author. He'd buy something like *War and Peace* and, while paying for it at the till, I'd ask him if he'd ever read anything else by Tolstoy. When he said no, I'd recommend *Crime and Punishment* and probably offer to lend him my own copy (with annotations in the margins, which would impress him no end). He'd have wild, curly brown hair and glasses, which would make him look very bookish, but when he took them off, he'd look incredibly sexy, although not that many people would've seen that side of him. We'd sit up at night, discussing literature and drinking red wine, and then coffee as the sun came up. We'd have huge arguments about Tolstoy and Faulkner, arguments that would end with him storming off into the night, usually accompanied by lightning and torrential rain, and I'd run after him without my coat or an umbrella and throw my arms around him, kissing him passionately, totally oblivious to the raging elements.

Unfortunately, the closest I got to living this fantasy was someone asking me whether we stocked any George Orwell. He was a man in his late thirties, early forties, with dark brown hair, that looked like it would've curled if he had let it grow a little longer, and beautiful deep green eyes.

'Orwell? Oh, yes, of course!' I enthused and hurriedly looked up on the relevant shelf.

'A fan are you?' he said, amused at my haste in finding what he wanted.

'Isn't everybody?' I responded, as my finger slid along the line of books I was searching through.

'I shouldn't think so. What's your favourite?' he asked and I glanced quickly at him.

'I haven't read them all,' I said, apologetically.

'Haven't you?' I felt there was something mocking in his tone, as though he hadn't expected me to have read any.

'*Animal Farm*,' I replied in an effort to sound more assertive. 'That's my favourite.'

'*Animal Farm*? Yes, well everyone's read that one.' He walked away as soon as he found what he was looking for and I wanted to run after him and tell him why it was my favourite. It was my favourite because I'd lived it, we'd lived it, were living it in Zimbabwe. I wanted him to say 'Oh, so you come from Zimbabwe'. I wanted to feel special and not just another shelf stacker.

The bookshop was managed by a Mr Parker. 'Call me Rupert,' he said on my first day. 'None of this Mr Parker crap.' He was a large, overweight man, who looked, from behind, like a baby elephant. It was the way his trousers sagged that gave this impression, that and the way he lumbered happily around the shop, never rushing, as though he were following the rest of the herd down to the waterhole.

He called me his 'Rhodesian Rose', although he wasn't really old enough to be excused the turn of phrase. I'd make tea in the morning before the shop opened and every day he took his first sip and uttered, 'Beautiful,' as though I had made something exotic, not just a humble cuppa. He irritated me, and he made my skin crawl when he came up behind me as I was stacking shelves and breathed down my neck about something or other. He had no interest in books; he couldn't see why anyone was interested in them, which seemed a little out of place for a man trying to sell them in order to make a living. I came to see him as indicative of a type of Britishness, that wearying cynicism and lack of enthusiasm for anything good, anything purely itself and not pretending to be anything that it wasn't. He could've had any job. He could've been selling doughnuts or used cars, it didn't matter. At the end of the month, he got a pay cheque and how he made his money wasn't important.

If I had stayed like this, living there and working at the bookshop, perhaps my life would've been very different. Perhaps... how many times do we say that? In September of that year I went to university and stayed there for the next four years.

It was there that I began to feel a dislocation from my surroundings. Life was unreal there, a constant round of drinking and partying, interspersed with the occasional lecture and seminar. I enjoyed it at first, especially after my frugal existence in London. But there was something meaningless about it, bottomless. I felt it was a place that would suck me in and spit me out, a place in which I could lose myself and never find the way back.

There were students there who barely lifted a finger, who were only there to avoid going on the dole, preferring instead to accumulate debt by living on endless loans. Then there were others whose speech was heavy with theories, ideas, postulations. But they had never been anywhere, never travelled, never experienced what they talked so fulsomely about.

At university, I realised that men like Jason were two a penny and rather clichéd. I went out with some of them, though no one for very long. They spouted their literature and their politics, but they were boring. It was almost as though they all read from the same book, although each uttered what they had to say with genuine enthusiasm, as though the ideas were really theirs. I found myself searching for authenticity, for someone who wasn't aware of what they were saying, who spoke without thinking about it first.

It was strange to live in a place where everything was so ordered and so precise. Lines and lines of shiny new cars in the early morning traffic jams; no beaten up hunks of metal holding everyone up until they could be pushed off the road; no coughing, smoking buses lumbering down the highways, smoke billowing out into the face of the following traffic. Instead, polite waves of hands from one motorist to another, letting someone in from a side street or waiting patiently for them to park. No reckless driving; no hooting, shouting driver speeding dangerously through red traffic lights, cursing you for having the decency to stop on amber.

In response, I tried to arrange so much of my life around the order I found in England, although nothing fitted in as well as English things. I felt awkward, clumsy, afraid sometimes to open my mouth lest my accent gave me away. Worse than anything was the boredom of routine, the dead weight of it. It sank like a stone between my ribs and every time I swallowed it hurt, but it wouldn't digest, wouldn't disappear. It rose and fell as I breathed; it rubbed against my heart and frayed its edges. I tried to counter it, to talk and chatter brightly but there were so many barriers that sprung up as I walked into a room. I answered all the patronising questions about Africa, about droughts and cannibals, lions and giraffes. I tried to ask about Chelmsford, Cambridge, the M1, but it was so trapped, so constricted a conversation that beat against the walls of its prison, but remained what it was, empty. It resounded with a painful hollowness in nightmares I had, nightmares of walls crumbling inwards whilst I slept, of the collapsing roof that sheltered me from the cold wind of England.

In many ways those four years were a time of discovery;

studying opened up a different world for me. I lost myself in what I did. But in another way, my life remained static, and I remained the girl I had always been, introverted and lacking in confidence. Whereas life in London had made me more outgoing as I was one among millions, at university I became self-conscious again. The light that fell on me was not the enchanted limelight of the stage; it was the bright overhead light of the operating theatre. Here my life was open to scrutiny and dissection.

It is not enough just to travel, if one wishes to change who one is. The greatest journey we go on is inward towards our selves, rather than outwards and away. You cannot change who you are unless you know who you are and what you are capable of, and that is what I had never known and why, finally, I couldn't move on. Having no base, no bedrock, no roots, I floundered in the freedom of England. I was soon lost, soon overwhelmed, like a tent in a storm, whose guy ropes come loose and leave it to flap and blow in the unrelenting wind.

Gran wrote to me throughout those years. Her thick letters on blue notepaper arrived every now and then, her sprawling handwriting announcing her latest news: her garden, who had come for tea, trouble with the car, politics. She told me about a new gardener she had employed, what his wife and children's names were, and their ages. Her letters read like conversations one might have over tea, full of minute, sometimes arbitrary, detail. I was almost surprised when they ended, signed with a flourishing 'Gran', so lulled had I been by their tone. They were one of the few tenuous links that I maintained with 'home'. They connected me across continents and mountains and rivers. They connected me through space and time; a link to my old life, my real life, perhaps, my self.

Tolstoy, of course, never wrote *Crime and Punishment* and I still haven't read it. Or *War and Peace*.

Chapter Twenty-one

I often thought of Africa when I left. She lay as a huge expanse of silence and solitude between my two lives. I reached out for her sometimes in the early mornings and expected to feel the warmth of her sun across my legs. I imagined the coolness of dawn to be around me, thought I could hear the sounds of a house waking up, the gentle calls of early risers to each other. I could never get over how real the sensations seemed and my eyes would open only to be met by the cold emptiness of my English room.

In the first four years that I was away from Zimbabwe, I returned twice. On both occasions, I spent night after night looking at the stars flung carelessly about me in the black night. To return inside the house brought about the dizziness and despair of claustrophobia. I'd awake late at night and sit staring out through the window, the curtains swept aside. The only thing more beautiful than the African day is the African night and I needed it, longed desperately to have it all to myself; at this hour it was all mine.

On my first trip home my parents picked me up from the

airport and, as we drove back into Bulawayo, I couldn't believe how much things hadn't changed. When you're away from a place, somehow you expect it to change with you. But there was the same petrol attendant at the garage, the same waiters at the restaurant in Haddon and Sly, the same missing letters from the local supermarket's sign.

There was one thing that had changed though. When I went to visit Gran for the first time, Miles was there, sitting with her outside. I felt uncomfortable, wanting to throw my arms around Gran, but feeling annoyed that he was there. He and Gran were laughing about something as I walked up the path and, when she saw me, Gran didn't move, but smiled and stretched out her arms. I had expected her to be more excited to see me, and I, in turn, just bent over and kissed her.

'You're looking well,' said Gran, holding me at arm's length and nodding approvingly at my figure. 'Isn't she looking well, Miles?'

Miles's eyes flicked over me. 'You need some sunshine, girl,' he said without a smile.

'Oh, don't listen to him,' laughed Gran, waving him away with her hand.

I suddenly noticed that Gran had a bandage round her left calf.

'What's wrong with your leg, Gran?' I asked, concerned.

'Oh,' said Gran, pulling a face, 'I did such a silly thing. I was watering the garden and got the hose wrapped round my legs somehow. I fell over and bumped this leg against that pot.' She pointed to a rusty iron flowerpot near the tap.

'Are you all right?'

'Oh, yes, fine. The doctor came and saw to me. She said

it would take a while to heal. My age!' she laughed.

'How long has it been like that?'

'About a month?' she turned and asked Miles, and Miles nodded his head slightly in agreement. 'Yes. About a month.'

'You never told me,' I said, resentfully.

'Well, what good would it have done? It's not life threatening.'

'Mom never told me either.'

'I told her not to.'

I didn't answer. I didn't like to think of Gran becoming old, becoming like other grandmothers: small and grey and shortsighted, racked with every illness going. I felt uncomfortable; more than that, I felt excluded, not just by Miles, but by my mother. More than that, I felt excluded by distance and time. Life wasn't allowed to change in this way. I stood up and told her that I was going to see Mandy and I'd be back later.

'Yes, yes, go, of course. You must see her,' said Gran, without surprise or any note of resentment or wish to have me stay a little longer. 'Come back and see me later. We can have supper together.'

I left without kissing her goodbye, something I never did. When I got in the car and looked at my watch, I saw I had been there less than ten minutes.

We did talk later on, over a supper of tomato soup and bread and salad.

'It's not homemade, I'm afraid,' she apologised, indicating, with a nod of her head, her leg. 'It keeps me back a bit.'

She asked me about my course and which books I was reading, nodding whenever she recognised any of the authors that I mentioned.

'Have you met anyone? Anyone special, I mean?' she asked after a short silence when she had leaned back in her chair and finished eating her slice of bread.

'If you mean a boyfriend, no. No one 'special', as you call it,' I replied, blowing gently on my spoonful of soup.

'No one?' she asked, surprised. 'Oh, that's disappointing. I thought you would've met someone over there.'

There was another silence. 'I feel sometimes that I don't fit in.' It was quite a confession for me to make, considering it was me who had wanted to go to England.

'Oh?' said Gran, looking at me, 'I thought that's how you felt about living here?'

I felt annoyed suddenly, as though Gran were trying to say that I didn't fit in anywhere.

'Well, maybe you'll come back,' she said, putting her elbows on the table and pushing her soup bowl out of her way.

'How are things going here?' I asked.

'Oh, fine, fine. Could be better though. This damn leg holds me up a lot.' She smiled, but I could see it annoyed her. 'Miles asked me to move in with him.'

The words took me by surprise but, seeing my face, she gave a short laugh. 'It's not the first time he's asked over the years. Now he says I'm a hazard to myself and he could look after me.'

'And?' I asked tentatively.

'And nothing,' replied Gran. 'I said no, like I always do. I'm too old for all that.' She laughed and leant over the table mischievously. 'Imagine what the neighbours would say?'

I gave a wry laugh. Gran had never cared what anyone said.

When I left for the airport two weeks later, I wanted her

to say that it was me that she wanted, me that she needed. I half wished she'd ask me to stay. But she didn't. Instead she wished me well and kissed me goodbye.

'Goodbye, Gran.'

'It's never goodbye,' she smiled and I thought I saw the tautness of her smile waver a little. 'Only see you later.'

'Enjoy yourself, Ellie,' she called from the steps of her house as I walked to the car. 'We only live once, you know.'

When I neared the end of my degree, although I had the opportunity to leave, the world loomed too close and threatening, like an old drunk who totters across the road in front of you and stumbles in your path, however much you try to avoid him and the embarrassment that such an encounter creates. I decided to apply for a scholarship for a Masters; I couldn't expect Gran to pay for that as well.

It wasn't easy though. Although I had a British passport, I was still considered a foreign student. When I researched the funds available for Commonwealth students, I was told that I was British. I discovered that there were bursaries available for refugees, immigrants, the disabled; for children of Portuguese fisherman lost off the EU coast, for Albanian and Romanian orphans born between 1975 and 1982, for Guatemalan pig keepers' children who wanted to pursue studies in micro-biology. In short, there was just about every kind of scholarship available for just about any type of person, except if you were a white Zimbabwean.

I knew that the only way that I would be able to do my Masters would be to win a bursary. I almost killed myself getting there, pushing myself to the limit every day, attending every lecture, every tutorial, writing every essay and every exam. In the end it paid off and I received a scholarship to continue my studies. At the same time this is when things really started to go wrong. I was like an over-wound alarm clock, unable to ring but pent up with unreleased tension. In losing myself in my work, I perfected the art of being on my own, filling my time with events and duties and ignoring a large hole that gaped somewhere within and which, with time, gradually unravelled more and more until it threatened to engulf me. Exhausted but seemingly happy, I returned to Zimbabwe for the second time since I had left.

Gran seemed different this time. She was short-tempered, impatient, almost bitter about something. I felt awkward the first few days that I was there. She didn't ask me any questions and didn't congratulate me on winning the scholarship. I almost got the feeling that she resented me being home and I shied away from contact with her. On the last day of my two week break, I went into Mr Patel's shop to buy some cotton and he came up to me, smiling profusely as he always did and rubbing his hands together.

'How's Granny?'

'Fine, thanks.'

'Granny very proud of you, huh?'

'Maybe,' I said, with a weak smile.

'No. No maybes. Is. Every time she come in here, she always saying about you. Very, very proud of you.'

I felt tears welling up and just smiled awkwardly and left. Why couldn't she show me that she was proud of me?

That night, I told my mother about the way Gran had been acting. She didn't say anything, just went on stirring the gravy she was making. Later on, she came into my room as I lay in bed.

'I thought you might want to take back some of Gran's fudge,' she said, putting a plastic bag on top of my suitcase. 'There's a packet of tea in there as well. I know you don't get good tea in England. It's not as nice as ours.'

I nodded and she came over and sat next to me.

'Gran doesn't mean it, you know. She misses you terribly when you're gone.' She leant across and gave me a hug. 'We all do.'

But it wasn't enough to keep me there. I had started on a journey and, however ruthless I must be, it was a journey I was bent on completing. To return would be to go backwards. I was doing well, that's what I told myself, and I could do even better.

I had learnt at an early age that life falls apart very easily; that nothing lasts forever; everything is destructible. It was perhaps because of this lesson that I sometimes felt that I was always waiting for something terrible to happen, something to destroy whatever happiness I had. I never had the courage to accept any state of joy; I shied away, afraid that it would desert me. If I never owned it, it could never leave me; I could not be left.

*

The phone rings again and I let the answering machine get it. The message box is full, however, and it beeps twice and then rewinds. Another missed call.

Chapter Twenty-two

By the time I was completing my Masters, Mandy was also in England, living and working in London. She had graduated with a Fine Arts degree from Rhodes and worked at an advertising agency, designing logos and slogans. She lived in a huge house near Earl's Court that was divided and sub-divided between the twelve people who lived there. They shared the rent and the bills, they shared the bedrooms and the living area, and the food. There was no space; but there was a lot of laughter and parties and booze, and it was a perfect way of saving money. Most of the people in the house were from South Africa or Zimbabwe, although there was a girl from New Zealand and a couple from Canada, too. I didn't want to mix too much with Zimbabweans for I didn't see what the point of travelling was if you only socialised with people from your own country. I suppose, too, looking back, that I suffered from a hurt pride as well. I had been dying to leave Zimbabwe and wanted everyone to think I was having a great time in England, and so the last people I wanted to see were those I had left behind. However, probably because of my feeling of rootlessness, I found myself going to stay with Mandy about once a month. Each time I would really enjoy myself and each time I would return feeling low.

I called Mandy.

'Come,' she said. 'Come to London and stay for a while.'

'I can't, I haven't finished the course.'

'Well come afterwards. Come when you're finished.'

So I did. I finished my Masters and moved to London. It was in August of 1998, a warm day, hot even. I arrived at Mandy's house with a suitcase and a rucksack; everything I owned. It was strange at first to have to share a room with two other people, more if it were the weekend. In another way, it was great. Having people around me all the time, I forgot the noise inside my head and covered up the hole, the space in my chest that the wind blew through and knocked against.

I got a job as a receptionist at a solicitors' firm called Lowrie and McNeal on The Strand in London. It was a temporary arrangement, only supposed to last a few months. The Canadian girl, Rebecca, who lived at the house, was going travelling in Europe for three months and needed someone to take her place whilst she was away. I was glad of the opportunity as it gave me a chance to earn some more money while I looked for something more suitable and it wasn't taxing, just answering the phone and meeting clients. It was a welcome relief after four years of hard study. I thought it would be good for me. I thought that that was all that was wrong; I just needed a break. I needed to be with people, to enjoy myself and live a little. I kept telling myself over and over that I would be all right.

It was while I was living at 19 Canning Road that I met Mark. His cousin, Patricia, lived in the house. She was South African, from Cape Town, and worked as a junior lawyer at a firm near Bond Street. She wasn't the most attractive of women; in fact, at first I thought her almost repulsive to look at. However, there was something that changed about her face as you talked to her, as though it was a lump of clay that the conversation moulded and formed as it progressed. You almost came to like it but, if you didn't see her even for a short while, you'd find her ugly again. It was if she became more beautiful the more she talked.

She talked about a lot of things, mainly South Africa: apartheid, Mandela, crime. Not only her, but her friends as well and I came to think that South Africans had little else to make conversation about. It seemed to obsess them, but I soon realised that at the heart of it all was an over-riding sense of guilt and shame, a need to talk their way through their country's history, a need to find a place within it, even from the distance of England. It was the first time that I really began to think about Zimbabwe. I found myself reading African novels more and more: Nadine Gordimer, André Brink, Doris Lessing. In our nightly conversations about whatever aspect of South African society was under discussion, I began to feel ashamed. I was even more glad to be away from Africa. I felt a deep sense of satisfaction each time I finished ironing my clothes or doing the washing up. Here I was doing the same thing as Jameson, and not complaining. I didn't need a maid or a gardener and I felt guilty for ever having needed one. When Patricia argued that the only way for South African society to move forward was for whites to do the same jobs as blacks, I agreed totally with her. When she criticised the practice by whites of not letting their domestics eat at the table with them, I nodded whole-heartedly and, when she said that there was no difference between black and white, I was the first person to second her.

Alone in my thoughts, I knew the situation was more complex than either of us acknowledged. It was just easier to take the blame for feelings of exile; it justified our present position and location, our decision to be away from the countries we professed to love so much. For Patricia, South Africa had not reached the stage that Zimbabwe was at. It was still in the blissfully positive state that characterises a new country. Their black elite were hailed, revered as the success of Africa. This is what all could aspire to be. The division between poor and rich was not then seen as the major problem. A black person is congratulated on doing well; a white person is castigated for having such money to live on in Africa while others are starving. 'I think the only way I could live in Africa now is as a poor person and in a hut,' said Patricia.

I met Mark when he came to London for an interview and stayed with us for the night. He was what I would call conventionally good-looking and really not my 'type' at all. Blonde, clean-shaven, with hazel eyes, he wore cream coloured trousers and a blue and white striped shirt with the sleeves rolled up, revealing long tanned arms, and brown lace-up shoes. In my teenage fantasies about the Russian artist on the run, I imagined us meeting and falling in love immediately. One look in each other's eyes would be enough to seal our fate forever. Meeting Mark was the closest I have ever got to experiencing that in real life. From the moment I saw him, I knew that we would be together. Patricia had told me he was English, but she was wrong. Mark wasn't English, at least not totally. He had been born in South Africa and had lived in England since he was fifteen. His parents were originally English and had moved back to Britain in the mid-1980s, although they continued to own property in the Eastern Cape, which they visited every year or two. His job involved being employed by big businesses to improve their marketing concepts. His company organised everything from product research down to press conferences and advertising. He travelled the world as one of the heads of the firm, making a lot of money as he did so. When I told him I was a receptionist, he didn't laugh or smirk and instead seemed genuinely interested in what I did.

'It's not forever,' I said, hoping to justify myself.

'What are you going to do next?'

'I'm not sure. I'm still looking.'

'It's OK to look,' he smiled.

We'd do things like have picnics in Hyde Park, go boating on the lake, watch black and white movies in dingy arty theatres, and write each other long, witty e-mails. This is it, I thought. This is what I have looked for and now I've found it.

It was Mark who persuaded me to go back to university and pursue a doctorate. We had been together for two years and I had remained all that time at Lowrie and McNeal, Canadian Rebecca deciding to take another job on her return from her travels. I didn't think I'd be able to afford to study again and the frugal life of a student was not appealing anymore.

But the life of a receptionist wasn't for me either and I began to feel that I had become what I feared. The crux came when one of the partners phoned me and said a Mr Ishiguro would be coming into the office that afternoon at two.

'Mr Ishiguro?' I repeated. 'Not the author, surely. Kazuo Ishiguro?'

'Oh you've heard of him?' said James McNeal, not even attempting to disguise the surprise in his voice. 'Wow.'

'Yes, I thoroughly enjoyed *The Remains of the Day*,' I replied, pleased that I could answer him with such confidence.

'It's not him. Don't get excited. He just has the same name. He's Japanese,' he added superfluously, for I hadn't thought he would be anything else.

Mark asked me to move in with him and it seemed like the perfect answer. He said that the only way for us to be together was to live together and what could be better than living with the person I loved?

However, almost as soon as I moved in, things started to go wrong. His flat was cool and light, painted white with black and chrome furniture and I had a distinctly uneasy feeling right from the beginning that I was arranging my life around someone else's. My books rested uneasily on his shelves and even my toothbrush looked apologetically clumsy next to his.

Our relationship hit a low. He wasn't moody or distant. Nor was he irritable, but he was cold, which is much much worse. We didn't do anything anymore, besides make endless cups of tea and do the washing up. He wasn't interested in what I was doing or in anything I said. Sometimes I think he preferred the receptionist that he had met to the scholar that he had persuaded me to become. In turn, I devoted myself more to my work and often studied till late at night and went to the library at weekends. We lived off take-aways and frozen meals. I didn't cook because, I told myself, I didn't have the time, but it was more than that. We never sat at the table and talked; often we didn't eat at the same time. I would come home late and find Mark eating pizza in front of the television, and at other times I couldn't wait for him, so I'd microwave my meal first and he'd do his when he came in. Such were our lives.

One day, when we'd been living together a year and a half, he mentioned a woman that he was working with, Moira Sharp. As soon as I heard her name, I knew that she was the woman that Mark would leave me for. Who wouldn't, with a name like that, a name like a knife? If she were a character in a book, I would underline it in pencil. He was talking about her in passing, in relation to a deal, but I knew. I think in my own way I had already started to let him go.

We went out one evening with colleagues of his to a pub near the Thames. It was a beautiful summer evening and I remember thinking that I should be happy, but inside I was falling apart. I felt bruised, damaged, as though I had internal bleeding. Mark never flirted with Moira. He never said anything about her or to her that alerted my attention. The way I found out that something was going on between them was through so minor, so insignificant an action that, had I been looking the other way, I wouldn't have noticed anything. It was a look he gave her, fleeting, lasting less than half a second, but he might just as well have pushed the hair out of her eyes or squeezed her hand or brushed her lips with his. I knew in that moment that whatever relationship I had with Mark was over.

It would have been easy to go on pretending, to share the same flat, the same bed, to walk into rooms as a couple, to go out to dinner every now and again, to be the Mark and Ellie who were cordially invited here and there, but it would not be easy, not possible even, to share the same spirit, which is what you do when you are in love, to be thinking of the same thing at the same time. And that is what I saw in the look that they shared. I saw that they shared the same spirit and no amount of persuasion and begging can bring back a spirit that has fled.

I was talking to Mark's secretary when I realised I knew what I was going to do. I was going to get up and, without saying goodbye to anyone, I was going to walk out of the pub and out of Mark's life forever. The air was warm on my face as I walked down the stairs. The river shone before me and I walked a little way before stopping to watch people on their boats, wending their way along. Others sat on benches next to the river, some were jogging alongside it, or walking or pushing prams, or just standing and looking at it like me. I kept saying to myself that I would be all right. In some strange way I felt relief. There wasn't an argument, there wasn't any shouting or crying; just me walking away.

I had walked quite a way before I realised that I didn't really know where I was going or what I was going to do. I didn't want to go back to the flat; it wasn't mine anyway. I just carried on walking, stopping sometimes, but mostly just walking. I didn't have a lot of money on me, only enough for a night out at the pub, but I did have my cheque book. I looked at it and thought it was my fault, the way things had fallen apart. I should have tried to patch things up a long time ago, but I hadn't really wanted to. I felt overwhelmingly tired suddenly and just wanted to lie down somewhere and go to sleep. I saw a taxi in the distance and, on a sudden impulse, waved it down.

'Where to, love?' asked the cabbie, chewing gum.

'The Fairtowers,' I said, getting in and sinking back into the seat. It was a middle of the range hotel about two blocks from where we lived.

I booked a single room and, after dismissing the suspicious gazes of the hotel staff who looked around for my luggage, I took the keys and went upstairs and I took my dress off and lay down on the bed, cooler and calmer.

Much later, I ordered room service: fillet of hake with a lemon and herb sauce, vegetables and a side salad. I had a small glass of dry white wine and toasted the rest of my life. It was mid-summer and the light came through the curtains and made the cutlery gleam, rather superciliously, I thought, for the hake was the real focus of my attention. I sliced through the soft white flesh and dug my fork into the overcooked broccoli. I remember thinking that from then on I would associate the taste of fish with sorrow and I was glad that I had chosen it from the menu, because I could live without fish for the rest of my life.

Chapter Twenty-three

I suppose there are those who will feel that I have skipped over my life in England somewhat, made light of it and not revealed too many details. The truth is that it isn't that important. As I said before, you cannot change who you are unless you know who you are, and that's what I had to find out. How little did I know that the time of reckoning would come so soon and in such a brutal way.

Mark moved out. He thought it was the decent thing to do, although really it wasn't very logical, as I couldn't afford the rent on my own. But he was gentlemanly in a way that only an unfaithful man can be and he offered to keep paying the rent until I could find somewhere else.

I continued to study and did some tutoring as well to help pay the bills. It didn't actually help that much, but I enjoyed it, more than the studying. I wrote and told Gran about Mark and she wrote back and told me to go with my instincts, but I never really knew what she meant by that.

I had a dream, not long after Mark moved out, that I was lying in a bath tub that was balanced precariously on the top ledge of the steel fire escape that ran up the outside of the flat. I was afraid that someone would walk out and find me there, naked, but, at the same time, I wasn't trying to get out. Instead, I was looking down at myself, through the water. For some reason, and dreams have no logic, I decided not to use soap to wash myself and to merely rinse my body with water. Along the sides of the tub, ran a thin brown line of dirt.

I told Gran about it in a letter. She was good at all that psychoanalysing and liked giving her interpretation.

'Why was the bath dirty if I hadn't washed myself?' I wrote. 'I would never get into a dirty bath. I always wash it out before I use it.' After years of sharing accommodation, I was almost fanatical about it.

I was surprised when she phoned me about the dream. Phone calls from Zimbabwe were expensive and rare.

'I've been thinking about your dream. Being naked in public always suggests a fear of embarrassment, of being shown up in some way.'

'Mmm,' was my only answer. I didn't want her digging around too much.

'Vulnerability, too,' she continued. 'Are you afraid of something or someone?'

Gran should have known better than ask such a blunt and direct question of me.

'Neither,' I said.

'It would also explain the height at which you were at. I know you don't like heights.'

'Right.'

'You're not dealing with something. You're sitting in clear water and deliberately not using soap.'

'Yes?'

'Well, then you can't be clean. Not properly. You're trying to ignore something and not deal with it. Clear water always has connotations of baptism and rebirth, but that is being undermined by the dirty ring around the tub.'

I didn't say anything.

'Do you see? Are you still there?'

'Yes, Gran,' I replied. 'I do see.'

'There's something to be overcome.'

'Interesting.'

'Any ideas?'

'No.'

'Well, think about it, will you, and tell me?'

'I can't believe you phoned to tell me that.'

'You're in trouble, Ellie, and I want to help.'

I paused.

'Ellie?'

'Thanks, Gran.'

'That's all right, my love. I do worry, you know.'

'I know.'

'Now, when are you going to get a proper job?'

That was the last time I ever heard from my grandmother. Three weeks later she was dead.

Everyone dreads that call in the middle of the night, that 'come quickly we do not know how much longer she has to live', or that, 'I am sorry to have to be the one to tell you that so-and-so is dead. It was quick. He did not feel a thing.'

I had a feeling of not knowing where I was suddenly as I stood next to the phone in the half-light of early morning. I thought: she died while I was asleep; while I was dreaming, her spirit was rising out of her body and leaving this world behind. Did it come here? Did it hover over my sleeping body and say goodbye? I didn't have time to say it, but did she? Did she stroke my hair? Did she lean over and kiss me like she did when I was a child and pretended to be asleep when she came into my room? Could she not have stayed, clung to her dying body and waited for me to arrive before leaving?

Death always comes as a surprise. Even those who have waited by the side of the dying and held their hand do not really expect the end. It is still a shock, they say, looking round crowded rooms for those they still expect to see. It is the one thing we can be sure of in life and yet it still comes as a surprise; we still feel cheated.

Part Two

Chapter One

One night when I was a child, I dreamed that I walked through a garden full of snakes. I had to make my way through a slithering mass that coiled coquettishly round my ankles in an evil mock coyness. Before me was an archway with a fat, thick python coiled around the top. Its eyes were narrow slits as it pretended to sleep, waiting, waiting for me to approach.

I could see Jameson some way off and called to him for help but when he turned around his face was covered in shiny blue scales and his eyes were yellow. A forked tongue flicked in and out of his mouth. When I woke up my pillow was wet. I had vomited while I slept.

*

Africa spread itself warm and brown beneath me as I stared out of the window of the plane. I began to feel nervous and claustrophobic. How many times had I longed for the warm brown earth and the star-crowded sky of Africa? Hadn't I cried myself to sleep, night after night sometimes, consumed with homesickness and longing? Now here I was. Home. A cold wave of reality washed over me that seemed to change the colour of the sky and the bush. The landscape looked empty, rather than spacious. It was deserted, unloved. The trees, the rocks, even the buildings looked ridiculous, as though someone had desperately tried to fill the landscape with things, but they lay unfinished, half built. I saw all the flaws of a country I had coloured with brilliant shades of orange, red, brown, deep green and blue. And now it lay before me, a pale watercolour, a land faded by the sun. Reality.

The last time I ever saw Miles Trevellyan was at Harare Airport. I had arrived in Zimbabwe that morning, but had to wait another day for a connecting flight to Bulawayo. It was three days since I had heard the news. Gran had been murdered by a burglar in the early hours of the morning. Suburbs was a bad area, the police told my mother. She had no security fence, no wall, no alarm and insubstantial locks on the doors. She was a sitting target, an elderly lady on her own.

When I arrived at the hotel I had booked in to stay overnight, there was a note waiting for me. Surprised, I opened it and immediately looked at the sender's name at the bottom. It was from Miles. He asked me to meet him at the airport that evening. He was leaving to go to England. Anger rose inside me at once. Gran was not even buried. Her funeral wasn't for a few days at least. Why was he leaving? Part of me was tempted to tear up the note and pretend I had never received it, but there was also a part of me that knew that that was not what Gran would have wanted. She would have wanted me to go and meet Miles.

He had already checked his luggage in when I arrived and was sitting at a table in the airport bar, smoking a cigarette and staring at his drink, occasionally stirring it with his little finger. It was a gin and tonic. He was wearing his trademark blue shorts and a white golf shirt. His long thin brown legs ended in *veldskoens* and short white socks. I didn't know how to approach him or what to say. 'Hi'? 'Hello'? 'Good evening'? I was glad when he looked up and saw me. He didn't smile, but gave me a brief stare before moving the bag off the chair opposite him.

'Sit down,' he said. It wasn't an order or a greeting. 'Would you like a drink?' I declined. 'Suit yourself.' He stubbed his cigarette out in an ashtray and blew smoke out of the corner of his mouth.

'So, you're leaving,' I said, more as an accusation than a statement.

'Yep. Everything's to be sold. There's nothing left now.'

He wasn't coming back, he told me. Ever. Everything he had ever owned was to be auctioned off: his books, his furniture, his car, even his record collection. The money was to be put in his savings account, but he doubted he would ever need it. It was useless anyway, he said. 'Mickey Mouse money.' I couldn't imagine his house empty and everything inside it gone. The realisation that we would have to do the same thing with Gran's house made me close my eyes for a moment and try to steel myself against the gathering tide of emotion. What made it possible for someone to spend seventy-seven years on the earth and yet have their mark rubbed off so quickly? Emptiness where once there had been life, spaces, blanks, where once there had been certainty.

'She's not even buried.' My voice came out in a dry whisper. I could feel the ache of tears in the back of my throat.

'I know,' he said, looking down. He rubbed his forehead with his hand. A couple of seconds passed before he looked up. His eyes were wet with tears and I was slightly taken aback at such emotion from a man I had always thought hard-hearted. 'I can't go... the funeral.' He stopped.

I nodded. I didn't speak in case I cried. There was another short silence and then he cleared his throat, 'There are a couple of things I would like you to do for me.' He was watching my face.

'Your grandmother had a son.'

'I know,' I said, looking him straight in the eye. 'Is that what you wanted to tell me?' My voice was obnoxiously flippant; it was a tone I had developed to talk to Miles in over the years.

'Obviously not. I was quite sure you knew that already, although she didn't like to talk about it.'

I didn't say anything. The fact was that Gran had never really talked to me about it. No one had.

'There's a photo of him in the drawer beside her bed. I want you to make sure it goes with her. There's also a beret, a green beret, army thing,' he said, tapping his head with his finger and resting it on his temple. 'She keeps it in the linen cupboard... at the top, I think. That was Jeremy's.'

'I know,' I said again with much more assurance than I felt. How did Miles know these things? I had discovered the beret by accident, but had she shown him?

'Promise me you'll make sure she has those two things with her.'

I nodded but his words seemed a little odd, as though I would have a problem.

'There's one other thing. I don't think I can have much say on the matter,' he said with a short laugh, 'but you could pretend it's your idea.' His voice faltered as he spoke and he reached for his cigarette packet. 'At her funeral I'd like you to read this.' He handed me a folded piece of paper. I opened it and read. It was one of Shakespeare's sonnets written in Miles's scratchy, unsteady hand. 'But thy eternal summer shall not fade,' he recited, pulling out another cigarette and rolling it between two fingers. I looked at him in surprise. 'Yes,' he said sarcastically, 'it's Shakespeare.'

'I...' I began, but he interrupted.

'You didn't think I knew any, did you?' There was a trace of a sneer in his voice.

'No, I didn't actually,' I said, riled.

'There's a lot you don't know about me.' He lit his cigarette and, half closing his eyes, blew out a long line of smoke. 'But you never gave me a chance. You were, are, always so self-righteous.'

I was stung. 'You never liked me,' I said defensively.

'Ja, well, it was hard. Like trying to get blood out of a stone.' He took another long drag of his cigarette and blew the smoke out of his nose. 'It's pretty ironic, isn't it, that I was the Shakespeare buff, not him.'

I was confused. Why was he comparing himself to Grandad? And with such bitterness?

'Still, we were fools regardless.' He pushed the cigarette butt down into the ashtray, squashing it with his thumb and forefinger. 'All fools. Old fools.'

He paused for a minute and then, staring off into the

distance, said, 'I asked her to marry me once. We were in Cape Town. She said no.' The corner of his mouth turned up in an ironic smile.

'She said not again. That was all she said, but I knew why. It was him; she was still in love.'

'In love?' I said, incredulously. 'He was in love with her, not the other way round.'
He looked at me strangely then as if he had just realised something. I thought his eyes narrowed slightly and his lips pursed together for a half second.

'Each man kills the thing he loves.' He nodded his head cynically.

There was another silence and he smiled distantly as he remembered something. 'Marry me, I said.' He looked down, the smile still on his lips. 'She said no, pretended she was some sort of feminist, that she was taking some sort of stand by not remarrying, but I knew. I knew. We were walking along the beach and there was this dead dog washed up on the shore.' He paused. 'It was very sad,' he touched his neck. 'It had a collar on. It obviously belonged to someone.' There was another pause and then, 'That's the strongest memory I have of that holiday.'

We sat in silence for a while and then he looked around, slightly dazed. He picked up his bag, slipped his cigarette packet into his shirt pocket and stood up. I stood too.

'My nephew might get in touch with you. He's the one dealing with the sale. I've given him your phone number in Bulawayo. Just in case.' We were at the departure gate now. He turned to me and sighed. He was an old man, Miles, a tired old man. 'Goodbye, Ellie.' He slung his bag over one shoulder and stretched out his hand to shake mine. I took it

212

hesitantly and he put his left hand on top of mine and held it there.

'We've seen the best of times, Ellie, the best of times.' His pale blue eyes were brimming with tears and he breathed in heavily. 'Adios, amigo!' he said, but this time there was no sarcasm in his voice.

'Goodbye, Miles,' I responded, but suddenly I wanted to ask him a whole lot of questions. The things he had said didn't make sense. Somewhere beneath the words was a meaning, like a crocodile swimming silently beneath the surface of muddy water. But he was gone, his bag over his shoulder and his boarding card ready in his hand, an ever shrinking figure as he walked through the departure gate and into the area beyond. That was the last time I ever saw Miles Trevellyan.

Chapter Two

It was the end of 2004. I hadn't been home for five years and, in that time, Zimbabwe had changed almost beyond recognition. The land invasions had unleashed a wave of terror and havoc that had torn through the country and left it bleeding and fearful. Those who could distanced themselves from it. They bought foreign newspapers and watched satellite television: Sky News, BBC World and endless repeats of *Friends*. They tuned into the weather report for every other country but their own and they tut-tutted over the Palestinian crisis or the atrocities in Iraq, but shied away from the violence in their own country, locking themselves away behind security fences, *durawalls* and intricate alarm systems. They applied for any sort of passport to which they felt even remotely entitled and bought foreign currency on the black-market whenever possible. The days of owning houses with big gardens and swimming pools were numbered. Town-houses and flats had gained in popularity as had remote controlled gates and vehicles with satellite tracking systems. Economically,

Zimbabwe was moving towards the standards of neighbouring Zambia and Mozambique, and socially it was becoming like South Africa, a country where many live in fear of being robbed, raped, hijacked or murdered.

I can't write anymore. Fifteen times, she was hit. Fifteen. Who counts? Who counts the bruises and the broken bones? Who counts the tears and the scars? Who counts?

*

When I arrived home, my father picked me up from the airport. My mother was in bed. Gran's death had carved dark shadows under her eyes. She got up when she saw me and drew me near her in a feeble but desperate hug. She looked rather eerily like Gran; her once soft chestnut brown hair was pinned back from her face with an old hairclip of mine, a streak of grey rising above each ear.

My grandfather was on the verandah in his favourite chair. He had a beer poured in a glass next to him but he seemed to have forgotten about it. We talked for a couple of minutes and then he went silent, looking out into the garden, not saying a word.

That night as I went to bed, I thought of how I normally loved the feel of fresh, clean, newly ironed sheets. I could almost smell the sun in the wind that had dried them. I usually relished it, that smell of sun and home, but now it made me unbearably sad and I lay in bed with my arms crossed, like a betrayed lover refusing to lie in the arms of the one who has hurt her.

The next day nothing much changed. My mother stayed

in bed and my grandfather spent another day on the verandah. Various drinks were left untouched next to him. He just sat and looked out into the garden. I didn't want to do nothing. I didn't want to just sit or lie down. I wanted to be active so I didn't have time to think. I took the keys for Gran's house and got in the car. Perhaps I should have told someone, but I just wanted to get away, to be close to her. I also needed to fetch the beret and the photograph, although I was yet to work out how to tell my mother of Miles's request.

I parked outside Gran's house and just sat for a couple of minutes. Her car was in the driveway still, that great blue beast I had known almost all my life. Once it had been something to look out for, an indication of where Gran was. It was almost a part of Bulawayo itself; everyone knew Gran's car. Now it stood, a quiet sentry, outside the house.

I sat gathering the resolve to go inside. I knew the scene of the crime itself had been cleaned up but it would still be strange. I had never been alone in Gran's house before. Eventually, I opened the car door and took a step outside. I tried to remember the last time I had been there and what I had thought and felt.

I went in through the side gate. It squeaked like it always had each time I came to visit and my heart skipped a beat. Why did I expect it to be different now? And yet somehow, I expected everything to have changed. I resented it for being the same.

Why do the birds go on singing?
Why do the stars glow above?
Don't they know it's the end of the world?
It ended when I lost your love.

The garden was wilting in the heat. No one had watered the flowers on the verandah or put the spray on the lawn. I thought it right that I do that first, and that if Gran were watching from somewhere, she'd be glad. The door of the shed was not locked and it opened with ease, but I was not prepared for what I found in there. Trays of seedlings, a small shovel and fork, a pair of gardening gloves that looked as though the wearer had just taken them off while she went away briefly and she'd be back any moment to put them on again. It was too much, there was too much of her and I reeled in grief. Outside, in the already shimmering heat of mid-morning, I leaned against the verandah wall and breathed deeply. I couldn't cry. I wouldn't allow myself. Not now. Later, later when it's all over I said. Later.

Having partly recovered, I re-entered the shed. The sun came through the window and trillions of specks of dust danced languidly in its heat. I grabbed the watering can and headed for the tap. The pot of mint that she kept beneath it, which usually thrived in the spray of water that fizzed out of the tap when it was connected to the hose, looked shrunken and limp. The tap gurgled and groaned before a burst of brown water exploded from it and I filled the watering can. I put the spray on, aware of the current water restrictions, but I didn't care. Bulawayo owed me one. Then, finding the right key, I slipped it into the lock and opened the front door.

I'm not sure what I expected. Ornaments tossed around the house? The furniture removed? Blood splattered on the walls? Instead, everything was in its usual place: the sofa and two chairs grouped cosily in the lounge, the tablecloth placed expectantly on the dining room table, the mirror hanging in the hallway.

Or was it? Gran would never have put a red cushion on the blue couch. I moved it and straightened the net curtains at the window. I ran my finger along the top of the coffee table and smiled ruefully. I could hear Gran tut-tut in faint disgust.

Gran's notepad lay next to the phone with the number of a plumber written on it and the name 'Martin' and 'Four o'clock Wednesday'. There was a flower doodle in the centre of the page. In the kitchen, I opened the fridge and found a slice of cheese quiche and a jug of milk. Half a bottle of white wine was in the shelf in the door. I hesitated. They should be thrown out, I thought, but it was too early yet. Besides, I was afraid to touch anything, afraid to reach out and feel what had last been touched by her.

I couldn't go into the bedroom. It was too early for that as well. For that's where it had happened, the murder. The scene of the crime. The linen cupboard was in the hallway. I opened it and stood back, momentarily overwhelmed by the smell of her. My heart contracted in grief and I wanted to pull everything out, rub my face deep into every sheet and pillowcase, cover myself in anything that smelt of her. But I couldn't, I just couldn't. Not now, I said to myself, not here.

Everything was packed neatly on the shelves, divided into piles of sheets, towels, pillowcases, tablecloths and serviettes. On the top shelf, there was an iron and a spare kettle. I stood on a chair and reached over into the back of the shelf. I expected to find the beret lying there on its own, like it was the first time I discovered it, but I couldn't find it. There were two cardboard boxes and an old plastic ice cream carton with what looked like broken pieces of a china ornament inside. I moved it out of the way and reached for one of the boxes. It was heavy and hard to pull out. I nearly fell off the chair, but finally managed to lift it down.

I'd like to think I was someone who never pried intentionally into someone else's business, but sometimes life has a way of throwing things at you and daring you to take the lead, even though you may not think yourself ready for the challenge. In the way of all good murder stories, the truth has a way of outing itself, of leaving a trail of clues that one must follow. It's just a pity that life doesn't have an inspector or a detective, a beady-eyed police officer who reveals the true story to a waiting audience, explaining the actions and intentions of all involved, wrapping it up nicely in the end with a smug smile of satisfaction as the credits roll up.

At first the box seemed to be full of invoice books. They were old with hard, navy-blue covers and 'Invoice Book' in broken gold lettering on the front. Turning them over, I saw something on their spines too, but the lettering here had faded and the most I could read was 'Jam' on one and 'ough' on another. I put them back in the box and looked up at the shelf again. Perhaps the beret was in the other box.

I managed to get this one down with little trouble. It was lighter and not as full as the first one had been. I found two more of the hard cover books and a cardboard coaster with a picture of a cocktail glass, complete with slice of orange and an umbrella, on it. 'The Grand, Beira' was printed beneath it and beneath that someone had written a number: 255. At the bottom of the box was a plastic bag. I took it out and peered inside. It was full of photographs.

I pulled one out and looked at it. It was Gran, a long time ago, in her swimming costume. She was posing, looking up at the sky, with her left hand behind her head. She had on a pair of sunglasses. It was a black and white photo, but I could see how dark her hair must've been and thought how glamorous she looked, her lips pursed together, her eyes away from the camera. I took more photos out. There were more of her in her bathing suit, some with her smiling, others where she looked disdainful, scornful of the person photographing her. There was only one in which she seemed her usual self, but this time the camera seemed to have caught her unawares, as though she was looking up from reading a book or a menu on which she'd just seen her favourite dish.

But it wasn't these that really caught my attention. There were other photos, photos of Jeremy: her son, my uncle, although I had never thought of him as such. Some were photos of him as a schoolboy, his hair parted to one side, his tie protruding through the 'v' of his jersey; others showed him on his back reading a book, beside a sandcastle, next to a wooden toy car, with a large brown dog. There was one of him as a baby, a round tub of a boy in a white vest, his smooth, bald head tilting as he smiled.

He was growing bald in other photos, photos that betrayed disquiet, an obvious unhappiness: photos of him in his army uniform. In one, he sat upon what looked like a hillside, looking out, away from the camera towards the horizon. His hands rested loosely on his shins and he was squinting slightly. His gun lay beside him. In another, he smoked a cigarette. In another, he sat outside a tent. This was the one in which he seemed the happiest for he smiled. I wondered how long it was after that that he was killed. He looked like Gran. Or rather, their eyes held the same look.

220

There was someone else in him, I could see, in the roundness of his features, but it wasn't Grandad. Some other relative perhaps?

Inside the plastic bag was another smaller bag, made from a thicker plastic, with the words 'Barbours' in red letters printed diagonally across it with the shop's address and phone number. It used to be Gran's favourite place to shop whenever she went to Harare. Inside that was a brown envelope and I opened it never suspecting what I would find. It was a death certificate. It was Jeremy's. There was the date of death: 21st February 1971. There was the place of death: Bulawayo. And there was the cause of death: suicide.

Chapter Three

Since that fateful evening when I found Jeremy's army beret and wore it proudly on my head, and then ran, arms outstretched, into the horror of Gran's eyes, into a wall of grief that had cemented itself firmer and firmer with each passing year, I had often speculated over the exact circumstances of his death. It wasn't that nobody ever mentioned him, because they did, but it was always in passing, as one might recall a one-time friend, someone not seen or heard of in a while. 'My brother used to do that,' my mom might say about the way I did something, or 'my brother had a teacher like that' or 'Jeremy didn't like maths either'. She never went into detail though and he remained a sketch to be filled in by imagination and supposition and coloured by death. For I never felt I could ask about him, as though when someone dies they become a miniature god, something to talk of in quiet whispers and not to be spoken badly about because no one should ever speak badly of the dead.

I didn't know how he died. I'd just presumed he'd been

killed in action because that was the impression created by those who missed him the most: his family. When people talk of heroes and 'what a waste of life war is', one thinks, don't they, of all the war movies they've ever seen, where soldiers die in slow motion gun battles, their mother's latest letter in their pocket, a picture of their sweetheart close to their skin? Heroes never take their own lives.

My hands shook as I looked down at the word: suicide. I suddenly felt scared, as though someone was watching. I looked behind me as though I expected to see a knife come thrusting through the air towards me. I picked up one of the books in the box and glanced at the first page. '1953' someone had written and crossed out 'Invoice Book'. I turned to the next page and found it covered in writing. In fact, it was full of writing, Gran's handwriting. She had obviously used the book as a diary. Every so often there was a date above an entry. 12th June, 1953; 13th June, 1953; 14th June, 1953. Sometimes there were gaps of a few days, sometimes a week, often longer. I picked up the other books; they were the same. The earliest one was 1947.

I read bits and pieces, some of it was hard to decipher, some of it was blurred by spots of ink. I felt afraid. I didn't want to be there anymore. I scooped out all the books and the pictures and stuffed them hastily into one box. Then I closed the cupboard and almost ran out of the house, the box under one arm. I had that feeling again, the one I had at the airport when I said goodbye to Miles. Something was beginning to take shape, to rise and come to the surface, like a body floating to the top of a river in which it has been dumped. Nothing stays hidden forever. There were questions I needed answered. No longer could I be kept in the dark

223

about Jeremy; no longer would I be satisfied with anything less than the truth.

As soon as I got home, I went into my mother's bedroom. She was lying down, but not asleep.

'Ellie,' she greeted me with a wan smile. 'Come and sit with me.'

I sat down.

'How did you get on?' Her voice was low and sad, but she was trying to make the effort to sound positive. I looked up sharply. 'You went to Gran's didn't you? I told Dad I thought you'd gone there.'

'Yes, I did.'

She smiled. 'It's as if she's still there.'

'There are some things I need to ask you,' I said, ignoring the temptation to indulge in nostalgic reminiscence. To prevent myself from holding back by asking about something else, I quickly added, 'Family things. About Gran. And... '

Mom nodded.

'I don't want to pry, but I need to know.'

She cleared her throat. 'What's this all about?' Her fingers played sadly with the tasselled fringe of her blanket.

'A long time ago, Gran told me that she had a son and that he was killed in the war.' I was prompting her to say something, but she didn't. 'Now this son, your brother...' I faltered. 'Well...'

'He wasn't killed in the war,' she said, as though she had only heard my first words. 'He was killed by the war.'

'What do you mean?' I asked, confused.

There was a long pause. Mom's eyes were fixed on the ceiling, but she wasn't looking at it; she was far away.

'He couldn't handle it. He was just a boy really. Twenty-one. That was Dad's fault. All his talk of war and how great it was.' She paused again and a smile played on her lips, as she remembered her brother. But then her face changed again and a film of sadness came over it. 'He was on a couple of days' leave and had come home. Gran and Grandad lived in Ilanda at the time. Grandad had trained to be a mechanic rather late in life and had been working at Fox's for about five years. It wasn't well paid and there were lots of arguments. The usual: money. There was never enough. I was still at school with a year to go until I finished. Jeremy wasn't himself. Very quiet. More than quiet. Subdued. As though life had been sucked out of him somehow. I remember how he sat at the kitchen table and didn't say a word. No one had been there when he'd got home and he'd just sat there for two hours. Didn't make himself a cup of tea or anything. Nothing. He just sat. I came in from school. I was at Townsend. It was close to where we lived and so I just used to cycle to school.' She paused again and thought for a while. 'I saw him sitting there. At the table in the kitchen. I was so excited, so happy he was back, and I ran up to him.' She stopped. 'He couldn't even put his arms around me.' She looked at me. 'He couldn't even do that.' She continued to fiddle with the blanket tassel. It seemed a while before she began again. 'I made him some tea and sat with him until Dad came home. He was frightened when he saw Jeremy. He tried to make him feel better, talking about rugby and cricket, and how we were going to win the war. But I saw the fear in him that day. An awful fear... he didn't say much, Jeremy that is, but he asked where Mum was a few times. Dad didn't seem to know where she was. He kept saying

'Out. She's gone out.' But we waited the whole day and she never came back.' She swallowed. 'Eventually, I took Dad outside and asked him what was going on. He said nothing, nothing was going on, but I knew it was. It was his look. Then he said she had done it before, stayed away all day. Never told him where she had gone. I hadn't noticed because often I was at school all day until five, but he said he phoned sometimes during the day and she wasn't there and later, when he asked her where she'd been, she said nowhere. But she had never stayed away the whole night.

'I asked him what was wrong with Jem and he said that he had seen this before, seen it with men in the War, the other war. They called it shell shock, he said.'

She stopped talking. Silence filled the darkening room for a minute or so.

'How?' I asked at last. 'How did he die?'

'Bullet. He put his gun to his head and…' She didn't finish. 'I was at school when they came and called me. They gave me tea, sweet tea, and as I sat there, it occurred to me that I had never been in the headmistress's office before and the thought struck me as rather strange. The curtains were a beautiful yellow chintz. I remember that. It was the first and last time I entered that office, but I remember the curtains. A beautiful yellow, like sunlight.'

'Dad found him. He had taken the day off work to stay with Jeremy. He went to buy some milk… he came home and found him.'

'What about Gran?'

Mom's eyes narrowed. 'She blamed Dad. And Dad blamed her.' I could see whose side she took.

226

'She didn't know,' I said, in some feeble and misguided attempt to stick up for Gran.

'Didn't know?' I could hear the anger creeping its way back into her voice.

'She didn't know he was at home.' I knew as soon as I had said the words that they were wrong.

'She should have been at home. And she did know. She knew! She knew and she didn't care!'

'But you didn't even know Jeremy was coming home...' I started.

'No! She knew he was there. She phoned in the late afternoon and said she'd be home soon. She spoke to him, to Jeremy. She told him she'd be home.'

'Where was she?' I asked the question, the question whose answer I thought would complete the jigsaw puzzle. Mom breathed in deeply, closed her eyes and breathed out.

'I don't know. To this day I don't know where she was. She would never tell me. Said it was none of my business, then said she was with a friend, but wouldn't tell me who. In the end I gave up. I suppose that deep down I didn't want to know.'

I got up.

'I'll make tea,' I said, moving towards the door, but she hadn't heard me.

'She was devastated. Inconsolable. But she never blamed herself. She blamed him, Dad. All his war stories. He tried. He tried to make up for it, but it was useless. Their marriage had always been a rocky one. Uncle Wally, he tried to help, tried to say things, but, again, it was useless. He was very kind. Organised things, made arrangements...'

'He lived in Bulawayo then, Uncle Wally?'

'No, no he didn't. He hadn't lived in Bulawayo for a long time. He lived in Harare, Salisbury. He'd lived there for years. He was doing some work, I think. He was an architect and sometimes he came down to the Bulawayo office for a couple of weeks or so. I thought Gran might have been with him, it would've made some sense, but she said no, she wasn't. It wasn't long after that that he moved to South Africa.'

'Why?'

'Why did he move? Well, why not? I suppose he wanted a new beginning. He hated it. The war, I mean. Made fun of us. The whites. Boy Scouts with guns, he said. And then Jeremy...'

'Why did you say it would've made sense?'

'Sorry?'

'You said it would've made sense for Gran to have been with Wally that day. Why?'

'Well, they were family, although we didn't see him often. He was doing some work in Bulawayo... I've just said that, haven't I?'

I nodded. 'What about Gran and Grandad? Afterwards. Why didn't they just get divorced?'

'It's not the done thing, is it?' said Mom, sarcastically. She gave a short, dry laugh and added, 'Much more socially acceptable to stay at home and argue.

'I couldn't handle it anymore, all the shouting, and so I left school. I didn't finish my 'A' levels.' She shot a guilty glance at me, as though I had accused her of being lazy or giving up. 'I would have failed them anyway. I met Dad soon afterwards. He was teaching at the time so he wasn't conscripted... well, you know all this.

'Then you came along. I needed help at first. There were complications and I had a hysterectomy. I was told I wouldn't be able to have any more children. So Gran and Grandad moved in with us. I was glad of the help, and she adored you. Sometimes I actually felt quite jealous.' She stared at me for a few seconds and her eyes filled with tears. 'It felt great. Like we were a family again.' Her voice broke. 'I felt I could keep an eye on her as well, although Dad said she'd never gone out again like that. But the arguments began again after a while.' She had started to cry. 'I wanted to change them. I wanted everything to be all right. I lost someone too!'

It was time to stop the questioning, at least for the time being. I didn't tell her about the diaries. I wanted to protect her, although from what I wasn't quite sure. But it wasn't just that; I wanted to solve this mystery on my own, once and for all. No longer did I want to be protected from the past. I took the box to my bedroom and locked it in the cupboard. Another secret.

Chapter Four

17th October, 1947

Dear G.

I woke today in the early hours of the morning and the first thing I thought of was you. There was a dull ache and, as I came to full consciousness, I tried to protect myself from the pain of remembering that you had gone. How strange it is to think that just a week ago, I woke next to you and watched you as you slept. You were lying very close to me, so close that I could feel your breath warm on my face. I moved back a little so that I could see you more clearly. You hadn't shaved and your dark stubble glinted red in the growing light from outside. Today, I lay and mentally traced the outline of your profile with my hands. I ran them over your smooth forehead, over your eyes, along your nose and down to your lips. I could feel the slight curve of your upper lip and the soft firmness of the bottom one, the dip of your chin. I am full of the grief of losing someone, of not being

able to explain what this is inside of me. It is too late.
Had we but world enough and time. But it is too late.

   E.

5, The Grove
Gorton
England

20th September, 1947

Dear Evelyn,
   I'm glad you told me what you did and, no, I will not
take a moral stance and admonish you for your actions.
Needless to say, though, your news did come somewhat
as a surprise.
   This man, G. as you call him, sounds quite charming
– and very 'you' – but he is, nevertheless, having his
cake and eating it, to use a cliché. My best advice to you,
if he is as unhappy in his marriage as he says he is, is
to force him to make some sort of decision – and quickly.
But until then you must stay out of it.
   My dear Evelyn, however discreet you may feel you
have been, I assure you there is always someone who will
have noticed – looks, glances; that sort of thing. The last
thing you want is for your reputation to be ruined. You've
mentioned before how narrow-minded Rhodesia can be.
It is the way of all small communities, believe me,
whether it be Bulawayo or a town in Hampshire. Promise
me you'll be careful.

It must be difficult working together, but you will have to make that break. Would it be possible for you to get a job elsewhere? Would you think of returning to England? Surely you cannot think of living there forever?

You say you love him, but you can love someone else. How much of this is the daring of the moment? Would you be so enthralled with him if he lived down the road with his mum and his dad and offered to marry you and give you everything he had? Why do we want what we can't possibly have? He's married, that's it. You must face it and try to meet someone else. Do they have many dances there?

Mine

19th October, 1947

My darling G.

I dream of you. I wake and think of you. I reach for you and you have gone. I dread to open my eyes and have them face the brutal reality that I am alone. Without you, I will be alone for the rest of my life. I am nothing without you. Nothing. I cannot face the emptiness. Nothing means anything anymore.

E.

Mine

20th October, 1947

Dearest G.

    I have taken to writing you these letters that I know I will never send, but I need to feel that I am speaking to you, that you are reading my words. Do you feel what I feel? What do you think about? Do you wake in the morning and think of me? Is it longing that you feel or peace that I am out of your life and that you can go back to your conventional existence without me knocking on the door and begging to come in?

    Do you think of me at all? Can you look at her and feel happy in your choice? Has she forgiven you? What has she said to you? That I am a bad woman, that I am a temptress? Or that I was just a whim of yours, our relationship nothing but something that men occasionally stray into. I'd rather be the former. I'd rather be bad, terribly wicked and debauched, than nothing. Don't let me be nothing.

    E.

There were more letters, twenty or so more. Some were in sealed envelopes, others loose. There were also bits of paper: notes whose yellowed folds spoke of more than the few simple words suggested. 'Lunch?' 'Club. 4pm. Y? N?' 'Ice cream. Park gates. 1pm.' 'Yours?' And often a more cryptic '52? Lunch.' Or '52. 6pm.' A code? An address? A person?

Besides the letter that I presumed was from Marjorie, which was missing the rest of its pages, there was only one other letter that wasn't written by Gran.

23rd December, 1947

My Dearest E,

An hour since I saw you last and yet it seems so long ago! I am obsessed with the thought of you. I think of you: of your smell, of your touch. Your taste. Why can't I get you out of my mind? I tell myself you are my mistress, an affair. I tell myself I am married, committed forever to someone else. What then is it that makes me want you so much?

I ask myself if it is because you have started seeing L. Am I jealous? Do I want what I can't have? Is it only the thought of you with someone else that makes me want you more? Am I guilty of the very trap of ownership that I decry? I want you. To possess you. I carry you inside of me. You are part of me and to see you with someone else is like a hand reaching in and pulling out, not my heart, not something as commonplace as that and found in the breast of every man, but a something, a something small but vital, a rare thing that has grown inside me.

I love you. What facile, overused words, but how else do I say it? Dearer than eyesight, space and liberty? I am Cordelia in front of Lear: there are no words to express how I feel.

There is so much about you that I don't know. I don't know what you're like in the morning. How you choose what to wear. Whether you have your tea in bed or at the table? Are you grumpy? I imagine you tying your hair up, clipping your earrings on, dabbing perfume on your wrists and neck. I imagine your dress sliding over your slip and the way you button it up. I imagine you rolling on your stockings and slipping your feet into your shoes. A touch of lipstick and rouge. I imagine I am there and I am lying in bed watching you and, when you are ready, you bend over me and kiss me and say you'll be back home for lunch. Home. Our home.

Could we live together, Evelyn? You are so much younger than I? Would you get bored? Would you look elsewhere? Would you still be faithful when I am an old man?

Perhaps this is all too late. How serious are you and L? Would we have a child? No one knows how much I long for one. It is perhaps my deepest and most hidden desire.

I know you wonder if I will ever leave my wife. I have known her for over twenty years. We don't have children, but we have a house, friends, family. Such are the ties that bind.

Perhaps I'm keeping you back and standing in the way of happiness with someone else. L? I must go. I want to stay. There is so much more to say and yet nothing. No other ways to say it.

All my love,

G.

I had started with the letters, thinking them easier to read than the ink-blotched diaries that seemed to run on forever,

235

one entry falling into another. But instead of helping fill gaps, they only created more. More questions and no answers. Who was G? What happened?

A long time ago, when I was at high school, Mandy and I got into trouble over a letter I wrote to her during a science lesson. 'I'm bored,' I wrote. 'Me too,' was her reply, 'and Mr Pringle's breath stinks of onions. He's just leant over me. I hope he wasn't looking down my top.' Mr Pringle confiscated the letter just as I was writing: 'He is a bit of a pervert on the quiet.' Mandy and I got detention for that.

'Never write a letter you don't want to be found,' said Gran as she, Mandy and I sat out on her verandah that Friday afternoon when our punishment was over.

'Well, people shouldn't read other people's letters,' said Mandy, taking a long sip of orange juice from the glasses Gran had poured us.

Gran nodded in agreement. 'Let me rephrase myself. If the letter is read by someone else, you shouldn't mind it. It shouldn't be something to be held against you.'

'What about love letters?' I asked. 'Surely those are private?'

'To a point,' said Gran. Mandy wrinkled her forehead in confusion. 'But after a while they become public property.'

'I've lost you,' said Mandy, putting her glass down and running her tongue over her lips.

'Let me put it this way,' said Gran, folding her hands in her lap. 'Think of all the great love stories. Percy and Mary Shelley, Winston and Clementine Churchill, Robert and Elizabeth Barrett Browning... who else? Well, you know what I mean. We only know about their relationships because of what they wrote to each other. They never burnt the letters

236

or threw them away. They kept them. Why? Because they wanted them to be found.'

I put the letters carefully back in their envelopes and into an old shoebox. Had Gran wanted them to be found? By whom and why? What did she want discovered?

When Mandy and I were caught writing about Mr Pringle, we weren't the ones who suffered the most as a consequence. We were embarrassed, but it was a joke. We were put into detention and weeded the athletics field for an afternoon, but that was it. It was Mr Pringle who was really embarrassed, left to wonder about his bad breath, boring lessons and whether most of the class thought he was a pervert or not.

I had a feeling I was about to experience some of Mr Pringle's pain as I delved deeper and deeper into Gran's past, but I had to know. I was determined to know.

Chapter Five

'I used to believe in God as a child.' My mother spoke softly, her wide, dark-rimmed eyes tired and strained. 'Mum made Jeremy and me go to Sunday school every week. We'd sing hymns and read bible stories. I knew all of them, all the stories. I used to think I wouldn't have minded living then, being Hannah or Ruth. It was as though the sun always shone in those stories. I could've lived in a parable, too, and never died. No one ever died in a parable.

'I stopped believing when Jem died. A man came to our house after the funeral. He had a bald head and wore a dark suit with a gold pen in his shirt pocket. He reeked of death, with his white notepad and his bible verses. I saw a different God then. A God who sought vengeance. A jealous God who took from you all you loved and then sent a man in a dark suit to quote bible verses at you and tell you about God's plan. "These things are sent to make us stronger," he said. All those sunny days in Canaan were a lie, a trick...'

'Were you happy growing up?' I asked after a short silence.

She didn't answer at first. Her bottom lip trembled.

'It's hard to say. What do I compare it to? There were happy times, yes. She was great fun, Mum. There were parties and dinners, but I think she was happiest with Jeremy and me. Especially Jem. She adored him.'

'Did you ever feel jealous?'

She stopped for a moment and thought. 'Yes, yes I did.' She breathed in deeply and let out a sigh. 'I always thought she loved him more.'

'Why?'

'Why did she love him more? Because he was a boy? Because he was the eldest? Because I disappointed her in some way? I don't know. She always said I was my father's daughter.'

There was another silence. 'I was never enough. Never enough. Even when Jem died, I couldn't give her enough support. She resented me for that. Because I wouldn't side with her completely. Because I comforted Dad as well. Yes, I suppose that's what it was.'

'Were they ever happy, Gran and Grandad?'

She nodded. 'Sometimes they got on. He loved her, you know? Worshipped the ground she walked on. But he wasn't the right person and he knew it and she made him pay.'

'Pay? That's a bit strong, isn't it?'

'It was just a feeling that was always there. A resentment. She hated him for loving her.'

Mom faded back into herself and was quiet for a long time. I got up to leave when she suddenly said: 'We went to Durban once. It was wonderful. We spent hours on the beach, making sandcastles, collecting shells, swimming in the sea. Mum would lie under her big beach umbrella. She

239

was very glamorous; wore sunglasses and a black swimsuit...
In the evenings, she'd bath Jem and I and then a maid would
come in and spend the evening with us while they went to
dinner. Down to the hotel bar or to one of the seafood
restaurants along the coast. I'd watch her dress: clip on her
earrings, roll up her stockings, slip on her shoes and squirt
perfume on her neck. She used to put it on the back of her
knees as well. I loved the smell of her...' Her voice broke and
she faltered. 'We were so happy.'

Later I looked through the pile of diaries: 1955, '56, '57.
1957 was the year they went to Durban.

3rd August, 1957

*We are having the most wonderful time and for the first
time I feel we are a family. We spend the days on the
beach with the children and the nights out dining. We
even had a dance last night after dinner. I didn't flinch
when L. put his arm around me and led me around the
floor. He makes me feel so beautiful, so utterly enchanting
with the way he looks at me, the way he presses his hand
into the middle of my back. At times like these I think I
could love him, I think I do love him in some fond sort of
way and, if only I hadn't loved G. first, I wouldn't want
for anything else but these adoring eyes. He's not a
challenge, of course, and I wonder whether I will bore of
him in the long run? But there are other things I can fill
my time with: the children, for one. I can cook and sew
and take them to all sorts of places and fill up my time.*

It probably only matters now, anyway. I will not need love when I am older, not physical love, just the love of children and a devoted husband. There are other things in life that are important. It's been three years since I last saw G. and I think I could face him now quite calmly.

5th August, 1957

I received a cable from G. this afternoon. He's here. I don't know what to feel. Excitement on one hand and nothing on the other. L. nearly caught me with the cable for we had just come in from the beach and he went on with the children to the milk bar for an ice cream. I stopped at the reception desk to buy a couple of stamps for the postcards that Francie and Jem wanted to send back to their friends, and suddenly the receptionist leaned over and handed me a telegraph. 'Arrived just this minute,' she said as I took it. I couldn't think at first who it could be from and, even when I saw the words, I couldn't believe it and had to read it through a couple of times. Am here. Will call. G. *I was just folding it and putting it in my handbag when L. came back and asked if I was all right. 'You look a bit pale,' he said. 'Why don't you go lie down? I'll keep the terrors occupied.' I shook my head, feeling guilty. 'Go on,' he insisted. 'You've earned it.'*
I had only been in the room about ten minutes when there was a knock at the door. The porter brought a message that a gentleman had phoned for me and would be phoning back in five minutes if I could wait at the

reception. I was so nervous, so anxious that L. not see me, so guilty of my emotions, that I nearly didn't go at all. Yet why? Why not tell L. that G. is here and arrange for him to meet us? Why do I continue with this subterfuge when only a couple of days ago I wrote that I could meet G. and not blink an eyelid? I thought I could stay and sit on the balcony and look out to sea and while I sat there the phone would ring and they would tell G. that I wasn't in or that we'd left. It wouldn't matter. I would just sit, watching the sea, my ears filled with its sound and the phone would ring and I wouldn't be there.

But I was. Of course I was. And I was there later that afternoon at the address he gave me: 52 Pioneer Street. I told L. I was going out souvenir hunting. Francie wanted to come with me and nearly spoilt the whole thing. She clung to my hand: 'Please, Mum, pleeaasse.' It was L. who stopped her. He could see I wanted to be on my own and, just before I left, he pressed some money into my hand and kissed me. 'Buy yourself something nice,' he said. 'For me too.' I tried to smile and kiss him back but my lips got the side of his mouth in a terribly clumsy attempt.

I spent part of the money on a taxi to Pioneer Street. It is a row of holiday houses just outside Durban. I felt guilty, yet I also felt I was punishing myself. I decided that I would just meet G. and talk and give myself a time limit. I would be deliberately cool and talk lots about the children. I would not give in to him, that's what I said. I will not let him control me like he used to.

It was hot, sticky hot, and my dress clung to me and I felt the glow of my skin under my make up as I stepped

242

out of the taxi onto the hot tar of the road. The sea seemed further away than it should for a stretch of beach houses. There was a small garden full of palm trees and a rickety couple of wooden steps up to a tiny verandah. G. was waiting. He had poured one drink and was just pouring the other when I arrived. The glass fizzed in his hand as he embraced me.

He smiled broadly when he saw me; I could tell he was nervous though.

'Thought you'd never make it,' he said, putting the glass down on the table.

I looked around. It was a simply decorated beach house. Not a cushion or mat was out of place. He obviously wasn't staying there.

'Where are you staying?'

'Margate, well, nearby,'

'By yourselves?'

'No.' He paused. 'We're with friends.'

'I didn't think you'd be allowed.'

'She doesn't know. I didn't know. It's been three years.'

'I know. How'd you find out we are here?'

'Grapevine. We've been thinking about getting away for a long time.'

'Whose house is it?'

'A friend's.'

'The Trumans'?'

He hesitated and then managed a wry smile. 'Yes. Good guess.'

He could see my irritation. 'Evie, please, we have one afternoon. One. The first one in three years. Let's not

243

spoil it, please.' He paused. I didn't look at him, fixing my gaze on the garden. 'I tried, I'm trying very hard...' his voice faltered. 'I think about you every day.'

I swallowed a large gulp of gin and tonic and focused on the long curve of the nearest palm. I do, too, I do, too! I wanted to shout. I wanted to cry so I held my glass against my mouth and let it pass.

'Evie,' he said, pushing my hair back gently. 'Evie...'

Later, as we lay in bed and he traced his name across my chest, his body moist and clammy next to mine, he said again that he missed me. 'Like an old friend?' I asked, laughing a little cynically and lying back against the pillow.

'More than that, Evie. You know that.'

'When did you arrive?'

'Last week.'

'Last week? And going?'

He moved uneasily onto his back and didn't look me in the eye. 'Tomorrow.'

My heart dropped, but why should I feel let down? What should I expect from him?

I didn't ask him anymore. We danced. There was a radiogram. An old one with a volume knob that didn't work and we had to strain to hear the words at first:

It's not the pale moon
That excites me,
That thrills and delights me,
Oh no, it's just the nearness of you...

But then we held each other and we were dancing so slowly anyway that after a while we could hear every word.

'What's the time?' he asked suddenly, pulling away from me. Those old familiar words.

'Old habits die hard.'

He pulled a face. 'Paul's coming at five to pick me up.'

'Paul? You must be joking!'

'I'm not. How d'you think I got here?'

'But me... I mean, the house...' I looked across at the dishevelled bed.

'Don't worry. I'll sort everything out once you've...'

'Gone.' I filled in the last word and pulled my hands away from his. 'I'll be quick.'

'No Evie,' he begged. 'It's not what I meant. Evie!' He ripped my clothes out of my hand and threw them across the room. One of them caught an ornament, which fell to the floor with a crash.

'How are you going to explain that?' I asked angrily, trying to get away from him. I wanted to smash up every single thing just to say that I'd been there.

'I don't care! I don't care! Evie, just don't go – at least not yet.'

But I did. My clothes felt even more uncomfortable than when I'd arrived and the only thing I wanted to do was have a bath, but I had to go to a few shops first. I bought Jem a kaleidoscope and Francie a pair of red rubber sandals.

'Couldn't find anything for myself,' I said to L. when I got back. 'Just a couple of things for the children.'

He wanted to kiss me, but I shied away and I saw

245

*again that look in his eyes. It's the first time I've seen it
these holidays, that look that says he knows I don't love
him.*

*'I want to change.' I said with obvious irritation. 'I
need a bath, too. It's been so hot.'*

*He smiled then as if that explained everything. 'Of
course. But don't take your time because you and me are
going dancing tonight.'*

'Dancing?'

'You heard me right. I'm going to take you dancing.'

I tried to smile. 'I'm so tired. The heat...'

'A bath will do you the world of good.'

*I tried this evening, I really did. I was getting ready
and L. came up behind me as I was doing up my zip.*

*'I'll do that,' he said and he kissed the back of my neck.
I wanted to recoil, to shiver, to shake him off, but instead
I turned around and kissed him. In fact, I kissed him
twice. The surprise and delight in his eyes was obvious
and later that evening he said that was the first time I
have ever kissed him first. I tried to enjoy myself. We
went dancing at some club in the centre of Durban. It
was smoky and loud, but L. loved it. I kept thinking
about this afternoon, wishing I was there with G.,
dancing naked to the old radiogram instead, and yet
hating him, hating him and hating myself for giving in,
remembering those words. Paul Truman was coming to
pick him up! Why is it that he remains such close friends
with people who obviously despise me?*

*How did we leave it? What decisions have been made?
Nothing, once again, nothing. I don't even ask. We are in*

too far to go back. There are too many people involved now. I have let myself down once again. I am his whore, his mistress. He commands and I follow. I should've let the phone ring and ring and ring. I should've watched the sea roll in and filled my mind with its sound. Why is it that I do not know how to say goodbye? I can't think what G. and I have done. We have destroyed not only our own lives, but the lives of everyone close to us. We will never get out of this relationship. Never.

Later, when we got back, I looked in on the children and saw Francie sleeping with her new red shoes on. My heart filled with such pain and I bent over her to kiss her goodnight.

Chapter Six

8th June, 1954

I wake at night sometimes and I think what have I done? Why have we started this affair again? He has been away from Bulawayo for five years and now he is back and I am with him and I cannot help but ask myself why.

I wonder whether I could run away, but I could not take the children if I did, and I could never leave them, never ever. I have destroyed my life, but I will not do that to them. A woman who leaves her children commits the greatest sin of all. A single woman who runs off with a married man may, at worst, be labelled a home breaker, and a married woman with no children might even be felt sorry for; it is her husband who looks ridiculous – is he a bore, a miser, a wife beater people might ask? That's the worst this woman will suffer. But a woman with children never leaves them. Never. Perhaps if I only had Jeremy and the truth were told to Leonard he would be heartbroken, but he would hardly be likely to tell anyone

Jeremy isn't, wasn't ever, his child. But not now with two. Now we are a family and women don't destroy families.

17th October, 1954

At least when I was single I could see an end: a decision would have to be made. But now we meet, we make love, we leave each other. Now there is no end. We turn in ever-increasing circles, faster and faster. No hope of an end, a decision. He once said that he could never leave her because of the 'ties that bind' and now I too am bound. What is the point? Every time we destroy ourselves a little bit more, every time we die a little death. Now there is no longing, only emptiness; no desire except the desire to die. But a woman doesn't do that either, does she? Wish to die.

Every night I say this is the end. It can't go on; it must stop. And then each morning hope is born again. It lies before me in each unlived hour and every day it ticks away, the hours empty, hope dies.

24th October, 1954

Today I was in town near the station and I thought I could get on a train and leave. Cape Town. Then England. Begin again. I would have, I really would have, except that I had a stew in the oven and I wondered what would happen if it burnt away and there was nothing for *them to eat. It seems ridiculous, but I couldn't help thinking: how would I feel if my mother left me and there was nothing to eat but burnt stew? And so I came home instead and there they were, all three, waiting for me. 'Happy Birthday' they all shouted when I walked in the door. There was a cake and streamers and Jem blew a paper trumpet, his pink cheeks puffing out in pride. Francie gave me a little present of three yellow daisies and then Leonard gave me a hard squeeze and a kiss on my neck.*

I cried then and they all stopped. I saw a shadow pass over Francie's face and her mouth drooped like she was going to burst into tears. 'It's all right,' I said, 'all right. Mum's just so happy, so happy.' And later as I lay in bed I thought: I am a fake. They love a fake. How they would hate me if they knew and I would lose them forever. Forever. It has to end, this time it has to end.

25ᵗʰ October, 1954

It's over. I've told him.

4ᵗʰ November, 1954

I calm myself; I tell myself that it's all right. Sometimes I find an order in life in which I can lose myself. Wake up, breakfast, morning tea at ten o'clock, lunch, afternoon tea at four, supper, bed. I look forward to each next stage and can't bear it if my routine is disrupted.

5th January, 1955

I have started going to church. A New Year's resolution of sorts. Have chosen to be a Catholic this time. The guilt suits me.

17th January, 1955

I don't know what I think of God. For most of my life I have imagined him to be a man, an old man at that. He wears white robes and sits in a grand chair flanked by angels in a place called Heaven. He's white. Should he be? I try to imagine him black, but can't quite do it. Should he have any colour at all? Should he be a man? I thought briefly today that God might be a black woman, a big black woman with breasts that heave and fall as she laughs, a deep rollicking laugh. Funny, but not an image that stays. Always I come back to the elderly white man in his white robes.

Perhaps we all imagine God to suit ourselves, perhaps what we imagine him to look like isn't important, or is it? My God is angry, vengeful, jealous. King Lear demanding absolute love from his Cordelia, and everyone else. The black, female God is caring, understanding. She knows what it is like to love; to love the wrong person. She pulls me into that huge bosom of hers and lets me cry. Her hands are soft and brown and comforting. She does not judge.

251

24th January, 1955

There are things no one tells you when you are growing up. Like where the sun goes during the night; the moon during the day. Like what thunder is and where babies come from. The meaning of dreams. Where we go when we die. They tell you silly stories about the sun sleeping and God being angry. About storks and angels. Father Christmas and the tooth fairy.

One day, someone asked their mother, 'Why are we here?' and was told a story about a far-flung eternity and snakes, women, men and a star above a stable. But it never answered Why? Why all this? Why wash behind your ears? Why tidy your bedroom? Why learn that 12 x 12 is 144? Why, when it's all going to end? When we're told that this life doesn't matter, that our souls will float upwards towards lovelier things, beyond the great blue sky? Why not die now instead of all this endless repetition: brushing teeth, polishing shelves, going to bed, waking up?

As a child, one expects something from life, a hope one often loses with age. Something is going to happen. Not now, perhaps, but then, when I'm older, when I'm a grown up. Eternity is then and there, stretched out across the sky in blue; in the tired old sun sinking down over the horizon and in the gold dust of evening; in the sunlight filtering through the shade of trees and the call of crickets on summer nights. In all that we expect will never end.

And then there's you. There, in the centre of the universe, ripping flowers apart in jest and wrenching great tufts of grass from the resistant earth in boredom,

252

squashing ants and laughing when birds fly away
because you clap your hands. The world will end when
you do.

21st March, 1955

I missed lunch last Tuesday because I was held up at the
bank. I experienced the most terrible feeling on my return
home. All the lunch dishes had been cleared from the
table. The remainder of the tea in the pot had gone cold
and I couldn't bear to see the plates with their crumbs
piled at the sink. I felt left behind, lost, as though life
could carry on quite happily without me, but I did not
feel relief, only desolation at how easily I could be
forgotten.

L. had gone back to work and the children were lying
down. I went into Jem's room and saw him asleep, his
Boy's Own *annual open next to him. I climbed on the*
bed and felt overwhelmingly tired as I curled myself
around him and fell asleep. I keep telling myself that this
will not last forever.

The rest of the diary was empty: smooth white pages with
the fine criss-cross lines of a ledger. At the back was a
photograph. It was very like one I had seen before, except
that it was taken from a slightly different angle. An elderly
lady, her handbag hanging by her side, her cardigan buttoned
up, sensible shoes on her feet. 'Mum, Matopos, 1953' it
says on the back. She looked like Gran, or rather Gran

looked like her, I thought, and for some inexplicable reason a line from a lecture I had once attended on Modernism sprang to mind: that the world changed more dramatically every ten years in the twentieth century than it had done every hundred years before. And yet there was something in her stance, in the way her body bent slightly forward, her chin lifted a little high that suggested a confidence, a knowledge, a belief in the world that is rarely seen any more. How wonderful to face life, knowing one's place, knowing what to give because you know what to expect, believing that nothing changes and never will.

Chapter Seven

12th May, 1960

The Rhodesians generally hate the winter, but it is one of my favourite times of the year. I particularly like the descent into winter around May and the ascent out of it in August. I was brought up to detest dust. Mother was forever dusting and I grew to believe it was something that must be gotten rid of at all costs. And yet here, I love it, perhaps, like Mother, not on tables and chairs, but outside in the sun. In winter everything here is brown. The bush grass is dry and brittle. It clutches the soft sandy soil, desperately hanging onto life.

I sat at the window today and watched the sunlight come streaming through the trees in the back garden. It was not the pale watercolour sunlight of England, but a bright, daring glow, one without the viscous heat of summer. It is warm in the sun, but the warmth does not heat the air so in the shade it is cold. Midges were captured in the light, dancing, fluttering with great excitement. The day shimmers with all the excitement and expectancy of an English summer's day.

The mornings are dark. Sunrise appears with a faint orange smudge on the horizon. The birds are up already. I want to snuggle under the blankets and not put a single toe out of bed. Yet the cold is to be embraced. It awakens and renews. I love the shock of cold water on my face, the crunch of frost on the ground, the spirals of warm air that I breathe out into the cold. 'Look, Mummy, we're smoking!' cry Francie and Jem as I walk them to school in the mornings. And then in the evening, that early bite. The search for jumpers to be put back on, a fire lit, a warm bath run.

12th August, 1960

I can almost taste the dust in the air. I feel like jumping up and down, turning circles. I feel like going on holiday. To the sea. Is it strange that this beautiful weather in a landlocked country should make me want to go to the sea? I feel I can begin again, that spring is nature's way of giving us second chances. Some might feel this way on the first of January: time to give up cigarettes, cakes, swearing. But by the second of the month those promises already begin to fade. Spring is not about giving up, but taking up. Out come the tennis racquets, the running shoes, the swimming costumes.

Tonight, as I passed Jem's room and looked in, I thought he was asleep and had just reached out to switch off the light when his eyes opened and he said, 'Sing that song you sing when you're happy.' I didn't know which one he meant and he started to sing, 'The trembling breeze embrace the trees, tenderly.' 'Oh,' I said, 'is that the one I sing when I'm happy?'

'Yes, it is,' said Leonard, who was standing by the door. 'That's the one Mummy sings when she's happy.'

4ᵗʰ September, 1960

I was at the park today. I took the children at lunchtime and we walked for a bit and then sat and had a picnic. There was a man nearby, an African man, a gardener working away at a new flowerbed. He didn't look at me until I greeted him and then I got the biggest, widest grin I think I have ever seen. He touched his hat and nodded a greeting back. 'What have you got there?' I asked, coming closer. There was a moment of surprise on his part and then he stretched his cupped palm towards me. In the middle of a clump of soft earth was a tiny orange flower. His hand shook a little as he pulled it out of the clod, shaking its spindly roots free. With excitement, I thought, not age. 'Marigold, Mamma,' he said and then drew the quivering seedling back into the safety of his body.

I can't help thinking Leonard is wrong. He thinks it's madness that the council plant non-indigenous trees. Who can hate a jacaranda? And it's not just trees he has it in for, but flowers as well, any kind of plant that 'is not naturally found in Rhodesia' to quote his exact words. But when I see the gardens filled to over-brimming with flowers in August, when I smell the sweet-peas, the yesterday-today-and-tomorrow, when the syringa blossom and the jacaranda's fall, when the air is thick with the suffocating heaviness of jasmine, I cannot help but think he is wrong. To see the African gardeners tend to the park with such loving care, to see, as I did, that hand outstretched: 'Madam, for you' and the look in his eyes, somewhere near the joy of a father holding his newborn child for the first time, the dirt under his nails, the soft mud crumbling off his hands. Pride in hydrangeas, petunias and marigolds. Leonard and I argued, of course, but he never wants to push the matter too far in case he wins. He is still afraid of losing me, afraid that one day I will walk out and say 'I don't love you anymore'. I see the look in his eyes, the nervous dart, the way they lower in surrender. Do I find it condescending or frustrating? No. But sometimes I feel overwhelmed, yes, that is the right word, overwhelmed by my power, my potential to hurt.

There was only one incident that seemed to threaten Gran's peace; one person, I should say, my mother.

8th July, 1961

I find her such a strange child at times and feel frustrated that I cannot seem to get past that strangeness. I always seem to have hurt her in some way. She looks at me with those big brown eyes full of longing and I know it will take more than the simple act of putting my arms round her to make her believe that I am on her side. She is reproachful. She watches me, not with suspicion for she is not a calculating child, but with hurt as though at sometime I did something terrible to her, let her down in some irrevocable way. Jem is easy: a hug, a kiss, fingers run through his hair, but not Francie. Francie is afraid of me.

A few days ago, a hornet began building a nest on the bulb of her bedside lamp. A strange place, but there it was working methodically and buzzing, it seems in glee, every now and then. Francie won't sleep without her lamp on; it is a habit she started very young and that we have unfortunately failed to break. But now she didn't want the lamp on in case the hornet got burned, so she cried and cried and insisted that she sleep with us. I tried to explain to her that the hornet may be there for a very long time and that she couldn't possibly sleep with us indefinitely. Leonard was sympathetic at first, but even he pulled a face the second night she came to our room.

I took her into her bedroom, holding her hand, and tried to show her there was nothing to fear in it. The cupboard and chest of drawers were closed and light came in from outside so the room was not completely dark. She sat on the edge of the bed, twisting her fingers round and round, her little mouth pulled into a gesture of angry defiance and still she refused, absolutely refused, to get into bed.

'We can't go on like this,' I insisted. I was tired and I could hear the hard edge of anger enter my voice. 'I'm going to switch the light on,' I said and reached for the cord, but her hand was faster and caught my wrist. She began to cry and tried to get between the lamp and me. 'It's a hornet, Francie, a hornet. It'll sting you. Why do you want to help it?' I breathed deeply, trying to keep calm, and pulled back the bedclothes and made a point of smoothing the sheet for her, but still that defiance. She pushed my hand away and yanked the blanket up again and suddenly I found myself shouting: 'Francie. Please!' and my hand reached for the switch and suddenly the lamp was on. Francie looked at me with absolute horror and then burst into tears and ran out.

Shortly afterwards Leonard came in and asked why I had killed the hornet. 'I didn't kill it!' I yelled at him. 'Look, it's alive' and it was true, there was the hornet still on the bulb, not at all flummoxed by recent events. But Francie would have none of it. She cried herself to sleep lying on the bed in Leonard's arms, he smoothing her hair and kissing her forehead and muttering all sorts of things to her. I watched her relax, I watched her let herself be comforted, be loved and I realised that she is never like that with me. She has never let me love her.

Chapter Eight

My grandmother's death never made international news. After all she did not live on a farm, nor was her murder thought to be politically motivated. The news teams did not flock to the scene of the crime or wait to interview my mother. It wasn't worth their while for it did not involve war veterans or provide enough material to point at an incompetent police force.

The police described it as 'cut and dry'. It was an obvious case of a burglary gone wrong. Someone had broken into Gran's house and she had woken up and discovered him in her bedroom. He was frightened and had hit her. He hadn't meant to kill her; he didn't even think she was in the house. A day later he was arrested. He still had the stolen goods with him. In court he pleaded guilty and was sentenced to life imprisonment. Outside the courthouse a police spokesman made a statement. He said he was glad that justice had been done. People thought that Zimbabwe was a lawless country, that one could get away with murder. They were wrong. The swiftness with which the police had dealt with this case had proved that.

My grandmother had been hit fifteen times about the head with the butt of an AK-47. There was nothing left of her face. The man who killed her was unemployed; he had been for several months. He used to sell curios at the market outside City Hall until the tourists stopped coming. The tourists stopped coming because of the violence they saw on their televisions in Britain, America, Europe, wherever. The violence they saw was against white farmers by their government. Perhaps they stopped coming because they thought it was only whites who were being targeted. Many black people had also died, but word of their deaths didn't always reach international news desks.

At first I didn't want to know the name of the man who killed my grandmother. I didn't want to know anything about him because I didn't want to feel sorry for him. I didn't want to imagine how he felt, whether he was remorseful, whether he worried who would feed his family when he was gone. The local newspaper had a picture of him on the front page. He was handcuffed and being led to the cells by two officers. He had on a pair of trousers and a T-shirt. Amongst the objects he had stolen were a tub of margarine, a bag of sugar and a jar of Cashel Valley plum jam. The police omitted to hand these back. Nobody ever commented on where this man could get a gun and I never understood why he had to beat my grandmother fifteen times.

In reality the police did very little in terms of catching him; he actually turned himself in, a day after Gran's death. They couldn't quite believe it down at Central, and at first laughed him off as a madman. Then he told them about the

262

scar, the scar on the underside of Gran's arm: the teapot stain. It was me, he said, I am sorry.

Gran was buried in a simple ceremony attended only by family. Over the years, many of her friends had died or moved away. Mrs van Heerden had died of cancer, Mrs Coetzee had moved to New Zealand, Mrs Patterson had gone to England and Mrs Benson was in frail care in an old people's home. Mr Patel was still around. He sent flowers, but didn't attend the funeral. I saw him in his shop the day before. Although to me he had always seemed old, there was a weariness about him now that was different. He leaned heavily against the counter, his tape measure still slung around his neck as it had been for years.

'One day, God's going to call us all,' he said, wagging his finger at me. 'And you must be ready. OK? Cause God's going to call us all.'

I didn't say anything, resenting the note of blame his voice carried, as though Gran should have been ready and waiting for the man who murdered her.

'I don't think I'll go,' he said, referring to the funeral. 'No, I will not go.'

Feeling the pressure of tears, I turned to leave the shop and that's when he called me back. I could see how hard it was for him not to break down right there and then for his voice choked as he spoke.

'I know your grandmother a long, long time. See?' The tears in his eyes made them look strangely bright and he seemed to try not to blink as he spoke. 'I know her way back before she even married.' He almost spat the words out at me and I half thought he would take me by the throat as he spoke. 'I know her. I know.' I stared at him, not knowing what to say and not understanding what he was saying. 'She never say goodbye, your grandmother.' He wiped the tears from his cheeks in an awkward flailing motion, like someone drowning. 'All the time only see you soon. You see, huh? That's what I will remember. Only see you soon.'

We tried to pick joyful hymns for Gran's funeral: All Things Bright and Beautiful and Make Me a Channel of Your Peace. We also sang I Vow to Thee My Country, a hymn Gran had once told Mom she had wanted sung at her funeral. It seemed rather out of place in the circumstances. Jeremy's green beret was buried with Gran. Mum held it all the way through the service and then placed it on top of the coffin. There were a number of bunches of flowers. A large one of white roses stood out in particular. There was a card and a message, but no name. It read: But thy eternal summer shall not fade. Miles, it could only be Miles.

Chapter Nine

'What do you want most in life?'

Mark and I were walking down Tottenham Court Road. It was two o'clock in the morning. Our second date, I think, or our third.

'I want to be happy,' I said and it sounded so meaningless, so clichéd, that I laughed and tried to make a joke of it. 'Yippee. Happeee.' I sang, like a newly escaped mental patient.

'Seriously,' he persisted, more seriously.

'Um...' I thought. 'I am being serious. It just sounds, you know, so...' I scooped my hands into the air to suggest what I didn't have the words to say.

'What would make you happy?' We had stopped walking and I stood for a moment, leaning against a phone box. I took a deep breath as though I was going to say something deep and meaningful.

'Chocolate ice cream every day. Breakfast, lunch and dinner.' And then I burst into laughter at the sight of Mark's face crumpling in the face of my fatuous behaviour.

'I want to know you, Ellie,' he said to me when we got to my door. I was tired but I smiled. It was a wonderful, romantic thing for him to say and at that stage I never thought it was impossible.

But what does it mean to know someone. I mean really know them? I got an email once, one of those forwarded things that you have to send on to ten other people within half an hour if you want good luck within three days. Ten Things You Didn't Know About Me. Mandy sent it to me and then I had to fill in my ten things and send them off to her and nine others. She said her favourite colour was red. 'You liar!' I said to her in another email. You never wear red. It's one of the things that people say to make themselves sound exciting to others. For isn't a woman who wears red bold, daring and ambitious? Isn't that why women bosses apparently wear red bras? It gives them confidence, write magazine psychologists. Or black bras. Not white, and definitely not skin colour. Who wants to fade into themselves?

I think of all the things that Mark probably never knew about me. I didn't like his stainless steel furniture, for one. Except perhaps the kettle and toaster. I don't like Tom Clancy novels or John Grisham. He could have worked that out, I suppose, on the basis of the fact that I didn't own any and he would never have seen me reading them. But had he ever noticed? Had we ever gone on one of those TV programmes where they ask couples about each other, how would we have scored? Tom Clancy was easy stuff, but what about other things? Shade of lipstick? Waist measurement? Shampoo? Did anyone ever write it all down and say here, this is me. You'll find everything you'll ever need in here.

'Tell me about your life,' Mark said to me, not long after he asked me what would make me happy.

'Where do I begin?' I replied, pulling a face of mock horror.

'In the beginning.'

I pulled another face. 'A bit of a tall order. Look, just ask me questions. Ask me anything. Just fire away and I'll answer.'

I suppose it made sense to begin at the beginning if I was ever to get to the bottom of this mystery. Bottom of the mystery! How like a line from The Famous Five that sounded! 'We have to get to the bottom of this mystery!' exclaimed Dick determinedly. Or with determination. Grave determination, even. Everyone in The Famous Five was gravely determined. And as a postgraduate student of literature I should know that there are no beginnings. In my beginning is my end. Who said that? I am the beginning and the end.

The oldest of Gran's diaries, that for 1947, was at the bottom of the box; its hard blue cover was dusty, yet the lettering on its spine had faded least compared to the others and the pages fell flat easily: much loved and much used.

9th January, 1947

He has renewed my faith in life. Only nine days since New Year and I can't imagine a life without him. Since

267

being back at work, I have seen him every day, but I try not to acknowledge him too heartily for I must not let my feelings show, although I feel they are written all over my face.

12ᵗʰ January, 1947

This afternoon we went for a walk through the park. He bought an ice cream cone and we sat on the grass and shared it. We couldn't hold hands or let looks give us away, but eating the ice cream, sharing the ice cream was our secret kiss. It reminds me of a time just before I met Timothy – how long ago that now seems! I'd just finished school and hadn't yet started work at Rumbolts. Marjorie and I decided to go to Margate for the day. It was spring; too warm for the coats we wore, so we took them off and walked with them over one arm. The warmth faded with the sun and we were glad of them again in the early evening. We had to run for the train, to be home before the blackout and the air raids. We shared a packet of chips on the way home. We hadn't enough money for a packet each, but there was a kind of blissful enjoyment in our frugality, as though they wouldn't have tasted quite so nice had we been able to afford two. Or was it the threat of air raids? Perhaps that was where our excitement came from.

15th January, 1947

He said he was going to come round today, but he got
held up at the Club. He telephoned from there to say that
he was having dinner with friends. He said he'd rather
be with me, but she will be there.

I am so disappointed. I've been looking forward to
seeing him all day. He goes away tomorrow for three
days. How can I live without seeing him?

16th January, 1947

One whole day without him. Two more to go.

21st January, 1947

I don't know. I just don't know. He hasn't phoned or been
round and he must have got back at least two days ago.
I can't contact him at all. It's wrong, the whole thing is
wrong and I should never have got involved in the first
place. It's all I can think about and I hate myself for ever
agreeing to anything.

22nd January, 1947

He's back! He came around yesterday evening and I was
so happy that I just couldn't pretend otherwise. I was
sitting at the window, having a cigarette and reading

when there was a knock on the door. I looked out and saw him. My heart stood still as I heard Mrs W. tell him that it was a little too late to call. I didn't know whether I wanted him to go away or not – to feel what it's like not to be able to see me and talk to me and to have a wall between us. I sat on the landing and was quite glad to hear him try and charm Mrs W. into letting him see me, but then I felt my heart drop again when I heard him say 'That's fine. I'll call back later in the week when I have time. Tell Evie it might be next week.' How could he give up so easily? Does he really only think of me when he has a moment to spare?

4th April, 1947

He appeared very early this morning – 6! I heard a tap on my bedroom door and yanked him inside when I saw who it was.

'What on earth are you doing here?' I whispered 'You'll get me thrown out!'

'Sorry. The front door was open. The maid was outside on the road talking to someone. She didn't see me slip in. I promise.'

My anger subsided. I was so happy to see him. We lay down together for a while on my bed. He said that this is what it would be like to wake up with me every morning. 'Just a pity about your wife,' I said and immediately regretted my words. I don't want him to think I think about a future with him. I would never force him to leave her. He has never mentioned it anyway. I must just be content for now.

He didn't have time to comment anyway because there was a banging on the door and Mrs W. was there, demanding to be let in.

'Room inspection,' she trilled through the keyhole, but I had a feeling she had a suspicion G. was there. Don't ask me how, the woman knows everything. Quickly, G. scrambled out of the window and stood on the little mock balcony while I let Mrs W. in. She glanced around, looked under the bed and opened the cupboard with such a flourish that I knew then she expected to find someone.
'All in order,' was all she said, before taking another look around and bustling out of the door.

'You go,' said G., climbing back in again. 'I'll find my way out when everyone has gone. Don't worry.' He kissed me and I went down to breakfast. All day, I was so happy that everyone commented on it at work. I kept thinking, this is what it is like to wake up next to someone, this is what it is like.

Chapter Ten

What do I know about her? When Gran first arrived in Bulawayo, she stayed at a boarding house run by an elderly Jewish widow called Mrs Wiesman. It was her only source of income and she ran a tight shift. All the girls had to be in by seven o'clock during the week and nine thirty at the weekends. Mrs Wiesman personally checked they were all in by banging her walking stick on each door as she walked down the passage. Each occupant had to call out her name. If anyone thought they were going to come home later than the curfew, Mrs Wiesman would thoroughly check the story out. She would phone up the Palace and ask what time the evening film would end or the host or hostess of the party one was invited to would be contacted and all details needed to be laid bare: who would be there, who was the chaperone, what type of music was likely to be played. Mrs Wiesman thought jazz a corrupting influence on young minds.

The boarding house was on Borrow Street, two roads down from Stoughton and James. It was a short walk to work in the morning and back in the evening. Gran made sandwiches for her lunch and would eat them in the park, sitting there at lunchtime with the other office girls.

Gradually she made friends, was asked out, went to the pictures, tea dances at the Grand, picnics, even a ball once at City Hall. Although Gran was a widow, she was only nineteen years old. Her life stretched ahead of her and she relished her new-found freedom.

All this she told me. Many, many times. Mrs Wiesman dressed in widow's black banging her stick on Gran's door; picnics in the park in the days when the grass was cut and flowers flourished and the river didn't stink and muggers didn't lurk. Dances at the Grand before it became derelict, before they nearly knocked it down, before they transformed it into what was going to be Bulawayo's first shopping mall like the malls the girls hang out in in *Beverly Hills 90210*, before the developers ran out of money and enthusiasm. Before, before... and yet, was any of it true. Really true? Ten Things I Didn't Know About Gran. One, she had an affair...

11th April, 1947

I went to his house yesterday. It is in Suburbs, a fine house built nearly fifty years ago. He has the most wonderful garden that I have ever seen, whether in England or here in the Colony. How fantastic that this is his 'second home', not his real one. He has a whole host of flowers and tells me he has even planted sweet peas. Anything can grow anywhere, he said, given the right conditions. He even says he's grown daffodils before.

273

Before he went inside, he picked me some bougain-villaea. 'Common as muck around here,' he said, turning it over between his fingers. 'So common and yet its beauty quite takes one by surprise. Full many a flower is born to blush unseen and waste its sweetness on the desert air.'

'You've said that before somewhere.'

'Probably. It's one of my favourites. Thomas Gray. Elegy Written in a Country Churchyard.'

I met his right-hand man, his manservant, Samson. He is a large African man, taller than the doorframe, a true Ndebele warrior. He's stocky as well – not the sort of man you'd want to pick a fight with. G. says he went to Burma with the King's African Rifles. I can imagine he looks quite foreboding in uniform.

We sat on the verandah and Samson brought a tray of tea, complete with the most delicious chocolate cake I have ever tasted, soft and dark and moist.

'Samson made it,' G. said with pride as he handed me a thick slice on a plate. 'He's a dab hand in the kitchen.'

He showed me round the house. It is not terrifically big inside: two bedrooms, living room, kitchen, bathroom and a library. In the latter, he showed me his collection of books, highlighting any favourites and retelling many of the plots.

'Not much crime here, I'm afraid, but help yourself if you find anything else.'

'What do you have in your main house if this is your second home?' I joked as my eyes scanned the spines of the books on the shelf in front of me.

'I don't keep my books there,' he replied, rather curtly.

I looked up. 'My books are private. This house is private. My wife hardly ever stays here. She doesn't often travel with me.'

I detected a sorrow, or was it a bitterness, in the words.

'When do you get time to read? You always seem to be doing something.'

'I love reading.' He was a little defensive in his answer at first and then he softened. 'I wanted to read Classics at Oxford, but my father wouldn't hear of it. I had to do something useful, so I went in for architecture at Cambridge. Poetry, poetry's my favourite.' He took down a volume and handed it to me. Collected Poems. 'Here. Read this.' It was an instruction rather than a suggestion. I didn't open it.

Samson announced lunch was ready, which we ate in the dining room: liver paté, roast beef and Yorkshire pudding, peas, carrots and roast potatoes (the last three from the garden, I was later told) and chocolate mousse. It was delicious. Samson carved the meat into thin slices and served the vegetables with silver tongs. He kept a tea towel over his shoulder throughout. He disappeared while we ate and then returned to remove our plates and serve the next course.

'Does he do this all the time? Or just when you have company?'

'Oh, all the time,' G. said, in surprise and I couldn't help a little smile. I wonder if G. has even made a sandwich before!

In the afternoon, we sat outside and G. read poetry aloud. His voice was strong and clear, almost defiant, in

275

the silence of the afternoon.

I have been here before,
But when or how I cannot tell:
I know the grass beyond the door,
The sweet keen smell,
The sighing sound, the lights around the shore.

'Will you stay?' he asked me, as the afternoon drew on. We sipped sherry on the verandah after tea.

'Mrs Wiesman...' I started, but he shrugged and said: 'She can be sorted out. What about you?'

'I'm not sure.' My stomach was lurching.

'I'll get Samson to make up the spare room. You can stay, we can have dinner, you can read or do whatever you want. Go to bed whenever you want.'

My heart dropped a little at the seeming innocence of his request that I stay over.

'All right,' I said quite boldly. 'All right, I'll stay.'

And so I stayed. Samson delivered a note to Mrs Wiesman to the effect that I had taken ill suddenly and would be staying the night at my uncle and aunt's. We had what he referred to as a 'light supper': slices of cold beef from lunch, baby potatoes, avocado and boiled egg and salad. There was a rice pudding for dessert. Samson bought coffee into G.'s study afterwards and we sat and looked at maps for an hour or so.

'West Africa is where I'd like to go,' said G., a lit cigarette in one hand, the other preventing the map from rolling up.

I looked over at the huge expanse of Africa, veined

with rivers and blotched with forests.

'We're very civilised here,' he continued. 'In comparison to other parts of the continent, we're years ahead, decades.' I detected a disappointment in his voice.

'Isn't that a good thing?' I ventured.

'Sometimes.' He was still intent on the map. His cigarette glowed orange and a small circle of ash formed on the end. 'At other times,' he said, turning to me, 'I think it would be quite exciting to go to a place that hasn't been discovered. Where there aren't postboxes and fire stations and neat little rows of suburban houses. Do you know what I mean?'

I nodded, but said: 'I don't think I'm one for a mud hut.'

'No?' he looked intently at me then and smiled. Then he turned back to his map. 'I'd like to just go, just go and go and go.'

I was surprised. For all his love of maps, I thought him someone who wanted the benefits of the Club, postboxes and a fire station.

'One day,' he said to me, taking my hand between his two, and I thought then that his 'one day' included me and I got a little shiver down my spine. One Day. I didn't sleep in the guest room.

G. dropped me off today. He came inside and spoke to Mrs Wiesman. It unnerved me how easily he lied to her about my illness, how he and his wife couldn't possibly have returned me in such a state. After he had gone, I turned to leave the sitting room and go upstairs, but she called me back.

'Evelyn.'

I turned and stepped towards her. 'Yes, Mrs Wiesman.'

'I want to tell you a story. Sit down.'

The room was hot for she hadn't opened a window, but the curtains were wide open and the sun burned through the glass, cutting little squares of light on the carpet. I sat in the armchair nearest the door, perching on the warm edge, ready to go. She stood in front of the mantelpiece.

'You see this man here?' She pointed to an old photo next to her elbow.

'Yes.'

'This one is my husband.'

She then opened a small mahogany box and looked inside. Her soft papery hands turned something over. It was another photo. Another man, this one older and more dashing. He had a small moustache and was wearing a pilot's uniform.

'This one, he break my heart.' The bluntness of her words caught me off guard. 'Girls don't marry the men who break their hearts. Girls marry men who look after them. The men who break their hearts take with them all the pieces.' She threw her hands up weakly. 'Nothing left for the nice man.'

I didn't say anything because I didn't know what to say.

'You think I not young once, Evie? You think I don't know what it is to love?'

'Thank you, Mrs Wiesman,' I said, standing up. 'Thank you, but I am not quite sure what you are

278

referring to...' I made for the door, but she carried on talking as though I hadn't moved an inch.

'His wife came to see me.'

I stopped.

'She say, don't take my husband. We have children. We can share him. Don't take him.' She laughed in a sneering way.

'Then the rabbi, he come to see me. He say you leave this man alone. He is married, he have children. But I love him and he tell me he is going to leave her. Then one day he is gone. They have left the country. South Africa.' She wagged her finger in the air. 'Not one word he say to me. Not one.' She paused. 'That day my heart is broken. That day I don't think I can get out of bed. Ever again. I do not think I can move.'

There was another pause and I moved again towards the door. This time she let me pass.

'Just remember they take with them all the pieces, Evie, all the pieces.'

My room seemed sad and forlorn. The glorious expectation I had felt the previous day still hung in the air as I entered, but dissolved in the empty light of a quiet Sunday. I opened the window and could hear voices laughing in the distance, carrying on the clear air from Borrow Street. I looked around the room; everything was in its place: the bed cover was straight; not even the book on my bedside table was at an angle. I sank slowly onto the edge of the bed, my bag dropping to the floor. What to do now?

This morning when I woke, G. was already outside

279

drinking tea on the verandah. He sat wrapped in a light dressing gown, but I dressed before coming out. Samson dutifully brought me tea, his eyes lowered when I said 'good morning' and 'thank you'. He poured the most wonderful cup of tea, just the right strength, but when I commented on this, he didn't answer. Perhaps he took it as an insult, I don't know. G. only smiled, as though I had complimented him!

Samson brought G. the Sunday paper and shortly afterwards announced that breakfast was ready.

'He's great, isn't he?' said G.

'Fantastic!'

'He learnt it all during the War.'

I raised my eyebrows.

'His C.O. in Burma taught him apparently. Wanted a good old English breakfast even though they were in the depths of the jungle, so he taught him. Taught him how to make a damn fine cup of tea, too.'

'Where did you go?'

'Wonderful chaps, the Afs. Some say they can't be taught, but this man's living proof they can. Living proof.'

Later, when we were eating, I said: 'You didn't answer my question.'

'Didn't I? Which one was that?'

'Where did you go? What did you do during the War?'

He finished his mouthful of food slowly and then took a long sip of tea before patting his mouth gently with his napkin and leaning back in his chair.

'I was here. I didn't pass the medical.'

'Oh? Why's that?'

'Heart problem. Small defect, nothing major.' He

laughed. 'No reason for you to look so worried. Just kept me out of the War, that's all.'

'What time do you want to go back?' he called from his bedroom as he got dressed. I was standing looking at a picture in the sitting room and my heart sank at the question. 'I don't want to rush you or anything,' he continued, coming through, straightening his cuffs and trying to put his shoes on at the same time. 'It's just that I have to go out later. Meet some chaps at the Club. I thought I'd drop you back at about nine.'

'Nine it is then,' I said, trying to inject enthusiasm into my words and wondering why he had bothered to ask.

He has a routine and I am not part of that. He will go to the Club, he will phone his wife, he will lunch with friends. He will drive home and Samson will serve dinner. He will have a sherry, smoke a cigarette, read some poetry and then fall asleep. I can be added and subtracted as is necessary, but I am not part of that routine.

Chapter Eleven

15th July, 1947

I haven't seen him for weeks. He has gone back to Salisbury.

20th July, 1947

He's back. Saw him in the office. He smiled, but he also smiled at Wendy Garnett and he asked her how her little boy is. I hate him.

22nd July, 1947

I did a really silly thing today. I phoned him at the Club. The porter said he wasn't in and asked if I would like to leave a message, but of course I couldn't. Well, I could have, but it's best to be as discreet as possible. I phoned again at lunchtime and was told that he was dining and, again, would I like to leave a message and, again, I didn't. I tried two more times and nothing. Eventually he phoned and asked if I had tried to contact him at the Club.

'No,' I answered, trying to sound as surprised as possible. 'I've been out all day. Busy.' I said the last word a little too definitely and it seemed as though my voice was a little high-pitched and I thought now he'll know. He'll definitely know it was me.

3rd August, 1947

He phoned me today and asked if I would like to join him and some friends for dinner at his house. I was apprehensive – his friends? But, of course, he treated me like his niece; I was introduced as such and treated, I feel, with condescending kindness throughout the evening. I will never be put through such an ordeal again!

Annette Truman is an American; she is loud, brash and crude. Although she is fairly stocky, she would be pretty were it not for the square set of her jaw and the way her mouth clamps together like that of a bulldog. She has the sort of dark curly hair that looks as though it has been oiled, and an olive complexion so that one might mistake her as a continental – until she opens her mouth, that is. She enjoys flirting with G., touching his arm, putting her hand on his shoulder, lowering her eyes provocatively when speaking to him and using her little girl voice for doing so.

Paul Truman is also loud. He's a Rhodesian by birth,

but spent about ten years in England at university and then in the War. He's the sort of man who wants to be everyone's friend, who wants to be thought well of by everyone. Ingratiating, that's the word. He thinks he's fun and makes lots of jokes and then laughs loudly. Annette's mouth pulls into a line of irritation when he does this; her lips completely disappear and she resembles a rather annoyed postbox.

He also has a habit of slapping G. on the back, which I can see doesn't always go down too well. He helps himself to the drinks trolley with aplomb and likes to give the impression of being tipsy, although I doubt he is. He thinks it makes him look risqué and exciting.

Samson once again served the most delicious roast pork with apple sauce, roast potatoes, butternut and green beans. There was mushroom soup to start and steamed ginger pudding to follow and then a magnificent selection of cheese and biscuits. I have never seen such a choice in my life!

But it was completely spoilt by the company present. At one point they were talking about the native situation. There has been some discussion recently in the press as to the standard of living provided by the authorities for the natives working in town. The majority of them are men who have to live in men's hostels in the townships. They are charged for what appears to be sub-standard accommodation and they are not allowed to have their wives and families staying with them.

'Well, it suits them down to the ground,' said Paul. 'They have their town umfazis and their kumusha umfazis. It's only do-gooder whites who think this is a terrible thing. The African man loves it, don't you, Samson?' Samson was just clearing the soup bowls when this comment was thrown at him. He didn't say a word, just piled one bowl neatly on top of another, his eyes meeting no one's.

'Paul says they can do it all night,' said Annette, blowing a blue stream of smoke into our midst. I waved it away with my hand. 'The men that is. And they aren't that fussy who they do it with – a couple of umfazis a night should keep them busy.'

G. raised his eyebrows, a smile playing round his lips. He didn't say anything and merely took a sip of his wine.

'These types who want equality between the races have got it all wrong, haven't they?' Paul was addressing G. 'They talk about it, but do they really want it? Do they really want Af children going to school with their children? Do they really want them sharing ablutions, eating at the same restaurants? For God's sake, would you want them at the Club?'

G. still didn't speak. He swilled his glass round and lit a cigarette. He was smiling though, but I thought it was more at Paul's enthusiastic outburst than at what he was saying.

'What is wrong with equality?' I found myself saying suddenly. G.'s eyes moved to me. He was interested in what I had to say. There was a shrug of irritation from Annette who blew out another plume of blue smoke.

'What's wrong?' repeated Paul with vehemence. 'I'll tell you what's wrong, they're not equal. They're not the same as us. It's just not there.' He tapped his head hard with his right forefinger.

285

'That's rather unfair, isn't it?' I said, keeping my voice steady and calm.

'Life's unfair. A survival of the fittest. We should know all about that, we're in Africa for God's sake!'

Suddenly G. spoke. 'Evie wouldn't know anything about Africa. She wants straight roads and flowerbeds and parks. Not wild animals.'

I felt his words as a reproach. He was still smiling though, looking at me intently, his eyes narrowing when he blew out cigarette smoke.

'I never...' I started and then stopped. Annette was staring at me with sly curiosity.

'Wait till you've been here a couple of years, dear. You'll change your mind soon enough.' She turned away, bored.

But G. continued. 'Evie's not the type to do anything adventurous. Not the type to travel without maps.' I stared at him, his mouth was widening into a red grin. 'Not like you, Annette. Do you know when Annette came here she hadn't even seen a map of Africa, didn't know where it was or what it looked like?'

Annette beamed in his praise and put another cigarette in her holder. She leaned across to G. who lit it for her.

'And that makes her adventurous, does it, being ignorant?'

She snapped me a look. Under the table, G. put his hand on my leg. I moved it. It made him smile more.

No one was listening to Paul who had launched back on to the subject of the native situation.

'I mean life's unfair, it's just unfair. Eat or be eaten.'

The last comment didn't seem to quite fit his

argument, but I didn't feel it worth arguing with his type.

'During the War,' he continued, 'there was a family here with five boys. Four of them went off to the War. All dead.' He banged the flat of his hand on the table, making the silverware jump. 'The powers that be decreed that number five stay here so at least the parents would have one surviving son. What happens? He's stationed at Thornhill air base, he's a flying instructor and one day he takes the plane up and there's engine trouble. Crash, he's dead.' He brought his forefinger down hard on the table and again everything jumped. 'Life-is-unfair.'

'That's a sad story,' I replied, 'but it hardly bears any relation to the situation of native people in Rhodesia.'

Paul gave a great sigh of irritation and rolled his eyes. 'Bears hardly any relation? For God's sake...'

'Shut up, Paul,' said Annette suddenly, but it wasn't for my benefit; she was bored and needed a change of conversation. She stood up and went over to the gramophone. She put a new record on to play without looking at what it was. It was jazzy and far too fast for dinner.

'Jazz is black man's music,' I said, my voice edging on anger.

She rolled her eyes and looked over at G.

'Your niece is far too serious for her young age,' she drawled, coming back to the table. 'She needs to go and have some fun.'

'Exactly what I told her,' said G., although he has told me nothing of the sort. 'Find herself a nice fella.'

Annette smirked and knocked back the rest of her drink.

287

'Get me another, honey, won't you?' She swung her glass provocatively in G.'s face. He took it from her and stood up.

'Excuse me,' I said, pushing back my chair. 'I just need some fresh air.'

The cool night air was welcome relief from the smoky dinner table. The shrill of crickets was comforting, as were the scents that reached me from the flowerbeds. It is such a beautiful time of year here, spring: the smell of dust and pollen is overwhelming. I walked round the garden for a while, not wishing to go back inside. Part of me wanted to walk out the gate, down the road and back to Mrs Wiesman's. Another part, that oh, so practical part, thought better of it.

I walked round the back to the vegetable garden and for a time wandered down each row of beetroot, lettuce, tomatoes, onions, carrots – the list is endless. The earth smelled damp and warm. I imagined everything growing silently in the darkness, spreading roots out, rather like treading water, but in earth, and floating lazily in each bed.

It was then that I noticed that the back door was open; light fell in a pool on the path. Someone was sitting in the doorway: it was Samson. He was sitting on a small stool polishing G.'s shoes. He didn't say anything. All I heard was the sound of brushing.

'Good evening, Samson,' I said, my voice loud on the still evening air. From the house I could hear the gramophone start again; another jazzy tune.

'Good evening, Madam,' he replied, but I don't think he looked up.

'Lovely evening,' I continued. What a very British thing to say. How many evenings like this has Samson experienced in his life, I wonder? I didn't take his absence of an answer as insolence. I don't think he sees me as someone he is entitled to converse with. Perhaps he finds it odd that any white woman would talk to him at all. I realised that Samson must've taken the coffee into the sitting room already or he would not be here polishing shoes.

'Is that you finished for the evening, Samson?'

There was a pause. 'Sorry, Madam?'

'You are finished?'

'Yes, Madam.'

'You must be relieved. Another day's work over.'

The brushing continued. 'Ah, no, Madam.'

I couldn't think of anything else to say to him, but he suddenly seemed the only person I wanted to speak to.

'You went to the War, the master tells me?' I immediately regretted such a question. It moved right away from conventional niceties onto something much deeper. What could he say? Yes, I had a wonderful time? Many people were killed? What a relief it's all over and we're now back to normal?

The brushing stopped momentarily and then resumed.

'Yes, Madam, I went to the War.' His voice was low and serious, but not sad.

Again, I was at a loss for anything to say. I stood for a while, looking out into the garden, looking up at the great expanse of sky and stars and suddenly I thought one day I will be dead and none of this will matter. This evening, the Trumans, G., the roast pork with apple *sauce, even Samson cleaning shoes in the darkness will mean nothing. No one will know, no one will remember.*

'Burma,' Samson said suddenly. 'I went to Burma with the King's African Rifles.'

I still didn't know what to say and fought to find appropriate words.

'It must've been quite an experience.'

'Yes, Madam.'

Again there was a pause and then: 'It was good, very good. And when I came back home, they gave me a bicycle.'

'A bicycle?'

'Yes, Madam, for active service. Every native soldier gets a bicycle.'

There was silence again.

'One day you must teach me how to cook.'

The brushing stopped and I detected a half laugh in the darkness.

'Ah, no, you must know how to cook better than me.'

'No, I don't. Unless it's beans on toast.' *I gave a short laugh, but there was nothing in response.* 'My mother,' *I explained*, 'never wanted me to cook in case I wasted the rations.' *I wondered if my words were lost on him.*

'Yes, Madam.'

Suddenly someone burst into the kitchen and opened the drawers of the dresser with great noise. It was Annette.

'Hey, Samson, where're the glasses? We're having champagne! Champers.'

She swung her head out of the back door, glasses in hand. Samson was on his feet in seconds. He moved the stool back for her. She caught sight of me in the darkness.

'Oh, God, there you are! I told the others you must have gone home. Samson, buya lapha!*' She danced inside again, Samson following, his khaki uniform, just a little too short over the ankles.*

Chapter Twelve

August, 1947

We had the most terrible row this afternoon. Last night, when Paul and Annette were leaving, Paul asked if they could give me a lift home and I said yes and jumped up, perhaps a little too quickly, and grabbed my handbag. G. was looking at me with mild surprise and Annette looked at him and then back at me and smiled slyly. She is such an open book, or maybe that look of sly suspicion is natural.

They dropped me back here rather late, but Mrs Wiesman had given me a key to the door before I left; she says she trusts me enough to give it to me, but I feel she only gave it to me because she doesn't trust me at all. Annette barely said goodnight. Her eyes were closed and she was lying back in the seat. Paul's sense of chauvinism sprung to life again and he insisted on walking me to the front door, although I said quite vehemently that he didn't have to. He wanted to kiss me, but I turned my cheek just as he leaned over and he got my ear instead. His breath was thick with alcohol. He squeezed my hand, too, and said that he hoped to see me soon. As long as I don't mention the natives, I thought!

Then today, G. came over. He was over-exuberant at first: he talked too loudly to Mrs Wiesman, his laugh a bellow in the small sitting room and she kept looking over at me and trying to read my face. He said he would like to take me out for an ice cream, but I said Audrey was expecting me to help her cut out a dress that afternoon, in about half an hour's time to be precise, so we didn't have enough time.

I could see he was taken aback. He is not used to me resisting him. He suggested a walk and, although I raised a weary eyebrow to show I didn't think much of his idea, I couldn't think of a suitable excuse not to.

We walked a little down the road; it was hot for it was only two-thirty and the heat has not lost its edge at that time. The wind caught the dust in light, orange swirls; everywhere there was an airiness, a lightness, almost as though you could run and leap and fly in one swift motion. But I did not feel light. I waited for some sort of apology, an explanation at least for last night's behaviour, but there was nothing, only this exaggerated jollity, his attempt I think to make me feel I imagined the whole thing, to make me feel I am too serious; that he meant nothing by ridiculing me in front of his friends.

I said little. At the end of the road, we turned to go back the way we had come. I knew he was aware that soon we would approach the boarding house and our conversation would come to an end. He stopped suddenly, but I walked on a couple of paces before turning round to face him.

'Do you know what you need?' he said, as though some great idea had just occurred to him.

'What's that?' My voice was flat and bored.

'Your own house, a flat at least. You don't need Mrs Wiesman and her boarding house rules.'

If he was expecting a reaction, it was delayed.

'I like where I am, thank you.'

'You don't!'

'I do, thank you.'

He opened his mouth as if to say something and then shut it again with something of a smile.

'I could arrange something, somewhere for you to live. On your own.'

A stab of anger made my eyes smart with tears. My throat was taut and my words came out strangely strangled.

'I don't need you, thank you.'

The smile disappeared and he reached for my hand, but I pulled it back, turned and ran the rest of the way back here. I closed and locked the door and then ran upstairs to my room, no longer able to keep back the tears.

Later

At about four o'clock, he came back. Mrs Wiesman was out. He grabbed my hand when I opened the door and led me to his car. I felt acutely conscious of such an action and wondered whether we were being watched by *anyone. We drove back to his house, neither of us saying a word. Tea was waiting on the verandah, tea and a huge chocolate cake. Before I was allowed to sit, he dashed into the garden and picked a sprig of jasmine from the hedge. Its smell was deep and rich. He put it between my hands, clasping them together with something like an element of desperation.*

'Don't ever leave me, Evie,' he said and then he drew me nearer until he was holding my shoulders, like they do in the movies and I had the briefest of inclinations to throw my head back as though I was in some terrible swoon, because of course I was. I thought he would say it then: I love you. I love you, Evie. But he didn't, not so obviously, although I knew what he meant. 'I'm sorry,' he said finally. 'Forgive me, I was such a fool.'

Tonight I opened my bedroom window the furthest it would go and leaned outside.

The night air was deliciously warm and voices floated out from other rooms. I tied the jasmine to the curtain, but all I could smell was HIS smell, that wonderful smell of him that is not an aftershave or cologne, but something that just can't be bottled or defined. How I love it. I love it when it is all over me and I can't think of anything else.

15th October, 1947

The heat is crippling. I wake before dawn and sit watching the sun rise. This is the coolest part of the day, but it does not last long. Every day the sky is blue, but even that is soon burnt out of it, leaving it painfully white, devoid of colour as I am devoid of energy. Suicide month is what they call it here.

I have told G. that we must end this relationship. It is going nowhere. We will get found out sooner or later. I would have to leave and he would probably lose his job.

'I don't want to leave her,' he said.

'I didn't say you did,' I replied, reeling at the impact of his words. So honest, so brutally honest.

'There are so many things I still want to do with her,' he continued, not listening to me.

'Do with her?'

He had his head in his hands, his fingers clasped round the back of his neck. There was a silence. He didn't answer my question. I lit a cigarette. It gives me confidence to smoke when I don't know what to say.

'Have you ever been unfaithful before?' I asked suddenly, although I didn't want to know if he had or not. My voice was oddly detached as though I were a psychiatrist asking her patient a question, and I would note down the answer and file it away after he had left. He sat up and sighed, closing his eyes.

'Yes.'

It was the answer I dreaded. I took another drag of the cigarette.

'How many times?'

He shrugged. I was smarting with pain, but I said nothing. The heel of my shoe had dropped from my foot and I concentrated on flicking it up and down, up and down, finding the rhythm some comfort.

'Does she know?'

'Yes.'

'About all of them?'

He thought for a second. 'Yes, all of them.'

'Are you going to tell her about us?'

His face creased into a sad frown.

'Evie, you're... different.'

I tapped ash on the verandah floor, even though there was an ashtray next to me. He could at least be original.

'Who were the others?' I strained to keep the note of detachment in my voice.

He shrugged irritably. 'I don't know. Women!'

'I should hope so.'

'Ah,' he covered his face with his hands, 'they were just women.'

'Just women?'

'Look, Evie, they lasted one, two weeks at the most. A bit of fun, nothing serious.'

He reached for my hand. I didn't move it away, but nor did I give it to him. With my other hand I threw my lit cigarette butt in the flowerbed, something I know G. detests. He sighed and took his hand away and we sat again in silence.

'She's all right with all of this, your wife?'

'No, she's not all right with it, but she puts up with it.' Then, as by way of explanation. 'She loves me.'

I rolled my eyes.

'She does. Look, we have a friendship that is stronger than any relationship.' He made relationship sound superficial, trivial in comparison. 'The friendship came first.'

'And our relationship can never compete with this, this

friendship, can it?'

He paused. His shoulders drooped. 'It's different.'

I turned away, but this time he moved squarely in front of me. 'Evie, you're different. I've never,' he paused, searching for the right words. 'I've never felt this way about anyone.' He ran his fingers through my hair, his hand dropping to my shoulder. 'Don't leave me.'

'What's the point?' I exclaimed, becoming suddenly animated with anger. 'What's-the-point?'

He sank back into his chair in defeat. My hands fumbled for another cigarette, but the packet was empty.

'You're right,' he said suddenly, and then more quietly: 'You're right.'

His smile was bright and forced when he at last turned to me again.

'I've been unfair. We need to end this, you're right.'

My stomach was tight with pain and thunder was roaring in my ears as I tried to maintain control. I pushed my nails into my palms.

'It's best,' I tried to say, but my eyes were already blurring with tears.

*

'There's an email from Mark,' my mother said as I came into the kitchen.

'Anyone else?'

'A couple of condolence messages. No one sends cards any more, do they?' She was hunting in the cupboard for a packet of teabags.

'Not in Zim,' I said, sitting down at the table. 'No one

sends Christmas cards in Zim.'

'Sad.' she said, pulling open a foil packet and taking a couple of teabags out. The kettle was just coming to the boil.

'What about Uncle Wally?' I said suddenly. 'Have you told him? Did you write?'

My mother's face creased into a sad frown as she poured the boiling water over the teabags.

'I don't know what to do about that one. I've thought about it. But he's so old. Would it be too much for him? Murder... I mean...' She stirred the tea slowly, the heat rising in little wisps.

'But surely he needs to know.'

'Well, that's what I mean. Does he? Does he need to know? I don't know how much contact they've had over the past ten or so years. She never mentioned him to me.'

'Perhaps he's dead,' I suggested.

'Perhaps.' The idea startled her, but then she said, 'No, Mum would've told me. Someone would've told her.'

'Perhaps they thought it would be too much for her.'

I wasn't being sarcastic, but she looked quickly at me then as though she thought I was.

There was a silence as we drank our tea. She stared off into the distance, her face still puffy with grief and lack of sleep, her greying hair pulled back into a loose, untidy ponytail.

'It's so easy to lose touch, isn't it? Even with your own family. So easy.'

Chapter Thirteen

Leonard Rogers, my Grandad, was new to Stoughton and James in late 1947. A builder, not an architect. Handsome in a conventional sort of way, wrote Gran. Self-consciously good-looking, the type of man who catches his reflection every so often in mirrors and shop windows and smoothes back his hair with a lick of his hand; the kind of man who knows what position best displays his good looks and frequently adopts that pose in the company of women. He is not the sort of man I find attractive, but there is this rather appealing little boy shyness to him that I find quite a relief after G. He is upfront, honest, has yet to learn the subtleties of flirting and yet, too, he has not learnt to manipulate or deceive.

They went to a Christmas ball together, although on New Year's Eve she stayed by herself in the boarding house while everyone else went out. Leonard had begged her to go with him to the dance at the City Hall, but she refused, citing a personal engagement made 'months ago'. Alone, she cried. G. was in Salisbury for Christmas and New

Year. There was even a suggestion that his work in Bulawayo was coming to an end. I looked at the letters again. I am full of the grief of losing someone, of not being able to explain what this is inside of me. Early in 1948, G. returned to Bulawayo.

8th January, 1948

He's going to leave her. He came to see me today – G. did! He looks older, although perhaps he is just more serious. Mrs Wiesman was surprised to see him and made an excuse to leave the sitting room soon after he arrived. She shut the door behind her, something she never does. We talked: the usual formalities. Questions that lead neither here nor there. I sat on a single chair, while he sat on the sofa, his hat in his hands.

'I'll leave her,' he said quite suddenly, as though he were answering a question I had asked him. I didn't say anything.

'I've thought a lot about this.' His voice had an air of finality as though he wanted me to stand up there and then and walk out the door with him, no questions asked. He hadn't been looking at me, but now he raised his eyes and looked for my reaction.

'What about your job?' I ventured. 'Reputation?'

He waved away my words with a shrug, but I could tell he was worried about that side of things. 'I won't be the first person to have ever got divorced.'

We both knew that wasn't the problem.

'And...? Your wife?'

He looked down again and then cleared his throat.

'It's going to be hard on her, but I'll make sure she's well provided for.'

'You've told her?'

'Not yet.'

'Not yet,' I repeated, hearing the words roll slowly off my tongue.

'It's going to be a difficult time. Are you prepared for that? People may talk...' I gave a cynical inward laugh. How many times have I suggested to him that people know and he has never believed me.

'Will we stay here?' I ventured again.

'Let's see how things go. If we can weather the storm. Perhaps the Union...'

I felt a surge of excitement, but kept calm.

'When?'

He shook his head a little too quickly. 'Not sure.'

'Not sure?' My heart was like a child's balloon that is blown up, but the neck not tied, and then let go of, so that it flies stupidly around the room, knocking into objects and people and then lies motionless on the floor.

'Soon.'

I didn't dare ask anymore. He stood up then and came over to me. Kneeling at my feet, he took both my hands and kissed them.

'I think it can work, Evie,' he said. And I kissed him back.

28th January, 1948

Samson has been giving me cookery lessons. I go there when work finishes early at three o'clock on a Thursday. At first, he was rather reluctant; he laughed, then he was bashful and then slightly diffident, as though he was offended in some way. But G. spoke to him and he gave in, conceding defeat.

Everything was ready for me when I arrived for my first lesson. He had a freshly ironed and folded apron waiting for me on the table. There was a large mixing bowl, a wooden spoon, a metal spoon, a knife, two teaspoons, a plate and a scale all lined up along one side of the table. Down the other was a line of various tins: sugar, flour, baking powder and a jar of strawberry jam. A yellow cake of butter lay on a plate next to some eggs.

'We are going to make a cake,' he said as he tied his apron firmly round his waist. I followed suit, impressed by his air of authority, although he was obviously nervous.

'Right, where do I start?' I said when I had washed and dried my hands and tied my apron on. I noticed that he had already switched the oven on and he had greased the baking tins. At first, I thought, perhaps he thinks me above this sort of task. But I was wrong. I was relegated to the tasks of weighing out ingredients – Samson told me all the weights for he doesn't use recipes at all – sieving the flour, breaking the eggs into a bowl – but not beating them! He beat, he whisked, he poured, he mixed and finally he baked a delicious Victoria sponge.

G. said it was delicious, better than ever, although I

told him that all I really did was weigh out the ingredients.

'Well then, Samson's been getting it wrong all this time!' He winked and gave me a kiss.

But I wanted to do it myself. I begged Samson the next time.

'I watched you, I know how to do it.'

He sucked his lips in and sighed.

'You concentrate on the supper,' I said, nodding over at a hunk of beef on the draining board, waiting to be cut up. 'Just let me try. Let me show you.'

It was a flop. I saw Samson's eyes dart over every now and then and once or twice he seemed about to say something, but stopped and went back to chopping up onions or peeling potatoes.

By the time G. came home, the sponge had been cut up and put in a trifle.

I could barely look Samson in the eye at first. Then I wailed: 'What happened? Why?'

Samson pulled a chair out and gestured for me to sit down.

'It is important that a woman can cook for her husband, isn't?'

I nodded, aware of his particular use of words.

'Why?' It was a question he wasn't looking for me to answer. 'Because the woman must show love.'

'And the man...?' I started but he held up a finger of admonition.

'The woman must show love, the man receives love.'

'But...?'

'No. This is the way it is. The man provides the food,

304

the woman cooks it to show her appreciation. To show her...' Here he paused, waiting for me to say in unison with him the word 'love', but I didn't. He completed the sentence on his own. He grabbed the unwashed mixing bowl from beside the sink, the wooden spoon still in it, and began to beat an imaginary mixture. He did this slowly but firmly, making a show of holding up the spoon, watching the mixture drop slowly, scooping it up again, smiling in satisfaction at the texture, its smoothness, its elasticity, its surrender to him.

'I'm sure I did all that,' I said with a laugh.

'No. No, you didn't use this.' He tapped his chest and I frowned. 'Love,' he explained. 'You used this.' He tapped his head. 'I see you, you are thinking about the time, you look at the clock, you think he is coming back now and you want it to be ready. So you go like this,' – he made an exaggerated hurried movement in the bowl with the spoon – 'you don't spoon the mixture into the tin, you scrape. You lick your fingers,' – I looked up questioningly – 'never lick your fingers. This is not for you, it is for him.'

'This man who taught you how to cook, Samson, your C.O. in Burma, he told you that did he, about love?'

Samson paused and looked down. He placed the bowl back on the draining board and turned back to the dinner he was preparing.

Over a couple of months, Gran became a successful cook and baker: chocolate cakes, swiss rolls, fruit loafs, buns, biscuits, doughnuts, scones. She ventured into soups and desserts and then into main courses: roasts, soufflés, stews, pies. But her real forte, it seemed, were cakes, especially Victoria sponge. Samson would stand by her side, urging her on, 'Whisk faster!' or 'More, more!' as he made the motion of beating with his hands. Gran was exhausted by the end of the afternoon, and sometimes it was only G. who took a slice of the warm, golden cake. 'You see?' Samson once asked her as they stood at the doorway of the verandah, watching him eat, G. oblivious to their presence, 'It's not for you. You see?'

For Gran, the period was one of excitement. Her culinary journeys brought her a sense of completeness that hadn't been there before. I feel like I have grown up at last, she wrote. They also brought her closer and closer to G. He came to expect her there once a week in the late afternoon, waiting, the table set, with cups and saucers arranged, fat slices of cake cut, the thick red jam oozing out. Or sandwiches might be placed on a platter, decorated with slivers of lettuce, or buns heaped on a plate, biscuits piled prettily in a pyramid. They would sit and talk as the sun set and the heat lifted and the cool of evening crept in.

If Gran stayed for dinner, they would have a sundowner, always a gin and tonic with a slice of lemon, and wine at the table. Samson was as proud of her as she was of herself, wheeling her achievements in with a certain flourish, presenting them to G. as if to say she loves you. This one, she loves you.

Chapter Fourteen

17ᵗʰ March, 1948

The most embarrassing thing happened today. At lunchtime I went for a stroll in the park and saw the most beautiful deep pink geranium I have ever seen. I know G. has nothing like it in his garden so I took a cutting and wrapped it in my handkerchief. After work I wandered over to his house, hoping to surprise him with it.

I walked in the gate and onto the verandah, all the time looking down at the flower in my hand. I was just about to open the door when my eye caught some movement to the side of the house. I looked up and there she was: Riette. And not just her, but Annette as well. They were standing together in that shared attitude of interest and concern that women have when they discuss gardening matters, but they had obviously seen me arrive and were both looking across. I started and drew my hand back from the handle: such familiarity is hardly going to keep me from suspicion. Annette said something to Riette and then turned her back to me. She was smoking a cigarette.

Riette came towards me, but she did not raise her hand in a wave or smile. I could have been a delivery boy or a messenger for all the signs of welcome she gave me.

'Hello!' I said with perhaps a little too much gusto in my voice. I could see she noticed it too, and replied with an equal lack of enthusiasm.

'Evelyn.' It was a statement, rather than a greeting. Perhaps she was merely confirming some suspicion she had.

'I didn't know you were here,' I said, trying to sound bright, but sounding instead rather strained and high-pitched. I immediately regretted my statement because what was I doing there if I didn't expect her there? 'I mean,' I tried to say everything in one flow but it came out rushed and nervous. 'I mean, I didn't know you were here until I was told. He... your husband... he told me you were here and I should pop in and say hello.' And then, as if this needed qualification: 'See how you are.'

'How nice,' she replied, although there was nothing in her voice or in her attitude to support this statement. She looked down at the flower in my hand.

'Geranium,' I said, again too brightly.

'I know.'

'I brought it for you.'

A queer smile, if it can be called that, flickered across her face then, pulling the corners of her mouth backwards briefly. But it wasn't a smile of appreciation; she was laughing at me.

'Oh, it's a cutting is it?' she said, peering over the

verandah wall at my hands.

'Yes.' She made no attempt to take it and I made no attempt to give it to her. 'Have you got a glass? I should put it in some water.'

She nodded inside the house.

'Samson will find you something.' She began to turn away back to the garden. 'Will you stay for tea? Annette is.'

I made a show of glancing at my watch. 'I have to get back,' I said.

'Perhaps some other time.'

'Yes, that would be lovely.' My hand was on the door handle as I spoke. 'I'll just take this inside.'

Everything seemed oddly alien inside the house, as though I was a thief, somebody coming to break in and steal something. The sofa and chairs in the sitting room, the brass bowl on the coffee table, even the pictures, many of them framed maps, on the walls, all seemed out of place. As I passed G.'s study, the door was closed: is this the only room in the house in which I exist? Hidden away to be taken out and pored over, lovingly explored and enjoyed, but ultimately to be put back on a shelf.

The kettle was just boiling as I entered the kitchen. Samson lifted it and poured the water into the huge teapot. A Victoria sponge stood on a stand, neatly sliced and sprinkled with icing sugar.

Samson looked up, his eyes briefly registering the situation, but he said nothing. Why does this continue to surprise me? Surely I don't expect him to comment on my affair with his master?

I showed him the geranium and he lifted a small glass

down from the shelf and filled it with water.

'Thank you, Samson,' I said with the same forced brightness I had used with Riette.

'I will tell him,' he said, without looking at me, 'I will tell the baas it is from you.'

I could have taken this further, I know. Left a message, something that conveyed another meaning. But instead I said too loudly and too cheerily: 'Goodbye!' I tried not to sound like an intruder, a conspirator, someone who destroys what is good and takes what they believe is theirs. I wanted, I want, to be normal, to be just me, Evelyn Saunders, putting a geranium cutting in water. A geranium cutting that I had brought for her, not him. I wanted Samson to be a domestic, a cook, a face that fades in and out of the background, not a co-conspirator, an aide in this terrible mission. I wanted to be able to walk out of the house and be thinking of friends I would go and see, a young man I was in love with, whom I would marry and bear children for. I wanted to be thinking of cooking and baking and taking up the hem of my dress. And then it suddenly occurred to me, as Samson stirred the teapot slowly and curls of steam peeled off and rose into the air, that everything I like, she probably likes as well. I can point to nothing and say this is mine, this is mine.

Chapter Fifteen

Two weeks after Gran's funeral, my mother received a letter from the firm of lawyers that Gran dealt with, asking her to make an appointment with regards to the reading of her will.

'You do it,' she said to me, passing me the letter one lunchtime as we sat in the kitchen drinking tea. Mom had begun to get up more, at least for the first half of the day.

I made an appointment for the next day, wondering how much Gran had to leave anybody; she had never been a well-off woman. A Mr Mpofu showed me into his office. He was a thickset man with a bald head and a jolly, laughing face. I imagined Gran enjoyed dealing with him. His office was large and comfortable with pictures of Victorian London on the wall. There was a filing cabinet behind his desk on top of which was a vase of artificial flowers and a school photograph of a little boy. His cell phone, which he kept glancing at throughout our discussion, as though it had rung silently and he had missed a call, he kept near his right hand.

'Now let's see,' said Mr Mpofu, smiling as he read through the will before summarising it to me, '"All my jewellery is to be left to my daughter, Frances McIntyre."' I nodded, not expecting very much else. '"My house, 52 Lawson Road, Suburbs, and all its contents I leave to my granddaughter, Ellie McIntyre." And that's it. There's only one provision that the garden is maintained in the manner in which she kept it and no alterations are to be made to the house itself.'

'The house?' I said, feeling that there must be some mistake. 'She can't leave it to me. She didn't own it... did she?'

'Yes, she did,' smiled Mr Mpofu, leaning back in his chair, one roll of fat easing up above his collar. 'She bought it when she moved in, about what, fifteen, sixteen years ago.'

He was watching my face. What did he know? I thought. What was it that everyone seemed to know that I didn't?

'How? She worked at Haddon and Sly. She never had any money. How did she buy it?'

Mr Mpofu shrugged, his mouth drawing up into an upside down smile. Then his face creased into an answer as he remembered something.

'If I remember correctly,' he said slowly, 'she didn't actually buy it.'

'Which means?'

'She was given it.'

'Given it?'

'Yes, someone in the UK gave it to her. I remember now. An uncle, I think it was that she told me.'

'An uncle... You don't happen to know his name do you?'

'I have the title deeds,' he said, looking through some papers. 'Let's see... Title Deeds for 52 Lawson Road, Suburbs... Cadwallader Lloyd. He used to own the house and he gave it to your grandmother when she moved in.'

'Cadwallader... used to own it... wait...' Wait, wait, wait, I wanted to scream. Just hang on here a moment. Let me just absorb all of this. '52... of course,' I breathed, gaining me a concerned look from Mr Mpofu. 'Of course, of course...'

*

4th April, 1948

G. came home early today. There was a huge thunder-storm and I wasn't baking because the electricity had gone. I was in the lounge, cutting out a sewing pattern, sitting cross-legged, a position that pulled my dress up mid-thigh. They, my legs, were smooth and brown and the red flowers on my dress picked up on their warmth. Whenever I looked at them, I felt a little more in love – with their strength, their youth, the tone of their muscles, their silky feel. And, too, with the sun that has browned them, the roads that have toughened them, the hands that have run along them.

I heard footsteps on the verandah and someone tried the door handle, but it was locked. I rose and opened it, hoping it was him, half knowing it was. It was. Without a raincoat, with only his hat for protection from the rain. His shirt and trousers were sopping wet, but he laughed as he stepped over the threshold.

'Why's it locked?' he asked, taking off his shoes and his jacket and giving me a big kiss.

'You never know who will turn up unexpectedly.'

He laughed and took me by the shoulders.

'No more,' he laughed, pushing me back onto the wall,

smoothing my face with his hand. 'We're going.'
I couldn't speak, couldn't say a word.
'Beira,' he said, kissing me. 'Are you coming?'

10ᵗʰ April, 1948

*As I write this, the train is whizzing into the night. I am
so excited, so in love. Every step of the way I thought
something would go wrong. Someone would notice the
way we have been behaving; someone would find the
tickets. I was even afraid of someone drawing conclu-
sions from the new blouse I bought! I felt as though it had
Beira written all over it! I've been afraid of smiling too
much and have tried my best to appear rather grim for
the past week. Once they discover my disappearance,
they'll probably go looking for a body!*

*I lie here and feel the movement of the train, the judder
and grind of the wheels carrying me away. G. will be
there to meet me. It's hard to imagine us walking around
like any other couple, arm in arm.*

14ᵗʰ April, 1948

*Spent the day at the beach. G. took photos. We are staying
in a beautiful hotel called The Grand. The balcony of our
room overlooks the sea. I have longed for it all these years.
Some part of me can't help but feel I have come home.*

Two weeks later, she married my grandfather.

*

'Someone phoned,' said my mother when I got home. 'Said he was Miles's nephew. Something about books. He's going to phone back later.'

'Books?' I repeated with a shrug. 'Maybe he wants to know what to do with all that trash Miles used to read.'

'He surprised me once,' said my mother. She was wiping the kitchen counter with a damp cloth, pushing it gently round in circles. 'He quoted something from Shakespeare, oh, I can't remember quite what now, King Lear, I think. And I said, 'Oh, so you've read it?' And he said, 'I've read all of them.' I suppose he thought I was being patronising, but I wasn't, I was just surprised. He was actually fairly well educated – I think. He didn't seem like that, but he was. He knew a lot of Shakespeare.'

'A lot of people quote from Shakespeare and don't even know they're doing it.'

'Do they?'

'Out damned spot.'

'I know that one.'

'Neither a borrower nor a lender be, that's Shakespeare.'

'Is it? I never knew.'

'Hamlet. You see.'

'There's that other one isn't there, from Hamlet? What's it now? Each man kills the thing he loves, that's it isn't it?'

'That's Oscar Wilde.'

'Oh, is it? It sounds Shakespearean somehow. My mother used to say that often.' She stopped and thought. 'I wonder what she meant.'

Chapter Sixteen

20th January, 1949

G. came to visit me this morning. He never said anything, but sat and held my hand as I lay in the white hospital room. The blankets were tucked in tightly and I could not raise myself to kiss him. He looked down at my hands, the sadness of it all written deep into his face. He used to say that my face was easy to read, that it spoke for my heart and mind. But today I spoke endlessly and mindlessly of bright, trivial things and tried to ignore the roar in my ears and the stabbing pain in my chest that ripped deeper the longer he was there. And it was his face that was full of sorrow.

'He's mine, isn't he?' he said as he held my hand, pressing it softy between his.

I shook my head. 'No.' My voice was thin and raspy. I tried to smile. 'He's Leonard's. Of course he's Leonard's.'

He nodded sadly. He had brought me a small arrangement of yellow roses, picked, he said, from his garden. I do not know how long he sat there, not saying anything, just holding my hand, turning it over, pressing it deeply. Eventually he left. He kissed my hand and left. I am alone.

*

Miles's nephew rang again. His voice held the warmth of a cricket player, a good all-rounder, 'a dependable chap', someone who could be called upon at any time to help a friend in need, guard the wicket or even sell off his uncle's belongings. He said he had something I might want to keep, something he felt he couldn't throw out or store away; something he thought I should have.

'Would you like to have dinner with me tonight?' he asked, quite out of the blue and I was momentarily lost for words. 'No' floated around somewhere, but I couldn't quite grasp hold of it and for a second or two I faltered.

'We're almost related,' he joked, 'and I've so few relations that I wouldn't mind adopting one more. Besides, I can make a really good lasagna,' he said, his smile oozing through the words.

'Um, OK,' I agreed, without much enthusiasm.

He gave a short, sharp laugh and I detected a slightly offended note in his voice. 'You don't have to.'

'What time?'

'Seven.'

'OK. Where do you live?'

I wrote down the address, folded it up and slipped it in the back pocket of my jeans.

'Don't forget.'

'I won't.'

'Make it six thirty,' he said suddenly. 'Pre-dinner drinks,' he said by way of explanation and then, in another voice, like a colonial aristocrat, 'Sundowners on the verandah as the natives come in from the fields.'

He was not a big man, taller than me, not thin, but not very well built either. He had brown hair cut very short and very deep dark blue eyes. Good looking? Yes, in a conventional way. A Nice Person. Likes to tell jokes, but not dirty ones. Sensitive. The kind of guy a girl can talk to, watch the odd soppy film with, depend on for deliveries of flowers: the New Man, Zimbabwean style. He lived in a townhouse in Famona, in a complex with some Spanish name, like Santa Fé or Santa Monica, one of those sort of names that is a popular choice for townhouse complexes, but has little to do with Famona or Bulawayo or Africa.

He appeared to be a collector of colonial and African art, for there were some prints of Bulawayo circa 1910 on the walls of the lounge and two African masks lay on a table as though he intended to put them up at some point. There was a Tonga stool and various carvings and a reed mat near the fireplace. On top of a small carved table were various examples of Rhodesian literature: *Great Places Washed With Sun*, *Rhodes: the Man* and *Gold Paved the Way*. I couldn't help feeling they were as much objects as the wooden masks.

'Nice place,' I said to him as I sipped a gin and tonic and watched him cook.

'This?' He looked about, as though seeing it for the first time and shrugged. 'Not bad. I haven't had a lot of time to do much to it. I've been in Zambia for the past three years

318

and before that I was in Harare – that's where I grew up – so Bulawayo's kind of new to me.'

'Why d'you move?'

'Oh, this and that.' He poured a thick white béchamel sauce over the sheets of lasagna, licking a drop off his fingers before wiping them on his apron. 'Em, excuse me, licking my fingers. You develop bad manners living on your own.'

'I know.' He looked up at me quickly and then put the pot in the sink.

'Why'd I move? Let's see. Job fell through, girlfriend left and, quite frankly, I didn't like the natives.' He laughed. 'All true, except for the last part.'

'What do you do now?' I ignored the prompt to ask about his girlfriend, hoping he wasn't one of those who indulge in exchanged sob stories as a way of chatting up women.

'Nothing, actually.' He put the lasagna in the oven and turned the timer on. 'Can't live without one of these,' he said, nodding towards it. 'It's a male thing, I suppose. I'd just forget it otherwise and have another beer. Which reminds me...' He went to the fridge and pulled out a Castle. 'Another drink?'

I shook my head and lifted my glass to show it was still more than half full.

'You'll have to do better than that,' he said in mock horror.

'I don't drink fast.'

'Cheap night out.'

He took a swig of his beer and looked over at the table, which he had set earlier. 'We're missing a spoon,' he said and rummaged through a drawer. 'Fact is, I moved to Bulawayo to have a new start, different perspective you

could call it. Ah, found one. Spoon, that is, not perspective.'
He placed the spoon on the table after giving it a quick shine
with his apron. 'I'd always thought of it as this slow olde
worlde type of place. I came here once as a child with my
dad to visit Uncle Miles and he took us out one morning
somewhere or other. It was early and we stopped at a
junction and had to wait for about three cars before we could
go and I remember Miles shaking his head in disbelief at the
traffic.' He laughed, but I detected a sorrow somewhere at
the thought of Miles. 'He was a cranky old bugger – well,
you would probably know better than me.' He stopped, as
though he waited for me to say something, contradict him
maybe, do the polite thing and insist Miles was nothing of
the sort.

'Cranky old bugger sounds right.'

He smiled. 'He's actually my great uncle, my dad's uncle.
It was just him and my grandfather and then my grandfather
died. Miles never married and I'm an only child so he was
the last remaining relative, besides my dad, of course, but he
lives in Australia and I'm here, so I'm It.'

'You're an only child, too?'

'Snap.'

'Where's your mom?'

'Dead.' He threw a spoon into the sink with a clatter.
'Committed suicide when I was four.'

The picture I carry in my memory of that evening is very
clear. When I think of it, it unrolls like a film reel in my
mind, each still entire and seemingly independently perfect,
yet needing what came before and what followed to give it
meaning and completeness.

Behind him at the dinner table I see his shelves of books and a collection of videos near the television. I tried to read some of the titles, but he was constantly aware of my eyes, of where they were looking. I didn't want to give the impression that I was interested in what he read and watched. I knew he was looking for that sign of recognition in my eyes, recognition that is of a shared interest, common ground, a subject on which he could say yes, she understands me; we share this.

The fact is that I didn't want such assumptions to be made. I didn't want someone to say that I was this or that in particular, especially when they didn't know the rest.

'What is it exactly that you do?' I asked as he spooned lasagna onto my plate and offered me Greek salad from a great wooden bowl.

He grinned. 'Can't you guess? I'm a chef.'

'This better taste good then,' I laughed. 'Or else you're fired.'

He seemed to breathe an inner sigh of relief at my more jovial manner. 'Wine?'

'No thanks. I don't really drink.'

'Hah! Famous last words!'

'Really, I don't drink.'

'Experience tells me that whenever someone says that, they drink. Now, would you like some wine?'

'No thank you.'

'Oh, fine, be like that then, but I'm going to have some.' He pulled the cork out with a fine pop and set the bottle on the table to breathe. An expert, I thought.

'I worked in a lodge on the Zambezi in Zambia for three years. It's where I met my girlfriend. She also worked there, managing the place, taking reservations, all that sort of stuff. Then the lodge closed down, my girlfriend went off with a hunter and I came down here in the hope of starting a restaurant, but it just hasn't happened. I've been here about four months and my funds are starting to run out. I'm going to try Mozambique in the New Year. I have a friend who wants me to manage a lodge there for him.'

'What's the problem?'

'Bureaucracy really. I wanted a house in Suburbs. One of those old colonial types – high ceilings, wooden floorboards, the lot. It's the council that's giving me gyp about it. Residential area, noise factor, traffic.'

'You like old things?'

'Mmmm,' he consented with a vigorous nod of his head. 'Love them.'

'I've got some old books you could have.'

'Great. They do look old, don't they? I mean, they're not just old books, they do look old?'

I was right, it was the look he was aiming for. He liked the look of old things and the books would give him the air of someone well read, someone who valued the past. It struck me then how like an English country gentleman he was, or at least that's what he aspired to be.

'Don't you want them?' he asked.

'I don't like them. They're old and... well, old. My Gran had lots. I don't know what we're going to do with half of them.'

'I know the feeling. Miles has left me with a mammoth task – which reminds me.' He started up and made towards a small table in the corner of the dining room. 'The very reason I asked you here tonight is to give you this.' He

322

returned with a manila envelope, which he passed to me with a flourish before sitting down again.

Inside there was a photo. I pulled it out and stared at it in surprise. It was a picture of Gran and I. We were standing next to Shirley, her enormous blue car, me with the door open and Gran looking at me, smiling. It was taken before we went to Miles's farm that afternoon years ago. I turned it over hurriedly.

'Where'd you get it?'

'I found it among some things. Papers, photos. I thought you might want it.'

'Thank you,' I said, not looking up.

'He really loved her, you know.' It was a statement meant to make me feel better, but it took me by surprise. My fork scraped noisily on the plate as I dug into the salad.

'Do you think,' he said, taking a sip of wine and giving the glass a slight swirl, 'Do you think she loved him?'

I put my fork down, trying hard not show my irritation with his question. I didn't think we knew each other well enough to exchange views on Gran and Miles's relationship. I resented his attempt at familiarity. At the same time I knew I could crush him with my sarcastic tongue, so I lied. 'Yes, I think she did,' I said, for heartbreak hung on the air and threatened to swamp us if I hadn't.

After dinner we sat on the verandah and had dessert. The air was heavy with the promise of rain, the heat almost suffocating. Lightning flashed, but it was still far away. I wondered whether the storm would be over before it reached us. The bullfrogs croaked, their beautiful deep voices competing with the shrill pitch of the crickets to be the voice of the night. We ate peaches in syrup, followed by coffee that he made dark and strong and bitter. His cat, Alfie, a great ball of ginger fluff, came and sat on my lap, falling asleep contentedly, his little fist of claws opening and closing around my finger.

He wasn't a secretive man, but what brought us together was our loneliness, our aloneness although perhaps he did not recognize that in me. I think he mistook it for independence of mind. I think this because of the questions he asked and those he didn't. I felt he wanted something from me, some sort of answer, that maybe I would solve something for him.

The rain moved closer. Ribbons of wind played boisterously with the tablecloth, which flapped across the table. It was still hot; I could feel the moisture on my face. I thought perhaps that I should impress upon my memory more clearly the aspect of that room, the feeling of the approaching storm, the music faint in the background, his blue eyes, the feel of the cat's claws digging into my finger, the taste of the coffee in my mouth.

He was doing all the talking, as lonely people often do. I think that's what it was; he found an audience in me; other people brushed him off. I liked that, being privy to the thoughts of others. And he did interest me, I'd give him that. I was afraid, though, of the time when I would be called upon to talk. I lived so near to the surface of my emotions that sometimes I felt their proximity as a physical ache. I appeared calm, but was bubbling away inside. I didn't want all that to come out. It would be too much, all that I suppressed laid bare like ornaments on a market stall for all and sundry to look over, inspect and handle.

What was the use of all this, I thought suddenly. If I had

wanted to talk, would he have listened? All these niceties and feigned interest in my life. I'm like one of his books, I thought, something on the shelf that never gets read. I decided I wouldn't see Tony again.

Before going to bed that night, I sat for a while looking out of the window at the sky. I tried thinking of England, of how it must be – snow and mistletoe, cold days and freezing nights; the way my fingers hurt when I forgot my gloves or when I scraped ice off the car. England. How I longed for it now; the banality of life there, the protection one felt from the world – double glazing, Yale locks, central heating, the News. If only I were there now, I wouldn't have to watch the sunset, those awful dying rays, and the dusk. How I hated the dusk. And Sunday mornings; the loneliness of them. At least in England I could lose myself shopping. The silence of Sunday can be kept at bay in England, locked out with the cold.

Something moved behind me and I jumped. But it was only the fan whirring round. I must have dozed, I thought. I lay down on top of the bed and sighed, slow tears moving down my cheeks.

The storm took a long time in coming. Only later did I hear the rain start to patter on the roof. Lying there I felt an ache somewhere near my heart for happier times, for times gone forever. I longed for her then. This was the first real rain since she had died. She would have loved it. 'Coming down cats and dogs.'

Chapter Seventeen

The top shelf of the cupboard in her bedroom, that's where I found it, her trunk. People are far more predictable than they suspect. Keys are left in flowerpots and under mats and a woman always keeps her diaries and letters in her cupboard.

'Miss E. Saunders, Passenger to Southern Rhodesia' read the fading inscription on the front of the trunk. It was overlapped in places with Union Castle and Rhodesia Railways stickers. Inside the trunk were dress patterns and photographs and theatre programmes and even a menu from the Cape Town Castle. There was also a picture that I had made her years ago when I was still at Attlee Primary: Father Christmas with a cotton wool beard and lucky bean eyes.

There were also four more diaries. Why they weren't with the others, I'm not sure, except that they were no longer the blue hardback ledgers from Stoughton and James, but proper diaries, designed to be such.

There were diary entries for early 1971, but nothing after that until the 80s. The old note of desperation and anxiety re-entered her thoughts. The war was on and Jeremy had signed up. Her marriage was crumbling: there were arguments, silences, great bursts of rage. She was worried. Jem might be killed. G. had reappeared and she went to see him every day.

19th January, 1971

G. phoned me this morning. What a surprise! I couldn't do a thing afterwards, but sit in a chair and laugh! I've tried to suppress it, but it's still there. It's still there.

21st January, 1971

I can't bear it. I can't bear the loneliness of being at home by myself. Leonard is working, Jem is away and Francie is at school all day. Why shouldn't I spend time with G.? After all these years apart, haven't I paid my penance? The children don't need me anymore and Leonard and I seldom speak a kind word to each other these days.

22nd January, 1971

Today we met. I went to his hotel and waited for him in the lobby and then I realised that the man in the corner reading the paper was him. How my heart stopped! How we forget the ravages of age and for one moment I thought, you fool, you fool and nearly turned and walked out. He is almost completely bald now with a stomach that sags over his trousers. When he saw me, his face lit up and he got to his feet at once. It was no scene from Brief Encounter, *I can tell you! Two middle aged people kissing lacks something of an air of romance.*

He said he was more or less a free agent for the day, that he is a partner now in the firm and can organise his time around me. We went out for lunch: a dark, rather dingy place decorated in the bottle green that is so popular these days. Then it was back to his hotel and to the bar: drinks, of course, where his hand moved to my leg and stayed. And then his hotel room.

Immediately, I thought, how different it all is from those long evenings at his house. He tells me he still owns it, but rents it out to tenants. What a word, tenants. I thought I'd feel sad, but I didn't. I like it this way. I like the absence of sentiment and emotion. I like enjoying myself with no thought of the future. I am glad of a place with no poetry, no expectations, no cosy meals, no heads bent over maps, no illusions, no promises, no romance. Just the hand on the leg: sex. A need.

14th February, 1971

There were flowers in the room today when I came up. He no longer bothers to meet me in the lobby. I walk straight in, press the button for the lift and then knock on the door of his room. This morning the door was slightly ajar and when I pushed it open, I didn't see him at first, only the flowers. 'For me?' I said with mock surprise. He smiled, he was putting on his cufflinks, and sang:

'We planned together to dream forever
The dream has ended, for true love died.'

He hummed the rest as he turned down his collar and then turned to give me a peck on the cheek. 'Happy Valentine's.' I smiled and kissed him back, but on the way home I couldn't quite help but think how conventional he has become. No more hand-picked posies or pressed petals, only florist bought roses.

15th February, 1971

Leonard has been asking where I go during the day. He said he phones and I am not there. 'Out,' I said. 'Shopping.' 'All day?' he asked. 'Yes,' I said, but of course he does not believe me.

17th February, 1971

He wasn't there at the hotel this morning. I waited in the lobby a full hour before going shopping. I went back at lunchtime, but still nothing so I went home and guess who was there? G.! He was sitting in the garden having lunch with Leonard and Francie. Francie was just pouring him a cup of tea when I arrived and looked so pleased to see me, wanting to surprise me with G. 'Look who's here, Mum!' she called excitedly as I came in the gate. 'Surprise!'

I could hardly talk as G. got up and made a big show of giving me a kiss and a hug. Later he told me what pleasure he had in doing that in front of everyone. He asked about Jem and when we'd seen him last. And then he and Leonard got into quite a serious discussion about the war. G. was irritatingly flippant about it all and I felt myself siding with Leonard the more he talked.

'Of course, you'll never win,' he declared at one point, leaning back in the wrought iron chair.

I know he wanted to see Leonard's reaction and I hoped he wouldn't react, but of course he did and I saw G. lapping it up in glee.

'Noooo,' he insisted. 'You're a bunch of boy scouts with guns, that's all. S.A.S., Selous Scouts!' He scoffed at Leonard's attempts to persuade him otherwise.

'It's got to come,' he said. 'Independence has got to come.'

'Why?' I burst in suddenly.

'Look at the whole of Africa at the moment,' he waved his hand in the air as though there were a big map of the continent in front of us. 'Winds of Change. It's inevitable.'

'I seem to remember you saying the same thing about colonisation a few years ago.'

Leonard looked up at me then, surprised probably at mention of a conversation at which he wasn't present. G. also looked up.

'And I don't go back on that,' he insisted. He's like a politician, I thought. He has an answer for everything, neither confirming nor denying anything. 'Colonisation,

330

then the desire for Independence, war, revolution, subterfuge.'

'And then?' said Leonard, 'What comes after that?'

'Self-rule.'

'Bloody chaos,' said Leonard.

G. shrugged. 'If you don't like it, leave.'

Leonard was really taking the bait now. He shifted his body in anger and almost growled at G.: 'It's my country. I'm not leaving.'

'Then put up with it. But you're going to have to change. Change with the country.'

Leonard was perplexed. Perhaps he didn't quite understand what G. was saying because he said, shaking his head with determination, 'You want me to change into a munt? Become like one of these flat-noses? Bugger off!'

G. was watching me watching Leonard and there was the smallest of smiles twitching the corner of his lips. I didn't like him having fun at Leonard's expense, however much he may have deserved it. And then quite suddenly, out of the blue, he said, 'Quite. I agree with you. And that's why we're leaving.'

I looked sharply at him and he looked me full in the eye as he told us they are moving to South Africa.

'Durban,' he said with relish. 'I love the coast.'

'When?' The word caught in my throat, so dry and rough it was with shock.

'Oh, next couple of months,' he shrugged. 'Sooner the better.'

I got up and collected the teacups together with a clatter.

331

'That's lovely,' I managed to say. 'The coast. Yes, the coast would be lovely.' And then I carried the tray in to the kitchen, tears blurring my sight and half stumbled over a doorstop that had been left in the way. I tried to steady myself against the counter, tried to breathe deeply, and hold back the tears, but I could see Francie approaching with the rest of the tea things and I made a mad dash to the bathroom. Oh God, I kept thinking, how does he manage to do it every time?

19th February, 1971

He has persuaded me to see him one last time. He leaves tomorrow for Salisbury.

'Why?' I asked.

'You know why,' he said, 'I have to go.' But I shook my head, tears choking my throat. That wasn't what I was asking.

'We're in too deep.' He sat beside me and pushed the hair out of my eyes. 'Too much has happened. It doesn't matter that the children are older or that Leonard is as unhappy as you are. We can't take away their past. We can't do that to anyone.'

I shook my head weakly and buried myself in his shoulder, holding on to his shirt, smelling that smell, that smell. I will never smell it again, I thought. He held me for a while and then handed me a drooping rose from the vase on the table. I'd had to keep the roses there for there was no way I could explain them.

'Red roses for a blue lady,' he sang softly.

'And if they do the trick,
I'll hurry back and pick
the best white orchids for her wedding gown.' I
continued. *Ironic, really.*

'Spend the night with me,' he said, *kissing my head.*
I sighed and said 'No.'
'Please.'
'No.'

20ᵗʰ February, 1971

He phoned me this morning and asked me to meet him
for a drink. I know what will happen. We will drink, we
will not make it to lunch, we will go back to his hotel
room, we will make love. I will stay the night. He always
wins, doesn't he? Always. But after that, I have made a
resolution, he is out, out of my life. I will forget him, I
will not put him before anything else, not me, not my
family. I will end it once and for all.

For at least ten years she never wrote another thing in her
diary. Later that day Jeremy would return. She was out. The
next day he killed himself.

Chapter Eighteen

As a little girl, I imagined what it was like to fall in love, to be in love, a love that put a sparkle in your eyes and a spring in your step, a love that was known from the moment you looked into each other's eyes. If you believe what they tell you in the movies, bells will ring and rose petals will fall from heaven. Couples stand looking longingly at each other, knowing, just knowing, they'll be together forever.

But what no one tells you is what happens when that moment moves on. The camera never takes you beyond the point of the passionate kiss and the whispered words. It doesn't show the day to day living of ordinary people. What happens when the magic wears off, when you suddenly decide that you don't love someone any more?

Perhaps people merely grow accustomed to each other. Minds mould together, weathered into place by the habit of years. After a while, one forgets the other's irritating ways or learns how to deal with them. You learn how to manipulate, to get your own way, to destroy.

For a while after my break up with Mark, I used to ponder

the strange dynamics of human relationships and came to the rather cynical conclusion that people are singular, separate and that any act of union is an insult to nature.

Perhaps the only love to be trusted is the other love, love for your family or a friend or a puppy. A love that doesn't demand roses and candlelit dinners, one that is not continually seeking to find itself reflected elsewhere, watchful, paranoid, selfish. But that love, family love, also destroys, doesn't it? It demands, it bullies, it cajoles. It kills. Each man kills the thing he loves. What was the rest of that verse? *By each let this be heard, Some do it with a bitter look, Some with a flattering word*. The coward does it with a kiss. The brave man with a sword.

The day that I found my grandmother and Miles together, something died inside me. It was as though someone had blown out a flame that has been burning for hours. The wick smoulders and smokes for a while afterwards; the wax, still liquid and hot, needs time to harden and cool, but eventually it does and you can no longer mould it with your thumb. Something came to a stop, an end, like the motion of a boat whose motor has cut out suddenly, leaving the vessel to bob aimlessly on the darkening waves. What was it that died? Perhaps it was some capacity to love or, at least, to believe in it the way I had, or maybe it was a capacity to trust, trust in something greater than myself. I felt sometimes that my life would not connect, that in each hand I held two pieces of my life that would not come together. Like two magnets of equal polarity, they could not meet.

23rd October, 1983

We went to Miles's house today, a small, old place on
Third Avenue. Ellie didn't want to come and I thought
perhaps I should have taken her home, but she would
have been so upset and probably never forgiven me. She
so looks forward to our time together and I know that she
misses me almost as much as I miss her. Francie told me
she found a calendar in her room on which she had
marked all the Saturdays and put exclamation marks
next to them and she crosses off the days until each
Saturday comes.

But she won't speak two words to Miles and she
changes completely when he arrives, from a little bundle
of fun who can't stop talking to a strange, dark creature
from whom it is difficult to solicit any conversation. Miles
keeps telling me that she'll come round, but she hasn't
so far.

She's not the sort of child to make a fuss over
anything, but today she completely overreacted to
something at Miles's house: a snake. A house snake, one
of those thin brown things that appear shyly sometimes
on a very hot day and want less to do with you than you
with them. Ellie has surely seen them lots of times before
and it was in the pool, the empty pool at the back of
Miles's house, and so it was hardly going to harm us if
it was down there! The poor thing couldn't even get out
and I was more concerned about helping it out onto the
ground than whether it would bite me or not.

Ellie started screaming, 'There's a snake, there's a
snake!' and I came running from the kitchen and saw

her jumping up and down and pointing, and I expected a python or a cobra, something huge and frightening and dangerous. But there it was, this tiny snake, exhausted, fumbling up the stone step of the pool and then falling backwards as it reached the lip and couldn't bend its body in quite the right way.

'It's all right,' I shouted, grabbing her hand. 'For goodness sake, calm down!' I said we'd wait for Miles to come back for he had gone out to buy some drinks and would be back in about ten minutes. He'll know what to do with it, I thought. And she clung to me, tears pouring down her cheeks, and obviously really shaken; there was no acting there. Miles was longer in coming back than I thought he would be and when we showed him the snake it had died. The sun was too hot for it. I felt awful, I really did. That poor snake baking on the hot concrete and us sitting inside waiting for Miles to come and remove it.

It reminded me of another incident, years ago, with Francie. Wally had come round one Sunday and was doing his uncle bit with the children, playing games, taking them for rides on his back, that sort of thing, when suddenly I heard a scream. It was Francie. I rushed outside and bumped into her running inside. I remember that it was getting dark and I thought maybe she's tired. Perhaps Wally should think of going now. Wally was walking to the house with Jem on his shoulders and waved and smiled as I came out with Francie in my arms.

'Nothing wrong,' he called. 'She just got a fright.'

'What happened?'

'A chameleon,' he said, gesturing over to the fruit trees. 'We were picking peaches and suddenly she saw this chameleon and screamed.' He set Jem down on the ground and stretched his back. 'She ran and the chameleon turned purple.'

Jem laughed, that lovely gurgling laugh he had as a child.

I turned to Francie who had stopped crying and was listening to Wally. 'It's just a chameleon,' I said gently, but she turned away and hid her face in my shoulder. And even later, when Wally had gone and the children were bathed and I was putting them to bed, she wouldn't talk about it. I got that look though, the one she gives me when I've been cross with her, as though I've injured her in some way.

'It's not that I don't believe you...' I started, but she turned away and looked at the wall. I sat with her until she fell asleep, her sad face relaxing little as I smoothed back her hair.

Miles's house. What do I remember about Miles's house? Brown was a recurring colour; a seventies' shade of brown, occurring sometimes on its own and sometimes with orange, usually in the shape of big flowers on sun filter curtains. The furniture was old as well and seemed to lack any sentimental value, as though it was just there, serving a purpose. This was apart from his record player, which he obviously loved for it was polished to a high gleam and the records were stacked neatly inside the little cupboard underneath: Dean Martin, Elvis Presley, Julio Iglesias, Roger Whittaker.

The only attempts at a feminine touch were some white crocheted doilies on two side tables and an arrangement of fake flowers, also orange, on the sideboard. There was also a photo; a close-up of three black women who looked like they were from the Sudan or somewhere like that, with funny things in their ears and noses and lots of necklaces. It was black and white and, although they were facing the camera, they were also looking away from whoever took the photo. There was something about them that reminded me of a wild animal, startled at the appearance of a human, that has been quite happily doing whatever wild animals do, that freezes for a couple of seconds, looking at the intruder with a mixture of fright and fascination before running away.

Miles saw me looking at it one day. 'Abyssinia,' was all he said, but I could tell he wanted me to ask him more, but I didn't. Nothing he had done could ever have been interesting to me.

There were yellowed pictures on the walls: those odd Sarah Moon pictures that were popular for a time in the eighties, printed on chipboard that was stained with the little dead bodies of flies and mosquitoes and sometimes the long brown drip of a water leak. There was also a framed copy of *If* by Kipling and I always remember those last lines, if I remember nothing else: 'you'll be a Man, my son.' I used to wonder why he had never married, never had a son to whom he could say 'you'll be a man' and slap heartily on the back, like they did in American sitcoms.

There was also, I remember, a collection of books in Miles's lounge: paperbacks with yellowing pages and covers that had fallen off and been stuck back with Sellotape that was now old and dry and falling off itself. One book I glanced through had a number of tiny ants squashed flat between the pages, which slid out, free at last, if too late for any resurrection. I found a hair in another. Nose hair? I used to wonder.

Books with pictures of heavy black revolvers on the front covers, women: sometimes frightened, needing rescue; at other times seductive, trouble. That smell of dust, cigarette smoke, that one could almost taste; all the years trapped between the pages.

I remembered that visit to Miles's house. Perhaps it was the first or second. Sitting outside in the white heat of an early Saturday afternoon, feeling the hot stones beneath my feet and squinting in the glare from the empty pool. There was a *braaivleis* and two concrete seats and a table. All were swept clean, but they were old, in a style I would now recognise as from the fifties, but which then just seemed to breathe age and decay towards me in waves of heat.

I remember seeing the snake, twisting this way and that, writhing at the bottom of the empty pool, struggling up the gentle curve of the step and then falling backwards as it just couldn't make itself turn in time. I remember screaming, screaming, 'Snake! Nyoka!' and Gran running out the house and grabbing me by the hand. Miles was somewhere else. 'We'll ask Miles to sort it out when he comes back, don't worry. Don't worry!' she had insisted and pulled me into the house.

I kept looking out the window, which was shut, for Miles. A fly was trapped between the mosquito gauze and the glass. It buzzed and fell, buzzed and fell, and each time I thought it had given up it would hoist itself up for another buzz. And another fall.

It seemed an age before I heard the crunch of wheels in the drive, a car door slam, the clink, clink of bottles knocking together, voices in the kitchen.

'So where's this snake then?' said Miles and for a moment I thought he was going to reach for my hand. I folded my arms defiantly, my hands tightly under my armpits, and ventured slowly outside. I saw the flicker in his eyes, a brief registration of my prickly behaviour, but then it was gone and the half-mocking smile returned.

The snake was still there, but it was dead, bent in an eternal slither towards the steps.

'Baked,' said Miles, picking it up by its tail and watching it hang limply.

'Dead?' I could feel the tears welling.

Miles threw it over the hedge and wiped his hands on the back of his shorts. 'Nothing dangerous. Grass snake. Get zillions of them in here.'

And he went back in the kitchen, cracked open a bottle of Castle and poured it into two glasses. Just like that.

Chapter Nineteen

5th December, 1984

Last night Wally phoned. I couldn't think who it could be when I got the call from the operator. 'Hold on, please,' he said after confirming my number. 'A call from the United Kingdom.' And then there was what seemed an eternity of crackling and fizzing over the line and then 'Hello?' Hello. Such an unsuitable word. It was hard to talk and the delay on the line didn't make things easier. Later I thought of the line, how they say the cable runs all the way along the seabed, how I was literally speaking to him across continents and oceans. Hello. As though all the years haven't happened at all.

'I'd like to come for a couple of months,' he said. 'I'm retired now, you know.' And I thought of course you are, but two months? I know what will happen. It is like a record we put on every time we meet. I swear not to get involved. We get involved. He leaves. I am devastated.

'That's a bit long,' I said. 'I only have a flat.'

'I know.'

'How did you get the number?' I asked suddenly, probably sounding quite suspicious and unwelcoming.

'Contacts,' he said, his voice taking on the accent of an American gangster. 'You can run but you can't hide.'

'Two weeks.'

There was a pause, which could have been due to the line that seemed to spit then with extra vigour.

'Wally?'

There was no answer. And just as I said his name again, he came back on: 'Yes, two weeks, Evelyn, that's fine.'

14th December, 1984

I can't seem to do anything. Everyone keeps asking me what is wrong. I see Ellie's face when she comes to the flat, looking round at the mess, the unpolished furniture, the plants that need watering.

'I'll do it, Gran,' she says, seizing the watering can and rushing off to squirt each little pot plant. I heard her today talking to them: 'It's OK, Gran's just a bit worried because she's got a visitor coming.' And then, as though one of the plants had asked a question: 'Yes, from England. Do you know where England is? It snows there at Christmas and you can make snowmen and ride on something called a toboggan. And fairies live there, but they don't live here because it's too hot and they're not used to the heat. And the mosquitoes.' She even got the polish out today and started on the coffee table.

343

Do I really want to see him? I have even more to lose now: Miles, Ellie, my sanity. I could've died then. I thought of it. Who would've missed me if I had simply got up and walked out into the waves? No one, but now they would. I can survive now as I survived then when he left me for the first time. He has left me so many times since then, yet none was as painful as that first time.

I had begun to ask questions. Where are we going from here? Will we stay in Beira and not go to the Union? How did Riette take the news? Has any sort of scandal broken out back in Rhodesia? He was dismissive. Laughed at my anxiety, my need for plans. I knew him well enough to know when he was being evasive. We were having drinks on the verandah on about our fourth night there and I suddenly thought: what if there is no plan? What has he really told me about the future? Nothing. And then it dawned on me that he never actually said that he was leaving Riette. All he said was that we were leaving. But people leave to go on holiday, don't they? Just because you leave doesn't mean you won't come back. He was reading the newspaper when I asked him. His hand moved slightly and the paper twitched.

'Mmm?' was all he said.

'I asked you a question, have you left her?'

He sighed and folded the paper up neatly. But he didn't look at me. He looked far away, out into the growing darkness of the sea. It was my answer.

'You haven't, have you?'

'No.'

I was suddenly aware of how ridiculous I must look, parading like a wife: black dress, smart shoes, handbag, shawl. My earrings, my necklace, my wedding ring from Timothy that I had replaced on my left hand out of a false sense of propriety. Everything pointed at me and laughed. You fool! Didn't you know?

'What's this all about?' I asked with a vague gesture towards the beach.

'It was just meant to be a holiday. Time for us to be ourselves, by ourselves. You took it the wrong way. What was I to do?'

'So you played along?'

'No!' he burst out, quite angrily.

'What would you call it?'

'I...' He was at a loss for words.

We sat in silence for a long time. I tapped my glass gently with one finger to try and stem the flood of tears I knew was waiting to burst forth.

'Evie,' he said suddenly. 'I'm not really adventurous.' I shook my head, but he carried on. 'I'm not the type to pack up my things and head off into the sunset without knowing where I'm going.'

'That's why you have a map,' I tried to joke, but my voice cracked and I had to look away.

'Even then. It has to be planned, my journey. I'm not impulsive. I don't risk anything.'

'You've risked your marriage.'

He drew in a long breath. 'Not really, Evie. Riette will always take me back.'

'Does she know about us?'

He nodded.

'What did she say?'

'Break it off. End it. Before you get too involved.'

'And you?'

He threw his hands into the air in exasperation. His eyes, I could see, were full of tears. 'What do you think?'

I excused myself from Wally with the need to go and powder my nose. But I walked straight out of the hotel and down the road. I walked with some determination and ignored the calls from taxi drivers offering lifts. I just kept on going, kept on walking until the sun had finally set and I felt I could slow and breathe a little more easily. I heard music: vibrant Portuguese music and some American stuff and laughter. The laughter of young people enjoying themselves. Groups of young men and women walked arm in arm down to the bars and restaurants. I am young, I thought. I have time. But I looked at the young men with their soft, clean faces, their well-meaning gestures of chivalry and I thought I can never go back. I will never be young again. I have not got older, I have died. Yes, that is what has happened, I have died.

15th December, 1984

I first told Miles about Wally a couple of months ago. We had gone to his farm, Ellie came too, but she was in one of her awkward moods with Miles. He does try with her, but she shuts him off completely and nothing he does ever seems to break through that hard outer shell that she grows when he is around. It was so incredibly hot and we had gone for a walk in the afternoon, which was probably a very silly thing to do and I felt very tired and drained when we returned.

I picked some leaves while on our walk, which Miles said you could make into tea and drink, if left to infuse in boiling water. Raymond, the worker at the farm, confirmed this, as did his wife who said it was good for sore stomachs. I felt this odd sort of pride in Miles that he knew something that the Africans did; that he knows the bush. It struck me then that he is the first man I have been involved with who has been able to develop in me an interest for the bush, for things African. Wally, with all his maps and pretensions of being a great explorer, always stayed in expensive hotels and would never have lasted two minutes in the bush unless he had taken a whole heap of luxury provisions with him. Leonard knows Africa but doesn't know the Africans, if that makes sense, and I think how peculiar it is to cut yourself off from the inhabitants of a continent and yet profess to love the continent itself with such undying affection. Of course Timothy knew the bush like the back of his hand, but I never knew him. All I saw was a Rhodesian lost in the tame jungle of England.

I felt safe then with Miles and later, too, when we sat outside and he poured drinks and I made sandwiches, I thought this is wonderful, isn't it? Here at least I am able to enjoy the security of love without the need for secrecy. For this is what love is, isn't it: me preparing sandwiches, him pouring drinks, Ellie reading a comic book. How it surfaces at unbidden times, reminding you that what comes later, in the darkness, is only the climax of what went before: making sandwiches.

That night I told Miles about Wally. Ellie had gone to bed and a great storm was whipping up outside so we moved into the lounge. Miles lit a paraffin lamp and poured us each another drink and we sat on the sofa and talked. He didn't say anything, but not because he is jealous or angry or feels that I am a scarlet woman, but because he understands. The nod of the head, the squeeze of the hand, the lack of questions. He understands.

Then we spoke about him. I asked him why he's never married.

'I've had my heart broken, too,' he said. Then he told me the story of when he was in Abyssinia during the War and what a strange place it was. Africa ruled by the Italians, who were so useless at being nasty or violent that he almost felt like showing them how to do it.

He had fallen in love. There had been talk of marriage, but one day she wasn't there anymore and later he found out she had killed herself.

'Why?' I exclaimed, feeling in the touch of his hand, his reliving of the moment.

'She had been raped. She was dishonoured.'

'By whom? The British?'

'An Italian. The one lousy, rotten apple in all of them.'

I thought for a moment. 'An Italian raped his own countrywoman? You could understand if he had been Bri...'

'She was Abyssinian,' he cut in. 'Amhara.'

'Oh,' I said quietly, and then: 'The photo.'

'She's the one on the end right. Abeba.'

We sat in silence for a couple of seconds and then he said, 'I've never told anyone that.'

348

And I said, 'Nor have I.'

I felt so happy at that moment, so incredibly happy, and later, when it rained, I crept out of bed and stole down the passage and out onto the verandah. It was so beautiful: the great slices of lightning, the orchestra of noise. It was as though this stage had been prepared for me and I thought then of King Lear, of how he goes mad in the storm. And I thought, I am the same.

And then suddenly I turned and there was Ellie. And I wanted to share it with her and not just her: Francie, Leonard, Wally, Jem. I wanted to give what I had held back all those years so I took her by the hands and we ran outside. Dancing, round and round and round. But the next day it had gone. Despite the rain of the night before, it heated up again. The sky was grey, that awful rained-out colour, but the sun was already set to work on spitefully drying up the puddles and the grass was humming with the noise of insects.

The leaves that I had picked the day before and placed in water had drooped and I thought happiness, true happiness, is only momentary. Or perhaps it is just me. Maybe that's why I was attracted to a married man. I lived for those pools of happiness, but what of the time between the rains?

I cried in the bedroom while I was getting ready and Miles came in and saw.

'What's wrong?' he asked, putting his arm around me. When I didn't answer, he kissed my forehead and said, 'Things will get better with time.'

'They won't! They won't!' I cried and Miles drew me to him and said, 'Ssh. Ellie's outside. Don't make her upset.'

When we got back to Bulawayo, Miles left us after lunch and I went to have a lie-down. I told Ellie to come with me, but she was bored, so I made no objection when she got up and went into the lounge. I heard her open the front door and go up the fire escape. I fell asleep then and had a dream that I couldn't remember on waking, except that something wonderful had happened and I felt very happy when I woke.

But then Frances rang and was in a state about Ellie. Had she cried for her? Had she brushed her teeth? What had we done over the weekend? Of course, I didn't tell her about the farm. What would be the point? She'd only worry and then accuse me of putting Ellie and myself in danger.

Ellie came back just as I was ending the call and told me she had been at Audrey's and that Audrey had given her tea and shown her photos of me and a man whose name begins with a 'W'. Really, Audrey, I thought, what are you thinking of?

The next evening I went upstairs and saw Audrey. I think she was expecting me for she looked a little nervous when she opened the door, as though I had a bomb behind my back. She asked me if I would like some tea, although it was already six, but I said no. 'Audrey, you nearly gave the game away to Ellie.'

'Oh?' she said, with feigned innocence.

'You know what I mean,' I said with a wry smile. 'Boyfriends with names beginning with 'W'. Photographs.'

She smiled a little embarrassed smile, a little pink in the face. 'No, Evelyn, I never said he was your boyfriend.

350

I remembered just in time. I said you never had a boyfriend.'

'Which picture is it? I don't remember one of all of us.'

'Don't you? New Year's Eve. The night Bill proposed.'

'Well, it's important no one ever knows, least of all someone in the family. Please, Audrey. Remember, he's Uncle Wally.'

'Of course, of course. Just the memory, you know.'

I had turned to go downstairs when suddenly she quite took me by surprise, saying: 'She's dead, you know.'

'Who?' I started, but I knew.

'Riette. Died a couple of months ago.'

'How did you hear?'

'Grapevine. One of the ladies I used to play bridge with.'

'Oh,' I said, not really knowing what to say. 'That must be sad for him.' But I knew what she was thinking. All this time, all this wasted time. For although Audrey never approved of the affair, she has always approved of love.

Chapter Twenty

14th December, 1984

Ellie loves him. Yesterday we baked gingerbread men.
Wally was very funny. I'd forgotten how good he is with
children and I felt a pang. Ellie could be our grandchild.
How different life would have turned out. But then she
wouldn't be this Ellie, but a version of her, I suppose. She
would come and stay with us. We would take her out to
different places. She would love him as she loves me. Is
that the way it would have turned out?

5th January, 1985

This evening I took Wally to the airport. As I write this,
he is probably somewhere over Zambia and I wonder if I
will ever see him again.

  'You resisted me this time,' he said as I kissed him
goodbye.

'You and me both,' I laughed, but it sounded strangely strangled, like an ironic 'ha!'

He paused and shrugged and I knew then that the fact that nothing had happened between us was the result of a supreme act of will on his behalf. I thought back then to that conversation I'd had with Miles on that terrible day just before Christmas when everything had nearly fallen apart.

We had been out the previous night to the Naval Club. When I say we I mean Miles and Wally and I. I thought then that he'd been great, Wally that is. He hadn't once asked me about my relationship with Miles or suggested anything about him and me, and I breathed a sigh of relief as I later lay in bed. I thought it's all OK. We've weathered it and survived and now he can go back home and perhaps we will keep in touch: Christmas cards, that sort of thing. The odd letter. We can be friends. It is possible.

Then early the next morning Wally left to go and see Annette Truman – she and Paul did eventually divorce; he lives in Australia and she has remarried. A wealthy builder, Wally told me, and I can hardly say I was surprised. People like that don't slum it for anyone. Miles arrived soon after and was in this odd, overly amorous mood and kept coming up behind me and putting his arms around my waist and kissing my neck, and I thought for goodness sake, Miles, it's not even eight o'clock. It was too much, too needy, too possessive, not natural and quite unlike him I thought.

Eventually I asked him what was going on. It had taken me nearly ten minutes to make a cup of tea, he

353

was so touchy! 'I'm jealous,' he said, reaching for me again so I handed him a dishcloth and told him he could help by doing some of the drying up. He threw it to the side and pulled a face. 'He's come to take you, hasn't he, that Pom?'

'What Pom? Oh, him, oh no,' I declared and told him, I was quite excited actually, what I had felt the previous night when lying in bed, that finally our relationship had moved into one of friendship, but Miles scoffed and folded his arms in disbelief.

'Friendship? The guy wants you. It's written all over his face. It's in the way he talks to you, the way his body language changes when he's around you. Friendship!'

'What's brought this on?' I said, hunting through the drawer for a teaspoon. 'I thought we had a great time last night.'

'Yep, until he started on all that poetry palaver.'

'What do you mean?'

'All that stuff about flowers blushing in the desert air and for whom the bell tolls.' He affected the accent of an English aristocrat.

I stopped. 'You're jealous!' I laughed and poked him in the stomach with the spoon. 'I don't believe that Mr Miles Trevellyan is jealous!'

'That's what I said, didn't I?'

'I thought you meant because of me. But it's his knowledge, isn't it? His upbringing.'

Miles shrugged his shoulders but an embarrassed smile crept across his face.

'But you know all that Shakespeare. I bet he doesn't know half of it.'

'Doesn't he? I'm sure he does.'

'Not as much as you do.'

I wanted to speak to him properly, to tell him what I felt, what I had thought the previous night, when this man appeared at the door looking for him. Trevor someone. He works with Miles and he needed to tell him something, but he ended up staying for ages! He was funny, I'll give him that, and he made us both laugh about this nutcase of a woman he's going out with who phones him up constantly and leaves messages for him all over town. But all the time we sat there and listened to him I kept thinking this is what I really want.

It was only later, when Miles had gone and Wally had gone out and I was left to turn the events of that afternoon carefully over in my mind, that I thought of Shakespeare again. It is nearly forty years since Wally and I went to see King Lear. I don't remember the exact production too well and I wouldn't have remembered the play at all had we not had such an argument about it afterwards. 'Love,' said Wally, 'true love is selfish, jealous, vengeful. We are brought up to think otherwise: love sacrifices, love forgives, love embraces. But it doesn't, does it? Even God is a jealous God. Thou shalt have no other God but me. Absolute devotion or absolute annihilation. God had the biggest ego of all, for who else had created a world full of people and then demanded they love him.'

'What about your wife?' I asked, knowing I was striking low. 'She forgives you every time. Doesn't she love you?'

He paused. He knew I had him cornered.

355

'Who loved Lear more?' I persisted. 'Cordelia, who was able to limit her words to the succinctness of 'nothing', or Regan and Goneril, who had felt what it was like for Cordelia to be favoured over them?'

'Aren't we arguing the same thing?'

'Your wife, which one is she? Cordelia or Goneril?'

I remember that he leant forward then, slightly embarrassed, and gave me a quick kiss. 'You win,' he said, but I hadn't really known what it was I had gained.

It wasn't long after that night that I gave him the watch. I couldn't quite make up my mind about the engraving and thought at first to have 'Had we but world enough and time', but decided against it in favour of an allusion to Lear, 'From Your Shadow', with the intention of suggesting that I was his Fool, his conscience.

And then that day, after the trauma of the afternoon, I thought again that he was right: that love is selfish. All love demands and destroys.

That evening, when everyone had gone except Wally and things were a little awkward between us because he knew that he had saved my bacon and I didn't know whether to acknowledge it or not, he suddenly said, right out of the blue, that my flat was too small and that he didn't know how I managed to live in it.

'But you like small places, don't you? Don't tell me, Mrs Wiesman's in the flat upstairs.'

'I don't know why you always have to be so condescending.' I was tired and drained after the events of the afternoon so I suppose my voice sounded a little strained and annoyed.

'I'm not.'

'You are.'

He pulled a face, 'Don't take everything so seriously.'

'It's my house,' I said, not relenting.

'Flat.'

'It's my home.'

He shifted in his seat, taking my hand in his and giving it a squeeze. I snatched it back and rose angrily. I stood by the window, looking out.

'All I meant was that I couldn't live here. It's too small.' He looked at me, for the first time a little annoyed too. 'For me,' he added. 'It's too small for me.'

I took a deep breath and continued looking out the window.

'Come and sit here,' Wally said more quietly. The edge had gone from his voice and he patted the seat beside him gently.

I got up and moved next to him, but I couldn't quite forgive him for what he had said and even after he'd gone out to the Club and I'd closed the door and drawn the curtains, I could still sense his words in the air, lingering pervasively, the way damp does when it rains.

I put on some music and lit the standard lamp. The pool of light was enough to read by, the rest of the room edging into darkness. Later on, I lay in bed and listened to the soft drizzle patter against my window, missing the warmth of Ellie sleeping next to me.

'She's your crutch, isn't she?' Miles said to me not so long ago. He was talking about Ellie. 'You won't do anything while she's around.'

I had laughed and said 'Of course not.' But he is right. And then that day I felt I didn't need her anymore. Not

357

in the same way. But she had appeared. I'd forgotten that I had mentioned making Christmas decorations with her, but there she was with her little bag, looking very bashful and awkward at the door.

I wished I had never made that arrangement, never promised her anything, for with Ellie it is best not to promise, for she will never forgive you if you can't do it. Making Christmas decorations was the last thing I wanted to do at that moment and she saw and her little face fell as if to say 'et tu, Brute.' The men were making fun of her, but nothing nasty. Trevor thought she was a boy though and I thought this is bound to provoke tears. I tried to say things that made fun of Miles, like his dancing last night, and she laughed and I sighed an inner sigh of relief because now she knew I was on her side again.

Of course what I did with Miles was silly. Where was Ellie? Was she upstairs like I thought? At one time I thought I heard someone on the phone. Perhaps it was Wally. There was such a commotion and banging. Leonard shouting for the door to be opened at once and then all of them looking in: Francie and Leonard, even Andrew. I got a convoluted story about her being missing and my heart had lurched and I thought not again, not again. But then there she was and I wanted to say that it was me, me who was missing, who had been missing all those years. It was as if they suddenly saw me for what I was: a fraud and a liar and a part of me, a big part of me, wanted to say: 'Yes, you are right. Here take me, do with me what you will.' And then another, much smaller, part wanted to say: 'You're all wrong, all of you.

I wanted to love you. I did love you. Look, here, like I love this man. Unconditionally.' But I have used him, too, haven't I? I have used him to be strong against the onslaught of true love, deep, selfish, undying love.

I slept with the curtains partly open and watched the light from the security lamp outside filter in. And then the real light, the grey-white light of dawn that hardened as the sun rose and burnt colour into the growing day. And now Wally has gone. Again.

Chapter Twenty-one

December came. Hints of unrest and further economic instability breathed uneasily through parched rainless days. I had never known such a dry end of year. Storm clouds gathered often and then dispersed. At night we tossed in sweat-drenched sheets and woke exhausted in the early morning heat. I slept with just a sheet to cover me and the windows open on the clear star-filled skies. The wind hardly moved and often, when I couldn't sleep, I would go and sit outside and think, the night thick and warm around me. Talk of people emigrating hung above us like the sky that stretched white-blue and unrelenting, a never-ending migraine.

4th April, 1990

Samson came to visit me today. I didn't recognise him. How old he looked: stooped, grey and saddened, yes, that is what it was. Saddened. Weary with resignation to a life that had promised him so much, but failed to deliver.

I could have asked him how he found me, but it is a superfluous question in a country that runs on a bush telegraph.

He wore a suit, an old grey suit, which was probably his best, and a white shirt that was frayed at the collar and cuffs, and shiny black shoes, slightly scuffed at the front. I wondered briefly if they were Wally's clothes, things he had given Samson when he had left his service. I didn't ask him what he had been doing all these years. I'm not sure I would have got much detail out of him anyway, so what was the point? But I offered him tea and I was surprised he sat when I motioned the sofa and didn't hover at the door as in the old days. He sat with a sigh that seemed to make sitting painful, as if he immediately regretted it and wouldn't be able to stand again without help from me.

He waited until I had brought a tray of tea. I opened a packet of Marie biscuits and put them on a plate. I was surprised, too, to see his hand dart out and clumsily grab one. He ate it and gulped the tea greedily before beginning to talk. We went through the rituals of asking about respective families and nodding as the current status of each family member was revealed. Then there was a slight pause and Samson said: 'Have you ever been back to the house? Number 52?'
I shook my head. I made a point of never even driving past it.

Samson nodded resignedly as though that explained everything.

'But you own it? Baas, the baas wrote to me and told me you are the new owner.'

361

'Yes,' I said and then stopped. How does one explain owning a house one never goes to?

'I went there once,' he said, his gaze shifting to the carpet. 'I was looking for you, but they said a white madam didn't live there.'

'I rent it out,' I explained. 'Through an agency. I don't have anything to do with it really. I get a cheque each month and once I paid for a new geyser to be put in.'

Samson's forehead furrowed in confusion. I could see him looking round the shoebox of a flat and wondering why I chose to live where I did. There was a silence and I was about to ask him if he would like another cup of tea when suddenly he burst out: 'Madam, have you seen it? Have you seen number 52?'

I thought for a moment that his eyes had filled with tears and I got this odd sort of feeling in my stomach that he was going to tell me that it had burnt down and lay in a pile of rubble

'What's wrong? What is it, Samson?' I asked slowly, placing my cup and saucer on the table.

'Ah, Madam,' he said, his right hand playing with the crocheted armrest on the chair. 'Baas, Baas is good to me all these years. All these years.' He threw his arm in an arc that seemed to suggest the eternity that he has known Wally. 'Since 1945. 1945! I was a young man. Back in Bulawayo after the War. Ah, I was so happy, so happy to be back in the place where I was born! But no job!' His hands collapsed by his side. 'So my baas – my other baas, Baas Reynolds, he say to me, Samson, look for job as a domestic. Cooking. White madams don't want to cook. They want a black man to cook. He find me other baas.'

362

'What happened to Baas Reynolds?'

'He go to England.' Samson flung his hand backwards as though England was behind the sofa. 'He was English. He want to go home after the War.' He fell back in the sofa, tired, I thought. Crumpled.

'But Baas Wally, he was good to me. Ahhh, yes. He was a good baas. He writes to me,' he said, turning towards me and his face brightening suddenly. 'Sometimes he sends me money. And he paid for my two sons for school. All the way from here' – he cupped his lowered hand in the African way of denoting youth – 'to when they finished. All the way! Uniforms, books, pencils, pens, eh, shoes' – he ticked off each item on his fingers and then clapped his hands above his head. 'Ah, yes, he is a good baas.'

I wondered briefly, cynically perhaps, if he had come for money. Perhaps Wally hadn't sent anything for a while. Perhaps he saw me as Wally's substitute in Zimbabwe.

I shifted in my chair and his eyes returned to me, as though someone had suddenly said 'and your point is?'

'But now the house, Madam. Ah, it's not good. Not good.' He shook his head sadly.

'Why? What has happened?'

'It is the garden, Madam, ah it's too terrible.'

'Why? Tell me what's happened?'

'Terrible.'

'It's dead, is it? Have they let it go?'

Samson shook his head sadly and looked at his hands. 'They do not know,' he muttered quietly. 'They do not know how to look after it.'

I gave up after a while and reassured him that I would go and check up on the house as soon as I could.

His eyes flickered upwards then and I thought I saw something quite sly in the look. Again, it occurred to me as to whether he was looking for money. Or perhaps he was looking for a job.

'Where are you working now?' I asked, putting the cups and saucers back on the tray. I saw his eyes hopefully regard the last Marie biscuit.

'I'm with my brother,' he replied with a sniff.

'Doing?'

'Take-aways. Buns, colas, pies.'

I smiled. 'You're wasted, Samson. You should have been a chef. Have you ever tried? The big hotels?'

He looked down at his hands again and said, 'Certificates. Everyone wants certificates.'

He got up then to leave and I lifted the plate with the remaining biscuit up to him. 'Take it. You need something to keep you going.' He took it with fake reluctance, folding it into his huge palm.

'We come from a different world, don't we, Samson?' I said before I shut the door.

He looked blank.

'Certificates,' I said. 'Who ever needed them in our day?'

8th April, 1990

I have decided to move into the house. After my visit there yesterday, I realise it needs somebody. Somebody to look after it, to love it. Somebody to live in it: shine door handles, polish floors, shake carpets free of dust.

I couldn't understand what Samson was on about when I first arrived – the garden, well the garden is beautiful. The roses! The smell! The clumps of jasmine that fall lazily over the hedge as though clambering out of the garden to greet you. I thought, I've been tricked. Somehow this is Wally's doing. He has put Samson up to this. He wants me to see it, to fall in love all over again, to be moved by memories.

But I couldn't help thinking there was something in it; something in what Samson had told me that made sense. And I could see why he couldn't explain it to me. There was something missing. And in the house too. Nice enough pictures, simple soft furnishings. It was clean and yet lonely, so incredibly lonely. And nowhere did I feel this more than in Wally's old study. There were no maps, no books, no desk or drinks cabinet. There was nothing but a camp bed, bare except for two folded old towels at one end and a man's dark jacket in a dry-cleaning bag laid out across its middle. Next to the bed was a little side cupboard with copies of The Watchtower on top. Loneliness saturated the air. A businessman lives there, so the agency told me. He's away, said the gardener who greeted me at the gate. Two weeks here, two weeks Harare and I thought, how incredible, some things never change. But lonely. No passionate affair is conducted here, it witnesses no secret rendezvous. One toothbrush in the bathroom, two dead flies in the toilet bowl.

But I wonder if I can ever make it mine? I always wanted it to be mine, of course. Mine and Wally's. I *never wanted to go back into the past and I don't now. I don't want to be surrounded by the ghosts of yesterday or dwell in memories.*

But when I went there this afternoon I was reminded of that time I arrived there, pink geranium in hand, breathless, excited, in love with life and madly in love with Wally and I walked jauntily to the door only to see Riette and Annette in the garden. What was worse than seeing her there was knowing that he knew she was there and he hadn't told me. I had to swallow that hurt, to bury it somewhere and tell myself I had no right to feel that way, that I was his mistress and, in allowing myself to be so, I was agreeing for him to be unfaithful to me.

And then there was the house, the way everything inside seemed to reflect her attitude: Who are you? What are you doing here? You don't belong. So here is my opportunity, all these many years later, to say 'all this is mine.' And make it so.

Chapter Twenty-two

The day before Christmas Eve I bumped into Tony outside the local supermarket. I had just parked the car and was reaching for my bag when I heard a knock at the window.

'Howzit going? Been busy?' he asked, looking in.

'I suppose you could call it that,' I said, reluctant to speak, 'I've been sorting out my ticket. I'm going back to England in a week or so.'

'So soon?' he said and I nodded.

'Time to get on with life.'

'Listen, why don't you come round for a drink tonight? Christmas cheer and all that.'

'I don't know... maybe,' I said, my voice flat and non-committal. 'I've got quite a lot to sort out.'

He must have noted my reluctance because he shrugged and said, 'Well, it's up to you. You know where I am. The invitation's there.'

'Thanks,' I said, trying to smile.

'See you later,' he said and got on his bike.

I don't know what made me go round and see Tony that

night. Perhaps it was the thought of another night at home with its doldrum silence and static conversation. Or perhaps, strangely, I felt some connection to Gran through him, and if, as it seemed, everyone else knew her better than I did, he might have been able to shed some light on who she really was.

'Come in,' said Tony, opening the door. 'I was just sitting outside in the back garden. It's too hot to be inside.' He was barefoot in a pair of shorts and a T-shirt. 'Would you like a drink?' he asked as we went into the kitchen. 'I'm having a beer but there is some wine and Cola. Cola?' He held up his hands in a question.

'Wine,' I said, without my usual delay in answering. It was a bad idea, I knew, but I felt like a wound up alarm clock about to ring out. I suddenly felt that I wanted to talk to someone, just talk and talk and talk, but I regretted coming around to see Tony. He wasn't the right person to speak to. I should have stayed at home, I thought, and written everything down in my diary. We went to sit outside. There were two sun-beds on the lawn and I could see that Tony had been lying on one, for a book and an ashtray lay next to it. There was a silence while we sipped our drinks.

'I don't know what to say to you, Ellie,' he said. I felt a sharp pain travel up my chest from the echo of the words.

'What do you mean?'

'I mean I want to get to know you, but there's this six foot wall around you.'

I stared ahead. I was a little surprised at his forwardness.

'With barbed wire along the top,' he half laughed, making a circular movement with his right index finger.

'You're not the first to say that.'

'I want to help,' he continued, 'but I can't if you won't let me.'

I was sitting on the sun-bed, hugging my legs and holding the glass of wine. Tony lay spread out on the sun-bed next to me. I thought of leaving but didn't do anything. The combination of wine and the fact that I felt suddenly tired kept me there.

'What do you want?' I asked, defensively.

'I just want to know you.' It sounded so simple.

'You're leaving,' I said.

'So are you. What difference does that make?'

There was another silence. A bird chirped and the sun dipped lower, taking its angry heat with it and leaving the world calmer and cooler, although nonetheless troubled.

'Well, what do you want to know?' I said.

Tony took a swig of his beer and drew his lips back, tasting the bitterness. 'This is not an interrogation.'

I looked away and there was another silence.

'What do you want in life?' Tony asked.

I sighed and put my head on my knees. I thought, I don't want any more unhappy endings.

'Tell me about your life, Ellie,' he said, quietly.

'I wouldn't know where to begin.'

'Begin at the beginning.'

'The funny thing is that the beginning keeps changing and everything that comes after it. It might make more sense to begin now.'

'OK. Begin now,' said Tony, filling up my glass.

'Would you mind if I had a cigarette?' He tossed the packet over.

'What are you doing your PhD in?' asked Tony. His eyes were closed, as if against the glare of the sun, although it had all but gone and the strange silver reign of twilight was taking over.

'Postcolonial literature,' I said, taking a drag of the cigarette and blowing the smoke directly above me, unlike Tony who blew it out of the side of his mouth. I supposed it showed how inexperienced I was at smoking but I didn't care. Life had begun to take on that half-rosy glow that drinking wine on an empty stomach produces.

'Really?' said Tony, obviously surprised. He paused and then, 'Post-colonial-literature.' He said it slowly and then sighed. The noise made me laugh and he started laughing too. Soon we were giggling uncontrollably. I couldn't put the cigarette in my mouth for more than half a second before I'd start laughing again. It was wonderful; the first time I had really laughed in months.

'What's postcolonial literature?' he asked, emphasizing the post as though it was the one word in the title he couldn't understand.

'Oh, I don't know,' I answered lazily, not feeling like giving a lecture on its origins. I'd had enough of all that standing in front of an uninterested class and trying to make them excited about Black Women's Writing or the Asian Diaspora. Who the hell really cared anyway?

'You must know,' said Tony, 'you've done a whole PhD on it.'

'Doing,' I corrected him.

'Doing, done, will do. What's it all about?'

I thought for a while, took a few more drags of the cigarette, and then answered. 'It's about longing for an ideal, some idea of perfection. The past, when everything was well and good.'

'I'm not quite with you.'

'Some feel they can't even speak their own language anymore because it's been corrupted by English. The irony is, would they really like to be living a life without all the advantages of colonialism, unaware they could actually write at all?'

A half-smile played on Tony's lips.

'It's a bit like the government here,' I continued. 'They go on about colonialism, imperialism and any other 'ism', as though they really don't want to be driving a Mercedes Benz or living in a home built like the White House or even... even going overseas on foreign spending sprees. All they actually long for is a hut somewhere without any modern conveniences and absolutely no modern transport.'

'There's a bit of a difference between postcolonial writers and African governments, surely?'

I ignored him, for I was slightly annoyed at his reaction to my speech and the way he had picked up that I had deviated from answering his original question to making a political comment. I was feeling so bitter and defeated I wanted to hit back, not at Tony, but at the world.

'What do you think it means, Tony, to have an identity? For anyone anywhere at this particular point in time, what do you think it means to say: "I am this" or "I am that"?'

'I think the problem is,' said Tony, getting a word or two in when he could, 'that we all want everything done our way.'

I looked at him, uncomprehending.

'We both want to be in control,' said Tony, 'both black

371

and white. The problem in Zimbabwe is that whites want to live first world lives in a third world country and can't understand when it doesn't work out like that. The problem with blacks is that they want to do things their way, but it's never really their idea. Their own idea. Democracy, for example. It's somebody else's invention. They talk of colonialism and the need of an African culture, but they wouldn't swap any of the benefits of colonialism for the chance to have their old way of life back.'

'That's what I said. That's exactly what I mean.'

'Instead of leaning on each other for support and acknowledging that we both need each other, we bring each other down, trample each other under foot. We both lose, Ellie. We're both losers. We've both lost.'

I tilted the bottle up against my lips for another swig of the wine, but Tony leaned over and took it away. He pushed the hair out of my eyes and kissed my lips.

'Don't drink anymore, Ellie,' he said. I suddenly felt very tired and very drunk. He took my hand and pulled me up and then led me into his bedroom. His bed felt cool and inviting as I lay down and he curled his body around mine. Holding his hand, I fell asleep.

Chapter Twenty-three

3ʳᵈ June, 1990

'My petunias are doing well this year,' I said and immediately regretted it. It sounded like something an old woman would say. I waited for the blow, for the bright patronising comment; an acknowledgement of my own self-proclaimed statement: I am old. Instead, he said, 'You could do with some fertilizer on the geraniums. And the roses need to be cut back. I could do that for you if you have a pair of secateurs.' I knew he was offering because that's what he wanted to do, not because he felt sorry for me. He sees the garden as something to explore, to keep alive, to add to, not as something set, static, never to be changed.

10ᵗʰ July, 1990

'I think I love you, Evelyn,' Jason said to me this evening.

'No you don't,' I half laughed. We were sitting outside having a hot toddy on the verandah. It was dark and cold but moths still flickered round the light so I had switched it off. We relied on a pale moonlight to give us some light. 'Not really.'

'I do,' he persisted. His earnestness suddenly made him seem young and I was reminded briefly of Ellie and her crankiness over going to the dance this evening with Vance. I had to try not to sound motherly or condescending.

'You love Rosie.'

I heard him suck his lips in and smack them out again. I could imagine the tips of his fingers touching each other, his hands making a triangle, like a doctor before he gives a prognosis.

'No, I don't,' he said, straightening up. 'She's just well, just there.'

'A travelling companion?'

'More or less.' He sounded completely dejected, but I knew any attempt on my part to try to make him feel better wouldn't be appreciated.

I placed my glass on the table.

'You remind me of someone.'

He looked up.

'Someone who also loved gardening and books. Poetry. He loved poetry.'

'Is he dead?'

I shook my head. 'No, just far away. Far, far away.'

'Do you love Miles?' he asked after a pause and I detected the slightest sneer in his voice as though no one could possibly love Miles and after all he is far more tangible an opponent than a slightly mysterious someone who loved poetry.

But of course I love Miles. He may not seem extremely loveable to many people. It is only with Miles that I feel a kind of peace, a love that neither demands nor accuses. Leonard, poor Leonard was so intricately caught up with my relationship with Wally and I could not love one without hating the other, and it was Wally, Wally who I truly loved. But now I see that love need not demand, it need not hurt, it need not require everything of one. I can go out with Miles tonight, we can have a fantastic time at the Naval Club and then I can come home, alone. I am not anxious about tomorrow with Miles. He will be there; I will be there. The absence of love, that kind of love, is a relief. To not feel jealousy, anticipation, loss. To never want more. To not have to wait for a telephone call, a foot at the gate, a hand on the door. To not feel the length of hours stretched into the tightness of hope, twists of despair. This now is a love that does not end. Love has no time limit, no required time. It flows on from hour to hour, day to day. Peace, yes, Miles has brought me a sense of peace.

He's cranky, but not bitter like Leonard; he loves Shakespeare, but he is not pretentious (like Jason?) or anxious (like Ellie?). He just is. He's unaware of himself, not trying to be anyone, not trying to make me love him for this or that reason. Just himself. I've never known anyone who is so comfortable in his own skin. And that is why I love him.

And then, too, he understands the nature of sadness, something that Leonard does not, which is why he is

*bitter. He allows me time to be alone, to grieve, to grow.
Every day I grow through the house. The garden. I extend
myself through rooms, loving the light, the dark, the
easiness of being alone. I no longer live in half a room as
I did when I was married, or when I visited here to see
Wally: given a certain time of day to call, knowing at the
end that nothing was mine or ever could be.*

*There was something pathetic about Jason, the way he
sat hunched over the table, the bitterness in his voice. I
wished he had gone to the dance with Ellie. She would
appreciate this intensity of purpose whereas I do not. I
am too old for this now, too old.*

I skipped ahead, looking, searching, for important dates,
wanting somewhere to find myself as I thought I was.

20th October, 1992

*I wrote to Wally this evening and asked him for some
money. It's not for myself – it's for Ellie. She wants to go
to university in the UK. She says she doesn't fit in here,
that she's dying, starved of culture and books and
learning. Wally will appreciate her predicament because
that's how I think he felt at times. That's why his study
was only his. He never wanted anyone to look in and
laugh, to tread on his dreams the way his father had.*

*Some months ago, I enquired through the British
Embassy as to whether I would be eligible for a pension,
but I received a letter last week informing me that, as I
have never worked in the UK, I am not. Recently, I found*

376

myself wondering what my life would have been like if I had stayed in England. I'd probably own a house, receive a pension, go on holiday to Majorca twice a year, complain about the weather, the government, tax. Live in a sheltered little world. Grey, but sheltered. In England you are someone. Not an important someone, but a life that is valued. What you think and experience matters. You can shout, complain, ask for more.

Africa gives you the knowledge that you are no one, that nothing lasts, that you are a very small creature on a very large continent and that you will live and die like anything else.

Chapter Twenty-four

15ᵗʰ September, 2004

I went to the station with Miles this afternoon. He went inside to book a ticket for his domestic worker who is going to Harare and I sat in the car waiting for him to come out. I can't believe it is the same place I arrived at over fifty years ago. It was a grand place then: spotless, with a restaurant and a bathroom. The nearby buildings were also smart: painted, well maintained. The hotels were not brothels, but respectable places to stay in. The line of palm trees into the town centre heralded something new, something to be proud of, a beginning.

Last weekend we went to the park. It is bare and brown, the worst I have ever seen it, worse even compared to all the drought years we have had. I could not find one gardener in the whole place. In a flowerbed, instead of the usual seed packet denoting what was planted, was a condom packet. It seems to be the order of the day now. There are condom packets everywhere now, and yet everywhere, too, the stench of AIDS.

I felt the same feeling this afternoon. A feeling of things dying and there being nothing to replace them. I saw no beginnings, only an end. Nothing new has been built there for a long time. The shops are dilapidated, sagging, ancient, tired. And yet posters still advertise hope: dances, bands, football matches. And that made me think that, because I am no longer a part of it and because it is no longer a part of white life, does it mean less now than it did to me then? Isn't there someone who arrives on the overnight from Harare, perhaps hours, even a whole day late, in an overcrowded compartment, stinking of orange peel and urine and greasy takeaway food, and yet feels that same sense of hope on arrival?

Maybe he or she doesn't see the row of slumped shops or the tyrannical eye of the power station, but the row of palms, not as tired ballerinas waiting impatiently to be signalled off stage, but as something fresh, something new. Perhaps I am just too old, too tired and too old. Perhaps when we are young, young and happy, we do not see the weariness in life because we have not experienced ourselves.

But then another part of me wonders, did it have to go like this? Could the shops and streets and palms not have stood tall for them, too? Does the train have to smell of urine and unwashed bodies? I see they use the old Rhodesian Railways carriages still; what better days they must've seen! But black people wouldn't have travelled in the same manner, would they? They would've travelled third class anyway. What was it like then? I never knew. Was Rhodesia bad? I'm not sure. Not all of it, surely? I find myself longing for clean streets, spotless public toilets, a competent police force. What has been gained? Independence. A shallow word in a country where freedom of speech is not allowed.

Did we treat black people as badly as they treat each other? Surely not, I long to say. But maybe it is not enough to be well fed or looked after. Somewhere one wants an acknowledgement: I am human. More than that: You and I – we are equal.

Ellie often writes and urges me to join the Movement for Democratic Change – at least attend a meeting or two and see what they have to say. And sometimes I have been tempted, but I have never been able to follow it through somehow. Perhaps I just don't believe enough in change. Perhaps I never have liked the idea in whatever form it took.

Of course there is a part of me that understands him; Mugabe, I mean. I understand the bitterness. After all, we both lost children. And one can never forget, can one, after that. Never ever. What eats him up, what poisons him, what sets him out to destroy anything new, anything conciliatory, is this awful bitterness. But not just that; his failure, too. I failed Jeremy. I couldn't rescue him, couldn't separate him from the mess I had made.

If hate, as Wally once told me, is the purest form of love, then all I see is an old man begging to be loved. His photo is everywhere: in the bank, in the post office, in some of the most rundown, dirty shops in town. He presides over everything, saying: All this, all this destruction is mine. And all because he wanted to be loved. Forgiveness is what he offered us all at Independence, but *he never really wanted to give it and now he doesn't want to receive it. And who would? Forgiveness nullifies anger and forces one to look at oneself rather than fixing all that hate on someone else. How we all hate looking at ourselves.*

Doesn't he feel guilt, people ask, but how many of us do? I never thought I'd be the 'type' of person to have an affair. Flashy. Done up. Hard. A home breaker. Someone who feeds on another's misery, who milks the bad time in their marriage for everything that it's worth: jewellery, money, nights in expensive hotels. Wally never bought me jewellery; we never stayed in a hotel until Mozambique.

Often we talked; talked and talked and talked and never made love at all. We'd look at all his maps and dream of all the places we were going to go. We'd drink cheap wine and eat cheese sandwiches on a picnic blanket on the floor, imagining that we were far away and different people.

Did I feel guilty? No. I tried, I sat in church and listened to the minister admonish those 'people of sin' who fornicate, who conduct extra-marital affairs, who drink and gamble and who never seek the forgiveness of the Lord. And all I thought as I left was that I am not guilty, except perhaps of feeling no guilt at all.

I think of that time, so long ago now, when she came to see me. Perhaps I shouldn't have been so surprised to be paid a visit by my lover's wife. I had been married to Leonard for about four months and had developed a habit of waking very early in the morning, around three, and sitting up to watch the white dawn of each day harden.

I used to think that I had seen a preview of my life, day after day, each day rolling into the next and I thought that if I could watch it happen there would be no more surprises: I knew what was coming before all those innocent sleepers did. I slept in the afternoon when the world retreated from the heat of the day and the roof creaked in lazy submission. I was pregnant, of course, so I got away with my strange sleeping hours.

It must've been about four o'clock when she knocked on the door and I opened it, bleary eyed, not even thinking about who it could be. It was her: Riette. She looked pale, I remember.

'The child,' she said, looking at my swollen belly. 'I don't mind if he comes to see it. If he's at all involved in its life.' She stopped and stared at me before continuing. I hadn't even asked her inside and she was standing rather gingerly on the front step while I leaned against the door for support. 'You'll let him, won't you? It's all he ever wanted, a child.'

I shut the door then, but I know she stood on the step for another couple of minutes before leaving.

3rd October, 2004

I have just written to Ellie and told her that I would like to come and see her in England. I have felt this way since that day at the railway station. Perhaps it is a sudden longing for order and cleanliness, or perhaps it is something to do with age. For years I have planned to make a trip back 'home', but I have always imagined it

382

to be a fair way in the future. Now I am seventy-seven years old and one is never sure how much time one has left. I'd like to go while I still can, while I have the energy and while my health is still good.

I wrote to Wally as well and told him of my plans. I never felt quite resolved about our relationship and I'd like now to sort it out. More than anything, I'd like to tell Ellie the truth. I want her to come with me to see him, to know him as himself, not this fictional Uncle Wally who has haunted our lives for so many, many years.

I felt a thrill of excitement as I headed a sheet of blue paper this morning. Dear Wally. How long since I wrote those words? I have always found it easier to express myself on paper. It's something about the written word; it has a power that the spoken word lacks. We riddle our speech with slang, ums, ahs and pauses, unfinished sentences, till it hangs ragged and useless about us. But there is no letter I have written with an unfinished sentence. Even the letters I did not send. When I look through them, I find a person closer to myself than perhaps anyone knows. I see who I really am, but I wonder if they do.

If I'd ever sent Wally the letters, I wonder if he would have been able to read the clues, to decipher what I was telling him. I don't believe it is possible to be anything but oneself in a letter. That's why they are such strong pieces of evidence in crime cases. But it's not only our handwriting that gives us away, it's what we write. There is nothing more important than that, whether it be a short note or a long tirade. There is nothing more important than that.

But suddenly I didn't know what to write. After all this time, what should I say?

Perhaps that's why she never sent the letter to Wally. I found it, in a long blue envelope, between the pages of her last entry.

7ᵗʰ October, 2004

When I die, I want to die here, in Africa. I want to die on a beautiful clear day in August, when the sky is blue and the sun is not yet high and hot, but diffused in the air, alive in what you see. That's when I want to die.

My grandmother died in October, before the rains started, when each day was saturated with the heat of the dying year. He said he didn't mean to disturb her. He thought she'd be asleep. He thought, too, that she wouldn't hear him or dare to confront him. She was seventy-seven years old. 'A good innings' someone said to me at her funeral. Could she not then at least have chosen her moment to die? The sky was not blue and the earth was not cool. Her face was beaten beyond recognition.

Christmas Day was hot and bright. As usual, I woke early and slowly rose from the bed. A faint headache thumped somewhere behind my eyes. On the shelf in my cupboard lay three presents, all wrapped in the same paper. Some sort of pixie type creature was blowing on a horn, leaning forward, his legs wide apart and his eyes closed as his cheeks puffed out. There seemed something slightly forlorn about him and I almost wanted him to put the silly horn down and catch his breath. The smell of pine from the tree reached me with pangs of nostalgia.

Christmas Day almost seemed to pass without anyone noticing. Grandad sat on the verandah, as he always did, looking out – where? At what? He wasn't bored, that I knew. He was trying to sort something out in his mind, like we all were. Cricket was on television and Zimbabwe weren't losing quite as dramatically as they had done for a while. Grandad maintained it was just luck; soon they'd be out – no one played first class cricket anymore. We all expected him to say 'not since the Rhodesian days' but he never mentioned them anymore and the void where the words should have been, reeled and swung, hitting us for six and leaving only a sense of loss, an ache for the way things were, imperfect as they had been.

Tony phoned.

'What are you doing?'

'Nothing.'

'Would you like to have dinner with me? Turkey, potatoes, pudding, the lot? I'll even throw a cracker in for good measure.'

'I don't think so,' I said, the flatness of my voice slicing through the jollity in his, rather like a pair of sheers clipping off a rosebud.

'Come on. It'll be fun. Promise.'

'I don't think so, Tony. I'll arrange for the books to be here when you want to collect them.'

'That's it?'

'That's it. I'm sorry, Tony. Goodbye.'

Part Three

Chapter One

1st January, 1947

I had the most wonderful New Year. I was really not looking forward to it – dreading it, even – as Shirley and Eddie left for Beira two days before. Shirley's the closest to what I would call a friend. There are the girls from the office but, well, that's all they are, girls from the office. Don't get me wrong, they're nice – friendly, good fun, but nothing more. Lesley and Ann did say for me to go out with them to the Grand, but I thought it best to stay at home. I felt very low. I could hear the girls next door getting ready – well, at least a squeal or two of excitement now and again.

At one point, there was a tremendous banging on my door and, when I went to open it, Audrey Faraday was standing there in just her slip.

'Oh, Evelyn, let me in!' she cried. 'Someone will see me standing here!' and she dived in under my arm and threw herself onto my sofa.

'What on earth is going on?' I asked. She has such beautifully pale skin, which that afternoon was glowing with laughter.

'I think he's going to ask me, Evie.' She stopped then and repeated herself, slowly but smiling all the while. 'I think he's going to ask me.'

'You mean?'

'Yes, I mean to marry him!'

'Oh, Audrey, well, that's wonderful, just wonderful.'

I threw my arms around her neck and felt that warm just-washed touch of her skin. I couldn't help but feel a terrible sadness, although I made sure Audrey never saw it. When she had gone, I lay on my bed and cried.

At about three o'clock that afternoon, Mrs Wiesman knocked on my door.

'You've a visitor, Miss Saunders,' she barked. 'He says he's your uncle from Salisbury.'

Surprised, I leapt off my bed, ran a comb through my hair and slipped my shoes on. I glanced at myself in the mirror quickly and wished my eyes weren't so puffy.

Cadwallader was in Mrs Wiesman's small sitting room. He had his back to me when I walked in and seemed to be looking at the ornaments on Mrs Wiesman's mantelpiece. He had his hands behind his back and he was holding his hat.

'Cadwallader?'

He turned and smiled. 'Evelyn! How are you?'

We talked for about half an hour. Mrs Wiesman kept the door open and I knew that she was probably listening from inside the dining room that adjoined her room. Cadwallader knew as well and kept saying some things really loud, like: 'I've heard from your mother. She says she's well and that Aunt Clarissa made her special mince pies for Boxing Day.' I wanted to laugh, but he cautioned me playfully with his finger on his lips.

Cadwallader is in town for about three weeks. He begins some work down here in the New Year so they decided to spend Christmas here with some friends. I thought it kind of him to visit and find out how I've been coping. On one level he seems like an archetypal gentleman: very polite and not particularly expressive with his emotions. Nothing much seems to worry him, perhaps because he has money and money does solve a lot of problems. But, on the other hand, although one might be excused for thinking him a little superficial, there is a depth to him that I sometimes catch glimpses of. He understands things, picks up on what is going on at a different level. He doesn't acknowledge openly that he does so, he suddenly surprises one with an attempt at an answer.

'What are you doing tonight?'

'Nothing,' I said, feeling a little embarrassed. I didn't want him to think that I had had no invitations for New Year's.

'How about dinner and a dance at the Club?'

'Which one?'

'The only one. The Bulawayo Club. Would you like that?'

I hesitated, thinking of his wife. I didn't know if I was in the mood for her. He seemed to read my mind. 'My wife's ill. She was going to come, but she's not feeling well. Bad back.'

I brightened.

Well, we had the most marvellous time. Cadwallader promised Mrs W. to have me back very soon after midnight. She pulled her lips in at first and shook her head, like a doctor who has diagnosed a terrible illness, but she relented in the face of Cadwallader's charm and he came to fetch me at seven o'clock sharp.

There were so many people there. The women in the most beautiful ball gowns (I borrowed something from one of the girls) and the men in tuxedos. I had a glass of champagne and felt the world spin around me as the band struck up. Instinctively, my foot started tapping and I couldn't wait to be asked to dance. Cadwallader introduced me to a whole lot of people – lots of single men and I could've danced all night with each of them and still had energy for more!

The food was tremendous. I haven't eaten that well since the time I went to dinner with Cadwallader and his wife in Salisbury. Cadwallader always introduced me as his niece and after a while it just seemed so natural. No one was suspicious – and why should they be? Don't we all take what people tell us about themselves as absolute truth?

And then suddenly I met him. George Granger, a friend of Cadwallader who served in Burma during the War. It is the first time that I have found myself really attracted to someone and it quite swept me off my feet. He must be about twenty-five with thick dark hair and the longest eyelashes I have ever seen on a man. He's a Rhodesian, but spent a lot of time in England, training with the RRAF. I didn't tell him about Timothy. I don't want to be a widow and what if he knew him? No, I just want to be Evelyn Saunders again. Cadwallader kept looking over at George and I talking. He smiled every time my eyes met his and raised his glass at me on one occasion. He seemed to be watching me with a fatherly air, looking after me and I felt so comforted that in this new, exciting, but rather overwhelming and at times frightening country, I have him to watch over me.

At midnight, we sang Auld Lang Syne and did the conga right outside into the street. Someone made a toast. 'Happy New Year, Rhodesia, 1947.' And then we all sang God Save the King. Shortly afterwards, Cadwallader said he must take me home so I said goodbye to George, after he asked for my address, and we climbed into Cadwallader's car. It was the most perfect evening. People were walking home, shouting and laughing and wishing each other a Happy New Year.

'George is engaged,' Wally said suddenly. He kept his eyes on the road. 'I thought I must tell you.'

My heart plummeted and I felt the sudden return of all the loneliness that I had felt earlier that day until Cadwallader arrived.

'Lovely chap. A bit mixed up that's all. The war.'

The war. How I hated it. Longed to be free from something that seemed continually to reach out its long tentacles and pull me back. How I longed to find someone whose life had not been corrupted by it. I tried to maintain a calm, composed exterior, but my words came out, hurt and broken 'Is there anyone here who hasn't had their lives changed by the war?'

Cadwallader shrugged. 'Probably not.'

I was silent for a while and then Cadwallader turned into a parking bay and switched the engine off.

'Sorry,' he said again, 'I thought I must tell you. That sort of thing happens a lot out here. I'll have a word. Tell him to leave you alone. Was going to, but I didn't want to cause a fuss. New Year and all that.'

'I don't need you,' I said suddenly. 'I don't need a knight in shining armour to look after me. I'm fine.'

I just wanted to go, to run and run and run. And maybe I'd get to the coast and I'd get on a ship and I'd sail all the way back to England and everyone would be there: Mum and Gregory and Marjorie and even the Clifton brothers, all waiting for me as the ship docked and I'd never, never, ever have to come back here again.

Chapter Two

I left Zimbabwe after Christmas. Back in England a cold wet January greeted me; I was glad. I didn't want sunshine or blue sky; even the gradually lengthening days irritated me. I didn't want anything to remind me of home, I wanted nothing to be the same. For three days I didn't leave my flat, preferring instead to sit cross-legged on a chair in front of my desk, bent over some piece of work. I was reading a lot of Wordsworth, though never one of my favourite poets and not someone to whom I attributed much praise. But ploughing through his praise of Tintern Abbey, I came upon the lines:

> *...but hearing oftentimes*
> *The still, sad music of humanity,*
> *Nor harsh nor grating, though of ample power*
> *To chasten and subdue.*

In those few words Wordsworth described the background music that I had heard all through my childhood, some kind of whispered tune that had the listener strain to hear it entirely, like a piano playing in a far off room.

When I was a child and afraid of death, I found solace in reading comics and books where no one ever got older and grew up and died. Now I found myself craving the same sort of immortality in the work I was doing. My research became another escape, another way of retreating into an imaginary world where the realities of this world could be kept at bay. I half wished that I could stay in my flat forever, perhaps ordering food when I needed it, but never having to leave the comfort and security of my little world. Such is the effect of winter too. Life is always that more immediate in the summer, forcing one to open windows and clear out clutter and face the sunshine outside.

I was preparing some questions for a tutorial group I was taking the following week. We were to discuss Wordsworth's Lucy poems. I turned to a clean sheet of paper in my notepad and wrote: Who was Lucy? Someone he knew? His first love who bore his child? His dead daughter? Does she provide a medium for him to express his feelings about death? Why did he write these poems?

I sat back, my pen suspended over the last word I had written, and looked at the list for a long time. I suddenly felt that I wanted to know, I wanted the mystery to be solved. I didn't want the usual tutorial session where we discussed various theories and ideas and then sat back and said, 'well, we'll never know for sure,' or 'it is difficult to say with any certainty but...' The study of literature suddenly seemed like a complete and utter waste of time. Where were the answers, where was the certainty? I picked up the telephone and dialled the number of the University. I asked to be put through to Dr Munroe in the English Department. He would know, I thought, he would know the answer. Who was Lucy? I wanted to know. I wanted to know who Lucy was. I was put through. I waited. The phone rang and rang. He wasn't in. I put the phone down, almost in a rage, and then strode across to my desk and pulled open the bottom drawer.

In it were all the papers I had brought back from Zimbabwe: the photographs, the letters, the documents. I was looking for the letter, the last one written to him but never sent, the one written in perfect copperplate in dark blue ink and folded neatly into thirds. The one addressed to Cadwallader Lloyd, 3 St. David's Walk, Cardiff, South Wales, United Kingdom.

I picked up the phone again and dialled Directory Enquiries.

'What's your number please?' said the voice on the other end of the line. I could hardly speak. His name sounded wrong in my mouth. I felt as though I would be doubted, told to repeat the name, told there was no possibility that such a person could exist.

'Hold on, please,' said the voice. I waited. It came back. With the number. My heart lurched. It was likely he was still alive. I could phone him. Now. This very minute. I could phone him. What would I say? Hello, this is Ellie, Evelyn's granddaughter. Hello, this is Ellie. I am Ellie. I know who you are.

Finally, I decided to say that I was Ellie, Evelyn's granddaughter, and over in England and hoping to see him. I picked up the receiver again and stopped. He would ask. He would say, how is Evelyn? I have not heard from her for a while. What would I say? I am sorry. I have bad news. Evelyn is dead. Or would I lie? She is well. She sends her love. She is sorry she does not have more time to write. Then I also thought, what if he knew already? Perhaps a friend had written and he knew already. Thinking the latter may be true and that he may be glad to hear from me as a result, I picked up the phone and dialled. I waited for the click, for the 'hello' or the 'good morning', or the 'Cadwallader Lloyd speaking, can I help you?' But it just rang and rang and rang. I put the phone down. I tried again. And again. No one answered. He was out. I could try later. But I wanted to speak to him now. In a fit of frustration I wrote him a brief letter, telling him who I was and that I wanted to come and see him. I ran downstairs and posted the letter in the post-box across the road. I kept on trying to phone him through-out the day and in the evening, too. No one answered.

I tried phoning him the next day too, but I was unsuccess-ful. And the day after that. I even tried leaving it for the whole afternoon, as if this would somehow make him be there in the evening. The following day, a large brown envelope arrived. I looked at the postmark with a start; it was from Cardiff. Inside was my letter, still in its sealed envelope. There was a note attached to it with a paper clip.

To whom it may concern, it read, I am sorry to inform you that Mr Lloyd has now moved to The Elms Nursing Home in Hereford. He suffered from a stroke at the end of last year and it was decided that it would be best for him to be in a place where he can be looked after as well as possible. I, as his neighbour and long term friend, have agreed to keep an eye on his house and cat and to redirect any mail that may arrive for him.

His condition has deteriorated over the past weeks to

such an extent that he is in no condition to either read or reply to any correspondence and thus I have not forwarded your letter. If you are a relative of Mr Lloyd's, or know of a way in which I could contact his family, please could you let me know as, in the unfortunate, but likely, circumstance that Mr Lloyd's affairs need to be wound up, I will need to contact them.

Please do not hesitate to contact me.

Yours,
Emerith Davies

There followed an address for Uncle Wally and a phone number. The next morning, for the first time in nearly a week, I got ready to venture outside, although this time it wasn't for the necessity of food, but for the necessity of a mind put at rest. I was also going to say goodbye to someone I had never known.

One train and two taxi rides later, I was at The Elms. The ease of travel, even the distance, didn't seem to justify the longing. From the outside, it looked like a typical nursing home, solemnly quiet red brick set in peaceful surrounds. Too much peace, I thought, as though it was to prepare its inmates for what was to come.

The reception area was typical too: light green carpeting, prints of wild flowers in brass frames, four single chairs covered in soft grey linen grouped round a wide, smooth table, a few choice magazines spread over it in a friendly arc. Very comforting, very quiet, very still.

There was an office off to the left, but no one was in it. The computer was on though and a red mug with a picture of a deep white smile, that looked quite sinister without eyes to ground it, rested next to the keyboard.

I was trying to read a notice, something about allergies, when the door, which was half open, flew backwards and in marched a plump nursing sister in a blue uniform, buttons up the front and watch pinned on the top of her left breast pocket, with black tights and black lace up shoes. Sensible shoes for sensible people. Following her was a man, a young man with dark hair that was greying prematurely at the temples and belied the smoothness of his skin and his youthful gait. He was wearing a suit, but had loosened his tie and looked harassed in the way that only young, inexperienced people can. It was as though he still had the price tags on the bottom of his shoes, as though the cellophane wrapper his tie was bought in was lying on his bed at home, as well as the cardboard backing from his shirt and the great big plastic bag his suit was folded into when he bought it at the last sale.

'I don't know where it is,' she said as she strode in ahead of him, her pony-tail jumping up and down in indignation. She rummaged through some papers on the desk with a brusque movement that suggested she didn't really expect to find whatever it was there. 'I put it here this morning, that's all I know.'

'Well, it's not here now,' he whined.

'Excuse me,' I intervened. 'I don't know if I'm in the right place, but I've come to see a relative of mine, a Mr Cadwallader Lloyd.'

'Yeah, it's through the double doors, left down the

400

corridor and it's the second door on your right. Didn't know he had any relatives,' she said as I left.

As I walked along, I wondered who I would find lying in Uncle Wally's bed. Would he be the same man I had met seventeen years before? The man with the big beaming face and the receding hairline? Would he sit up and smile and joke. Would he sing *Mona Lisa* and *A Nightingale Sang in Berkeley Square*? It was early in the afternoon. Would he even be awake?

I wasn't prepared at all for what I encountered when I walked into Wally's room. He was asleep, lying on his back and breathing with his mouth open. His breath was shallow and every now and then it seemed to miss a beat and he spluttered. His face was no longer like the sun of my childhood paintings, but rather like a deflated balloon. It was thin and drawn and his skin clung tightly to the hollow recesses of his cheeks, which were crisscrossed with tiny blue and purple veins. The sheet was drawn up under his elbows and turned down. His arms lay still and lifeless, one connected to a drip.

I took his hand in mine with an intimacy that would've been presumptuous had he been aware of my presence. His palm was a hard, dry yellow, but the back of his hand was brown except for the veins which rose blue and fat across it and the liver spots pitted here and there, as though a child had flicked paint carelessly across them. He didn't respond. I looked at him. He had hardly any hair left; a feathery white half crown was barely visible.

On top of the small cupboard next to him were a jug of water and two glasses. There wasn't a book or a magazine, a bar of chocolate or an apple even. Nothing else but him. This was Wally, Uncle Wally, who had once played with me and tickled me until I screamed. This was the man who had once held my grandmother as they danced and when they made love, the only man she had ever truly loved and for whom she had borne a child.

I sat for a long time. Another nurse came in. She appeared to be pleased to see me. No one ever visited.

'He's on his own,' she said, as she tucked in his blankets and smoothed the sheet down, completely superfluous actions as he hadn't moved an inch since I'd been there. She was a large woman with a mass of brown curls pinned back with a tortoiseshell clip. Her large light-blue eyes seemed younger than the rest of her as did her neatly clipped nails at the end of her short plump fingers. There was something warm about her, something that for some reason reminded me of tea and hot toast on a winter's day.

'You're the first person who has ever come to see him.'

'How long has he been here?' I asked.

'About two or three months,' she said, pursing her lips and thinking. 'Since October, I think. Yes, October.' The last two words were accompanied by a decisive nod.

I nodded once in return. Gran died in October.

I must've sat for nearly an hour, watching him, holding his hand. Outside a flurry of soft snow floated down, melting as soon as it touched the earth. Gradually the sky darkened and another nurse came in and drew the blinds. Eventually I got up and put my scarf and coat on. I could hear a trolley being wheeled along the corridor; tea was being served.

On my way out, I stopped and spoke to the nurse at the reception area. It was the large nurse I had spoken to earlier.

402

She was putting files away in a cabinet and didn't look my way at first.

'I'll come back tomorrow,' I said.

'OK,' she said cheerily and then turned and saw me. She looked surprised but then smiled and said, 'Well, that'll be nice for him. As I said, you're the only visitor he's had.'

I went the next day and, a week after that, I visited again. It was a Saturday afternoon. A doctor was bent over Uncle Wally when I arrived and two sisters stood on either side of the bed, dutifully answering all his questions and nodding at any suggestion he made. He gave me the briefest of glances when he was finished and left the room with the brusque determination of a man with little time to waste.

One of the nurses, it was the large, jolly one, came over to me while the other recorded Wally's state on a sheet pinned to a clipboard at the foot of his bed. I had that feeling again, of hot tea and warm toast with the butter soaking in, and for a moment I wanted her to put her arms around me and hold me close. She probably had children, I thought, a boy and a girl who waited with eager anticipation for her to come home every evening and who sat on her lap and read books while she stroked their cheeks and kissed their hair.

She led me out of the room and into the corridor, looking back as she did so, as though she was afraid that Uncle Wally would hear something.

'It's not good,' she said in a low voice. She was wearing a navy blue cardigan and, as she spoke, she gently folded back the cuffs, something she probably did for her children and unconsciously applied to her own dressing. Then she folded her arms and picked a stray piece of cotton off one sleeve, absently examining it for clues as to where it had come from.

She turned her attention back to me. 'Not long now. He's very weak.'

I nodded.

'Is there anyone you'd like to call? Any other family? Anyone... ?'

I shook my head. 'Not that I know of.'

She looked puzzled. 'Your mother? Father? I'm sorry, I don't know... I mean, isn't there anyone?'

'My family live in Zimbabwe,' I explained and saw briefly her mental attempt to locate it in time and place. Her thoughts seemed to alight on something.

'Oh, Zimbabwe. Hasn't that been on the news lately?'

'Yes,' I said, but didn't elaborate. I wanted to defend it, leave it in peace and wished it were better known for Victoria Falls than violence and anarchy.

'And you're the only one over here?'

'Yes. I'm a student.'

She gave one long nod of her head and sucked her lips in as though something had just made sense.

'How are you related?' she asked.

I began to answer when she suddenly touched my arm and said quickly, 'I hope you don't mind me asking.'

'No, of course not. He's... he's my uncle.'

She nodded. 'I see.'

'Great-uncle really. On my mother's side.'

'Yes, I thought he was a bit old to be just an uncle. Oh, well, it's nice you're here. It's nice for him to have someone here.'

She had begun to walk away when I suddenly called after

her: 'Does he... did he... before... when he first came... did he ever ask about anyone? Did he ever mention anyone to you?'

She thought for a second or two and then shook her head. 'He mentioned a man who was looking after his house and I think he had a dog. He mentioned the name but I've forgotten it. I'll ask Mary. See if she remembers anything.'

'What about things? Personal papers... I mean, not papers, but well,' I sought frantically for the right words. 'A book, even! He doesn't seem to have anything. Nothing, nothing to say... well, to say who he is.'

Her forehead was furrowed into a frown. 'I'll ask Mary. She might know, but I don't think so. I don't think much came with him.'

I sat with him into the evening. Someone came in and reminded me that visiting hours were over and, although I nodded and made mental moves to leave, I stayed where I was. The same nurse returned a little later and told me it was all right, I could stay as long as I wanted. She had obviously been informed of Wally's condition.

It was around six when I felt Wally stir. I had begun to doze and didn't know whether I had quite seen right. His eyes opened slowly and he gazed at me without focusing. His right hand twitched in mine. He drew in breath noisily and then, quite unexpectedly, spoke.

'Ellie,' he wheezed. My chest contracted and I leaned forward eagerly. I could hear my pulse thumping in my ears.

'Yes,' I whispered back, my voice almost as hoarse as his.

'You haven't changed a bit.' I bent low to hear the words, loathe to ask him to repeat them.

'You haven't changed a bit,' he said again and, for the briefest of moments, I saw the man I had met so many years earlier. There was the flicker of a smile that lent a rotundity to his now shrunken face, that blew it up, like a child's balloon. He breathed out and it was gone.

I was stuck for words.

'She told me you were over here. You should've come to visit.'

Tears welled in my eyes and I looked away.

'I'll come and see you every weekend until you're better.'

His top lip half curled in an attempt at a laugh.

'Had we but world enough and time,' he whispered back. 'You like books, I hear.'

I felt someone hold me by the throat. I couldn't speak so I just nodded.

'Good.'

He was silent for a while after that and then said, a little louder than before: 'She's gone, hasn't she?'

I nodded.

'I knew she had. I couldn't feel her anymore.'

The tears had started and I wiped them away with the palm of my hand, roughly, without remorse.

'She loved you,' I blurted out. 'She loved you her whole life through.'

He didn't answer at once and appeared to think about it for a while. He closed his eyes and made a strange moaning noise that made me alarmed at first, but then I realised that he was singing.

'You made me want you... And all the time you knew it... I guess you always knew it... You made me happy, sometimes you made me glad, but there were times you made me feel so bad...' His last words disappeared into a wave of coughing.

A nurse put her head round the door.

'Go and get some sleep. We'll call you.'

'I think he might be getting better,' I said enthusiastically. 'He spoke! His eyes opened.'

'It happens,' she said, as though I had been talking about the appearance of measles spots or bruising after a knock, not someone's life.

'I'd like to stay.'

'We'll call you. We've got your mobile number. We know where you're staying. Get some rest.'

I left shortly afterwards. I left the nursing home with its light green carpets and comfy chairs, its framed prints of wild flowers and interesting magazines about the countryside and animals and nice people. All the things that prepare you for the silence that replaces the music, the record that plays our whole life long, the tune that we sing one final time before we leave this strange and broken world.

Uncle Wally died. He was sleeping when it happened. I was sleeping when it happened. They phoned me in the morning. Could I organise things? There was some paperwork and would I let the rest of the family know? Oh, and could I come and pick up his belongings? There were things I'd have to sign for and then that would be all. All I need do. They could organise the funeral if needs be; there was an undertakers that they dealt with, a nice man, very reputable... if I could just let them know.

Everything was ready when I arrived. A little too ready. The body had been removed. There wasn't even a bed in the room. The jug and two glasses were still on the top of the cupboard, exonerating themselves quietly from any hand in the business. There was a small bag of clothes and a packet

407

of unopened Polos, which suddenly looked so completely ridiculous that its very absurdity threatened my precarious composure and I shoved it in the bag.

'There's this as well,' said the nurse, handing me a brown envelope. Inside was a gold watch. I'd seen it before, so many years before. I turned it over in my hand and saw an inscription on the back. Holding it up to the light I read: From Your Shadow 1948.

I fought to hold back the tears but they were coming fast. Great convulsions shook my body as I covered my face with my hand.

Chapter Three

'Don't cry,' said Cadwallader, pulling a large handkerchief out of his pocket and passing it to me. I took it
ungraciously.

'Rhodesia's a hard place,' he said, quietly, looking
straight ahead and running his hand slowly around the
steering wheel. 'Any country's hard when you move, but
Rhodesia's really hard. Settler society. Everyone looking
for permanence, everyone striving to be a success. It's a
make or break country.'

'You're all right,' I said, rather rudely. 'You've been
here a while. You've got money' – he started to laugh –
'and a big house...'

'Yes,' he replied, a note of sorrow, or was it sarcasm,
in his voice. 'I'm used to it.'

We sat in silence for a while longer, me dabbing my
eyes, Cadwallader looking straight ahead.

'At Cambridge,' he suddenly said, 'they used to call
me Taffy. Taffy Jones. All right, boyo? they'd say, in a
mock Welsh accent. Either that or they'd beat me up.'

He gave a short, sharp laugh. 'I had a friend, English chap, Charles Trent-Smythe. We played rugby together and one day I scored the winning try. I was a hero suddenly. Forget Taffy and boyo. Suddenly I was one of them. English, no longer from the Rhondda Valley or Llanfairpwllgwyngyllgogerychwyrndrobwllllantysilio-gogogoch, as they liked to tease. We were in the pub, drinking of course, and this friend of mine, Charles, he says suddenly, "I would like to make a toast, to Llywelyn ap Gruffudd" and this whole pub goes quiet. "Who the..." I hear someone say, but Charles says it again: "To Llywelyn ap Gruffudd" and suddenly everyone follows suit, just like that. Afterwards I said to Charles, "Charles, what on earth were you thinking of" and Charles says "He was a prince. Llywelyn ap Gruffudd, was a prince. More than that, he was the only Welsh ruler to be recognised as such by the English."

'Point is,' said Cadwallader, after a short pause in which I had made no attempt to say anything. 'Point is, I know what it's like. And that's why Rhodesia is the ideal place for me. Here I am a someone. Here I am Llywelyn ap Gruffudd without anyone telling me I am. Over there, I'm Taffy until told otherwise.'

I sniffed. 'You're a man,' I said.

He pressed his lips together and started the engine of the car.

'Come on, I'll take you home.'

He didn't park right in front of the boarding house; Mrs Wiesman's sitting room light was on.

'Happy New Year, Evie,' he said, taking my hand in his. 'For what it's worth, eh?'

Then suddenly he leaned over and kissed me, not a cursory kiss on the cheek, but a proper kiss, a long, soft, searching kiss on my lips. I didn't start or move away. He leant back in his seat and rubbed his forehead. He was obviously unhappy with himself.

'Go in,' he said. 'You'll get into trouble.' But I didn't move. I think I was too mesmerised by what had just happened. Then I picked my evening bag up off the floor where it had dropped and fumbled clumsily with the door handle.

'Sorry, sorry, forgive me my appalling manners,' he said, jumping out and rushing round to my side of the car. He opened the door and offered me his hand.

'Goodnight,' I began, 'thank you for a wonderful...' but he shook his head and clutched me to him.

'I like you, Evie, I like you a lot.' Then he squeezed me tightly and let me go.

'I'd better walk you to the door.'

Here I sit, two o'clock in the morning, trying to gather around me my feelings, trying to reason what happened. I think I love him. I think this is what love is. I think tonight only confirmed what I have known for a long time. Oh, dear God, what am I to do? Will he see me again?

3rd January, 1947

Cadwallader came to see me again today. I was so excited, yet so apprehensive that he was regretting what happened and that he'd come to tell me that things

411

couldn't possibly go on. I tried to prepare myself for it and have a reply ready – something like 'Under the circumstances, it is best...' or 'I've met somebody since I saw you last. We're engaged to be married in April.' How ridiculous! I can't believe how I've been feeling. I don't understand it. I never felt this way for Timothy and I married him.

Is this what love is like, for I can't stop thinking about him? I don't know what I'd do if he called it off. I was looking out of the window and saw him cross the road to the house, so I did have a little prior warning of his arrival! I quickly combed my hair and straightened my dress. I thought of putting some lipstick on, but then I thought that would look too eager and not natural enough. I did squirt some perfume on though – that lavender that Mum gave me before I left. I hoped it didn't smell too strong and too recently sprayed. One must never appear too eager! I heard him knock on the door. Nobody went to open it for about a minute. I began to get quite anxious that he would go away, thinking nobody was in. Then I heard him knock again and the door was opened.

'Oh, Miss Saunders,' called Mrs Wiesman up the stairs. 'Your uncle's here to see you!'

I left it a couple of seconds before going downstairs. I didn't know how to look, whether to smile, or only smile politely, or to try and look Greta Garbo – mysterious (which I just can't do!). I think I managed an odd smile and perhaps looked as though I was eating as he looked sheepish and asked me if he was disturbing my lunch. 'Of course not,' I said and let him in and then didn't know whether I sounded too keen.

'Are you busy?' he asked, looking around.

'Just cleaning my room,' I said and immediately regretted it. What have passion and cleaning to do with each other? 'Such a chore,' I added.

We sat rather stiffly in Mrs Wiesman's sitting room, him on one side of the coffee table and me on the other. I could hear her clock ticking methodically.

He sat down and we made small talk while I fingered a crocheted armrest on the sofa. Mrs Wiesman came in shortly with a tray of tea and two dry biscuits. It was a treat she did not afford every visitor. I wondered if she would add the cost onto my month's rent. Cadwallader talked about work and said he'd be in Bulawayo for at least another month. I tried not to sound pleased, tried not to sound particularly interested. My heart was thumping and my hands shook a little as I lifted the teapot. The tea was grey when I poured it out.

'Sugar?' I heard myself say, as though from far away. He shook his head, but accepted a biscuit.

'Is there something wrong?' he said eventually, looking rather dejected. His jacket really didn't suit him and seemed to hang rather despondently on his shoulders. 'I don't bite.'

I smiled nervously and wished to goodness that I could be more in control. I felt girlish and silly, like I was meeting someone behind the bike sheds for a ciggy.

'Come and sit next to me,' he said, smoothing the space next to him with his hand. I shook my head and motioned to the door. He sighed. Then he stood up, took my hand and pulled me up. He glanced out of the door

413

quickly, closed the door slightly so it was only half open and then pushed me up against the wall.

Here, I suppose, was my perfect chance to back off, to call things off, to say 'we shouldn't', 'we can't', 'I won't'. But I didn't. I let him put his arm around me so he was holding the back of my neck with his right hand. He pushed my hair up and held it back. And then he kissed me. He wasn't drunk, he wasn't joking or crying or desperate. He was just him and I was just me and we were kissing.

5th January, 1947

He brought me flowers today. I was doing some mending and there was a knock at the door. I looked out of the window and saw him and then ran downstairs and opened the door before anyone else could. Do uncles bring their nieces flowers? Apparently he picked them in the park!

He told me not to call him Cadwallader; everyone calls him Wally, but I must call him something else, something that only I will know him by. Llywelyn ap Gruffudd? A bit long-winded! LaG? No, that sounds like something left behind. LG? What about just G.? Just G., just for me.

Chapter Four

Mark moved back in. He was alone again, of course, and said I needed someone to look after me. To be honest, I found the thought quite appealing. He was the devil I knew and I was all for clinging to what I knew, devil or not.

I put Gran's house on the market, but didn't receive many offers. Not many people want to live in a place where someone's been murdered. It was broken into twice in the year after her death, but there was nothing to steal except tap fittings and brass doorknobs, all which remained untouched. But I wasn't worried. I didn't even know if I wanted anyone to live there. No one but me knew what it meant to her.

I suppose there is a point in all lives when the will to live and the desire to begin again begins to take shape and grow. My life that had drifted along, flat and lifeless and numb, began to waken slowly to a new consciousness and I began to feel that the time of mourning had passed.

I was standing on the platform of the tube station about a year after Gran's death. It was cold and dark and only five thirty in the afternoon. I stood waiting, staring out, looking for the golden eyes of the train to appear. As it snaked its way towards me, the green letters EALING BDWAY shone out, a mechanical glow worm in the black evening. For the first time in a long while, I felt a sense of contentment. Here was something arriving to take me away. Back home. It would do it every evening. A sort of rhythm started in me and I felt myself click back into the beat of life.

On the tube, three men with accordions got on and tried to strike up a tune. It was awkward at first and very out of tune. A couple of passengers looked as though they wanted to laugh or gave a harassed roll of their eyeballs. I felt an urge to join the men, to get up and sing along. In my teenage fantasies, this would be the time when I would meet my artist who could also sing and play the banjo. But these were three rather middle aged and worn men just trying to make a living. I dropped some coins in their cup, pulled my scarf closer around my neck and stepped off the train. I was smiling.

And so life could've carried on this way. And I could've been happy in a pleasant, contented sort of way: marking under-graduate essays, supporting Mark in his career, hosting the odd dinner party, seeing Mandy twice a week, reading in the library, looking forward each year to the Spring, counting the long dark winter days away, immersing myself in academia, in theories and hypotheses. Losing myself again.

But life, life changes very quickly and I was not ready for what happened next.

Miles died. My mother phoned to tell me she had seen the announcement in the *Morning Mirror*, an e-mail newsletter that had replaced *The Chronicle* as the foremost announcer of births, deaths, engagements and marriages in Bulawayo. Among advertisements for jobs, cars, houses for rent and sale, there were some that offered to look after your elderly relatives if you were in England and they were rotting away in some uncared-for old folk's home, or if you lived in Australia and needed a loved one's grave tended back home. That sort of thing.

My mother forwarded me a copy.

Miles Trevellyan (Corporal, King's African Rifles) 1920-2006. Uncle of Ronald Trevellyan and great-uncle of Tony. Peacefully in Bournemouth, UK. 1st February 2006. Funeral to be held at St Mary's Church, Bournemouth on Saturday, 8th February at 3pm. All enquiries to Tony Trevellyan - tonyt@yahoo.co.uk

I didn't expect to ever see Tony again. I presumed he was in Mozambique somewhere, cooking prawns in an expensive guest lodge. Although his great-uncle had died, I didn't expect him to fly over to the UK for the funeral, just arrange the costs maybe and send a wreath of flowers. So it was with some surprise that I opened the door to him two days later.

'Tony?'

'Ellie...' He bent over and gave me an awkward kiss. It was early in the morning and I hadn't brushed my teeth. I moved away. He seemed offended.

'Miles has died,' he said, still standing in the doorway and looking quite perturbed. It was rather a strange meeting for two people who hadn't seen each other in over a year.

417

'I know,' I replied. 'Would you like to come in?'

He seemed to deliberate, as though he had flown thousands of miles to deliver those words and now that his mission was complete, he'd fly home again. Then he came inside, put down his rucksack and unwound his scarf.

'I got your address from your mom. Did she tell you?'

'No.'

'Oh. I thought she would have.'

'Perhaps she forgot.'

He paused. 'Perhaps she knew you wouldn't want to see me.'

'That's not true.'

He didn't answer, but a weary raise of the eyebrows showed that he didn't believe me. He moved into the living room and sat down.

'Nice place,' he said, with a slow pat on his knees.

'Not really.'

He raised his eyebrows again in that same way, as though he felt he could never do anything right.

'Tea?' I asked.

'No thanks,' he replied, as if, by doing so, he was refusing me authority over him.

'How're things?' I asked, in an attempt at small talk. Tony was sad and strained and obviously uncomfortable in my flat, in my presence.

'I've come to ask you if you'd come to Miles's funeral. It's on Saturday. In Bournemouth. I could pick you up. I've hired a car. It starts at three.'

'I don't know...' I started.

He drew in a sharp breath. 'Why not?'

'It's just...'

'Just what?' His irritation with me was obvious. 'You didn't like him. I know that. So what? The man's dead. I've flown six thousand miles to say goodbye. I'm not even asking you to get on a train. I said I'd pick you up.'

'Are you sure you don't want tea?'

'I don't want tea. I want you to come to Miles's funeral.'

'Why?'

'Because.'

'Because why? He didn't like me, I didn't like him. Just because he's dead doesn't mean I have to like...'

I was cut short. 'Is there anyone you do like?' he exploded.

'What... what d'you mean?'

'I mean anyone, anyone who isn't strange, odd... anyone you do like?'

'Of course...'

'Name one. Just one. Anyone will do.'

'Tony, I...' I stopped. 'Perhaps you should leave.'

'Yes, perhaps I should,' he said, standing up. And he left.

I don't know exactly what made me change my mind. Perhaps it was my memory of Tony's strained angry face or some feeling of guilt for my act of coldness towards Miles. Or perhaps it was the photo, the one of Gran and I and Shirley. I kept it on my desk and every time I raised my eyes from doing some work, there it was. It struck me anew that the photo was of me and her, not her and Miles, and that perhaps he had seen something that had passed me by.

St. Mary's Church in Bournemouth was the last place in which I expected Miles's funeral to be held. He was the type not to want a funeral at all; the type to wish to be buried in a cardboard box or fed to the chickens, something out of the ordinary like that. St. Mary's was too English, too genteel, and also too cold, too remote to care tuppence for Miles and who he had been and what he had done. Yet somehow I couldn't help feeling that Miles was sitting somewhere nearby, maybe in a back pew, smoking a cigarette and having a laugh. At my expense, of course, always at my expense.

Tony was sitting in a front pew with his head bowed. He turned on hearing my footsteps along the cold stone floor and looked surprised to see me, but he said nothing and turned back to face the altar. Miles's coffin lay closed upon the bier. An organist played soft slow music and the priest shuffled papers on the pulpit and looked at his watch. There was no one else there except for one elderly man who had gone to sleep. I could see why Tony wanted me there.

It was brief, the service. If Tony had prepared a speech about Miles's life and what he had meant to him, he did not read it. I was surprised, though, at the priest's mention of Miles's wartime exploits, his time as an Italian prisoner of war and his eventual escape. Just when I thought it was all over, Tony took something out of a small case that was beside him on the pew, got up and stood next to Miles's coffin. He had a small trumpet on which he played The Last Post. The priest looked down, biting his lip, not because he wanted to cry or laugh, but maybe because, like me, he saw the ridiculous sadness of the end of one man. No great honours, no tearful mourners, nothing to leave behind.

Tony and I decided to get lunch somewhere. Relations had thawed somewhat between Tony and I. He was obviously glad to see me and I felt my previous behaviour forgiven. He was emotionally drained, but attempted the occasional joke, a coping mechanism I imagine he had learnt from his father after his mother's death. We shared a chocolate brownie for dessert, although I ate most of it, Tony turning up his nose after one bite.

'Too much baking powder,' he said, but I shrugged and carried on eating.

Later that afternoon we walked along the pier and had an ice cream, although it was far too cold and the wind whipped my face with unusual vigour.

'We're being typically British,' I said, licking my ice cream and wiping my eyes at the same time. The wind made them water.

'How so?'

'Well, it's February, there's one day with blue sky and suddenly the whole world's out eating ice creams and talking about Summer! It's bloody freezing!'

He didn't say anything and for a while we continued to eat our ice cream and stare out across the grey-blue sea.

'Uncle... Miles,' Tony said suddenly, 'told me once that the ice creams in Ethiopia were the best he'd ever tasted.'

'Ethiopia! Crikey!'

'It was Abyssinia then. An Italian protectorate.'

'Mmm. I know,' I replied matter-of-factly.

He ignored me and continued. 'Italians, he said, always made the best ice creams.'

'I feel there's a message here somewhere,' I said, finishing the last of the ice cream and folding the paper over the stick, ready to be thrown away. I put my hand out for his, but he was lost in thought.

'The message is even your enemies have something to

give. He said something like that. No one is totally despicable. Certainly not the Italians. He liked them, you know. Never bore them any grudges.'

He handed me his ice cream stick and I threw them both in a bin behind me.

'Very moving,' I said, my usual cynical acerbity returning.

'Ellie,' he said suddenly, leaning back on the rail. 'Ellie, come to Mozambique with me.'

'Don't tell me they make great ice creams there as well.'

'Seriously, Ellie, listen to me. Come to Moz with me. We'll be there a few weeks doing the sourcing, all that sort of thing, and then we can go back to Bullies. We can start the restaurant. Your Gran's old place. A fish restaurant in Bulawayo. I can cook and you can take orders' – I pulled a face – 'or, or write a book, look after the garden, whatever, teach postcolonial literature at the university... whatever! Just come. Come with me.'

I held the icy rail with both hands, welcoming the cold, feeling the salty wind whip past my face, watching a tiny buoy bob up and down just beyond the pier, rolling this way and then that, a tired little speck just doing its job. It was one of those life-changing moments that I held in my hand and I felt dizzy as I looked over the railing into rollicking sea beneath me.

'I have a boyfriend, did you know? The flat you came to the other day, we live there together.'

'Do you love him?'

I rolled my eyes. 'Don't try that one with me.'

'I'm sorry. I... look. I just have this... feeling. You and I. All the things we could do.'

I didn't say anything.

'If there wasn't a boyfriend, would you come?'

I sighed in irritation. 'You can't ask those kinds of questions. They're too... too hypothetical. How do I know? Everything would be different. I can't answer that.'

He shrugged sadly. 'OK.'

We were both silent for a while and then he asked, 'Do you think you'll ever go back to Zim?'

'To live?'

He nodded.

'No.' I watched the surprise register on his face.

'Why? Why not?'

I paused and thought for a bit. 'I had a childhood that was riddled with lies and secrets. No one moved on. That's how people are in Zim. Either they are immersed in the past and can't move out of it, or else they pretend it never happened. And us – we're the lost generation, growing up on snippets of lies, stories, anecdotes, jokes. It's not enough to live on what your parents told you. We need more. We have to stop making the same mistakes. We're stuck in a cycle of lies and secrets, lies and secrets.'

He was confused. 'What are you talking about?'

'The only way I can live in the present is to live here. This is the present.'

'I still don't get it.'

I moved closer to him and put my hand on his arm. 'It's not you, Tony...' I began, but he put up his hand and waved me away.

'Right. It never is, is it?'

'Honestly, it isn't. It's Africa. It's not my home any more. This' – I waved a weak arc in the air encompassing the grey frothing sea and half the pier – 'this is me.'

'I don't believe you.'

'It's true, Tony. I never belonged. I never will.'

'You mean to say in the whole continent there's nothing for you? Everyone else is the same and you are different?'

'I...' I began but he stopped me dead.

'Oh, forget it. I give up. Stay here, marry your boyfriend, read books, hide yourself away for the rest of your life. I just give up.'

I declined his offer of a lift back to London. He said nothing, but a deep sigh said it all. He took me to the station and left me at the ticket booth.

'Goodbye,' I said and, in an attempt at being amicable, 'Good luck.'

He looked at me, his lips pursed together in anger. He still thought I would change my mind.

'Miles didn't want to go to East Africa. He wanted the Mediterranean or Burma. He thought it was just a desert, you see, he didn't expect to find the finest ice cream in the world.'

'Have a good trip back,' I said in response, ignoring his attempt to find another moral in the ice cream story. 'It was nice seeing you again.'

Chapter Five

Never use a teabag twice, Gran always used to say. And she was right. The first time you get a nice strong cup, the next something weak and anaemic-looking. It never pays to use a teabag twice

Mark and I were all right for a while. Comfortable. Quiet walks in the country, followed by quiet lunches at country pubs. Quiet nights in with videos and takeaways. Quiet conversations. A quiet drink once in a while.

He became very protective of me, very considerate. He changed TV channels if I asked him to and did the washing up every night. He wanted to look after me for some reason, almost as though he thought life would snap me in two if he wasn't around.

I set about cementing my life in Britain and breaking off the pieces of my old life that still clung to me. I threw away all the postcards I kept on the fridge that were from Zimbabwe – pictures of Victoria Falls and African curios and waterfalls of the Eastern Highlands. I took down a water-colour I had in the lounge of the Matopos and even a pair of wooden salad spoons with carved giraffe handles found their way to the nearest charity shop.

I dealt with a backlog of post as well: copies of bills from 52 Lawson Road that were forwarded to me by Mom who paid them all initially; unopened letters from Gran's lawyers about the house, even a letter from Emerith Davies about Wally's cat that I still hadn't replied to. There were phone calls to make, letters and e-mails to write, but I was doing it. I was managing, and I couldn't help but congratulate myself on my efficiency, especially when Mr Mpofu emailed to say that someone was interested in the house, a family, in fact, who could pay cash up front, in pounds. The house could be sold within weeks.

Everything was fine until I started having the dream. I dreamt it was dark, very dark, and I stood outside Gran's side gate wondering whether to go in or not. Then I lifted the latch and walked purposefully up the path and onto the verandah. I tried the door, but it wouldn't open, so I smashed a glass panel, like they do in films, and opened the door from the inside. No one heard a thing. I walked into the lounge and down the passage to her bedroom and there she was, lying asleep. Then she turned over and opened her eyes and saw me. 'Ellie,' she said, 'it's you.' And I realised then that I was him, I was the murderer and I looked down at my hands and there was a gun, an AK-47, and I was going to hit her, to hit her and hit her... and then I'd wake up. Screaming, sweating, crying. 'I'm sorry,' I shouted. 'I'm sorry, Gran, I'm sorry!' Mark was always there. He'd put his arms around me and hold me tight next to him, rocking me and smoothing my hair. 'It's just a dream,' he'd say, but it wasn't.

Mark believed I was suffering from something called Post-Traumatic Stress. He suggested I 'see someone'. There were plenty of bereavement counsellors out there; there were even support groups who could help: LOL – Loved Ones Lost – or Families against Murder or even just the good old Samaritans. He could get me numbers, contacts, recommendations. I just had to say yes.

But I had no intention of booking an appointment to see some friendly counsellor in a community centre. Shoestring is the word that sprang to mind. Damp carpets and school-room chairs, informative posters on the wall, a kettle and two mugs, a nice, friendly, earnest counsellor filling in forms and then filing me away.

Then Mark suggested I write it all down. Write an article is what he said. Send it to a newspaper or magazine. Zimbabwe was in the news, it was topical. I might even get paid.

'Where do I start?'

'Start at the beginning,' he answered simply, but I didn't know where that was.

15th January 1946

Today I said goodbye to everybody. My trunk has been sent on ahead and all I have to carry is my small leather suitcase and my handbag. Why then does it feel like the heaviest luggage anyone has ever had?

Last night, I took my ring off and wrapped it in a hand-kerchief, my best one, the blue with white lace. I'm travelling under my maiden name as well. I just can't bear the questions, the looks: averted eyes or brief glances left and right to see where Mr Broughton is. I'm taking the ring with me, but I won't wear it again.

This morning, Dad took me to the station. I didn't want him to; I'd rather have taken a taxi and had no one to wave me off from the platform, but he insisted. Gregory wanted to come, too, but I was determined and said no. Mum didn't cry. She had been peeling potatoes in the kitchen when I came downstairs and said I was ready to go. She just washed her hands, dried them on her apron, one finger at a time as she always does, and then she put her arms around my neck and kissed me. Her hands were cold and clammy and I could smell the dirt from the potatoes. It was so commonplace that I started to cry. I realised then that life would go on without me. Don't cry, said Mum sharply, and she wiped my eyes with the corner of her apron. You're a married woman now. This isn't your home any longer. You belong there. Why then did I feel like such a child?

Dad carried my suitcase for me and we walked down to the station, which has always seemed so far away and yet was so close today. He wanted to buy me a newspaper and, although I protested, he insisted. He put my suitcase down in the waiting room and went off to the little station shop, his hand in his pocket as he walked and I knew he was counting his change and hoping he had enough. He came back with The Telegraph *and a packet of boiled sweets – for the journey, he said, as though I had thought they were to be kept for supper or eaten with my breakfast the next morning.*

While we waited, we talked of such arbitrary things: the weather, train times, how much longer we'd be using ration books. I wonder why we resort to such trivial conversation when time is so short and there is so much left unsaid. I felt my heart would break as I kissed Dad goodbye. I wanted to hold on to him, to hold on to his smell and the feel of his arms tight around me, to be able to feel him and smell him whenever I want to and wherever I am. I felt his cheek rough and bristly on my skin and I thought, this is what it is like, this is what it is like to say goodbye.

'Goodbye, Dad,' I said as I leaned out of the window of the train. It started to move.

'It's never goodbye,' he replied and, then, as the train began to hiss and steam, he called, 'Only see you soon.'

Chapter Six

20ᵗʰ February, 1946

It's awful, awful, awful! I want to go home! When I arrived in Salisbury, there was no one there to fetch me. I waited three hours and all the other passengers had gone. It was terrible, just terrible. I sat in the waiting room and ordered a cup of tea and a bun. The lady behind the counter looked really put out that I had ordered anything at all and took an awful long time to bring it across, even though I was the only person there. It's usually Sod's Law that, as soon as one gets comfortable, the person one is waiting for arrives. So I thought I'd chance it and try and play Fate at its own game, but no such luck! I ate the bun and drank the tea so slowly that I didn't enjoy either. The tea went cold and I wanted to cry.

Just then, a tall, very dark young man walked in in a great hurry and looked around. He didn't see me at first and went over to the waiting room and tried the door. On finding it locked, he swore and rattled the handle in the hope of attracting someone's attention. Not succeeding, he turned and saw me looking at him

'Evelyn?' he hazarded, the look on his face a mixture of guilt and anxiety.

'Yes,' I said, standing up and taking his proffered hand. 'And I presume you are Robert?'

He smiled briefly and told me that everyone calls him Bobby.

He seemed to suddenly remember where we were and hurriedly started apologising. He said it was 'Ma's fault' and that she told him to go and buy some grain for the chickens and he got held up and that's why he was late. He said he'd told her he couldn't go 'there' and be back and down here in an hour, 'but that's Ma'. What she says goes apparently. He picked up my case and asked if it were all, but I said that there was my trunk as well, which was in the stationmaster's office. I pointed out the direction and he made his way toward it quickly. I followed behind.

'You're a bit late, my boy,' said the stationmaster to Bobby in a headmasterly way. 'This young lady nearly stayed here the night.'

Bobby was terribly apologetic – very much like a schoolboy who has been told off. He seemed a little afraid, a little nervous. He picked up the trunk too quickly, not quite realising how heavy it was and dropped it awkwardly again. He looked very embarrassed.

'Too busy to pick up a young lady just arrived from England?' said the stationmaster, continuing with his reprimand. 'What sort of a welcome is that for her? You

need to learn some manners, young man.'

'It's all right,' I said, intervening, for the stationmaster was obviously put out that he was no longer to be my knight in shining armour. 'He's here now.'

'Hmph,' was all the deposed hero had to say about it before he picked up my trunk and followed us outside. The stationmaster heaved the trunk rather unceremoniously into the back of the car, which is a very old 1920s Ford. It's very battered and I'm honestly quite surprised that it went.

'I suppose you're used to a Rolls Royce,' Bobby said as we got inside and he started the engine.

'We don't have a car,' I replied. 'My family, I mean. My father can't drive and we don't have enough money, anyway. I usually take the bus or walk.'

'Well, you'll be doing a lot of that,' he said, lighting a cigarette and throwing the match out onto the pavement. 'Walking. You Poms won't give us enough petrol to run like we used to. We're rationed here to two gallons a month.'

There was an accusing tone in his voice as he looked sideways at me and blew smoke out the corner of his mouth. I wondered whether he blamed me for his admonishment by the stationmaster or whether he wanted to see what my reaction was.

'We have rationing in England, too,' I said in reply.

He raised his eyebrows in a way that said he didn't believe me and then drove forwards into the traffic.

The house is very small and dark. From the outside it looks bigger, probably because it has a verandah that runs around it. The houses here are all bungalow level, I presume because they have the space to build them like that, but for all the supposed extra space, the inside of the house is tiny and the windows are all small and remind me very much of the cabin windows on the Cape Town Castle!

When I arrived, it was getting dark, so I couldn't see much of the garden, but now I know that there is a large chicken run in the back and a washing line. There are no flowers in either the front or the back garden, only a couple of miserable shrubs near the gate and a few long-dead pot plants on the verandah. Inside the house, it is as though time has stood still, even the air doesn't circulate. There is a small front room, the door to which is permanently closed, and I only know it is such because Mrs Broughton disappears in there once a day at four o'clock and Marie, she's Bobby's wife, takes her tea there. The first door to the right of the passage is the kitchen, which is perhaps the largest room in the house. There is a an old wooden table and six chairs in the middle of it where we eat our meals, all except Mrs Broughton who has hers in her room. There is one large built-in cupboard at one end in which all the dry food is kept. Vegetables are stored on the bottom shelf. Outside the kitchen door is a large stone sink in which Marie does all the laundry once a week. She also buys meat once a week and cooks it the same day. It is then placed in a meat safe, which is like a cage with coal on the top. Water is poured over the coal and runs down the sides of the safe, keeping the meat cool. The legs of the safe are placed in small bowls of water to prevent ants climbing up.

What pictures there are on the walls are of the bush in bright, garish colours that, even from what little I have seen, I would never associate with Africa. In my bedroom, there are framed faded cross-stitched pictures of deer running in woods and The Lord's Prayer. *The latter hangs above my bed, rather like an epitaph!*

Mrs Broughton is tall and thin and gaunt. She has grey shoulder-length hair, which she has pinned back above her ears with a comb, and grey eyes, if that's possible, which are the strangest eyes I have ever seen, being totally devoid of all emotion. Her face is deeply lined, probably a result of too much time in the sun as a farmer's wife, and around her mouth are deep sad lines that drag her mouth down into a permanently sorrowful look. She stands very straight at all times, almost as though someone is prodding her in the back with a stick and is so thin she looks as though she will fall over at any moment. She must once have had a lovely figure, but varicose veins bulge out of her calves, thinly veiled by the stockings she wears.

Marie is also thin, but with dark hair that is thick and curly and which she pulls roughly back into a ponytail. She wears the most old-fashioned dresses, mid-calf in length and far too big for her. She also wears black lace-up boots, which I haven't seen since I was a little girl and Mum used to wear them. Over her dress, she wears a large white apron. Marie hardly says a word. She seems obliged to stay in the kitchen where she does everything from the washing of clothes to the cooking of every meal. Bobby and she have a young son of about two or three, Colin, who seems to spend his whole life crying. He clings

434

to Marie whenever I walk into the room and appears afraid of his father and grandmother, who take little interest in him at all.

Mrs Broughton was in the front room when I arrived and Bobby went to call her. The strange thing was that he closed the door behind him when he went in and again when he came out with her. Mrs Broughton took my hand in hers, which was cold and damp, as though she had sat with her hands immersed in water for two hours. She let it go quite quickly as though the whole ceremony was just too much for her and had used up her last reserve of energy.

'Pleased to meet you,' she said, without much of a smile. 'Marie will give you some supper, if you go in the kitchen.' She nodded to the door on the right.

I turned my head to follow her gaze and, when I turned back, she was halfway gone, back through the door into the front room. Bobby caught my eye and shrugged. He showed me into the kitchen where Marie was cooking at the stove. She turned shyly when she saw me and greeted me with averted eyes, as though I were the queen come to stay.

Supper was a fatty beef stew with green beans. It reminded me of hospital food, the food that one eats when one is ill, that slides down your throat and wrestles to stay there as wave upon wave of nausea greets you

At six o'clock, Mrs Broughton reappeared in the doorway, holding what appeared to be a Bible.

'Marie, I'll have my supper in my room,' she said. She glanced at me and gave a slight nod of her head. Later I found out this is her way of saying goodnight. She then

disappeared up the passage and I could hear the door of a room close. Marie arranged things on a tray for her and took it in. When she came back, Bobby stood up and said, 'I'm going out,' and that was it, he was gone. Marie washed the dishes, said I wasn't allowed to help. She poured hot water into a jug and took it to my room so that I could wash. When I appeared fifteen minutes later, she was gone and the kitchen was in darkness. From a room, I could hear her talking to Colin and telling him to hush in case he woke the house. It was only a quarter to seven. I turned back to my room and closed the door. It was the first night of my new life and I wanted to go home.

Chapter Seven

Gran always said that the way to a man's heart was through his stomach. She wasn't the first to coin the expression, but it meant more coming from her. I remember her telling me, 'a man is not interested in how interesting you are, whether you are an expert on medieval history or nuclear science, or whether you are the most gorgeous looking woman on God's earth. There is one thing that makes even sex pale into insignificance and that is food.'

After my episode with Tony, I was desperate to make things work with Mark, if only to prove to myself that I had made the right choice. Mark and I still lived on takeaway meals and frozen food, but I began gradually to try and make a proper meal for supper, even if it was just an omelette to begin with, and although even that flopped. One day I decided to be quite brave and asked Mark if he'd like to invite anyone back for dinner. He was surprised, but happily so, and duly asked a colleague and his wife round one night.

What to make kept me occupied for a while. I couldn't overdo things and produce some great extravagant dinner; I would seem too eager to please. Nor could I do beans on toast. I wished Gran were around so that I could ask her advice. The next best thing, however, was her *Good House-keeping* cookbook that I had brought back with me, more as a memento of her than to actually use. I flicked through the pages carefully. Some recipes had been more often used than others and the book naturally fell open at certain pages where the spine had cracked. Still, everything seemed too formal and perhaps not modern enough.

While turning the pages, a cutting slipped out. It was from a newspaper: yellow and rough. It was for *coq au vin*, my grandfather's favourite. I decided to try my hand at it, feeling that any recipe where you have to add wine would give me a feeling of being a real chef. Soup was all right for a starter: soup can never be pretentious like crumbed mushrooms can. For dessert I chose to make chocolate brownies with ice cream.

Cooking, I found, gave me a great deal of satisfaction. Gran was right when she told me that it is the ultimate form of giving. 'You can taste love in a meal,' she always said. What you cook, what you eat, is an expression of yourself and what you feel for others.

Mark was impressed. He came up behind me in the kitchen, put his arms around my waist and kissed my neck. His chin was bristly.

'Smells nice,' he said, looking over my shoulder and into the soup pot. He dipped his finger in and tasted it. 'Tastes nice, too.' He kissed me again. 'Know what I think?'

'What?'

'I think... you'd be a great mum.'

Instinctively, I backed away and then, realising what I had

done, made it look as though I was reaching over to check something in the recipe. I was too late though. Mark had felt my hesitation and his face fell.

'Think about it,' he said, giving me a squeeze. 'We'd get married first, of course.'

I was frozen to the spot. Mark moved away.

'I'm going for a shower. Call me if you need a hand.'

Simon and Rachel were on time. They arrived with a bunch of flowers and a bottle of South African white wine. Chardonnay, I think it was. Simon was tall and wiry with a friendly, open face. I imagined he played tennis or squash, and enjoyed watching rowing and cricket. Rachel had long, straight blonde hair, figure-hugging clothes, short jacket, boots, a gold chain round her neck and a french manicure.

'You're from Zimbabwe?' commented Simon half way through the soup, which Mark had taken upon himself to compliment me on twice already.

'Was,' said Mark, before I could say anything.

'How long have you been over here?'

'About ten years.' I replied. Suddenly it seemed a very long time ago that I had left. 'I've been back a few times, of course.'

'You must have seen some changes.'

'It's almost unrecognisable,' said Mark, interjecting again before I could say a word. Never had I said to him that I found Zimbabwe 'unrecognisable'.

'Well, I wouldn't go that far,' I started, but he interrupted me again.

'Your gran wouldn't have been murdered ten years ago, would she?' he challenged me. Simon blinked and stopped, his spoon halfway to his mouth.

'Your gran was murdered? Gosh, I'm so sorry.'

'Yeah,' said Rachel. 'How terrible.'

I didn't think it was the time or the place to mention Gran's murder, so I didn't say anything, took a big gulp of my wine and mentally shook Mark for bringing her into the conversation.

'There's a lot of that now out there, isn't there?' said Simon. 'White farmers. Was your gran a farmer?'

I burst into laughter and Simon blushed. 'Sorry, sorry,' he said, 'I'm a total ignoramus. Just what one reads, you know.'

'It's all right. If you'd known my gran, that's all. No, she wasn't a farmer. She was very much an urban person. She was murdered at her home in the suburbs.'

'Terrible,' said Rachel again. 'I have an aunt in South Africa who was hijacked last year. They threatened to cut her wedding ring off her finger if she didn't give it to them.'

Everyone shook their heads.

'Pity about Zimbabwe,' said Simon, chasing a crouton around his soup with his spoon. 'I hear it used to be a beautiful country.'

'It is. It still is,' I started to say, but Mark cut me up again.

'It's the way of all tin-pot democracies,' he said with finality.

'Do you think it will get as bad as Rwanda?' asked Simon. 'I watched a film once...'

I stood up and scraped my chair back. Everyone looked up in surprise. Simon hadn't finished talking.

'More anyone?' I asked, at the same time reaching over for all the empty bowls and stacking them one on top of each other.

'No thanks, that was lovely,' said Simon.

'Lovely,' echoed Mark and toasted his wine glass at me. Irritated, I left the room without smiling. In the kitchen I poured myself another drink and leant against the kitchen counter. I had my eyes closed when Rachel came in and asked me if I needed any help. Embarrassed, I waved her away and made some excuse about being tired. She insisted that she help with something and I almost snapped at her to leave me alone, then I gave her a bowl of new potatoes and asked her to put them on the table.

Back at the dining table, Mark poured himself his fourth glass of wine, but Simon declined by putting his hand over the glass.

'Not for me,' he said.

'Come on, Simon, you're not driving,' insisted Mark, but Simon shook his head. 'You need to learn a couple of things from our Zimbabwean over here,' he joked. 'They all get pickled out there in the colonies and then it's work as usual the next day. Isn't that what it's like, Ellie? Blue sky and booze, isn't that what you once told me?'

I pushed Mark's plate rather roughly towards him and some of the sauce spilled onto the tablecloth. I didn't answer him.

'Well then,' said Simon with a good-natured smile, 'You must be glad to be here in civilisation. In fact, really, apart from the occasional word, I would say you have quite a good British accent. Wouldn't you say so, Rachel?'

Rachel nodded and took a mouthful of food.

'We're working on it,' said Mark.

'Of course, you're not a true Brit yourself, are you?' said Simon to Mark.

'I left South Africa a long time ago,' he replied with that same sense of finality. 'I don't consider it my home anymore.'

'A lot of people complain about Britain, but there's a lot to be said for it, isn't there?' Simon looked to Rachel for confirmation of his statement and her eyes met his and she nodded.

'Very true.'

It wasn't until I served the chocolate brownies that it suddenly dawned on me what was happening. Everyone oohed and aahed and said how wonderful they were, but to me there was something wrong. I had that feeling you get when you can't remember someone's name and the more you think about it, the more it eludes you and, for some unfathomable reason, you always think it starts with a completely different letter to the one it actually starts with. And then suddenly, when you're not thinking about it, the name suddenly appears. 'Of course,' you exclaim. 'Of course!' That was how it was when Tony's words came back to me: too much baking powder. Reality hit me like an express train.

Chapter Eight

22nd February, 1946

My job is to feed the hens. I go out each morning at six, sweep the coop, feed the hens and collect any eggs. It seems the only thing I am expected to do at the moment – or is it the only thing I am to be trusted with? I feel a lot of suspicion towards me in the house, as though they expect something particular of me. I can't work out whether this is to do with me being English or whether it is due to me being Timothy's wife and widow. I don't know what to do with the rest of my day. Marie says she doesn't need my help and Bobby is gone all morning and afternoon: he works on a chicken farm, just outside the city. He returns at five o'clock, dirty and grumpy and wanting his food. If he doesn't go out in the evening, he's in bed by seven o'clock. When he goes to bed, Marie sits in the kitchen, rocking Colin back and forth in a chair. On the nights he goes out, she goes into the bedroom and shuts the door. My day seems to begin and end at six o'clock. There's not a book to read, nor even a newspaper, just the persistent ticking of the kitchen clock.

On the first morning, Marie made me breakfast, Bobby had already gone out, and I offered to help but she turned up her nose and said, 'I'm all right.' We sat there for about half an hour and suddenly she said, 'Ma will be up soon,' and I thought that meant that she'd come in and we'd talk, but what it meant was that Marie took her a bowl of porridge and some tea on a tray. 'Go and sit in the garden, if you like,' said Marie who began to make pastry, so I sat on the verandah for a bit, but there was nothing to see or do. I don't understand why I'm expected to do nothing.

3rd March, 1946

Once a week, Marie goes into town. She puts on a faded navy blue dress, a long, old-fashioned thing again, and a straw hat that is broken in places, which she has then tried to cover with cheap fake flowers. I picked it up this morning because it had blown off the hat stand onto the floor and, when I turned it over, I noticed the holes. She grabbed it from me and pushed it down on her head, without even a glance at the mirror. She wears no make-up and appears to scrub her face in the morning because it always looks red and raw at breakfast. I said I had a hat that she could borrow and she said that she 'doesn't borrow hats', as though I had head lice or something equally evil!

She takes a big straw basket with her everywhere and

a big black purse in which all the housekeeping money is kept. Bobby counts it in the evening and checks the change against every receipt. Mrs Broughton sits with him while he does it, which is very peculiar. It seems the only thing she takes any interest in.

She sets off with Colin on one hip and apparently catches a bus two roads down from here. She returns in the evening with the basket full and covered with an old white cloth. She unpacks it herself and puts the purse high up on a shelf. Colin is usually asleep or crying.

I don't know what Salisbury is like, except for the station and it appears I never will. Am I to stay here for the rest of my life? Even Marie, poor strange Marie, gets out of the house once in a while.

10th March, 1946

A frightening thing happened this morning. I thought I can't sit and do nothing for another day, so I thought I'd pre-empt Marie and do some cleaning without asking. After breakfast, she went out to hang washing on the line and so I opened the door of the cupboard and took the cleaning materials out from where I'd seen her put them away last night. I thought I'd start in the front room and so pushed the door open, which was very stiff. I don't know what I expected to find. The room is kept so secret, the door always closed and even the curtains closed. But there was nothing out of the ordinary, except that it was perhaps the nicest room in the whole house. There was wallpaper and chair covers and crocheted mats on the

445

table. It looked clean. It was stuffy, though, and the sun hitting the back of the curtains at that time in the morning, made it quite warm. I drew the curtains and was just opening a window, which was very stiff and didn't seem as though it were opened often, when Marie came dashing in and grabbed me by the arm. She pulled me with such force that I flew backwards and knocked over a vase. It didn't break, but rolled slowly across the wooden floorboards. Marie pounced on it, inspecting it for damage.

'It's all right,' I started to say, referring, of course, to the vase, but she was furious, the most animated I have seen her since I got here.

'You have no right to come in here,' she said angrily.

'No right...?' I started, completely dumbfounded. Does someone need a right to enter the front room?

'Never, ever come in here again,' she admonished me. Her chest was heaving and she breathed heavily to regain composure. 'Not without permission.'

'Permission...? I'm sorry,' I said, still not knowing what I'd done wrong. 'I didn't know... I didn't mean...'

'It's all right,' she said, calming down and taking the polish and duster away from me with a rough yank. 'Come out.' She closed the door behind us and began to walk away. 'Just don't do it again.'

I stood for a moment, totally and utterly in shock, before I made my way to my room and sat on the bed. My hands were shaking and sweaty and I wiped them on the bed cover. I heard Mrs Broughton's door open and her footsteps press gingerly down the passage. There were voices and I imagined Marie explaining the whole awful episode to her mother-in-law.

Chapter Nine

3rd April 1946

Last night, I went out with Bobby. It's the first sort of entertainment I've experienced in the whole two months I've been here. It was a problem, but I was willing to withstand all sorts of treatment in order to get OUT of this house.

At breakfast, Bobby asked me, in a hushed and secretive voice, whether I would like to go out in the evening. To a dance! Of course, I said yes. I could hardly contain my excitement and delight, although Bobby put his finger on his lips and pointed to his mother's room. 'Seven o'clock' was all he said to me before picking up his hat and disappearing out the back door.

Marie stood at the sink most of the morning, peeling potatoes silently and looking distantly out of the window. I swear she wears that apron to bed! She didn't say anything to me, just looked at me as I was leaving with those large doleful eyes. I asked her if she'd like to come with us. Baby Colin was lying on the floor, crying as he always does, and she scooped him up and carried him out of the room without an answer. Nothing was said to Ma Broughton and we slipped out of the house quietly. On the way to the hall, I asked Bobby if Marie wanted to come with us, or whether she wanted to go with him and I could've stayed behind, but he shook his head and turned his nose up.

The Wednesday night dance is quite established here. Someone plays the piano and everyone dances. Apparently, there's often a man who comes and sings and everyone says he sounds just like Glen Miller, but he wasn't there last night. At ten o'clock, tea and coffee is served. Last night there were a couple of plates of sandwiches as well and someone had made a cake. Bobby said he hadn't seen a cake served there for at least a year, butter is still so short. He said they must've known I was coming and got things nice and ready for the English girl. The Rhodesians seem to think the war was fought and won here and here alone. What I don't know about rationing isn't worth knowing and yet they all seem to think I expect something grand all the time.

What I can't understand is why Bobby comes here at all. I was always of the opinion that one didn't need a social life after marriage! Well, I had a good time and met so many people. They all asked if I'd be there next week and I looked across at Bobby and he shrugged and muttered 'we'll see what we can do', but I can't imagine being let out again, two weeks in a row!

14th April, 1946

Well, a strange turn of events happened yesterday. It was about lunchtime, just before, when Bobby came to me in the kitchen. I was making chicken soup and had just put the bones on to boil when he came in. Marie was outside, bringing in the washing, and Mrs Broughton was in her room, probably lying down. She takes a nap before and after lunch and yet never seems any the more rested for it. Bobby sidled up to me while I stood at the stove and peered over my shoulder at what I was cooking.

'I'm going out tonight,' he said suddenly. I wasn't sure whether he was inviting me or just telling me.

'Where to?' I asked. 'The usual?'

'No. Somewhere different this time.'

'Oh? Where?'

He tapped the side of his nose conspiratorially and smiled a sneaky smile.

'Tell me,' I said, hoping that no trace of the longing I felt to join him could be detected.

'Ace of Spades,' he said in a whisper, with a quick glance at the door, to make sure no one was there. 'Want to come?'

'How?' I asked, holding the spoon still in my hand, as though the very act of stirring the pot would alert Mrs Broughton to our plans.

'Same time,' he whispered back. 'Be ready.'

I nodded and he moved away towards the back door.

'Oh, Bobby,' I called, my voice suddenly loud above the bubbling soup. I lowered it again quickly. 'What is it? What is the Ace of Spades?'

'Night club,' he whispered back. 'Wear your dancing shoes.'

I was apprehensive about the whole thing all day and kept looking across at Mrs Broughton during lunch to see if she suspected anything. She sipped her soup slowly and invalid-like, lifting the spoon weakly to her lips, trying the liquid and then lowering the spoon despondently, as though disappointed with what she thought was something else, much like, I suspect, she greets life, with suspicion and despair.

She didn't finish her soup, which was no great surprise as I haven't seen her finish anything since I've been here. I offered her a piece of bread, but she immediately raised her hand in protest, as though I had suggested she run a mile down the road. She retired back to her bedroom shortly afterwards, with a brief direction that her tea be brought to her there. Marie arranged the tray for her: half a cup of black tea, a small jug of milk and two tablets from the array in the bathroom in an old egg cup. Marie takes her her tea twice a day, every day, and I'm made well aware that this is a ritual in which I shall most certainly never participate. As if I want to.

No one spoke through the whole of lunch; there was just the odd clunk of spoons in bowls, the occasional slurp from Bobby and the persistent drip of the kitchen tap.

'That tap's driving me round the bend,' I said at one point, in an attempt to break the silence. No one said anything. No one even looked at me.

'Have you ever had anyone in to look at it?' I asked. The silence deepened. 'A plumber, perhaps?' I made the

450

obvious suggestion in what I hoped was not a condescending tone. But it was too bright, too chirpy a note that
I trilled and it fell loud and heavy amongst us. Bobby
moved his chair with a slight jerk and it scraped the tiles
underfoot. He cleared his throat uneasily but didn't speak
and kept his eyes on the soup. Marie patted her mouth
with a grey handkerchief and, with her eyes glistening,
said, 'Timothy was always good at that sort of thing.'
Her voice was just above a whisper, yet it seemed to grate
the air into ribbons of sorrow. Mrs Broughton put her
spoon down and made to get up.

'I'll have my tea in my room,' she said and glided,
pale and thin to the door. Marie went outside, ostensibly
to throw the rubbish away. Bobby looked up at me with
what looked like menace in his eyes.

'Why did you have to bring him up?' he growled when
she had gone.

I didn't, I wanted to say, but held my tongue.

'See you later,' he said, picking up his hat. 'Don't be
late.'

The rest of the afternoon went like clockwork, which is
not difficult in this household. At four o'clock, Mrs
Broughton appeared for tea. She took it, as usual, in the
front room, alone. Marie carried it in on the tray: a cup
and saucer, teapot and milk jug, teaspoon and one dry
biscuit on a plate. Half an hour later, Marie collected the
tray. There was a small pool of yellow-brown liquid at
the bottom of the cup and the biscuit had a corner
removed. Bobby and I had our tea at the kitchen table
while Marie washed Mrs Broughton's cup and saucer.
She stood drying them dreamily by the window as I said,

'Won't you have some tea, Marie?'

She turned her head ever so slightly towards me, the rest of her body still facing the window, and replied in a low, flat voice: 'No.'

Bobby stirred his tea violently with his spoon and let it clatter into the saucer. He looked angrily at me, gulped down the tea and left the room. I had no idea what I'd done wrong. As Mrs Broughton passed the kitchen on the way to her room, she looked in and said, 'I'll have my supper in my room, Marie.'

Marie nodded acquiescence and Mrs Broughton turned to go, her hand on the handle of the door. Her eyes briefly passed over me, she sucked her lips in and then was gone.

At five thirty, Marie took Mrs Broughton's tray to her room. A knife and fork replaced the teaspoon, and a small dinner plate with one helping of carrots and one helping of shepherd's pie replaced the teacup and saucer. There was a small tumbler of water and the eggcup, once again, with two tablets inside. When Marie had gone, I noticed that the rolling pin lay on the breadboard, although there had been no cause for her to use it that day. I don't know why, but it struck me as strange.

At six o'clock, the tray was removed and brought back to the kitchen. Bobby looked up from the newspaper he was reading as Marie brought it in and raised his eyebrows. She nodded once and he looked back at the paper. Fifteen minutes later, he stood up and told me to be ready by seven. I looked at Marie and she looked across at me.

'You'll need to do the dishes before you go out,' was all she said.

452

At seven o'clock, I was ready. I left my room and met Bobby in the passage. He was standing stock still, the top half of his body leaning over towards his mother's room. He put his finger on his lips and I stopped and listened too. There was nothing, only silence. He motioned for me to move down the passage and out through the front door. I looked towards the kitchen, but the door was closed. Outside, the air smelt so fresh that I felt quite overwhelmed and had to force back my tears. It was as though the streets and the pavement, even the houses next door and opposite us, were part of a different world to which I no longer belonged.

I could hear the music before we even reached the Ace of Spades. It was calling to me, begging me, to come dancing and leave the gloom of the house behind for just a couple of hours. Inside, Bobby asked me if I'd like a drink, a proper drink, something alcoholic.

'Gin and tonic,' I said, feeling a thrill of excitement.

He nodded and returned shortly afterwards with my order and a whisky and soda for himself. A couple of his friends arrived and joined us at our table. I felt self-conscious at first for they looked surprised at seeing him with a woman who wasn't his wife, but he introduced me correctly as his sister-in-law, Timothy's widow, and there were the appropriate utterings of condolences from them and my appropriate thanks in return. I tried to look a little tearful, but couldn't quite do it. Not for the first time, I felt a charlatan, a fake, and was convinced the others could see it and didn't believe me.

During the course of the evening, I looked across at Bobby occasionally, at his sad, handsome face and felt

453

so incredibly sorry for him. Here, in the company of men his age, in the presence of the music, the laughter and the cigarette smoke, he gained a certain confidence. He leaned easily back in his chair and talked – no, not just talked – conversed, something I hadn't seen him do at home. One hand played nervously with the edge of the table and he tapped his foot a little too quickly for the beat of the music, but his eyes lost that angry, needy look they often hold and I got a glimpse of what could be, what had been even, before Timothy's death, before the War.

I had a wonderful time. I danced with four or five different men to anything from the jitterbug to a slow waltz. How wonderful to feel again a man close to me, being held in someone's arms, if only for a short while, and feeling again, that beautiful sense of life, full-bodied and warm just a heartbeat away.

At ten o'clock, Bobby looked at me, tapped his watch and put out his cigarette. I noticed he had only smoked half and wondered what the rush was. He suddenly jumped up and wished everyone a goodnight. I had to walk quickly to keep up with him and he could barely hold the door open long enough for me to go through. Once outside, he slowed a little, the night air seeming to calm him. About halfway home, I tried to make conversation, but it was hard going and stilted.

'I really enjoyed the evening,' I said.

There was no reply.

'It was so nice to get away. So nice to have a dance.'

He looked sideways at me and said, 'We won't be able to do it every week.' It was a warning, a signal to me to keep quiet.

'Oh, I know,' I said in reply. 'I never expected we would. I just thought I'd say something that's all. It was nice and I had a lovely time.'

He softened and managed a resigned, rather pained, smile.

'I don't go there very often. I don't have enough money. I wish I could've bought you another drink.' He had only bought me the one, but I'd made it last all evening.

'I don't mind,' I said, soothingly, 'it's the dancing that I love.'

'I noticed.' He paused. 'I don't like dancing.'

'Have you ever tried it?'

He raised his eyebrows and pulled his bottom lip over his top lip. 'Once. Hated it.'

'I can teach you,' I said.

'Nah.' He shook his head.

'Why not?' I persisted.

'Told you, I'm not interested.'

'Because you think you're not good at it.'

'S'pose so.'

I stopped. He walked on a couple of steps and then, realising I wasn't walking alongside him any longer, looked back. I held out my hands.

'May I have the pleasure of this dance?' I said, with mock ceremony.

He turned back on his way and I ran to catch up with him.

'Oh come on, Bobby!' I cajoled. 'Don't be so bloody serious!'

'Forget it,' he said, a note of nastiness entering his voice.

'Why?' I said sharply. 'There's no one around. It's just us...'

'I said no!' he suddenly shouted, turning to me. 'I don't want to dance here or there or anywhere!'

I stared at him in amazement and he turned, embarrassed, and continued walking.

'And it's never just us,' he added, more quietly. 'Not in this place.'

'What do you mean?' I asked and he shook his head.

We had reached the house, which greeted us dark and foreboding; not a light was on.

'Go in,' he said, sitting on the verandah step and lighting a cigarette. I hesitated and he waved me away with his hand. His eyes were glistening with tears. To save him embarrassment, I followed his orders. I crept along the passage in the dark and closed my bedroom door behind me. Light from a street lamp came in through the window as I undressed and climbed into bed. About fifteen minutes later, I heard the front door open again.

'Bobby!' called Mrs Broughton from her room. The footsteps in the passage stopped and then I heard him call back.

'Just me, Mother. I thought I heard a noise outside.'

There was no reply, just the soft sound of a door closing and the creak of a bedspring.

Chapter Ten

The next evening, Mark came home with a couple of DVDs and a Chinese takeaway. 'So you don't have to cook again,' he said to me with a kiss. In the kitchen, while waiting for the microwave to 'ding', I text-messaged Mandy: 'Where are u?' She was at The Leopard's Spots, a South African pub in Ealing.

'I have to go out,' I said to Mark, who had made himself comfortable on the couch, remote ready in his right hand. 'It's Mandy. She wants me to meet her somewhere.'

He looked disappointed. 'Is it urgent? It's cold outside.'

'It's always cold outside,' I replied, rather severely. 'I won't be long. Your food's ready.'

And so it was that I found myself there that night. It was heaving with Springbok-jersey-wearing South Africans, drinking cans of Castle and dancing to Johnny Clegg.

And we are the scatterlings of Africa
On a journey to the stars
Far below, we leave forever
Dreams of what we were.

Mandy and the others had been drinking a lot since leaving her flat where they'd had Amarula shooters and a couple of rounds of beers. They were sitting and sharing stories of Home over a shared plate of potato skins and dip, reminiscing in the sentimental way that prolonged drinking engenders. Things that didn't mean anything throughout one's life in Africa become invested with a particular air of geniality. Bottles of Zambezi and Castle produce a sense of pride in the person drinking them; the eating of *biltong* is accompanied by shouts of joy and relief. A sip of beer transports one back to Harare or Bulawayo or the River and one almost expects to feel the sun on one's face. This was made in Africa. I am touching Africa. It's the closest one can get. I hated it and yet I drank. I hated it yet I laughed at all the jokes and bought another round. I hated myself because I gave in. I stopped swimming against the tide and let the water close in above me.

I don't remember much after that, except being hauled into a taxi and it stopping and the driver telling us all to get out because I'd been sick on the seat. 'I'm sorry, I'm sorry,' I tried to say, the words thick and clumsy in my mouth. 'Something I've eaten,' I tried to add. Mandy was laughing. 'Typical Ellie,' she said. 'It's never your fault.'

Mandy took me back to her flat, which she still shared with seven other people. Someone pulled off my jeans and then I was helped into bed. I wondered briefly if the sheets were clean and whose bed it was, but for once I couldn't care less.

They all left the room. I lay in its cold stillness. Listless, heavy with pain, I turned over on my side. An incredible urge to retch surged through me then. The room spun around as my mouth filled with the taste of salt. I clutched at the bedclothes yet felt completely out of control. Something was bearing down on me. I felt a force pushing against my chest from above. When I closed my eyes, I was dragged downwards. Down, down through the darkness, that great black abyss that existed within me, a bottomless cavern in myself.

And then up to the top again. It was like swimming to the top of a swimming pool, breaking through the top of the water, fighting for breath, reaching through the surface.

As I opened my eyes, the light in the room seemed to have gained in intensity. There was something sinister about it, as though it were the light of an operating theatre. Then my stomach heaved and heaved. It wouldn't stop. I gasped for breath, but it wouldn't let me inhale. Everything I had ever drunk or eaten seemed to be there, spewed on the floor and the bedclothes and down my front. There didn't seem to be anything else to give, yet my body seemed to want to be rid of every part of me, as though I were diseased. Was this how I was going to die? Renouncing myself in an expulsion of vomit? All my hate and loathing spewed next to me and on me. Would I drown in a sea of sick?

The retching stopped almost as violently as it had begun, leaving me alive and out of breath. There was blood on my lips and chin, but the room had slowed and seemed steadier. I fell asleep for a long time and when I woke it was very dark and silent. I got up weakly and had a bath. Then I pulled the sheets and duvet off the bed and lay down on the bare mattress. I slept again. This time until morning.

Chapter Eleven

25th April, 1946

I have had the most terrible news. A telegram arrived this morning. Dad has died. He had a heart attack two days ago. They have left me alone with my grief, looking at me with lowered eyes, but not saying anything. Bobby managed to say he was 'sorry' and Marie squeezed my shoulder and gave me an extra spoonful of porridge this morning. Mrs Broughton was told the news while she was in her bedroom and, when she came down, she gave me a nod of her head, but said nothing until I was drying the dishes. 'What was it?' she asked, suddenly. 'Heart?'

'Yes,' I said, the word wheezing out of my throat, so tight was it with tears.

She just nodded and walked away. Did I expect anything more?

I walked up to the church after I had finished my morning's work. Marie didn't look up when I said where

I was going. She was down on her hands and knees scrubbing the back step.

'Take your time,' she said. 'I can do everything here.'

Not being a Sunday, the church had a different feel to it, a different kind of quietness, one not expectant of being broken. I cannot explain the feeling of freedom that I experience every time I walk in, how much the atmosphere itself is different. Today, it seemed even more welcoming.

I sat and prayed for a long time. Dust danced in slants of sunlight. Although it has been getting cooler recently and I am told that 'winter is on its way', I do not feel it is cold, like the Rhodesians do. Mrs Broughton is already wearing a brown cardigan and Bobby wears a jersey in the early morning.

I was suddenly disturbed by two African men in overalls who walked up the aisle, talking away at the tops of their voices. When they noticed me, they suddenly went quiet.

'Good morning, Madam,' they said and took off their caps.

'Good morning,' I said.

'I hope we are not disturbing you, Madam,' said the taller of the two. 'We have to do some measuring.'

I noticed then that he had a tape measure in his hand and the other had a small notebook and pencil.

'Well, don't mind me,' I said, but they didn't seem to understand and they stood there, looking down at their hands as though they had been reprimanded. 'Carry on. It's fine, please.'

'Thank you, Madam,' they said in unison and walked

up to the front of the nave where they began to measure part of the wall. A white man then appeared. I'd say he was in his late thirties with a receding hairline. There was something very confident about him. He didn't swagger; it wasn't an arrogance that he exuded, but a strength, something that said he was capable of facing the world. He didn't see me, but walked straight up the aisle and addressed the two African men. His voice was louder than theirs and he seemed to just give them orders, but suddenly one of them started laughing and then they all did. He must've said something funny to them.

One of the African workers then remembered me and signalled to the others to quieten their voices. That's when the white man turned and saw me. He held up his hand in an apology and then walked over.

'Good morning,' he said. He had the poshest voice I think I've ever heard, except for the king talking on the radio.

'Cadwallader Lloyd,' he said, offering me his hand. I shook it.

'Evelyn... Saunders.'

'I'm so sorry to disturb you, but we're measuring up for a memorial. We could come back later if you'd rather... One doesn't expect to see anyone here on a Monday morning.'

He had the most beautiful pair of blue eyes, the blue of the sea along the coast of South-West Africa. He had a very honest, open face, the face of a man with nothing to hide.

'No, no,' I said, and insisted that they carry on with their work. I couldn't tell him, of course, how wonderful

462

it is just to see other people, to know that the world hasn't ended elsewhere, but carries on, living and dying every day.

The two workers were standing still, waiting for their orders and this man, Cadwallader Lloyd, turned and waved to them to carry on.

'We won't take long,' he assured me and turned to go back to them when I asked:

'Is it a war memorial?'

'Yes. They're going to have the main one at the cathedral, but they've asked one for here as well. Something smaller, of course. It may be just an inscription. Full many a flower is born to blush unseen and waste its sweetness on the desert air. Something poetic like that.'

'That's beautiful,' I said, and I asked if I could write it down, which I did in my little notebook. It's by someone called Thomas Gray, apparently.

'Are you all right?' he suddenly asked me. I suppose my face was all puffy from crying. I told him that I had just received some bad news, the death of my father.

'Goodness,' he said, 'that is awfully bad news, isn't it? I say, where do you live?' He glanced at my bare left hand. 'Are you staying with people?'

At that point I just burst into tears. I didn't care. I just couldn't think straight. I have never felt such an emptiness in my life before and hope I shall never feel it again. He took out a big handkerchief and offered it to me and I took it gratefully.

'Back in a moment,' he said, and went over to the workers. He said something to them and they put the

tape measure away and walked quietly out of the church, their eyes deferentially averted.

'I've sent them for an early lunch.'

'Oh, I am ever so sorry,' I began, but he brushed my apology away and sat down next to me.

'Where are you from?' he asked and that was it. The whole story just tumbled out. Timothy and Dad and the Broughtons. Even the Ace of Spades (I got a raised eyebrow then!) and the incident in the front room. Everything.

'Goodness,' he said, when I'd finished and then he didn't say anything, not a thing for a long time. In fact, we sat so long in silence that I thought he must be thinking of a way of making an escape from me and my strange story, so I thought I'd help him out. I stood up.

'You've been very kind,' I began and he started quite noticeably.

'Oh, dear, no, don't go. Evelyn, sit down. In fact, no, would you like some tea? I have some in a vacuum flask. Sandwiches too, sardines.'

I accepted and, sitting there in the quietness of the church, eating a sardine sandwich and drinking a strong cup of tea, I felt the weight of the world shift slightly. I have found a friend, I thought. A friend.

27ᵗʰ April, 1946

Before I left, Cadwallader asked me to have dinner with him and his wife at the weekend, Saturday. I didn't think I could. The Broughtons – would they let me?

'Tell you what,' he said. 'Tell them that I'm your uncle.'

'Uncle?'

'Yes, tell them that I'm a distant relative also living in the Colony who has contacted you over your father's death. Someone you haven't even met.'

'How then have we met?'

'I'll write a letter. Give me your address and I'll write you a letter.'

'All right,' I agreed and felt a surge of excitement. 'I'll wait for your letter.'

It arrived this morning. Marie carried it in, looking at the back of the envelope before passing it to me. 'Post,' she said, as though I received it every day. 'Local.'

I feigned surprise, not very well, I thought, saying 'Oh, who could it be?' rather like some pantomime character. I read it a couple of times before announcing, 'It's from my Uncle Cadwallader.'

No one said anything.

'He's asked me to dinner on Saturday night.'

Still no one spoke.

'He says he'll come and fetch me.'

Still nothing.

'Well, that's very kind of him,' I said, standing up and pushing my chair back with a slight screech. 'I'd better go and write a reply.'

I just hope, hope, they will let me go.

1st May, 1946

I have never felt someone dislike me so intensely – and I do not mean Mrs Broughton, I mean Cadwallader's wife. In fact, everything went well with the Broughtons. I told them again that I was going out and had my letter at hand to show them if they asked, but no one did. Cadwallader came to fetch me. Bobby was sitting outside on the verandah smoking when we left. I think he was envious of Cadwallader's car, which is big and new and shiny.

'Goodnight,' I said, as we walked down the steps.

'Yep, goodnight,' said Bobby.

I can put up with Bobby's rudeness; it is born of a complex he has about himself, but the rudeness of Mrs Broughton and the rudeness I experienced last night at the hands of Mrs Lloyd are something else.

Mrs Lloyd, I was never told to call her anything else, was in the kitchen when we arrived, supervising the cook. Cadwallader ushered me through to a large lounge and offered me a sherry. I was quite taken aback at the splendour of the place. It is beautifully furnished and decorated with a mixture of European and African art. The sofas and chairs are covered in exquisite Sanderson linen, cream in colour, the same material as the long curtains on the french doors, which lead to an outside area where I could see more chairs and a table. There is a crystal chandelier and a beautiful carpet on the floor and a huge drinks trolley, complete with ice bucket and tongs. How my heart leapt to see such refinement after being in the desert such a long time!

I asked about Cadwallader's work and he told me that he is an architect and works for a firm called Stoughton and James. At the moment he's working on the War Memorial, but there's also a tremendous amount of building going on throughout the Colony. 'It's opening up. The British Government is encouraging people to move out here and why not, everything's here, servants, sun and...'

'Booze,' completed a voice from the doorway and I turned and saw Mrs Lloyd for the first time. She is a tall woman with long mousy blonde hair, the type of woman who could be quite good looking if she were to wear a little make up and put a curl in her hair, for it is most terribly flat and lifeless.

'Blue skies and booze, that's all there is here,' she said, walking in and taking the glass that Cadwallader offered her before sitting down. He remained standing next to the drinks trolley. She took a sip of her whisky and handed it back to him with a shake of her head. 'Too strong, darling,' she said and then turned to me and said, 'All these years married and he still can't quite get it right.'

'That's the nature of being married isn't it,' I joked. 'Isn't it true that the majority of husbands don't know their wives' favourite food?'

'Is it?' she said, looking at me over the brim of her glass.

I didn't know what to say and then Cadwallader tried to joke that it worked the other way round too. That many women didn't know anything about their husbands or else why did they knit them the same awful jersey every year or give them the same awful socks for Christmas.

'You forget I don't knit,' she said, drawing each word out with a sneering languidness. 'And I've never given you socks, have I?'

There was another awkward silence and then she asked me what I liked doing hobby-wise.

'Reading,' I replied.

'Oh,' she said, still staring at me, her tone one of disappointment. And then, as though it were almost too much effort to ask, 'What kind of books?'

'Crime.'

She gave a slight sneer. 'We have a detective in our midst, Wally.'

'I always like a good whodunit myself,' he said. 'Agatha what's-her-name, that sort of thing.'

'Christie,' I said, and I got that look again, that one that tried to take me in and digest me slowly, before spitting me out.

'The Banfords are late,' she said suddenly, looking at her watch.

'They'll be here just now,' he replied, sipping his drink.

'The point is they're late, whether they'll be here just now or not is irrelevant.'

Cadwallader shrugged.

'Can I get you another?' he asked me, his tone obviously more gentle than when he spoke to her. She heard it, too.

I started to say thank you, although I had about a quarter of a glass still to go, when she cut in and said, 'For God's sake, let the girl finish her drink, will you?'

I was uncomfortable with such tension. My parents were never ones to argue in public; in fact I have always considered it quite bad form to do so. I was therefore quite glad when the Banfords did arrive.

The rest of the evening was very much the same. She interrupted, contradicted or corrected everything that he said and he fended her off with playful banter. Mrs Lloyd absorbed herself with the Banfords for the rest of the evening, giving me the most cursory of glances now and again and not asking me if I'd like seconds when she asked everyone else. An African servant served the meal, which was mushroom soup, roast lamb, vegetables and trifle. At the end of the first course, I made to collect the soup bowls, when Cadwallader, who was sitting at the head of the table to my right, put his hand on my arm and stopped me. Mrs Lloyd and Mrs Banford exchanged looks. I didn't realise the servant would also clear the dishes. I felt incredibly spoilt. I have never known people who have had servants.

After the meal we sat in the lounge again and more drinks were poured, but I declined.

'Go on, night cap,' said Cadwallader.

'If she doesn't want it, she doesn't want it,' said Mrs Lloyd.

'I'll have it,' I said, my voice strong and defiant. 'Thank you, that's very kind.' I got the longest stare of all then.

Before Cadwallader drove me home, he had a rather heated but hushed conversation with his wife in the hallway. I couldn't make out what either of them was saying.

'Come over any time you like,' she said as I left, but her voice was flat and expressionless and she seemed to be looking over my shoulder while she spoke.

'Thank you,' I said, wanting to add, 'but that's very unlikely.'

'Does everyone have a servant?' I asked Cadwallader in the car on the way home.

'Of course. Why, don't they?'

'No, not the Broughtons.'

'You don't do it yourself, do you?'

'Yes, with Marie. She does most of it.'

'Heavens.'

Inside the kitchen, Marie had gone to sleep in a chair with Colin on her shoulder. I thought Bobby must be in bed, but he came in the front door just after I did. He flicked his cigarette out into the night and closed the door without a word.

'Have a nice evening?' I whispered.

'All right,' he said, tugging off a shoe.

'Goodnight,' I said as I went to my room, but there was no reply.

Chapter Twelve

10th May, 1946

After not hearing from Cadwallader for over a week, I received a letter today, asking me to meet him at the church. I told Marie where I was going, although I didn't mention whom I was going to meet, and she just nodded. I hadn't finished all my chores, but I said I'd do them when I got back.

Cadwallader was talking to the African workers when I arrived and just waved across while he carried on showing them something. I slipped into a front pew and flicked through a hymn-book while I waited. My eyes alighted on I Vow to Thee My Country, *which we sang so often at Sunday School as a child. I don't know if I could sing it here. I don't feel anything, not yet anyway, and I doubt I will stay in this country longer than the end of the year.*

When Cadwallader came across, he was smiling as though he had something to give me.

'Evelyn, I've been thinking,' he said after we'd exchanged courtesies. 'The reason I asked you here today is because I had the most wonderful idea last night. Now, hear me out.'

I closed the hymn-book and put it back in its rightful place.

'As you know, I work for a firm of builders called Stoughton and James. We have an office in Bulawayo, a city in the South of the Colony – you would have passed through it on your way up here.' I nodded. 'Well, I've made some enquiries and they need a secretary.' I started to say something and he held up his hand. 'Let me finish. I've got it all worked out. I can find you accommodation there. Nothing special, but affordable, probably in a boarding house. I'll give you the money for the train and I'll arrange for someone to meet you there. You can start work next month.'

He paused to see the effect of his words.

'The Broughtons...' I began.

'You can't stay there, Evelyn. Not for the rest of your life.'

'But what do I say?'

'You don't have to say anything. I'm your uncle. I'll arrange to come and see Mrs Broughton and express my desire that you, as my niece, move to Bulawayo to earn your keep. Don't worry, I'll sort it out.'

I still don't know if it's the right thing to do. Cadwallader insisted and kept asking me if I really wanted to stay here any longer and, of course, I said no. 'That's settled then. I'll come and see Mrs Broughton tomorrow morning.'

472

11ᵗʰ May, 1946

This morning I woke early and went out to feed the chickens. I had just finished sweeping out the coop, when I heard a noise on the far side, so I went round the back and was rather surprised to find Marie sitting there. I was even more surprised to see her smoking a cigarette. She started slightly when she saw me and her mouth half opened and then closed and she gave a shrug and looked away. There is not much point in trying to make an excuse when you are well and truly caught red-handed. She was sitting on an upturned crate, her back against the wire of the coop, squinting slightly in the glare of the morning sun. I don't think she spends a lot of time out of doors.

'Hello,' I said.

She took a deep drag of the cigarette, blew out a cloud of smoke and glanced at me with a nod of her head. 'Morning,' she said.

'Mind if I join you?'

She shook her head and moved sideways a little so that I could sit next to her and offered me the cigarette. It wasn't quite what I meant, but I took it anyway and inhaled deeply and blew strong blue smoke out my mouth. I was surprised I didn't cough, but my chest felt tight and I rubbed it gently. Neither of us said anything for a long time. We passed the cigarette back and forth until it was a smoking stub. Marie grudgingly put it out and then sat with her arms folded across her knees.

'When are you off?'

'Couple of weeks.'

She nodded.

'Ma OK about it?'

'I think so, from what my uncle said.'

'It's the best thing you can do. You'll die here.'

I wanted to say I know, but it seemed cruel. I was getting away while she stayed. I didn't say anything and we sat for a long time, again in silence.

'He's not your uncle, is he?' she said quite suddenly.

'No,' I answered. 'No, he's not.'

'He's married.'

'Oh, it's nothing like that! Nothing like that at all.' I was completely taken aback at the thought. She gave a brief nod of her head and looked away from me.

'Did you love him?' she asked, again the sound of her voice, clear and bold in the crisp morning air taking me by surprise. Then she coughed and said, well whispered really, 'Tim. Timothy. Did you love him?'

In another situation and another place I would have lied and said yes, yes I did love him, but I felt a need to be honest, not just with anyone, but with Marie. She had invited me into her confidence, let me see her smoke and not scarpered like a frightened rabbit when I found her behind the coop.

'No.' And then I added, 'He didn't love me either.'

She smiled then, not maliciously or accusingly, but with something like relief. It was brief, merely turning the corners of her mouth momentarily, and then it was gone.

'To tell you the truth,' I continued, 'I don't know very much about him. You probably know more.'

She was drawing circles in the sand with her finger while I spoke. Sitting there with her knees pulled under

474

her chin, her feet bare and her dress tucked between her legs, there was something very childlike about her, as though we were having a break from playing hopscotch and just now we would stand up and resume our game. Her hair fell in front of her face and I saw, too, a momentary beauty. Years briefly fell away and she wasn't overworked and under-appreciated Marie, but a young girl whose life stretched ahead full of promise.

'He's not the father,' she said, turning to me, her eyes brimming with tears.

'Who?' I asked stupidly. 'Bobby? What do you mean? Baby Colin...?'

She looked straight ahead at the fence. One of the posts was leaning to one side.

'He's Tim's. Tim's baby.'

My mind reeled. I felt slightly sick from the cigarette and put my hands on either side of my face as I tried to steady the world.

She looked at me and this time there was a hint of triumph in her eyes.

'Me and Tim, we were going out... he was training here in Salisbury, but we never thought he'd actually be needed. He knew the bush like this,' she held up the back of her hand. 'They wanted him to do tracking. One day he was here, next he's off to England.' She nodded her head towards me as though he had been sent to me specifically. 'He came back once, but he was different, angry, but he said he was going to get out. He'd come back, we'd get married...' Her voice broke and she was silent again, except for her rasping breath as she tried not to cry.

'Then he wrote. Said he'd got married. Sorry, he said.' She broke a small stick into two and peeled the bark off.

'I wrote back. I'm pregnant, I said, but I never got an answer. I was going to kill myself. I didn't care. I didn't want to live. My uncle, that's who I lived with since my folks died, would've killed me anyway. And then Bobby came to see me. Tim had told him. We went for a walk and he brought me an ice cream. He wore a suit although it was much too hot and it made him sweat. We sat on a bench in the park and suddenly he put his hand on mine and said 'Marry me.' I said no at first, but then we walked back to the house and it was as though there were no other options, but death. So I said yes and he went inside and spoke to my uncle while I waited on the verandah. A week later we got married.

'I should've got rid of it, I suppose, but I've heard of other girls… things going wrong. There were no other choices.'

I sat quietly and breathed deeply. My palms were sweaty and I longed for another cigarette, just so that I'd have something to do with my hands.

'And Bobby?' I ventured. 'That was very noble of him…' I wasn't convinced of my own words and I was right.

Marie gave a brief sardonic smile. 'Don't you know? Bobby doesn't like women.'

I didn't know what she meant at first and then gradually it dawned on me. Thoughts circled my head and gradually came and took their correct places. Something began to make sense.

'Come with me,' I said after another brief pause.

Marie gave a short laugh.

'No, really, come with me to Bulawayo. We'll make up a story. You could also be a widow... you could begin again.'

She turned to me again, this time her eyes full of tears and defeat. 'I can never, ever begin again.'

'You can!' I urged.

'No,' she whispered. 'You go, go on your own.' She smiled. 'Write to me.'

'What on earth is going on here?' I burst out. 'What's going on with all of you? Mrs Broughton and that bloody room, Bobby and his nights out, you and Colin? Why can't you leave? Why?'

'Shh!' she admonished me quietly, taking me by the shoulders. 'I've made my decision and I'm better off than the others, you know. Bobby – what can he do? Ma Broughton?' She shrugged and laughed. 'She talks to Timothy in that room, you know?'

'Talks?'

She nodded and laughed again. 'She says he appears to her and they sit and talk. That's why no one is allowed in there. She only wants him. She's not interested in the living.

'I went in there once when she was sleeping and I sat for a whole hour, hoping that Timothy would appear. I was going to tell him a thing or two...' she was crying now and laughing. 'He never appeared.'

'Grief,' I said, trying to sound the voice of reason, 'grief does funny things to people.'

'She's always been funny,' said Marie with bitterness. 'Her old man left her when Bobby was little. He *saw the light. Timothy ran the farm, since he was about twelve. They lost it when he went to the war. Debt. Bobby doesn't know anything about farming.'*

There was another silence and then suddenly she said: 'What've you got to wear down there in Bulawayo? You got any nice dresses stored away in your trunk?'

I shook my head. 'No. You all think I'm the queen or something. I haven't got a lot.'

'I'll make you something,' she said, standing up and brushing the back of her dress.

'Make me something?'

'Yes, something nice. I haven't made something nice for a long time.'

Chapter Thirteen

15ᵗʰ May, 1946

Marie took me shopping today. It is the first time I have been into Salisbury since arriving here all those months ago. We got the bus right into the centre and did all the grocery shopping first. In the bus, all the Europeans sit in the front and there is a section at the back for the Africans. I don't think it's right, but Marie says they smell and why would you want a kaffir *sitting next to you anyway? Most women here seem to walk in pairs. Not all of them wear hats; Marie says they are very expensive. I am shocked that the Africans have to move off the pavements if a European is approaching. Marie does not seem at all surprised by this and asked if it's not the same in England. I told her I have only ever seen one coloured person in England and that was in London at a railway station. She couldn't believe it! 'You're lucky,' she said.*

We went to a place called Cecil Square, which is

shaped like the Union Jack. It's not far from the railway station and it's where the taxi rank is, although Marie would never dream of taking one, they are far too expensive. Petrol is rationed here and there are not that many cars on the road.

For lunch we went to a place called Shorties. I was surprised to see Marie buy what the Americans call a hotdog. I've never had one before, but I tried it and quite liked it. Perhaps not so much tomato sauce next time.

I couldn't quite believe all that is available. I went into a bookshop, Kingstons, I think it was called, which for me was like walking into Aladdin's cave. What a selection! They had magazines and newspapers as well, all of which can be delivered to your doorstep. The Broughtons have nothing, not even a newspaper to inform them of the news!

At the supply store, everything Marie asked for was carried down off the shelves, weighed, cut if necessary and wrapped in brown paper, which the shopkeeper had a huge roll of on the counter. How it thrilled me to be part of life again. Marie was asked if she was paying cash or on account, but she said quite firmly cash, gripping onto that large black purse like it was the key to her very existence.

Finally, we went into a material shop-cum-haber-dashery. A rather strict and foreboding lady stood behind the counter with a tape measure round her neck. She must've been in her fifties, quite stocky, with thin lips and pale skin that contrasted with her brown hair.

We chose two pieces of cloth. Marie insisted on two: a pale blue and an olive green. Both cotton. She asked to see their collection of ribbon as well and the strict, foreboding lady lifted a small drawer of ribbon onto the counter so we could look through it. Every piece that Marie unravelled, the lady pounced on and wound round her hand before placing it back in the drawer.

'We'll take these two,' said Marie, indicating two pieces that matched the material. She also chose buttons and two reels of thread.

'Are you in need of a pattern?' the saleslady asked, as though we were schoolgirls playing house.

'I've got something,' Marie replied, without looking up from her purse, which she was rummaging in.

Everything was folded neatly and Marie put the package in her basket. She refused to let me carry anything, although Colin did let me occasionally carry him before bursting into tears and insisting his mother do so. Then she insisted we go for tea before we make our way home.

We went to a place called The Lounge, a large tearoom with swing doors. Marie ordered us a pot to share and two scones.

'Marie, how are you going to pay for this? Will you let me give you something?'

She waved me away with her hand and concentrated on getting Colin sitting properly with his bib on.

'Seriously, I've seen how Bobby checks all the receipts and counts the money after each shopping trip you make.'

'Don't worry,' she continued dismissively. 'I have my way.'

When we got home and had put away all the groceries

and left the purse on the table with all the receipts, Marie motioned me to her room. She took the package from the material shop with her. In her room, into which I had never been before, was a chest of drawers. The top drawer was locked and Marie took a key out of her pocket and unlocked it. Inside, it was full of patterns. They had never been used.

'Marie,' I gasped. 'All these patterns...'

I turned them over: patterns for dresses, patterns for skirts, patterns for blouses and shirts and suits. Even a pattern for a ballgown. Right at the bottom was a pattern for a wedding dress.

'Marie...' I said again, picking it up and running my hands over it. 'Oh, Marie.'

Marie smiled ruefully, took it from my hands and pushed it to the back of the drawer.

Later, she told me how she afforded all the patterns and the material she had bought for me that day. She sold eggs to the Lavender Lady.

25th May, 1946

I'm going at last! The steward has just come round to make up my bunk, but I am too excited to sleep. I miss Marie. She and I have become very close in the last couple of weeks. She has taught me how to sew. The first dress she made herself and then insisted I make the second one myself! 'Listen,' she said. 'Listen very carefully and watch what I do.' And I did it! I made it. I promised to write, but I doubt she will return the favour.

Cadwallader picked me up and dropped me at the station. I was so excited, but so nervous as well. He held my hand while we waited, a very fatherly thing to do and I appreciated the gesture.

'I will come and see you when I am next in Bulawayo,' he said. 'And I'll telephone you over the next couple of days – make sure you're all right. Send me a cable if there are any problems.' Yes, very fatherly and I am in need of a father at the moment.

Goodbye Salisbury! I am going to Bulawayo, Bu-la-way-o, Bu-la-way-o.

Chapter Fourteen

Buddhists believe that the soul remains on earth for some time after death before it leaves forever. I felt this was true of Gran. I used to think I'd seen her sometimes. On the tube, at the market, in the High Street on a crowded Saturday afternoon. Sometimes I just felt she was there. I'd hear a piece of music or someone would say something that Gran would've said and I'd look up sharply, expecting to see her there. Once, I caught a very strong smell of lavender perfume in the air as I walked home from the university. It didn't seem to belong to anyone or lead anywhere; it was just there.

Another time I was just coming out of a tube station and passed a busker at the top of the steps. He was playing A Nightingale Sang in Berkeley Square on a violin, and for a moment I felt the earth spin. A great ocean of tears threatened to well up inside, so I stood still for a few moments and then went a few steps beyond him and then stopped and went back. I stood while he finished playing, catching his eye from time to time as his head moved with his instrument. 'That was wonderful,' I said when he finished.

'Wonderful.' He smiled shyly and nodded his head in thanks and surprise when I pulled out a ten pound note and dropped it in his hat.

But I'd got it all wrong. I wasn't listening. When I was a child and Gran would read to me, she'd make me listen to the story carefully and ask me what it was about afterwards. If I got it wrong, she'd tell it to me again. And that's what she was doing now. Telling me again because I wasn't listening.

It was something that Tony had said that set it all in motion. Not the bit about baking powder, something else. It was that afternoon of Miles's funeral, I think, when we'd had that argument because he wanted me to go to Mozambique and I was adamant that my new home was in England.

'You know the problem with all of you ex-Zimbos who live here?'

'I'm sure you'll enlighten me if I don't.'

'You all live in some... some... fantasy land!' he cried, tapping his head viciously with his hand.

I rolled my eyes, but didn't say anything.

'You're just like those postcolonial writers you told me about. You want everything to be perfect, to be whole, to be... to be in some original state of happiness, as though there ever were such a thing. All of you, you all move away because you can't stand reality.' His back was towards me, heaving with anger. Now he turned and faced me, little pinches of white around the mouth, gesticulating wildly to prove his point. 'Africa is Africa. It's as simple as that. Accept it and move on. Forget this idea of some golden age when everybody was well fed and happy and had a good job

485

and a bright future and all the rest. See Zimbabwe for what it is, not as some failed annex of 1950s Britain. People carry on living. They go shopping, they go to parties, they visit friends. For heaven's sake, they eat ice cream while bombs drop! They don't stop because there's been a change of government or the crime rate has risen! You see what the press photographer sees: the poverty, the corruption, the decline. You only see what's missing, not what's there. If only you did it the other way round, you'd be surprised with little pools of happiness.' He stopped, slightly out of breath as though he had just run a race.

'Write a different story, Ellie.' His voice was suddenly soft, the anger subsiding. 'A different ending, at least.'

But what in the end makes a good story? Gran didn't have much time for modern thrillers; she dismissed my praise of *The Silence of the Lambs* as 'misguided', as though I had fallen into some sort of trap in thinking it a good film. She had said that it was gruesome at the expense of depth, as were many contemporary films and books. The villain is a mass murderer, a nutcase, someone who looks and acts strangely. They keep their victims in cellars or cages, inflicting the incredible pain of torture, both physical and psychological, all because they had a strange relationship with their mother and hated their father. The act is so awful, the method so complicated and the murderer so twisted that one can distance oneself from the crime, thinking, 'I would never do that.'

But the old-fashioned crime, the Agatha Christie whodunnit, this is a true exposition of the human psyche. She, Gran believed, understood what drove the ordinary person to murder: the old lady, the vicar, the housewife; all were capable of the greatest sin on earth. And that in the end is what is so unsettling: it's you, it's me. No one can say, 'I wouldn't do that.' Behind the murders are jealousy, hatred, envy. Love. How many crimes are committed in its name?

It is not only the murderer who is unbelievable these days, but the detective, too. Forensics, CCTV footage, lie detectors. Gone is the knowledge, the understanding of human nature, of the reasons why people do what they do. Gone, too, is the attention to detail: not just body language – the shifting of feet, the wringing of hands, the eyes that do not meet the detective's full on – but little things: the colour of a handkerchief, the shade of a lipstick, the type of ink used in a pen. All these are overlooked.

The answer to the mystery lay, not in the act itself, but what led up to it. All that is thought irrelevant, everyday, ordinary. All that doesn't make the headlines.

Tony was right, of course. There was so much more to Zimbabwe than made the headlines. But the anger, the violence, the slow burning of a country. Who could ignore it? When market stalls go up in flames and the police stand laughing? When old people die of starvation? When Death is as welcome and common a visitor as any other to those dying slowly of disease? When the only available medicine is paracetamol, which cannot kill the pain. Does one dare look for beauty, for happiness, in such a land of sorrow? Better one live far away and, in refusing to return, refuse to condone.

I shrugged Tony off at the time, but I began to think more and more about his words, more and more about him. I felt it was time to put my life into perspective. I didn't want to be one of those people who end up living in some place like Surrey or Upper-Middlecombe-Under-Wye, who sit and dream of the good old days, ordering *biltong* over the internet and drinking Zambezi Lager like it's *manna* from heaven. I don't want to have a Rhodesian flag up in my living room and I don't want to write the memoirs of my African childhood. I don't want to live in the past.

Many things seem so much clearer and less threatening. If I stand back from the world, it is now not with my old feelings of alienation or irritation, but to watch, half amused, as the world turns frantically by. Below those cool waters that now run through me, I know that I am deeply hurt, and perhaps always will be. What is different is that I now feel I have the power to survive.

I like to think that wherever Gran and Wally and Jeremy are, that they're together. Of course, Miles is probably there, too, and Riette and I'm not quite sure where they fit in, but I like to think that they're at peace: no more hiding, no more secrets. I realise now that's why she left me the house, 'the house and all its contents'. Because she wanted me to find out, to read her letters and her diaries, and for everything she had kept to herself for all those years to be at last known to someone else. She had picked me to confide in after all. Perhaps I was her closest friend and, if I was the person to whom she could confess so that her burden of guilt could be lifted, even if after death, and she could rest in peace, then who was I to deny her?

One day I couldn't feel her any more and I knew then what I had to do. I had to leave my little hole where I had hidden away. The answer was not in the Spiritualist Church, nor was it in my academic article on 'The Rise and Fall of

White Zimbabwe'. The answer was in life, in living.

And so it is time for me to go. A car door shuts, a phone rings somewhere in the house, not with the short sharp insistent trill I have heard for the last few weeks, but with something like the soft rush of water on a beach or the long calm call of crickets on a summer's night. Go, it says, go now.

For the first time in a long time, my thoughts are on the future, not the past. I see the clear blue water of the Mozambique Channel, I see the fish restaurant in Bulawayo, Gran's house with the garden full of flowers, the wide open sky stretching on and on and on. I will learn how to cook expensive meals, how to serve customers with a smile, how to run our own business. I will learn which flowers to plant when, how to read the vagaries of each season's passing and, who knows, I may even learn to dive.

Extracts

The Unquiet Grave, Palinurus (Cyril Connolly), Hamish Hamilton, 1945

Part One

Chapter 3:   'Unforgettable', Nat King Cole, written by Irvin Gordon, 1951.
'You'll Never Know', Nat King Cole, written by Gordon and Warren, 1957, © WB Music.

Chapter 4:   'Smile', Nat King Cole, written by Chaplin, Turner and Parsons, 1954.

Chapter 5:   'Let's Face the Music and Dance', Nat King Cole, written by Irving Berlin, 1962.

Chapter 9:   'When I Fall in Love', Nat King Cole, written by Heyman and Young, 1957, © Chappell & Co.

Chapter 10: 'The Nearness of You', Ella Fitzgerald and Louis Armstrong, written by Washington and Carmichael, 1956, © Famous Music Corp.

Chapter 11: 'Smile', Nat King Cole, written by Chaplin, Turner and Parsons, 1954.

Chapter 13: 'You are My Sunshine', written by Jimmie Davis, is used by kind permission of the publishers Peermusic (Pty) Ltd.
'Mona Lisa', Nat King Cole, written by Livingston and Evans, 1950, © Famous Music Corp.

Chapter 10: 'Elegy Written in a Country Churchyard', Thomas Gray.

'Now Sleeps the Crimson Petal', Alfred, Lord Tennyson.

'Sudden Light', Dante Gabriel Rossetti.

Chapter 15: 'The Ballad of Reading Gaol', Oscar Wilde.

Chapter 17: 'A Blossom Fell', Nat King Cole, written by Barnes, Cornelius and John, 1944, © Mistletoe Melodies Ltd, 1 Wyndham Yard, London WlH 2QF, used by permission.

'Red Roses for a Blue Lady', Dean Martin, written by Tepper and Bennett, 1948, © Chappell & Co.

Chapter 18: 'The Ballad of Reading Gaol', Oscar Wilde.

'If', Rudyard Kipling.

Chapter 20: 'You Made Me Love You', Nat King Cole, written by Monaco and McCarthy, 1967, © Sony/ATV Tunes.

Part Three

Chapter 2: 'Composed A Few Miles Above Tintern Abbey, On Revisiting The Banks Of The Wye During A Tour', July 13th, 1798, William Wordsworth.

'You Made Me Love You', Nat King Cole, written by Monaco and McCarthy, 1967, © Sony/ATV Tunes.

Chapter 4: 'Solitude', Ella Wheeler Wilcox.

Chapter 10: 'Scatterlings of Africa', Johnny Clegg, written by Johnny Clegg, 1987.

Acknowledgements

This September Sun is a pure work of fiction both in terms of plot and character. However, while researching the historical background to the novel, especially that which takes place before the 1980s, I did draw on the experiences of some of the people I interviewed. In particular, I would like to thank Mr and Mrs Ballantyne for relating their experiences of living in Salisbury in the 1940s and Mr Ballantyne's time in the RAF, the late Mrs Redfern for sharing her memories of arriving in Rhodesia as a young nurse and Mr Norman Pratt for giving me much information about daily life in Rhodesia in the 1940s and 50s as well as detail on the railway system. My Mum, Fay Rheam, who was always willing to research any detail, however small, for me at the National Archives when I was unable to, has always encouraged me in everything, but in particular in my writing. Thanks to my Dad, my sisters, Kelly and Francesca, and my partner, John, who have all read various chapters at various stages and given me their opinion, whether I liked it or not! I'm grateful, too, to Jane and Brian of 'amaBooks who faced many difficulties in order to publish this novel, but who remained optimistic throughout! Thanks, too, to The Writers' Coven in Singapore, for whom I wrote the first chapter of the novel. I finished it at last!

PARTHIAN

Award-winning
Welsh Writing

www.parthianbooks.co.uk